Delicious praise for the COLD CEREAL SAGA:

"Totally original and wholly brilliant."   —Eoin Colfer,
bestselling author of the Artemis Fowl series

"With an off-the-wall sensibility that fans of the author's *The True Meaning of Smekday* will recognize with delight, Rex brings together unconventional allies to be hunted by agents of the huge Goodco Cereal Company."
     —*Kirkus Reviews* (starred review)

"Rex takes his magically delicious premise seriously, finding the thin line between absurdity and comedy."
     —*Publishers Weekly*

"The story is filled with wildly imaginative elements and clever wisecracks, but the humor is couched within a rich, complex plot that's filled with engaging characters and concepts."
     —*SLJ* (starred review)

"An expansive cast of colorful characters keeps the surprises coming."   —*The Horn Book*

"Will leave readers anxious for the sequel."   —ALA *Booklist*

"Flat-out fabulous."   —Bruce Coville,
author of *My Teacher Is an Alien*

"Second helpings, please!"   —Jonathan Stroud,
bestselling author of The Bartimaeus Trilogy

AND NOW BACK TO
THE NEWSROOM

In lighter news, a trio of Florida kids say they've proven that a new breakfast cereal really *CAN* make you *smarter!*

For more we go to Miami Public Television's Marcos Horchata.

Marcos?

BRAIN FOOD?

9.

SCIENCE FAIR
BREEZY PALMS
ELEMENTARY

REPORTER

It's Science fair season at Breezy Palms Elementary, and fourth graders Amy, Max, and Varga Luna needed a project.

Then Amy saw a commercial for a new cereal: Peanut Butter Clobbers.

Um, I saw the commercial on television? And in the commercial the guy says the cereal will make you smarter.

So I thought...maybe we could make an experiment to see if it really does.

LIVE

REPORTER

For two weeks Varga Luna ate nothing but Peanut Butter Clobbers morning, noon, and night. Max ate only a competitor's cereal, and Amy ate as she normally did.

Then we compared our homework scores before and after the experiment.

My scores stayed the same.

Mine, too.

VargaLuna, you singlehandedly ate seven boxes of Peanut Butter Clobbers over two weeks.

Did your scores improve?

LIVE

Your tie is pentagonal. It's covered with an interlocking pattern of tiny lizards. The lizards are based on the work of Dutch artist M. C. Escher. You're either an Escher fan or else a fan of tiny lizards.

If I concentrate really hard I can guess what you're going to say before you say it.

LIVE

I'm bothering you. It's because you're a firstborn, aren't you?

Your name can be anagrammed to make ROACH HARM TACO.

What were you asking us?

Nothing. This is Marcos Horcha—

HA, MACHO CARROT.

Marcos Horchata reporting.

ARM TORSO CHA CHA.

UNL
CHA

ADAM

UCKY

RMS

REX

THE
COLD CEREAL
SAGA
BOOK TWO

BALZER + BRAY
An Imprint of HarperCollins*Publishers*

Also by **ADAM REX**

COLD CEREAL: The Cold Cereal Saga, Book One

THE TRUE MEANING OF SMEKDAY

FOR TEENS

FAT VAMPIRE: A Never Coming of Age Story

Balzer + Bray is an imprint of HarperCollins Publishers.

Library of Congress Cataloging-in-Publication Data
Rex, Adam.
  Unlucky charms / Adam Rex.
    p. cm. — (The cold cereal saga)
  Summary: "Three kids must save the world from the diabolical schemes of an evil
breakfast cereal company, which has been luring magical creatures to our world
through a rift in the time-space continuum"— Provided by publisher.
  ISBN 978-0-06-206006-8
  [1. Cereals, Prepared—Fiction. 2. Magic—Fiction. 3. Adventure and adventurers—
Fiction. 4. Twins—Fiction. 5. Brothers and sisters—Fiction.] I. Title.
PZ7.R32865Unl 2013   2012026714
[Fic]—dc23   CIP
                                                                              AC

13 14 15 16 17   CG/OPM   10 9 8 7 6 5 4 3 2 1
❖
First paperback edition, 2014

For Dr. Marie Rex, who is a teacher today

CHAPTER 1

Samantha Doe was going to miss her big red coat. It was by far the warmest thing she'd ever worn, and she'd worn it every day for more than three months, and you couldn't help getting attached to something like that. On the inside it was furry, like a pet. It even had the word DOE on the pocket. Samantha loved her big pet coat. But she was going to have to give it back.

She'd been in Antarctica for fifteen weeks—twice as long as she'd been told. She could swear near the end that Goodco was just grasping at excuses to keep her there. And then there was that business with her laptop.

One of the Goodco people, one of the big men who didn't seem to have any scientific credentials at all, had come to her dorm room and asked why she hadn't been sending any personal emails to her children.

Samantha had, in fact. She'd sent Scott and Polly each

an email every day since the Saturday after Thanksgiving. A hundred letters. But she said, "Well . . . since it's *personal* emails I'm not sending, I don't see how it's your—"

The man brushed past her and grabbed her laptop off the bed.

"Hey!" Samantha said. But she stepped back. She was suddenly afraid of this big man. He'd just come in from the cold night, wearing the same sort of coat Samantha wore, that everyone wore. Red on the outside, furry on the inside. On him it looked like an animal he'd turned inside out and was flaunting, like a warning. He scowled at the screen.

"You haven't sent an email to your kids since December first," he said. "And they've never emailed you back?"

Samantha wanted to fold up into herself. Scott and Polly wrote her all the time—what was this guy talking about?

"Here—" the big man, this massive man, told her. "This. Where did you get this software?" He showed her the screen, and a file she'd never seen before. It was called 2003 TAXES, and it was nested inside three folders named for sugar-free candy recipes and a fourth titled PHOTOS OF MY UNATTRACTIVE AUNT. She'd never noticed any of these before, either. Her laptop had a lot of garbage on it.

"Why . . . why does it matter?" Samantha asked the man, who was heaving, who could not possibly be

getting larger, could he?

"It matters . . . it *matters* because it's counteracting the spyware *we* put on your computer. How did it get here?"

Samantha didn't know, though her mind turned back to a drawing Polly had sent, months ago, that took a suspiciously long time to download. Anyway, the big man dropped her laptop carelessly on the bed and thundered out before she could answer, or get indignant, or even ask what he'd meant by *spyware*.

She stood awhile, aware of the shallow tide of her own breath. She wasn't so sure about this Goodco anymore. She didn't care how beloved their cereals were.

Afterward she checked, and it was true: all the old emails to and from her kids had vanished off her computer, as if they'd deleted themselves. All of Scott's curious messages, wanting to know every last thing about the strange phenomenon she was studying. Even Polly's drawing of a cat with a unicorn's horn, gone. She sat on her bed and thought for a long time.

The next day she demanded to leave on the next plane out, and over the following weeks Goodco delivered one feeble excuse after another why she needed to stay. But then finally, when they gave their permission, an unscheduled flight made ready to leave right away—a woman at the Kiwi base had slipped in the shower, and Samantha could hitch a ride on her medical transport. She landed in New

Zealand, and gave back her red coat, and caught a plane to Los Angeles, and then another to Philadelphia. Scott and Polly and their father, John, would be meeting her at the airport—or so they said in an email she could no longer find five minutes after she read it.

She deplaned into the terminal, exited the secure area, and almost didn't see the chauffeur holding a sign with her name on it. She wasn't looking for her name, after all; she was looking for her family. But she approached the uniformed man with a little frown on her face.

"I'm Samantha Doe," she told him. "I wasn't expecting a driver."

The chauffeur tucked the sign under his arm and fished something shiny out of his pocket.

"I've been instructed to give you this," he said, and handed her a small gold octagonal hoop.

She turned it in her hand. "What is it? It . . . heh . . . it looks like a miniature particle collider."

"Put it on."

"What?"

"I've been instructed to tell you to put it on."

"Instructed by whom? My ex-husband?" she said as she slipped the thing onto her wrist. Then, wincing, she asked, "Was it always glowing?"

And then she was gone.

● ○ ★

Thirty feet away, Scott gasped. He couldn't help it. There was no flash of light, no puff of smoke. His mother was just there, and then she wasn't. She wasn't anywhere. She wasn't anywhere in the whole universe.

"GO GO GO GO!" shouted someone in the crowd, and then ten ordinary-looking men converged on the startled chauffeur and seized his arms—Freemen, laying in wait for Scott and his friends to show themselves. Members of the Good and Harmless Freemen of America, a secret society of creeps who did Goodco's bidding. Scott's heart started pounding against his chest like it wanted out— and why not? The last time he'd seen so many Freemen in one place, they'd tried to dissect his friends.

"What the—" sputtered the chauffeur as the Freemen held him fast. "Lemme go! What happened to that lady?"

The surrounding men, in their plain clothes and scarves, looked to an older Freeman in a black cowboy hat and duster, who stood apart and scanned the faces in the crowd. Then he turned to the driver.

"Who hired you?" Scott heard him growl.

"Some old guy," said the chauffeur in a high voice. "Look, what's this about?"

"It's the wizard's work," the man in black told the others. "Must be. Fan out, he might be close."

The man in black was both right and wrong—the wizard was close, but the wizard wasn't a wizard.

Scott started to move, but Merle laid a hand on his shoulder.

"Stay put," the old man said.

Scott's wig felt itchy. His fake glasses felt fake. In his black wig and big black glasses, he felt like Clark Kent. A kind of bizarro universe Clark Kent who removes his glasses and for some reason his hair to reveal that he is actually a perfectly ordinary blond boy with a mild peanut allergy.

Well, not so ordinary, really. He was part fairy, on his father's side. Plus he had a leprechaun in his backpack.

"Is he really Merlin?" another Freeman asked the man in black. "They say he turns people into animals."

"I *wish*," huffed Mick, the leprechaun. Merle could only do a few cool things, and he was already doing most of them.

"*He's* the reason all the magic left our world," another man told his fellow Freemen, glancing around, his voice the reedy voice of the True Believer. "*Merlin*. He's why it's all trapped in another dimension with the elves and fairies."

"Not true," Merle muttered under his breath.

"And now he's trying to ruin the Fay's Grand Plan to bring the worlds together. Him and his friends. He's *powerful*—"

"He's just a very old man who knows some card tricks,"

insisted the Freeman in charge. "Nothing more. But . . . assume he could be anyone. Check the women for Adam's apples."

The so-called wizard just to Scott's left in the gift shop was not Scott's father. This man in a Mets sweatshirt and an identical pair of thick black glasses was a time-traveling scientist named Merle Lynn, and the glasses had been his idea. Each pair had a tiny light in the bridge that flashed thousands of times per second, too fast to see, and did something weird to the occipital lobe in the brain of any person looking directly at them. Scott didn't understand the details, but the upshot was that anyone staring you in the face would be transfixed by your glasses and not really notice anything else about you. These glasses were your secret identity. So even though there were evil men in the airport looking for Scott and Merle right this second, they paid no attention to the old man and the boy in the wigs and glasses standing stiffly by the Ben Franklin bottle-cap openers.

The Freemen were splitting up, showing people fake badges and asking them questions. Or maybe real badges—the Good and Harmless Freemen of America had a wide reach.

"They're coming," Scott whispered. "Why are we just standing here?"

"If we let 'em come to us, we'll look like a couple a'

nobodies with interesting glasses. If we move, we'll be a boy and an old man trying to leave. Your call."

Scott exhaled slowly as a Freeman in khakis and a pink shirt walked right through the gift shop and showed them a very authentic-looking police badge. Scott's wig felt like a pile of hay. He tried to maintain eye contact without looking like he was trying to maintain eye contact, which was quite a trick.

"Sorry to bother you two," said the Freeman. "But we're looking for a person of interest. Elderly Caucasian male? Mind if I ask you why you're here?"

"Waiting for my brother," Merle answered. "His flight's late."

"And which flight would that be?" asked the Freeman as he produced a smartphone from his jacket.

Had he really been paying attention, the Freeman might have noticed Scott and Merle tighten up inside their winter coats. Even the backpack flinched. But the fact that he hadn't yet registered that he was already looking at an elderly Caucasian male meant the glasses were doing what they were supposed to.

"From Dallas," said Merle.

The Freeman frowned at his phone. "You're in the wrong terminal. The only flights from Dallas are arriving into D and F. This is C."

"Son of a gun. Well, thanks for the help."

"Sure," the man told them. "You're free to go."

But they didn't. Outside the gift shop an old woman was shouting, "HOW DARE YOU?" to another Freeman who had apparently just asked her to prove she wasn't secretly a man.

"Whoop. That looks like trouble," the pink-shirted Freeman said. And he turned to leave, but here were these two people with glasses, still staring at him like idiots. He turned back.

"Everything all right?" he added. "You don't want to keep your brother waiting."

"Right," said Merle, and he tried to back away without looking away and accidentally knocked a City of Brotherly Love snow globe off a low table. And still he did not look away.

"Oopsie," Scott said weakly.

"Brilliant plan, this," said Mick, knowing he could only be seen and heard by a very few. "A disguise that requires eye contact. Maybe later I'll tell yeh abou' my idea for a bulletproof necktie."

The Freeman backed up. He squinted. He peered at Scott and Merle as if they were one of those posters that look like noise but that reveal a dolphin jumping over a heart if you cross your eyes just right. Then he took a picture with his phone. A picture of Merle and Scott in which their glasses would not flash but would rather perch awkwardly on their suddenly recognizable faces.

"Um," said the Freeman. Then Merle waved a white wand at him and the man fell, snoring, in a heap.

This wasn't magic, either. It was more like a futuristic Taser, Scott recalled as he and Merle plowed through people and Liberty Bell ashtrays and dashed back toward the parking garage.

"There!" shouted the man in the black hat. "Those two!" Nine men peeled away from whomever they'd been interrogating and sprinted after them.

"YOU ARE NOW ENTERING THE MOVING WALKWAY," said an electronic voice as Scott and Merle scampered shakily onto a low-walled conveyor belt for people who didn't appreciate having to walk a tenth of a mile to get to their cars.

"Your fault," yelled Merle. "Just sayin'. No reason we had to get this close."

"I had to see her," Scott answered, probably too low to hear.

"Archimedes," Merle said into his wristwatch. "Bring the van around."

The narrow moving walkway created some confusion for nine men running abreast, so a number of them ran down the center of the carpeted hall instead and fell behind.

"Any o' them wearin' those pink goggles?" asked Mick.

"I don't think so," Scott answered. He didn't want to look. "I think they're trying to blend in."

"Aces," Mick said, and he zipped his cauliflower face out of the backpack. Then he hopped atop the black rubber handrail and ran back toward the Freemen.

"What's he doing?" shouted Merle.

Scott watched Mick curl into a ball and tumble down into the narrow alley of the walkway.

"I think he's bowling."

Freemen tripped and knocked against one another and bounced off the handrails.

"YOU ARE NOW EXITING THE MOVING WALKWAY."

Scott and Merle vaulted onto the carpet again and through the exit, and then they were standing in an alcove, a recessed bay of doors set into the airport building where it met the edge of the four-floor parking garage. They stepped out among the concrete pillars and ramps of the garage, where they were joined by a barn owl and a white van. The former flew to Merle's shoulder as the latter screeched to a halt in front of them.

They had no intention of getting in the van, though. The parking garage only had one narrow exit, and it was sure to be guarded. Mick caught up, and the three of them ran right around the van and hid themselves behind a huge gray column between two SUVs.

Merle spoke to the mechanical owl, Archimedes, and Freemen began pouring through the doors in time to see the white van peel away again.

"Blockade all C garage exits," one Freeman said into a walkie-talkie as the others moved to pursue the van.

"Wait!" said the man in the black hat. "He's tried this trick before. There's no one in that van."

"Great." Scott sighed. "They're getting smarter."

"Listen," said the black-hatted man, and the others listened. "Silence. He's still on this floor."

The Freemen stepped lightly, spreading out, bending to check under cars. When one drew close, Merle put him to sleep with the Slumbro and Mick helped drag him behind the pillar.

"Can you bring the van by again?" whispered Scott. And with his fist and a pair of running finger legs, he acted out a little scenario.

Merle raised his eyebrows and nodded. He gave the Slumbro to Scott and set about trying to explain the plan to his supercomputing robot owl. Scott flicked the wand when a second Freeman rounded the pillar, and they stacked him on top of the first one.

"Gettin' cozy back here," said Mick.

Scott heard an engine rumbling close, closer, but then it was only some lady in a blue hatchback. He whispered, "How long before the van gets back?"

"Maybe a minute."

A minute felt like a long time just now. The Freemen seemed to be everywhere—had more arrived? Maybe some of them were only passengers. A flight attendant pulling a pair of suitcases passed too close, and Scott put her to sleep before he could stop himself.

"Shoot, sorry," he hissed. "Sorry." Mick put her with the others.

Then Scott felt the van's congested engine draw near. Merle was hesitating.

"Can't do it yet," he groused, and nodded at a clutch of passengers entering through the alcove that separated the terminal from the garage. "Regular people in the way." Then they cleared and he added, "Archie, peel out."

Nearby they heard the fuss of the engine, the shriek of tires, the high whine of a belt that probably needed replacing. The van lurched forward, and so did Scott, Merle, and Mick, four bodies running at once toward the same finish line, and Scott really hoped Archimedes had a firm grasp of the geometry of the situation.

"There they are!" shouted someone, and a dozen undercover Freemen in their polos and chinos began to crab walk back through the sea of cars toward the terminal entrance. The fat white van hurtled around the corner, and Scott, Mick, and Merle crossed directly in front of it at top speed, with Archimedes flapping behind.

The van was braking now, filling the garage with a kind of angry whale song.

They threw themselves back into the bay of doors, pitched through those doors and into the terminal, then turned just in time to see the reeling white van parallel park itself neatly inside the alcove.

It was close. The driver's side mirror was nearly touching the door glass. Freemen tried to squeeze through a gap between the van and the wall, but Scott reached through a crack in the terminal doors and put them to sleep.

"Hold back!" the Freeman in the black hat ordered.

On the terminal side, a man with a duffel and a suntan and rubber sandals was just starting to take in the scene.

"Hey," he said. "My car is out there."

The black-hatted Freeman stood out of range of the wand and glared through the gap.

"That was your mom that disappeared, wasn't it, kid?" he asked. "What did you do to her?"

"We sent her into the future!" Scott called back. Exactly a year into the future, to be precise, but they didn't need to know that. "She's *safe* from you people!"

"C'mon," Merle urged. Mick climbed back into the backpack.

"Is this some kind of flash mob or something?" asked the man in the rubber sandals. "Are you going to move that van soon?"

"Sorry," said Scott, and he and Merle proceeded to leave.

"But my car's out there. I need it for driving."

"Sorry!"

They jogged back the way they had come and turned toward a down escalator to baggage claim.

"Stop right there!" someone shouted, and they turned to see the same Freeman who'd interrogated them in the gift shop, running down the moving walkway.

"What's he doing awake already?" said Merle.

Scott squinted at the Slumbro. "You know you have this set on NAP?"

"What? Give it here."

The escalator was crowded, so they fast stepped down some stairs.

"She's . . . she's really safe, right?" asked Scott. "Just in the future?"

"What can I say that'll make you believe me? I double-checked the math. Archie triple-checked it!"

"And Emily checked it too?"

Merle sighed. "Yes, Emily checked it too."

The Freeman was negotiating the escalator behind them and speaking into a walkie-talkie.

"Repeat, subjects are entering C baggage claim. Over."

Baggage claim was a wide tiled hall encircled by doors and big windows, filled with people and luggage and luggage carousels. You could turn in either direction to head outdoors, where the curbsides were packed with shuttles and taxis.

Scott was beginning to understand how to spot the Freemen. They all appeared to be wearing at least a little pink—a scarf, a shirt, maybe a hatband—and a number of them were coming to join him at the base of the stairs. So was a bald and topknotted Hare Krishna in white robes, who'd been slouching over a rattling tambourine and handing out pamphlets near two suitcases in a corner. Everyone else in baggage claim had been doing their best to ignore him, such that most had not even noticed his tall stature or the fact that he'd been chanting "Hairy Christmas" for twenty minutes. But now, standing straight, he towered over Goodco's pawns like the white king on a chessboard.

Scott and Merle stopped on the stairs about a half flight from the bottom, so the Freeman on the escalator just passed them, slowly, with an embarrassed look on his face.

"All right, you two," another Freeman in a pink tie said to Scott and Merle and, to a lesser extent, Mick. "You can't put us all to sleep."

"Can't we?" Scott whispered.

"Prob'ly not."

"Um, sir?" A Freeman addressed the tall figure in

white. "This isn't safe here—please step away."

Just then the Hare Krishna's two suitcases unzipped and released a brown-skinned boy and a pale and dainty little girl. And the tall figure threw off his robe and stick-on topknot to reveal a blockheaded monster of a former librarian. Nearby people gasped, and a family of four burst into applause.

"It's the bigfoot!" cried one of the Freemen, turning from Biggs to Emily. "And the girl!"

"And the boy!" said Erno. "Who's also super scary!" But it wasn't clear that anyone was paying attention.

They had every reason to fear Emily, who actually *had* turned a woman into a donkey a couple of months back. But she couldn't control that sort of thing, so when Merle began wanding people to sleep and Biggs starting lifting Freemen over his head, she and Erno just joined Scott on the fringes and tried to stay out of the way. Ordinary people all around the hall screamed or called for the police. The room was clearing fast. Mick leaned over Scott's shoulder.

"I should get in there," he said. "Start punchin' kneecaps."

"Maybe we should stay together."

"When I thought about all this going down, I imagined us doing something useful," said Erno.

"Can you remember what it was?" asked Scott.

Erno chewed his lip. "It was always kind of hazy."

More and more Freemen. The crew from the parking garage had found their way to ground level and entered baggage claim from the outside. Biggs was surrounded but still fighting. Merle was essentially hiding behind a small pile of Freemen and shaking his Slumbro beside his ear.

"That can't be a good sign," Scott muttered.

"Some of 'em have guns," said Mick. "Why aren't they usin' 'em?"

"Was that Mick talking just now?" Emily asked.

"You could hear him? You're getting better."

"Yeah, but I couldn't understand him. It just sounded like a little mosquito."

"No, that's right," said Erno. "That's what he sounds like."

"Shut it, lad."

"Mick was wondering why they weren't using their guns," said Scott.

"They're going to," Emily said. "Now that all the real people are gone. Watch."

Baggage claim had emptied out. The luggage carousels were choking on unclaimed bags. Freemen glanced about—no witnesses now.

"I better put a scare into them," Emily said.

"What, you?" said Erno. "What can you do?"

"Please. You *know* I've been studying pop culture," said Emily.

"Is that what you call watching a lot of TV?"

Erno and Emily hadn't been allowed television or movies growing up, so lately Emily had been making up for lost time. "I've been catching up on all the horror movies from the last thirty years, and apparently there's nothing scarier than a little girl acting spooky."

"Puppets," suggested Scott.

"Okay, yes. Puppets or a little girl acting spooky. Bonus if she's wearing a pretty party dress. Which I *am*."

"I don't understand," said Erno.

"What if I talk like thiiiiis," she sang.

"Geez. Yeah, do that."

Emily stepped forward, slowly, but jerking now and then as if she herself were a puppet guided by an unsteady hand. Freemen turned and noticed. With a blank face and dead eyes, she raised her arms and slowly sang "Pop Goes the Weasel" in a ghostly voice.

"Oh *no*," a man whispered. Freemen started backing away.

"Look out, something bad's gonna happen! Like in that movie with the puppet."

"She turned someone into an *owl*!" said another.

"That's the wizard's owl. It was always an owl."

Meanwhile, Emily exhausted "Pop Goes the Weasel" and started in on the national anthem.

Merle made his way over to Scott.

"Slumbro's on the fritz. It isn't holding a charge anymore."

"Does it need a new battery?"

"Hope not. They haven't been invented yet. You think this ploy of Emily's is gonna get us out of here?"

"Can't be worse than any other part of our plan."

Two Freemen lost their nerve and ran for the exit.

"You heard them upstairs," Scott told Merle. "They're afraid of you too."

"Good point," said Merle, and he pocketed his wand and waved his arms around, chanting in Latin.

*"Admonitio! Insani magica tempus!"**

What followed was a lot of tripping, running every which way, and repeated orders from the black-hatted Freeman to "STAND YOUR GROUND." But then the tinted doors of the south baggage claim entrance opened, filling the hall with light, and in glided a lovely, horrible woman. Emily dropped her act and suddenly looked every bit the little girl she was. Biggs roared. Merle muttered something that wasn't Latin but was no less exotic.

"Nimue," whispered Scott. Perhaps she heard, because she fixed her eyes on him and smiled.

"Freemen!" the woman sang. "Behind me!"

The remaining men scurried to her side like children. She looked good, which could only be bad. It meant she'd

---

* "Warning! Crazy magic time!"

22

been feeding on stolen magic and had glamour to burn. Her black hair was pulled up and piled atop her head in glossy ringlets like a tangled telephone cord. Her dress was red as a wound, with a bodice of crow's wings and milky pearls. It was hard to take your eyes off her.

It was so hard, in fact, that no one noticed a girl dash into the hall through the opposite entrance.

Nimue raised her slender arms, looking only at Scott. He could guess why. They'd foiled Nimue last time because she was weak and she didn't know Scott's True Name. He felt certain that she wanted him to know now that she'd figured it out, or was currently so powerful it wouldn't matter either way.

"We should run," said Scott.

"Can't outrun this." Mick sighed.

Then, suddenly, Polly was at his side. Scott turned to his little sister and said, "What are you do—"

"Lift me high!" said a small but confident voice that seemed to come straight from Polly's gut. She raised her hands, and in her palms stood a tiny black-skinned man, no larger than a toy, brandishing a birch-bark shield the size of a postage stamp.

"MACBETH DOE!" shouted Nimue, and a cold flash of roiling light tumbled toward them. "MERLE L—"

Then the light spasmed, rippled, and the woolly haze of it spun down into a single thread that plunged into the

center of the birch-bark shield and was gone.

Nimue gagged, wide-eyed, and pitched forward. The Freemen at her sides caught her before she hit the floor face-first.

"Yay, Prince Fi!" shouted Polly. The tiny man shuddered as the shield glowed fitfully like a loose lightbulb. He shook it until it was nothing but dead wood again.

Scott leaned close to Polly. "I thought you were supposed to stay in the car."

"Yeah—like Dad could keep me in the car."

"P-PIXIE?!" spat Nimue. She struggled for composure as the Freemen advanced. "How on this sterile doornail of a planet do you have a freaking pixie?!"

"It's kind of your fault, actually," Erno told her.

"Remind us to tell you about it next time," Merle added, fiddling with his watch. "Kids?"

"YOUR FAULT, MERLIN!" she screamed as they ran for the north doors and the Freemen followed. "EVERYTHING'S BROKEN, AND IT'S YOUR FAULT!"

Biggs burst through first, carrying Emily under one arm, and soon they were all in the sunlit, airy freedom of the outdoors. Two white vans bucked up onto the curb, clumsily—one because it was being controlled remotely by Merle and his wristwatch, the other because it was being driven by Harvey. Harvey was half man, half rabbit, and all jerk. He had just the right mixture of self-regard and disregard for everyone else that you wanted in a getaway driver.

In a moment Biggs had the back of Harvey's van open, and then they were face-to-tiny-smoldering-face with a fluttering, fire-breathing finch. Blue sparks pitched from his beaky nostrils.

"It's us, Finchbriton!" Mick said quickly. "It's us! Snuff it!"

Finchbriton chirruped and flew to Mick's shoulder as everyone piled into the van. Scott and Polly's dad was already there, and when he saw Polly he grabbed her shoulders and pulled her close.

Merle knocked on the roof. "All in! GO!"

The van lurched forward. The second van followed.

John hugged Polly tight—a desperate, crazy hug.

"You are crushing me," announced Prince Fi from somewhere in the middle.

"What did I tell you?" said John. "*What did I tell you?*"

"I thought they might need our help," Polly murmured. "And they did."

"I wished to be of service," said Fi. "The girl should have let me go alone."

The Freemen called for their vehicles and started their pursuit, but then the remote-controlled van opened its cargo doors and released the helium balloons, and the roadway was all fat colorful pandemonium, and by the time they cleared the vans had traded places, and the Freemen followed the wrong one.

"Am I in trouble?" Polly asked her father.

"You're . . . I don't know, grounded or something."

"Am I grounded too?" asked Merle.

"Everyone's grounded."

CHAPTER 2

December and January had been a strange couple of months, and that was saying something—November had been filled with magic animals and dark dealings in secret temples and an exploding cereal factory.

After the cereal factory exploded, Scott and his new sideshow of a family had gone on what his father insisted on calling "the lam." And here was the problem with that.

Scott's party included

- four children;
- an old man;
- an internationally famous showbiz personality;
- an eight-foot-tall librarian who needed to shave his body three times daily or thick, luxurious hair would surge from all but his palms, soles, and a T-shaped patch of face;

- a pixie prince who could hide in your pocket but who rebuffed any attempt to put him in a pocket because it was demeaning;
- a fire-breathing finch who didn't satisfactorily understand which occasions were and were not a good time for fire;
- a cat that tended to rub up against one's legs as if it didn't realize it had a six-inch unicorn horn coming out of its forehead;
- and a duo who were invisible to all but one in ten thousand but who otherwise appeared to be a two-foot-tall leprechaun and a man with a rabbit's head. And the reason they appeared to be a leprechaun and a rabbit-man was because that was what they were.

Scott and Erno and Emily had made a little game of dreaming up ways their group could be even more conspicuous than it already was.

"We could add a clown," said Erno.

"We could wear big sombreros," said Scott.

"I respectfully disagree about the clown," said Emily. "People avoid eye contact with clowns. The clown could actually be a big help." And you could almost see her make a mental note: *Hire Clown.*

"We could all get parrots," Scott said. "Parrots that scream all the time."

"We could get one of those inflatable gorillas they put on car dealerships."

Incidentally, *"Hire Clown"* was actually a pretty good description of their getaway philosophy so far.

"People tend to behave like it's the movies," Emily had lectured to the group. "So the Freemen will be watching all the airports, because that's what you do when you're trying to track people down. But do you know what people on the run never do in movies? They never take hot-air balloons. They never hire a mule train or a paddleboat down the Mississippi. They don't go on luxury cruises. We're going to do all those things."

John raised his hand. "Can we get motorcycles with sidecars? I've always wanted one."

Emily shrugged. "It's your money."

They'd been spending John's money like it was cursed, or on fire. He was their own personal Scrooge McDuck.

And so in this way they'd stayed a step ahead of Goodco and the Freemen while they made their plans. They'd rented an ice cream truck. They'd taken something called the Charleston Choo Choo. After leaving the Philadelphia airport, they abandoned their white van in a Center City garage and hired a guided tour across the Delaware on an amphibious vehicle called the Duck. In New Jersey, thrillingly close to Goodborough, they piled aboard a party bus custom painted to say CONGRATULATIONS ALEX AND STEVE.

"Weird being this close to home and not going there," Emily whispered to Erno. But Scott and Polly had not lived in Goodborough long enough for it to feel like home. Their home had just vanished a year into the future, postponed.

"Three hundred and sixty days until she's back," Scott told Polly.

Each of them staked their claim to a section of the bus. Biggs and Harvey and John traded shifts driving; Erno and Emily selected adjacent bench seats. Scott shifted around based on wherever seemed to be the quietest place to read at any given time—he was on his second book of King Arthur stories, trying to learn all the ins and outs. Polly taped off two whole rows, named the area Fancylvania, and tried to talk Prince Fi into an official state visit. But the little pixie camped instead atop the ceiling-mounted television—the only spot outside the bathroom where he could be certain not to have to watch it. And everybody avoided the bathroom.

The party bus seemed almost specially designed to give you motion sickness, what with its pulsing neon and disco ball and bad transmission. Every time they hit a bump it played Kool and the Gang for three minutes, and they hadn't been able to figure out where it was coming from.

"I don't know this song," Merle told Scott. "Is it from your generation?"

"I think it's more from my mom's," Scott answered. "Or her mom's? People play it at weddings, or . . . parties . . . or—"

"Or whenever they want to 'celebrate good times,' yeah. I sorta picked that up from the lyrics."

Scott smirked. "I can't believe I'm asking this, but . . . have you been born yet?"

"Heh. Later this year, actually. About a month after the fairies take over. If all goes well, I'm thinking of gatecrashing my own baby shower."

"That's weird."

"It is what it is." Merle shrugged. "In five years I enter kindergarten. In sixteen I graduate high school, in eighteen I invent time travel to the future but not the past. In nineteen years I go so far into the future I pop up as Merlin in the next universe, and in about fourteen billion years you and me have this conversation again."

"No." Scott winced. "No, that's not right. You were

trying to invent time travel so you could go back and prevent the invasion, right? If we stop the fairies from invading, you'll never invent time travel, maybe. The next universe'll be different."

"Or maybe I do all of this, every time. Maybe I always fail. Maybe I always say, 'Maybe I always fail.' Every twenty-eight billion years I sit on a bus and say that."

Mick crawled over the back of Merle's bench and thumped down beside him. "If yeh believed that, yeh wouldn't be sharin' this pig's breakfast with us."

"If I be*lieved* it, I'd know I don't have a choice, and I'd be doing it anyway."

Scott sighed. "This is why I don't like time-travel stories."

At fourteen Merle didn't like time-travel stories either, if only because they never had anything useful to teach him. But he'd read and watched them all.

As a boy he believed that time travel must be possible because it felt possible. Natural, even. When a terrible thing happened, didn't the human mind keep looking for solutions, even after the thing had passed? *If I could just not have been so loud, I could save them. If I could only have been more brave.*

Every new technology seemed to be preparing human

33

minds for the time travel discovery that could only be right around the corner. Instant replays. Undo buttons. Games that let you save your progress and face the boss monster again and again. After his parents were gone, Merle had a lot of time to himself, and he filled it with physics textbooks and books of folklore and crackpot websites. Friends were a distraction. When the past was repaired, he would have all the time in the world for friends.

At his high school graduation, he was a full four inches shorter than the next shortest boy.

The ceremony was watched over by the usual trolls, the same sort of Redcaps that surveilled any gathering of more than twenty humans these days. But after Merle threw his mortarboard in the air with the rest of his class and pushed back through the crowd to find his aunt, he found her standing stiffly beside a tall and stately elf. A sickeningly familiar elf.

"It was a . . . a *lovely* ceremony," Aunt Meredith said haltingly, as if she were fighting for breath. "Such a . . . *orderly* ceremony. The graduates weren't any problem at all—"

"I am not here as a peacekeeper, lady," the elf said in that way some of them had, where their voices seemed to come at you from everywhere at once. "I want only to congratulate your nephew. Privately, an' it please you."

Aunt Meredith was snuffling. She pulled her fingers

across her eyes. "Allergies," she murmured.

"It's okay, Tante," Merle told her. His heart was going sour in him. "I'll meet you at the el stop."

Other graduates and their families passed, giving them a wide berth, watching out of the corners of their eyes. Aunt Meredith lingered a moment, uncertain, but when Merle nodded again and jerked his head, she bustled off and left him alone with the fairy.

He was one of those regal, Tolkienesque elves that made you feel fat and unlovely. Six-five, lean, sloe-eyed, with short green mossy hair. A soldier's haircut. A strange mix of both human and fairy sensibilities: a silk hoodie, leather shorts, wristlet braided from dandelion greens, Converse One Stars. Off duty, obviously—only the pink dragon insignia on his red cap told you he was a

35

captain of the Trooping Fairies of Oberon.

People his aunt's age and older loved to tell one another how unnatural it all still seemed, even fifteen years on: spotting a centaur waiting to use an ATM, assorted gnomes at Coney Island, the Questing Beast sniffing garbage cans outside the Pick 'N Save. They said it with this tragic air, as if it wasn't a gift to have memories of the world as it was before. Merle would give everything to be surprised by the sight of an elf under his high school bleachers.

"Do you remember me?" asked the elf.

Merle huffed. "Is that a joke?" He felt faint.

The elf pretended to watch other graduates pass.

"My name is Conor, by the by."

"Right. Sure it is."

"I want you to know I took no pleasure from that day. I assayed only to do my duty."

"Then your duty sucks. You have an evil duty."

"If that were so, then my glamour would have failed me, and I would have died, and your mother would have lived. My actions were just."

"Don't give me that bull. Her gun backfired, is all. Don't you . . . don't you *dare* tell me you won because the universe *wanted* you to."

The way Conor was glancing around, Merle wondered if he was waiting for all the other humans to clear out. What happened when there were no more witnesses?

Maybe then the elf finished what he'd left undone, six years before. At last they were alone, and Conor frowned at his feet.

"You're being watched, Merle."

Merle felt a chill. "What, right now?"

"Always."

Merle hiccuped, nervously. Whenever he'd imagined this scenario, he'd always carried himself with a little more dignity. He hadn't been wearing a black satin gown, for example.

"They suspect what you're up to," Conor continued. "My superiors. They haven't seen fit to share their suspicions with me, but . . . I remember seeing you before, Merle."

"Yeah. *Six years ago June.* I remember that too."

"No, not six years. Centuries. I observed a dispute over a tower that would not stand, and you were there. And yet you were older, no longer a boy. I think you understand me."

Merle thought maybe he *did* understand. A thrill ran through him.

"And . . . you're telling me this why?"

Conor looked up finally, studied Merle awhile before answering.

"You know, the Fay have always taken human children," he said. "I might've taken *you* that June day.

Raised you as my own. You weren't so old."

Was that some kind of weird threat? Merle hiccuped again, felt empty-headed. Darkness creeped like a stain around the edges of his sight.

"I wonder if I did right, leaving you there with your mother and father. I wonder if I could have taken hold of a wheel then, stopped it spinning. What threads might be lost if I had?"

"You talk a lot," Merle slurred, swaying. "Is it your glamour making me feel like this? You hoping for a mysterious exit? I'm not going to faint, so you'll just have to look me in the eye and leave."

"Take care, Merlin," Conor said. Then Merle drooped, and fade to black.

After a couple of years at university, Merle had a reputation for being obsessive about western European folklore and brilliant at quantum physics, and not much else. It was understood that if you needed an explanation of the Pauli exclusion principle or wanted to know who built Stonehenge, you should get someone to let you into basement lab three, because day or night that's probably where Merle was.

A couple grad students poked their heads in.

"Hey—Merlin."

"Yeah, hey—Merlin."

"What," said Merle. He didn't look up from his soldering.

"Hey . . . how many pookas in a quark?"

"How many . . . ," Merle repeated idly. Then he turned his head to scowl at them. "How many pookas in a quark? That doesn't even make sense."

"What's the problem?"

"Well . . . you presumably have a lot of quarks in a pooka, but pookas in a quark? One's a subatomic particle. The other's one of the shape-shifting Fay. Don't you know the difference between physics and fairies?"

"*I* do." The first grad student scoffed. "I just didn't think *you* did."

The other student laughed.

"That's really funny," Merle told them. "Come closer and I'll show you how a soldering iron works."

"See ya, Merlin."

"Yeah, see ya, Merlin."

Professor Strohmer entered as they left. He stood and watched Merle work for a moment before speaking.

"You're back in the lab already?"

"Not back in it; still in it. Hey, watch the hoses. That's liquid helium you're tripping on."

Strohmer picked the remains of a microwave burrito off an adjacent stool and sat down. "You smell, Merle. And I hope you realize I'm only telling you this because you smell. You need a shower and you need to go to sleep."

"I have classes."

"You do have classes. You have my class, for example. And you know as well as I do that you're going to skip it and hide in here all day with your . . . chimera."

Merle clucked his tongue. "What do you mean, chimera?"

"Well . . . ," the professor began, adjusting his glasses. "It can mean a few things. But I meant 'something hoped for which is nonetheless impossible.'"

"It's not impossible. Just . . . very, very hard."

"I know what you're trying to build, Merle. And why. I heard about your parents."

Merle flinched. "How did you hear that? I never told—"

"I'm sorry. Word gets around. But we're talking about time travel, Merle. Time travel to the *past*, no less. It's science fiction. It's a f . . . it's a—"

"*Fairy tale?*" Merle said, turning. "You were gonna say fairy tale, weren't you."

"Merle—"

"You notice how members of my generation don't use that phrase? I wonder why that is."

"I think I've been giving you too much leeway, Merle."

"Hey—you know what else chimera can mean? It can mean a mythological monster made up of different animal parts. Like a griffin or a sphinx? And I know sphinxes are real, because there's one LIVING ON TOP OF THE LAUNDROMAT NEAR MY HOUSE."

"Okay, calm down—"

"I HAVE TO ANSWER RIDDLES TO USE THE CHANGE MACHINE."

Strohmer got up from the stool. "I'm going to try this again some other time."

"Wait," Merle said, and stepped back. "Sit down. I'm sorry. I'm just a little . . . off. I haven't slept in two days. But I can't leave the lab just yet. I'm waiting for something."

Strohmer had his hands on his hips, watching Merle like he was watching a dog rolling in filth, wondering if he should correct the behavior or just let nature run its course.

"You know I respect your opinion," Merle added quickly. "Your work with fairy metals is the main reason I chose this school."

Everyone knew by now that Fay treasure couldn't be trusted. Maybe some satyr would pay you in gold pieces, more than he should have, even; but if you didn't go and spend them quickly enough, you'd find you had a purse full of buttercups or some such.

Professor Strohmer had been the first to recognize that those buttercups must have been imbued with a kind of energy when they were changed into gold, and that they released this energy again when they changed back. Other scientists took his research and found a way to stabilize the gold somewhat, so that it held its energy like a battery and only let go a little at a time. Suddenly any mundane thing could be powered by fairy gold, with unpredictable results. Even old guys like Strohmer had to admit that what they were doing might not strictly be science anymore.

Merle had a robot owl that he'd hacked and tinkered with, and this owl had a fairy battery that would keep it running for centuries.

"Those fairy metals have given us a lot of things," Strohmer reminded him. "We're going to beat global warming because of fairy metals."

"Uh-huh."

"I'm just saying . . . maybe this whole crusade of yours is a little misguided? The resistance movement your parents were a part of has all but died out. I know we've lost some things, some freedoms, but . . . have you read the new paper in *Nature*? The average human lifespan has increased by almost five years just since the Fay came! Some believe that a baby born this year may live to two hundred!"

"Yeah, a lot of animals live longer in captivity," Merle muttered.

The professor exhaled, then slapped his legs and rose

from the stool again, looking for his exit strategy.

"Hey, speaking of kids, whatever happened to your toy owl? I remember when you started here, that thing never left your shoulder."

"He's helping me with an experiment," said Merle.

"Well . . . when he gets back, tell him I said you should both power down for a while."

"If I did my math right, you can tell him yourself in . . ." Merle consulted his watch. "Six minutes."

Merle must have had a look on his face. Strohmer eyed him suspiciously.

"What happens in six minutes?"

And then, suddenly, Archimedes was there. He appeared, flapping, just above their heads. He clasped a golden octagonal ring in his talons.

Strohmer started and tripped over the helium hose in earnest. Merle was short of breath. "Okay. Wow. It worked." He checked his watch again. "I guess I got the math wrong, though."

"What just—" Strohmer sputtered. "Where was he?"

The owl landed and held the ring out to Merle.

"Nowhere. He was nowhere. I sent him into the future, one year ago."

"Why is it always a year?" Scott asked now, on the bus. "Couldn't you just have sent Archie five minutes into the future?"

"Could," Merle admitted. "But then I'd never have seen him again. Remember, the earth's always looping around the sun. In five minutes, the planet and everything on it would have moved five thousand miles to the right, and Archie would've popped up in empty space somewhere. Same with your mom. In a year the earth'll get back around to exactly where it was when she left, and she'll materialize in the same airport terminal."

Scott pictured it: his mom appearing suddenly, a little woozy maybe, wearing a bracelet made of fairy gold and wondering where her chauffeur had disappeared to.

Their tire grazed a pothole, and the music started playing again. Tiny spotlights fractured off the mirror ball and swam in schools around the inside of the bus. The

44

unicat chased these around while Finchbriton pecked at the mirrors.

"Here's what I don't get," Scott told Mick. "You say most Fay aren't spellcasters. Your magic is like really good luck. So how do you turn worthless things into gold?"

"We don't," said Mick. "I mean, not deliberately. It's like . . . yeh know when you're walkin', an' yeh think yeh see somethin' valuable on the ground maybe? Silver, or a diamond, or even just a quarter. But then yeh look closer, an' it's only a candy wrapper, or a piece o' glass."

"Sure."

"Well, when one o' the Fay thinks he sees a treasure, he's almost always right."

"Hey," said Erno, and he glanced over at where Harvey was sleeping, then back at Scott. "Hey, your dad's still driving the bus, right? Because the TV says he's at a French disco."

John (or rather Reggie Dwight, or rather two goblins masquerading as Reggie Dwight) was shown exiting a cab and entering the club above the caption "'Knight' Out on the Town." Then they flashed a few clips of Reggie from his movies and music videos, and then they showed the cab-to-club footage again in slow motion.

"What was that?" John called back from the driver's seat. "You say I'm on the telly?"

"I would never say telly, but yeah." .

45

"Who's got the remote?" asked Emily.

"Hey, Fi," said Scott. "Can you reach the volume?"

"I see no volumes," Fi answered.

"I got it," said Polly, and the bus speakers blared with the voice of the entertainment reporter, which had all the artless tenor of a toddler announcing to a crowded room that she has to go tinkle.

". . . cameras inside, but sources say he danced the night away with nearly everyone in the club. Vive la différence! Including this American college student studying abroad."

A redheaded girl tried to keep from grinning before the cameras outside the club. She wore a tiny T-shirt that showed that she was from Colorado, or Wyoming, or just a fan of rectangles. "I asked if I could take his picture with my phone?" she said. "So he took my phone and he put it in his mouth."

"In his mouth?"

"It was a really small phone. Then he swallowed it? Then he said I could get my pictures back in twenty-four hours. Do you think that means we have a date? I gave him my number, but he didn't write it down."

"Did he punch anyone?"

"He punched three people."

"Tell us about the punching."

"He punched one guy who asked to be punched 'cause

his girlfriend's a fan? Then he punched a girl I think by accident 'cause of his dancing. Then later he punched a guy who wouldn't let him cut in the bathroom line."

"ARE YOU KIDDING ME?" John bellowed from the front of the bus. "Oh my lord."

Goodco had only targeted John in the first place because they were rubbing out knights—it was nothing personal. But now it was like the goblin impostors were going out of their way to behave badly.

"All the better to make John look like a lunatic if he tries to tell the world what Goodco's up to," Emily suggested.

"My career is *over!*"

"Shh!" Erno shushed back.

"Those goblins are ruining my life!"

"*Shhh!*"

The cameras had gone back to Entertainment News Central or whatever they called it. The show's logo rotated on three big screens, and the anchorwoman stood rigidly in front of them like a pedestal with a smile on it.

"Reggie Dwight's bad-boy behavior began when he punched Queen Elizabeth II at a horse racing track last November. Fans of Reggie Dwight and royal watchers the world over want to know when the singer-actor and the Queen of England will sit down together and bury the hatchet. Sources close to the queen say that Her Majesty is still upset over Sir Reggie's unprovoked attack, but officially she's keeping 'mum.' It could be that rambunctious Reggie won't rest until his queen says 'good knight.' Now in celebrity baby news—"

"TURN IT OFF TURN IT OFF TURN IT OFF," said Prince Fi from atop the TV, where he crouched in a ball with his arms wrapped around his head. Polly did as he asked. Fi sighed and uncurled. "Like the foul wind of a thousand harpies," he explained, straightening. "Every television is surely swarming with demons too coarse for Pandora's box."

"Yeah, it's a pretty bad show," Erno agreed.

Despite having no good times to celebrate, they hit another bump.

CHAPTER 3

In Halifax, Polly wrapped John's head in bandages, save for a bare strip around his eyes that she covered with sunglasses and a thin slit over his mouth. If anyone asked, they were going to say he'd burned himself horribly somehow.

"We could tell people you were looking down the barrel of a flamethrower," Polly suggested.

"And why would I have done that," John sighed.

"To see why it wasn't working. Like in a cartoon."

"We could say you took a hot omelet to the face," said Merle.

"Couldn't it be something a little more . . . heroic?"

"Are you okay?" Scott asked Emily. She was rubbing her temples. She didn't look like she'd slept.

"Just a headache," she answered with a feeble wave. But you couldn't help but get Scott's sympathies with the word *headache*. He used to have migraines all the time. Every

49

time he saw magical things, actually, but he'd finally gotten used to them, and his headaches had mostly gone away.

"Weird dreams," Emily added absently.

They abandoned the party bus and walked down to the water toward a massive white cruise ship that rose like a cathedral from the dock. Harvey carried the unicat, which he was calling Grimalkin in defiance of every other name that had been suggested so far (Pointy, Stabs, Cat Stabbins, Lance, Pierce, Al Gore), in the hope that he'd be able to sneak quietly on board without getting either of them noticed. Mick and Prince Fi played gin rummy in Scott's backpack.

"Welcome to the *Canadian Diamond Queen*!" said a polo-shirted young woman when they reached the end of the queue. Then she put the brakes on her smile a little bit. Her attention swerved to avoid the giant and the man in bandages and finally parked itself on Merle. Here was someone familiar: a senior citizen, just like the last fifteen passengers she'd admitted. You could see her struggling to find the common thread that bound him to everyone else. Carnies? Circus people?

"Carnies," Merle told her.

"Uh-huh. Well! Welcome aboard! Make sure to have your picture taken with one of our cast at the top of the gangway!"

"Cast?" asked John. "You don't mean crew?"

The woman jumped when he spoke. "We . . . call them cast."

"Everyone wants to be in show business," John muttered as he passed. "Did you see how she flinched?" he added when they were out of earshot. "What, just because I burned my face I'm not allowed to speak?"

"You didn't really burn your face," Scott reminded him.

"Maybe she expected you to be mute," said Merle.

Erno said, "Maybe she expected you to cackle about how you're going to show all those fools, those fools who thought you were mad."

They entered the ship and plowed past the photographers. "We wrapped my face so I could be anonymous," John groused. "This isn't anonymous, this is just a worse kind of famous."

The inside of the ship looked like a floating Cheesecake Factory. It looked like a huge fancy gift shop. It looked like the tomb of King Hallmark III.

It also looked like Biggs was going to be doing a lot of slouching. The guest areas, with their hallways and cabins, were all narrow and low ceilinged. The rooms themselves were barely larger than the beds, with closets the size of bathrooms and bathrooms the size of closets. But each had a dozen free movies on the TV and chocolates on the pillows and a balcony that overlooked the ocean. Finchbriton met them on one of these balconies.

"There yeh are," Mick said to him. "Wanna join me under the bed? 'S roomy."

Mick and Harvey, who both preferred the undersides of beds, were sharing a room with Scott and Erno. Polly was rooming with Emily and Grimalkin. John was with Merle, Biggs was by himself.

"Come to our room, Prince Fi," said Polly. "I'll make you a little apartment out of a dresser drawer."

Fi sighed. "Thank you . . . no. That would be unseemly. I shall share quarters with the boys."

Polly hugged her shoulders. "Yeah, you're . . . you're right. Unseemly."

After a safety drill the ship got under way. And Harvey got immediately seasick.

"Why didn't you tell us you had trouble with seasickness?" Scott asked through the balcony door during a brief spell in which Harvey had either just finished or was about to commence vomiting onto the balcony below.

"HOW WOULD I KNOW?" Harvey sputtered, shivering. "I'm a pooka! I uthed to live underground. I went through a hole in the univerthe to get to thith turd of a planet. I've never thailed an ocean before."

"Yeah." Scott tried to sympathize. "Mick told me all about how he just turned up in this world suddenly, in a baby carriage. I guess it must have been a weird surprise for you too. When you made the Crossing, I mean."

That's what the Freemen had called it in their secret papers: the Crossing. The Walk Between Worlds—when a person or animal from the shrinking magical land of Pretannica traded places with some other person or animal here.

"Yeah, big thurprize," Harvey answered. "Didn't thee it coming."

"So . . . how did it happen with you?" Scott asked the pooka. "How did you make the Crossing?"

"I would love to have thith converthation with you? But I'm thuper busy. Thith boat ithn't going to throw up on itthelf!"

Polly stepped out onto the balcony and plunked down into a plastic lounge chair. Harvey watched her out of the corner of his eye, as if she might weave him a friendship bracelet if he wasn't vigilant. She watched him back, appraisingly.

"I like your ears," she said.

"I wish I could thay the thame," he replied, wobbling.

"I think you must have been a really important fairy back in Pretannica," she continued, undeterred. "Girls are experts on this kind of thing. Like you must have been a prince or a jack or something."

Scott stared at his sister. Harvey did, too. "Showth what you know. I wath a *king*. Harvey the First of the

Lepusian Kingdom."

Polly nodded. "In my homeland I was known as Princess Babyfat Von Pumpkinbread. Before I was adopted by *commoners*," she added, indicating Scott. Harvey gave Scott a sneer.

Scott frowned. "Hey, I was just—"

"Leave uth! Leave uth before I—" shouted Harvey; but he didn't finish his sentence, unless the remainder was "vomit," in which case he finished it spectacularly.

Scott pulled his head back in.

"So wait . . . ," said Erno to Mick. "A five is higher than a king?"

"If it's a trump, yeah."

"This game is stupid."

"Harvey's pretty sick," Scott mentioned.

"The mongrel has brought it upon himself," said Prince Fi, who struggled to hold playing cards that were nearly as tall as he was. Like at any moment they might seize him and bring him before the Queen of Hearts, and then off with his head. "Hares are meant to eat vegetable matter, are they not?"

"I think he might have gotten some relish accidentally on his last hot dog," Scott offered.

"Harvey's got a little glamour left," said Mick. "It'll sort him out."

Scott watched them a moment, then shrugged. "All

54

right, whatever. I'm going to go play video games."

The thing about a moving cruise ship was that you couldn't get *too* lost. There was never any need for the parental admonishment, "Don't go too far." Unfamiliar adults, who in any other situation might have reported an unattended child or even tried to corral him like he was an unleashed dog, tended to ignore Scott even more than usual. Over the next few days he ate a sundae for breakfast, saw three movies while floating in a heated pool, failed to watch any whales during a whale watch, and accidentally took a Zumba class.

The fourth night was a formal night, which meant that everybody was expected to dress up extra nice for dinner. John had taken them to a tailor, so all the men and boys had tuxedos. Even Mick, who could wear the clothes off a ventriloquist's dummy if he took them in a bit. Even Biggs, who'd been greeted as if he were the natural disaster the tailor had been preparing for all his life.

Only Harvey couldn't come to dinner. His stomach had settled, but his rabbit head was still a rabbit head. If anyone saw Mick, his size could be explained by dwarfism or Made-Up Disease Syndrome or whatever. But Harvey? Harvey was stuck, and getting cabin fever. He claimed he could handle it after decades of confinement at Goodco headquarters, but in truth he'd been sneaking out while the rest were at dinner and idly stealing things from both passengers and crew—bath towels, cell phones, cocktail shakers, sunglasses and shoes left poolside while their owners swam. He didn't keep any of it; he threw it overboard—he wasn't a *thief*. It was only to pass the time.

On this night, servers flitted about in feathery masks, offering the adults free champagne. Violinists circled like mosquitoes. There were grand staircases that served mostly as backdrops for having one's picture taken, since every other passenger exclusively rode the elevators, of which there were twelve. But the staircases were nonetheless wide and made from great slabs of polished marble with gleaming gold banisters. Only if this gold could have been peeled back to reveal chocolate might the cruise have gotten any more stupidly self-indulgent.

John had a personal rule against using elevators if stairs were available, so they were always shooing photographers out of the way as they descended to Triton's Promenade Deck for meals. Passengers who had never considered using the stairs nonphotographically turned now to watch Scott's group make its entrance: first John, with his bandaged face and sunglasses; then massive, monstrous Biggs; and then . . . Polly and Merle. You could see their disappointment—just one wolfman or a Dracula away from a solid theme.

All food was included in the price of the cruise, so when their waiter came to the table Erno indulged his new habit of ordering the first three things on the menu and deciding later what he actually wanted to eat. Scott ordered two things himself, but the second was for Mick. Mick sat in an empty chair and tried not to grumble when the server always took his utensils away.

Their food came. Scott thought he knew what salmon looked like, so he was surprised to find a spiral of green foam topped by a puff pastry covered in yams.

"I think they brought me the wrong thing," he said. "I don't see any fish."

"We need to discuss our plans," said Emily.

"Oh, wait—I found it."

"We're going to want to move fast once we reach England," Emily added.

They had two good reasons for going to the British Isles. Papers in the Freemen filing cabinet Emily had memorized said that the real queen was being held captive in Avalon, in the west of England. And they also had indicated that Prince Fi's pixie brothers were prisoners of the Goodco U.K. headquarters in Slough, a town west of London.

"Perhaps I should reach out to . . . some other knights while we're near London," John suggested.

The table swooned with silence for a moment. Merle said, "Yeah. Yeah, maybe that's a good idea."

"Just as a sort of plan B, you understand."

"Right."

Eventually they all expected to run afoul of a colossal pink dragon, and only knights could beat dragons. But Goodco had been quietly getting rid of knights, so the only one who was preparing for this was John.

Scott had noticed his father's confidence slipping. One day John would behave as if he was destined to slay the largest dragon in two worlds; the next you could tell he was thinking that a proper knight should be known for something more valiant than performing his own stunts in a stage production of *The House at Pooh Corner*.

Scott swallowed a yam. "You can do it." He shrugged. "Slay Saxbriton, I mean."

John's head lifted; even through the bandages he looked like someone had just given him a tiara and a dozen roses. "Do you think so?" he asked, with such a rainbow of a smile on his face that Scott found he couldn't look at him.

"Sure. Maybe. I don't know. Maybe we should get some other knights anyway."

"Hmm," Emily mused. "Not to be indelicate, John, but who do you know who isn't already dead?"

Merle coughed. Everyone picked at their food. Scott excavated a piece of salmon from inside its pastry shell.

"A few people. I know Richard Starkey."

"Who's he?" said Erno.

John nearly choked on his Roasted Winter Vegetable

58

Tower with Bacon Lardons. "Richard Starkey? Drummer for the Quarrymen? Only the most important rock-and-roll band of the twentieth century?"

"Oh."

"We should warn him," said Emily. "Where does he live?"

"In the Holland Park district of London, in a house formerly owned by the painter Frederic Leighton," Scott answered, his cheeks still full. Then he frowned at his own mouth, if one can do such a thing.

"Ha," said Erno. "That might be the first time anyone's known anything Emily didn't."

Mick was glancing back and forth between Scott and his plate. "Wait a minute," he said, pointing at the fish. "Is that . . . ?"

Scott nodded furiously, his eyes wide.

"The Salmon of Knowledge!" gasped Mick.

"The . . . what?" said Emily.

"The Salmon o' Knowledge!" Mick whooped. "First caught by the great Irish hero Finn McCool! One taste an' yeh gain ultimate wisdom. Yeh know everythin'! But I thought Finn killed it centuries ago."

Scott shook his head. He pushed the bite of fish around with his tongue. "Dere's ahways a Salmon ub Knowwige. Iffit dies, one ub iss shildren eecomes da new Salmon ub Knowwige."

"How do you know all that?" asked Erno.

Scott pointed at his mouth.

"Oh, right."

"Iss too mush," he added, wincing. "Too mush knowwige. Can't concendrate."

"Finn got all the wisdom o' the world from just a wee bit o' salmon fat that got on his thumb," Mick explained. "For the rest o' his life he could suck that thumb an' answer any question."

"Scott's the new Emily," said Erno. Emily scowled and crossed her arms.

Scott was shaking his head again. "Finn ried."

"Ried?"

"He . . . didm't tell da troof. He rost . . . *lost* all da knowwige as soon as he swawwowed! Juss rike I'm going to! Finn juss *bretended* to know ebrything."

Emily huffed. "Typical. Boys."

"'Tis a wonder the Salmon ever came to be in this world in th' first place," said Mick.

"Rifts open petween da worlds in oceans, too," said Scott as he pushed his fists against his eyes.

"It's hurting him," said John. "Scott, you should swallow."

"No!" said Merle. "Wait. We could learn a lot."

"Everyone ask him questions," said Mick. "Help him focus."

"Maybe he could guess what word I'm thinking of right now," Emily muttered.

Scott stared at Emily in shock.

"*Useful* questions," suggested Mick.

"Okay, um . . . ," said Erno. "We spoiled all that Milk-7 back at the Goodborough factory. Did we stop Goodco from putting out a cereal with Milk-7 in it?"

"No. But dey onwy haf enough to sell it in big cities at first. Dey're trying to get more dragon milg agross so dey gan sell it ebrywhere."

"Shoot."

"That doppelgänger of mine . . . ," said John. "The goblin Reggie Dwight. What's *he* up to?"

"Da goplins are in London, regording your negst album."

"Good lord. Can they sing?"

"But lissen," Scott spat. "Goblin Reshie Dwight is gonna meet wif goblin Queen Erizabef. Live, on gamera. Dey're gonna bretend to make up, wike eberyone wants dem to."

The table fell silent.

"This is big," said Merle.

"If we get close enough to goblin Reggie, I can take his place," said John. "I could expose the goblin queen as a fake."

"How many goblins does Nimue have, anyway?" asked Erno.

"Seben."

"We should split up," Emily said quietly. "One group helps Scott's dad, the other rescues the real queen."

"It's going to be dangerous," said John.

"Too bad we can't all take some of that chemical that makes everyone huge and strong," said Erno. "Like it did for Biggs."

"Didn't make everyone bigger," Biggs mumbled. "Just the boys."

"Is Emily right about the queen being held in Avalon?" Erno asked Scott.

"I . . . dunno? Yeah, I dink so. Ish . . . hazy."

"That's weird," said Merle to Mick. "Shouldn't he know?"

Mick shrugged. "Maybe they've got the location protected by a spell?"

"I guess it's a good thing I memorized *an entire filing cabinet*, then," said Emily bitterly. "I mean, it's no *magic fish*, but—"

"Wait," said Scott. "Yes. Afalon. In Somerset. Deffinidly."

"You can see her?"

"Yeb. She loogs . . . weird? Dere's someding weird about her."

"What a super-useful piece of information," said Emily.

"You're being mean begause you habben't been

sweeping," Scott told her, and their eyes locked.

"Sweeping?" said Erno.

"Sleeping," Emily corrected. "It's no big deal."

"And also you're sgared. Sgared you'll get dumb now dat you're nod daking the Milk."

Emily curled up in her chair. "Why'd you say that?"

"Id's drue."

"That doesn't mean you had to say it."

For a moment nobody could think of anything to add. Biggs cleared his sinuses.

Scott grimaced. "It'sh breaking up in my mouf! Too delicate. Hafta shwallow soon."

"I'm not surprised," said John. "The chef here is quite good."

"He shtudied at Le Cordon Bleu!"

"I had the salmon last night," said Erno. "It was really flaky."

"The shecret ish a citrus marinade!"

"Maybe we should stick to business?" said Emily.

Polly made a noise, and everyone flinched.

She'd been uncharacteristically quiet that evening. Normally she could keep two or three conversations going all by herself. Now she simply asked, "Will my . . . will Prince Fi ever forgive me?"

Scott just breathed a moment. "Can't tell the fujure, Pully. Onwy the present."

"Maybe I made him mad when I said he could sleep in our dresser drawer?" Polly said as she tore a piece of bread into little pills. "Like maybe it reminded him how I used to make him live in a shoe box? Back when I thought he was a toy?"

"He'll forgive you," Scott answered. He had no idea if it was true.

But just then he knew Fi's story. He knew everything there was to know.

CHAPTER 4

The prince himself had remained in Scott and Erno's cabin, and from atop the television he was watching an oblivious old woman with headphones clean the floor with a stick vac. He was only four inches tall, but his proud eyes and regal bearing made him appear five, easily. His indigo tabard brought out the faint blue of his dark face.

"I expect you cannot hear me through your ear cradles," Fi said. "Can you? No. Still and all, I will honor you with my speech. For though you are lowborn and gruesomely ugly, you will be audience to the story of Prince Fi, last son of Dun Dinas."

The maid didn't answer. Nor did she look up, which gave Fi a certain freedom of movement, and he paced the television like he was treading some high stage above an imaginary crowd of pixies assembled on the bedspread.

Pixies were not naturally invisible to humans, like the Fay; but after ten months as an inanimate toy, Fi was possessed by a powerful need to fidget, not to mention the kind of recklessness that comes of having very rich parents.

"King Denzil XXXIII and Queen Rosevear had four sons: Fee, Fi, Fo, and Denzil. And we were all happy on our islands, away from the savage humans and inhospitable Fay. Beautiful Lady Morenwyn often stayed at court, and my brothers and I undertook contests of courage and skill to win her hand. And the sun never set on the pixie empire. Nor anywhere else, I'm given to understand.

"But darkness fell nonetheless. Morenwyn was

kidnapped by her mother, the witch Fray, and stolen away to a secret island. My brother Denzil was oldest, so the honor of rescuing Morenwyn fell first to him. He took up our grandfather's peerless sword, Wasp-Mare, and sailed east in an enchanted boat. And was not heard from again.

"Next was Fo. And Fo chose the girdle Giantkiller, which gives a pixie the strength of a man, and the Hammer of the Jötnar, cold forged from ice that neither breaks nor melts. And he sailed south in an enchanted boat and was not heard from again.

"The honor of saving Morenwyn should have next fallen to me. But while I made my preparations, impulsive Fee slipped into my chambers and took Armaplantae, the Living Armor, and the bow and quiver of the great pixie hero Cornwallace, whose arrows always flew straight and true. And he sailed west in an enchanted boat. And was not heard from again.

"Here I asked around to see if anyone knew of a fourth enchanted boat, but no one did."

In the cruise ship cabin, Fi paused while the maid went to her cart for fresh towels. He cleared his throat as she returned. Her headphones buzzed with the waspish sounds of tinny Europop.

"The pixies have a great talent with birds," said Fi.

"We speak to them in their own language and may even persuade them to serve as mounts, though we do this but seldom—a bird who has let a pixie ride on its back will never be accepted into polite society again. In happier times the witch Fray had sometimes flown to the castle on the back of a red-billed chough. They were monstrous black birds, some as many as seventeen inches long, but I hunted the sea crows across coastal cliffs with the best weapons left to me. I wielded the marginally enchanted sword known as Carpet Nail, and for protection a thin scrap of birch bark that I have named Hoarskin."

It wasn't a dry throat now that made Fi cough. He could call his shield anything he wanted, but he knew he couldn't make it special—it was merely one of the sort carried by every member of the pixie infantry. Hardened by resin, these shields were really only useful against fairy magics. *All* pixie magic, rare though it was, tended to cancel out fairy glamour, and vice versa. It would surely offend Fi's pixie pride to admit this, but their oil-and-water magics were the only reason the Fay had not taken the pixies' islands generations ago.

"On the third day of my hunt I found a mangy old crow that stood apart from the rest of the flock. Indeed, if he dared come near, the others would peck at his head and

neck and beat him back with their wings. A pariah. But I let him close. I speared him plump grubs and earned his trust. And when I was near enough to whisper, I told him, 'Take me to your mistress.'"

The maid arranged and straightened the bedclothes and struggled with the contents of one of her pockets. Her beige uniform was really too tight for her, Fi noted, and it gathered in the pits and folds of her plump body. She was like a polyester walnut.

"I soared north, over the Irish Sea, stiff fingered and shivering as I held tight to the bird's scruff. And when we neared the Isle of Man, I . . . oh, dear." Fi trailed off and watched what was shaping up to be an epic clash of forces, suitable for song or myth. The maid had gotten her hand stuck in her own pocket and couldn't get it out again. She looked like she was playing tug-of-war with a dog.

"You'll have to let it go," Fi advised, though of course the maid couldn't hear him. "You can't hold on to whatever's in there and pull your hand out at the same time, woman; give it up!"

But with a spirited pull and a rip, the maid proved Fi wrong and produced a small white envelope from the ruined pocket. She stood still a moment, panting, then leaned over the bed and placed the envelope on one of its pillows. The pixies had their own written language, but Fi was reasonably certain that the name of the boy, Erno, was written on the front.

"Every other evening a little dark maid has left a chocolate on that pillow," Fi told her as she fixed her smock and made to leave. "Tonight, a secret message. What game is this?"

In the end, Scott had not so much swallowed as sensed the salmon dissolve, like some helpful spirit evanescing back into the unknown. The séance was over.

"It's all gone." Scott sighed. "My head feels like an empty circus tent."

"I was *going* to get the salmon," muttered Emily. "It was my second choice."

"I knew that," said Scott, holding his head and pointing.

"I totally kinda remember knowing that."

Everyone stared at their plates for a moment.

"This dinner was fun," said Erno. "What's for dessert, the Cheesecake of Courage?"

CHAPTER 5

The next morning John found Scott and Polly out on deck. He'd been jogging a circuit around the ship—sneakers and socks, shorts, hoodie, and bandages—and he stopped and rounded back after he passed their lounge chairs.

"Isn't it kind of awful, running with your head all wrapped up?" asked Scott as John sat at Polly's feet, breathing hugely and evenly.

"The worst part is changing the bandages at night," John answered, "and finding all these tiny bugs trapped in the gauze. I mean, do they really like gauze, or is this just the regular number of face bugs?"

Polly didn't say anything. The silence was conspicuous. Her face was cycling through expressions like a traffic light—hopeful to cautious to halting, then back to hopeful again.

John put a hand on her shoe. "Fi will come around. Just

give him time. Getting treated like a little plaything . . . it was a big hit to his ego."

Polly sniffed.

"Maybe you can give her some tips," Scott told John. "You actors have huge egos, right?"

John laughed. Or huffed, or something—it was hard to tell through the bandages. "Just the opposite, really. The best actors have no ego at all. No ego makes it easy to play a part, become somebody else. But it can also make you want to be loved by everyone. And when you need love that badly . . . you never stop being afraid of rejection."

"I don't think Fi's like that," Polly said.

"No," John agreed. "I think Fi *does* have an ego, and it's been bruised by all that toy business. He just wants to forget, and you're not letting him."

"I'm being nice!" Polly protested. "I've been extra nice ever since I found out."

"Yes—you're so *very* nice that it's like a box of chocolates every time you speak. He wishes he could move on, but you keep giving him big Mylar balloons that read SORRY FOR YOUR HUMILIATING EXPERIENCE."

Polly winced and chewed it over.

"My two bits, anyway," said John as he rose to resume his run. "See you in three and a half minutes." Then he charged off like a fit mummy.

After a pause Scott felt compelled to admit, "That

74

might have actually been good advice Dad gave you just now. I mean . . . assuming it really *was* Dad. Could have been anyone under those bandages."

"It was Dad. He's smart."

"Maybe when you cover up his face he gets smarter."

One very early morning the *Canadian Diamond Queen* docked at Dover. They had an official disembarkation time, which they ignored, and instead sneaked out through the luggage bays.

"Hey," said a man in a jumpsuit as they passed. "You're not supposed to be here."

"That's so true." John sighed through his bandages. "I should be sleeping in my big feathery bed after a night on the stage, dazzling my adoring fans," he added, and patted the man on the arm. "Thank you for saying so." Then he joined the others down the loading platform.

Erno sidled up to Emily. "So you haven't been sleeping?"

Emily shrugged. "Nightmares. I keep dreaming of Mom. I mean . . . *my* mom."

Erno nodded. They'd been raised as brother and sister, and Erno had to remind himself sometimes that it wasn't true, too. "How do you know it's her?"

"In my dreams I know what she looks like. When I wake up I can't remember. She's always looking for me, calling my name. But she can't find me. I try to call out to her, to tell her where I am, but my voice won't work." When she saw Erno's concerned look, she added, "It's nothing. Maybe bad dreams are a side effect of not taking the Milk-7 anymore." She glanced over at the envelope Erno was holding, the envelope he'd found on his pillow the previous night.

Erno had examined every inch of the envelope and its contents. He'd inspected it for fingerprints, knowing full well that he hadn't any other fingerprints to compare it to. When he thought no one was looking, he'd sniffed it.

"It couldn't have been Mr. Wilson," Emily told Erno. "How could he have known we'd be boarding that cruise ship? Why would he sneak on board dressed as a maid and . . . not even say hello?"

They passed quickly through the loading dock and bribed their way around customs. Erno read the enclosed riddle again, aloud. He was trusting Emily to handle this bolt out of the blue from Mr. Wilson, even though she'd been a bit high voiced and fidgety ever since learning about it.

> The new year has a week to wait till waking.
> The water's almost frozen in the well.
> The hours of the day
> pass swiftly by, then drift away,
> and yet there's nothing, less than nothing left to tell.

"He sounds depressed," said Emily. Erno continued:

> Soon the final days are numbered, then forgotten,
> and the new year's hardly worth the time it's taken.
> By degrees the hourglass reckons
> all the minutes, all the seconds,
> and the next year still has weeks to wait to waken.

"And that's it," said Erno.

"I don't get it yet," Emily groused, rubbing her temples again. "But . . . I will, don't worry."

"I'm hungry," said Polly.

"There's a grocer's," said John. "You lot stock up while I give Sir Richard Starkey a call."

Harvey sighed and thumped down on the concrete by the store entrance with Finchbriton and Grimalkin. Merle and Biggs veered off into the produce section for fruits or vegetables or some nonsense. The rest of them paced up and down aisles, grabbing bread and cheese and odd British snacks they would later regret. No one said as much, but all of them—Erno and Emily, Scott and Polly, Mick and Fi—were dreading the inevitable cereal section, as if it were lying in wait like the killer in a slasher film. Then, there it was: cheery boxes, cartoon animals, photo after photo of tumbling cereal pieces splashing up goopy crowns of whole milk. Nearly half the cereals were Goodco brand.

"Weird," said Erno. "In England, Koko Lumps is called Soy Capitán."

Scott paused in front of one box in particular. "There it is," he whispered. "Peanut Butter Clobbers. 'Now with Intellijuice.'"

"It's already out?" said Erno. "When did it come out?"

Mick leaned out of Scott's backpack to look. He groaned and said, "The queen on the Clobbers box—that's just me in a wig, innit?"

"It's not *just* you in a wig. You're also wearing a dress."

Prince Fi, for his part, couldn't take his eyes off the Puftees. Or the three blue-skinned Puftees Pixies on the box front. There wasn't much of a family resemblance, but apparently it was enough to get him thinking about his missing brothers.

"We should be talking about rescuing Fee, Fo, and Denzil," Fi said, clenching his little blueberry fist against his chest. "There is a correct order to things: we find my brothers, and my brothers help us rescue this human queen."

"Fi's right!" said Polly. "I mean, probably."

For a moment no one spoke. Scott waited for Emily's rebuttal, but she was off in her own little world.

"I . . . I don't know," said Scott. "This meeting between the fake queen and the fake Reggie Dwight is a really big opportunity, and it's happening so soon. We can't miss it. The whole world will listen to us about Goodco if we show them the queen's just a big puppet."

Fi was silent. Everyone was, and Scott felt like a jerk. Eventually Polly asked if Fi would like to be picked up.

"You may place me astride your hair tail," he told her.

"Ponytail."

"Yes," said Fi. "That." He still wouldn't go in a pocket. Polly lifted Fi atop her head, and he straddled her hair tie like it was a saddle. Scott suspected that he preferred to think of Polly as just a weird horse.

They should get out of the cereal aisle, Scott thought. They should keep moving. But he wanted to tear all these poisonous boxes off the shelves. He wanted to kick them around the store. Emily, he thought, had other ideas. She touched at the corner of one of the Clobbers boxes lightly, like she was worried she'd scare it away.

Intellijuice (or ThinkDrink, or Milk-7) was a chemical additive Goodco had developed after testing it out on Emily for ten years. Actually, *chemical* was a polite way of saying "mostly dragon barf and saltwater," but it made people smarter. It opened doors in their minds. One day soon Nimue would throw those doors wide and storm into those minds, and a million kids would become her private army of sugar zombies.

Maybe Emily was worrying about this. But Scott thought she looked more hungry than worried.

Erno noticed this, too. "C'mon," he said. "Let's go."

"Wait," said Emily. "Look."

She'd pulled a box of Clobbers out a bit, and now they could see Scott's last school picture printed above a recipe for Clobber Bars.

"Oh boy," said Scott.

Erno pulled other boxes out at random, and they found pictures of Emily, Merle, Polly, Erno, Biggs. HAVE YOU SEEN ME? was printed beneath each, with a phone number and a web address. They were all too stunned for a moment to move. Then Scott quickly straightened the boxes. "Leave the groceries," he said, and they walked quickly, but not too quickly, out of the store.

John met them out front in a truck with a squarish cab and a boxy cargo area.

"I got us a lorry!" he called from the driver-side window. "Just bought it off the driver around back! Paid way too much." The sign on the side said it had been carrying Poppadum Crisps in Minted Lamb, Bubble 'n' Squeak, Baked Bean, and Prawn 'n' Pickle flavors. The kids reread the sign a few times, but it kept saying that. They piled into the back.

Biggs drove and shared the cab with Erno and Emily. The rest sat around an electric lantern on the cold steel cargo floor, feeling it rattle against their butts as the lorry rumbled toward London. John undid his bandages and scratched his face.

"We could play a car game," Polly whispered to Fi, in the corner.

"What is a car game?" asked Fi. Polly considered how to answer, but she couldn't think of any games that didn't need at least one window to look out of.

The unicat (who'd apparently forgotten what had happened last time) stalked Finchbriton. It crept close, its body low and discreet but its tall tail twitching like it was advertising the Grand Opening of a tire store. Then it crept too close, and Finchbriton whistled a puff of blue fire that lit the tips of its whiskers. They burned down like fuses and ignited a little explosion of activity as the cat leaped up, and back, and ran around and around the truck interior, full tilt and sticking its claws in everyone. Then it went to sleep.

"You could tell me about how you got here," Polly suggested, kind of softly, kind of not wanting the others to hear her asking. Fi didn't respond right away, and she was on the verge of repeating herself when finally his voice descended like a deflating balloon.

"The lady Morenwyn had been kidnapped," he began. "Taken by her witch of a mother, the lady Fray."

CHAPTER 6

"Why was she a witch?" asked Polly.

"She was a sorceress," Fi answered. "The only one born in a generation. Pixie magic is rare, but powerful. We aren't all possessed of little glimmers like the Fay."

"But why not call her a sorceress or . . . enchantress or something? Seems like a witch is just a sorceress who doesn't get asked to parties."

"Do you want to hear this story?"

"Sorry."

"One by one my brothers quested to rescue Morenwyn, and one by one they disappeared. Only I was left, so I hunted for a sea crow that Fray might once have used as a steed, and when I found such a creature I asked it to take me home to its mistress."

"You can talk to birds?" asked Polly.

"Forsooth."

"Can you teach *me* to talk to birds?"

"No," said Prince Fi. "So: I flew north over the Irish Sea on the chough's back, shivering from cold, shivering with the thrill that soon I would see my brothers again, and sable-haired Morenwyn. In my reverie I'd scarcely noticed that the bird was plunging down toward

something jagged and dark rising out of the ocean, like a colossal bit of backbone. Then I saw this was a castle, larger and stranger than any I'd seen. It was squat and bowlegged, jutting up from a forsaken strip of rock and strutted with buttresses and staircases too monumental for any pixie. Blunt stone towers jutted out at impossible angles like new antlers. A web of windowpanes comprised the whole of one end of the fortress, as delicate as a snowflake but tall as a tree. The chough sailed toward it and might have taken me directly into Fray's sitting room if I hadn't the presence to leap off its back and onto the parapet."

"Parapet?"

"Yes, parapet. The . . . toothy bits on the tops of castles."

"Oh, right."

"How I wished for the ancient times of story and song when the great Spirit had cloven the hours 'tween night and day. I might then have waited for cover of darkness before acting. Instead I steadied myself against the salty wind and vaulted over the parapet. I slid slowly down the sloping castle wall and caught hold of the first window ledge I encountered. And now I pried open the wide windows with my sword and tumbled into the warm scarlet bedchamber of the most alluring pixie woman on a thousand shores.

"Morenwyn leaped to her feet and dropped her sewing. She had been mending some white sail or tent that lay curdled all about on the floor. Now she stood, tall and proud, brandishing her sewing needle. Her hair like a storm cloud, her face as rare as a night sky. The lost stars, remembered in her eyes."

Here Fi seemed suddenly to compose himself, and shift uncomfortably atop Polly's ponytail.

"So she was pretty?" asked Polly.

"No, not *pretty*. Not merely *pretty*. She was the dream

of the world. She looked down on me, kneeling in the folds of that white tent, or sail, and sighed.

"'And finally Fi,' she said. 'Goody.'

"'Lady.' I bowed.

"'That's the last of the princes, now. Who's next after you lot, the dukes? Are the dukes going to rescue me next? Just tell me how long I've got before it's butlers and washerwomen.'

"'Lady,' I said. 'I am here for my brothers, and for you, if you need a champion. Do you need a champion?'

"Morenwyn covered her plum mouth then, with her fingers. 'You're asking?'

"'I am asking if you require rescuing.'

"I didn't get my answer," Fi told Polly, "not then. For the window beside me shattered, and the white hand

of a giant yanked me out by my cloak. I was whipped through the air, half choking, and understood that Morenwyn was mending neither sail nor tent as a shirtless monster of a man dangled me in front of his thick, bovine face.

"He was on the tallest landing of a staircase outside her bedroom. It sickened me that he'd been watching us there.

"'Gentle!' Morenwyn called from the window. 'Don't hurt him!'

"'Won't.' The giant grinned. 'Much.'

"'I like to think,' I rasped, 'that she was talking to me.' And then I reached as high as I could and drove my sword beneath the giant's black fingernail.

"He howled and I dropped, holding my shield like a canopy above me to slow my fall. I caught hold of his leg on the way down and slid into the rolled cuff of his pants, where I huddled and waited. It was nauseating, being lurched this way and that as the giant turned about on the slick bricks, searching for me. He peered over the edge of the landing to the rocks below.

"'Where he go?' the monster bellowed. 'You see?'

"I heard Morenwyn say, 'Sorry, Nim, lost track.'

"The monster rushed off and wist not that he had a passenger. He took me to the mouth of a dry sea cave and down beneath that cathedral of rock, to a fire pit where sat four other giants in queer and mismatching dress.

"'Pixie man!' my giant, Nim, told them. 'Help me find!'

"Three of the giants jumped to attention and made ready to follow. A fourth giant, wearing only his undergarment, hesitated. Nim took a serious tone.

"'You come also, Rudesby. New ones must come when Nim say.'

"When this Rudesby spoke, his language was strange, the accent unfamiliar.

"'Pleez.' He seemed to plead. 'Aye juhst haave too tahlk too thaat tynee wumman. Aye dohnt beelahng heer!'

"Nim grappled with Rudesby and pulled him along by the ear, and that's when I jumped free of his pant leg, dashed across the sand, and tucked myself into the shadows until they were gone.

"'Pleez!' Rudesby struggled as Nim led him aboveground, his voice getting washed out by the sea air. 'Aye juhst wahna goh *hohwm*!'

"I ventured deeper into the cave, this cave that must form a hollow under Fray's castle, then scrambled up a set of steep and rough-hewn steps until I noticed another staircase of pixie proportions running parallel to the first. I climbed for an age, toward faint light. Finally I came to find a kind of metal grate, albeit one so large I could just squeeze up through its openings, and found above it the largest room I have ever seen.

"I think you'd call it vast even by human measure. Vast enough to hold hundreds of humans, or even to play a match of that sport of yours, with the basket and the ball?"

"Basketball," said Polly.

"Yes. Basket and ball. What is the sport called?"

"It's called basketball. That's what we call it."

"Ah, of course. You are the poets of the new world. So: I could see that the castle was immense on my approach to the island, but never could I have guessed that below Morenwyn's bedchamber it housed little more than one cavernous void, lit on its end by the tall leaded window I'd seen outside. Here was a room like the belly of a whale, with stone ribs buttressing the margins, each curving to the floor and pointing toward a golden monument in the center. The monument was almost ten pixies high, broader than it was wide, taller than it was broad. It was inlaid with silver, symbols, jewels, and it looked like a flaming sword against the ruby sky, framed in that vast and faceted window.

"The air in here was teeming with motes of dust.

"An animal voice screeched in the darkness, high above. I crept around the edge of the chamber. I had no wish to see the golden monument any closer—there was something distinctly Fay about it—and my duty was to my brothers. And to Morenwyn, I thought, if she would have me.

"But then the dust in the air shone like fire, the room lit with ten thousand tiny lights.

"'Aha,' said a voice like a growling house cat. 'Fi, is it? You princes are positively interchangeable.'

"A pixie woman stood far off, on the dais near the base of the monument. I don't like to say that she looked like her daughter, but of course she did. She resembled her daughter like the charcoal resembles the tree. She was dressed in the rags and ribbons of a hermit.

"'Well met, Lady Fray,' I said, and touched at the pommel of my sword. 'You keep a lovely home. Airy.'

"'Yes, I do think the airiness is its best feature.'

"Anyone else would have cluttered up the place with furniture, things. But you know all a person really needs is one good gold monolith.'

"'That,' Fray agreed, 'and I find nothing really complements a monolith like a stupendously large tapestry.' Fray gestured to the wall opposite the giant window, and now I saw something that before had been shrouded in darkness: a woven tapestry depicting two overlapping spheres, stabbed through their hearts by some sharp stake, and all the heavens torn asunder by fierce light. And beneath that: a multitude of people great and small, all weeping. 'I wove it in a day and a night,' Fray added, though this could only be a lie. 'I don't remember a moment of it. But I emerged from my trance

with cracked and bleeding hands and looked at what I'd created—a vision of the end of all things.'

"I didn't know what to say. It was a bit modern for my tastes.

"'So,' said Fray, stepping forward. 'Here for Morenwyn, I suppose?'

"'That is her decision to make. I'm here for my brothers.'

"Fray lifted her brow and nodded, as if in approval.

'At last, a worshipful son of Denzil. What a shame. Be a sport, will you? Make a pretty speech about freeing my poor daughter and leading the armies of pixiedom to my doorstep. It makes this next bit so much easier.'

"Fray whistled, and the floor grate lifted. Five giants, the same five I'd seen underground, climbed up into the chamber and formed a half circle around the monolith. The one called Rudesby was still being manhandled by the others. Fray gestured and muttered, and hurled a dart of light from her fingertips that struck the stone floor where I'd been standing only a moment before. I didn't think my pixie shield would protect me from this witchcraft. But I maneuvered to keep the golden tower between us, thankful at last for its Fay magic. Fray cast another spell, but the monument blew it like a wind, swept it off course.

"'Nim?' said Fray.

"'Rudesby!' barked Nim. 'You first! New ones always first!'

"He prodded Rudesby in the back, and the half-naked giant stumbled forward. 'Aye'm saahry!' he told me, advancing. 'Pleez dohn't hurt mee! Aye haffa wyfe in Sanfransisgoh!'

"He lurched at me, bent at the waist, fumbling with outstretched arm. I ran up the length of that arm, stabbed him in the ear, then leaped off his shoulders. Grabbing hold of his underpants, I arrested my fall, then dropped again to the floor behind his left heel and sliced his tendon. He dropped, clutching his head.

"'Tapping owt!' Rudesby said, slapping the floor. 'Aye'm tapping owt!'

"'Worthless,' grumbled Nim. 'Clara! Tom-Tom! Marty! Go!'

"Fray came around the golden tower, calling forth some new spell from the ether, but now her own giants blocked her sight. The three of them surrounded me, but like the pixie heroes of old, I confounded them. Three giants hunting the same pixie could only get in each other's way. They struck heads, crossed arms. I sliced one in the toe, and he was compelled to tackle another, while the third searched for me among their flailing limbs. But then I made my great error and saw nothing protecting me from Fray's mischief. She spoke, and I was blinded by light, and a moment later I could see but could not move.

"Again, some piercing voice called out from above.

"'There,' said Fray. 'By the Spirit, you're a clever mouse. I see why she likes you.'

"Fray stepped aboard Nim's hand and disembarked again after he'd brought her only inches from my face. To say that I strained with every muscle against Fray's enchantment would be a lie. I could not do even that. Only my mind raged against its cage.

"'Wonderful thing, this magic,' said Fray. 'I wish you

could see yourself. It's like the thinnest coat of glass. You needn't eat, or drink, or even breathe. You'll never die. But you'll never move again either, so here's hoping you end up someplace with a view.'

"She circled around me and was joined again by her giants.

"'This world is truly dying,' she whispered in my ear. 'I know I've said that before. And when I said it before, all the kingdom turned against me. Suddenly all my useful little spells, the magic arts that enchanted *your own sword and shield*, branded me a witch. Well, now—here's good news: I'm going to send you to a place without magic. A tedious groan of a place. You were so good with my giants, so I will send you to a world of giants.'

"'Mother,' said Morenwyn behind her.

"'Daughter.' Fray turned and answered. 'You've been attracting flies again. Look at this dirty little thing I've caught.'

"'Mother, I think he's different.'

"'Oh, they're *all* different. Our differences make us special, darling—I think I saw an embroidered pillow once to that effect.'

"'I'll deal with Fi,' said Morenwyn. 'Please. Leave me with him.'

"'We can't let him go, Morenwyn. If he told the elves—'

"'Why would he tell the elves?'

"'Morenwyn,' the witch said flatly. 'You know what's at stake.'

"I thought they both might have looked across to the tapestry then. It was hard to say. Morenwyn sighed.

"'I will do what needs to be done,' she said. 'But *I* will do it.'

"'Fine. Good. I'll leave Nim to help you.'

"And Fray and the other giants did leave us then. Morenwyn stood before me. I would have bowed if I could.

"'You always stood out, Fi,' she said. 'Even at your father's court, even when you were all stumbling over one another to impress me with your contests. I could tell you let Fee win sometimes.'

"I could neither confirm nor deny this at the time, though in the interest of accuracy I'll admit it's true.

"'Of course you know that Fee was here just before you. He didn't ask me if I wanted a champion. He had me three-quarters rescued before he even asked me how I was doing.'

"I smiled then, in my mind.

"'I was never kidnapped. I liked neither the warp nor weft of the future they were weaving me at court, so I sent for my mother. I *tried* to tell Fee this. Then Mother caught Fee, and she brought him here.' Morenwyn strode briskly toward one wall, and Nim lifted me up and followed. Where she stopped there was a low stone stall, a pixie-sized stall, jutting out from the wall, and an octagon traced in chalk. She seemed to be taking some care not to get too close. 'All of your brothers were brought here. Did Mother tell you about the doors?'

"*No,* I whispered back in my thoughts.

"'Mother learned from her travels that the world is shrinking, dying. She meditated on this for a long time. And then she had the vision of the tapestry! And she learned more. There are doors all across the world, and they can't be seen. Most, most by far, only open and close for a moment, and rarely in the same place twice. They lead to another world. A world, as my mother told you, without magic. A world without pixies or elves or any magical creature, she thinks. She's explored but a little of it.

"'But some of these doors, certain special doors, are open for weeks at a time. Rarer still are the doors that are always open. The Fay are desperate to find such doors. And we have four of them.'

"She gestured at the chalk octagon.

"'This one goes to a kind of twin England. We know it to be filled with humans. Now look up there.'

"She raised her arm straight in the air, pointed at

something too high and too dark to see. But then she tightened her fingers, and the motes of light far above us burned brighter. A crooked tower tunneled up from the castle ceiling. Across the base of it was strung a strong net. Near the top of it perched a dozen eagles.

"'There's a door up there, too. It opens onto a cliff face high above a desert. From time to time a human on the other side falls through and trades places with one of our eagles. We catch him in our net, and he joins our . . . happy family. I'm told Nim's grandfather came here this way.'

"'Yes'm,' said Nim.

"'The one they're calling Rudesby joined us only weeks ago.'

"She paused and looked at the tapestry.

"'There's a door there, too.'

98

"After a moment she motioned to Nim, and he carried us both past the golden monolith and to another corner. There was a larger stall here, a gaping octagon.

"She stepped down lightly onto the floor. 'The Fay want to find doors so they can escape this world, invade another, but Mother says they've turned wicked. She's foreseen that the fairies will tear both worlds apart with their folly, and she fears that you'll reveal her secret, tell them about these doors. She'd have me send you through that first door, to the human town. Like she did your brothers. I think . . . I think Mother's too careless in sending good pixies there. I won't send you through the second door either, which I understand leads to certain death. And the third's a frozen desert. But this one,' she said, nodding at the octagon, 'nothing ever goes in or out of here.'

"Nim set me down inside the stall, right in front of the octagon. He set me down facing the wall.

"'Mother says we'll have to go through to the other world one day, too. She says our world is drying up. I think she's saving this door for us. I'll send you through, and you'll be awaiting us when we come! Surely by then mother could be convinced to undo her spell.'

"'Good-bye, Fi,' she added. 'May the Spirit keep you.'

"I did not know what I was waiting for, then," Fi told Polly. "I did not know how the rifts worked, that a body had to change places with something of similar size on the other side to make the Crossing. So I stood rigidly in silence for a while, listening to Morenwyn breathe behind me."

Fi was quiet. The road rumbled along beneath them. "Then what happened?" asked Polly.

Then Fi had felt a sensation as if something was moving through him, and a second later he wasn't in the witch's castle anymore.

"Oh," Morenwyn said to the wriggling fish that had taken his place. "Oh, dear."

CHAPTER 7

Fi had barely registered that he was underwater before he was swallowed by a different fish. A fish that had been fixing to eat the one Fi had just traded places with. The inside of a fish is generally less diverting than the outside, so Fi was left alone with his thoughts. He thought of the great pixie hero Cornwallace, whom the

legends said had also once been swallowed by a fish, and had cut his way to freedom with his enchanted dagger. But Fi could not lift his arms, so he contented himself by merely wishing the fish misfortune, and would have been pleased to learn that it was eaten by an albatross a few moments later.

Still and all, getting swallowed by an albatross was nothing if not a step backward. And one relatively unimproved by the fact that the albatross was shot by a tuna fisherman that same afternoon.

The fishermen of the *Albacore Four* had been watching a World Cup match, and South Africa had just won, and Jerry had taken his gun up on deck to celebrate by shooting at the sky for a bit. The sky, disgruntled, threw something back: a great white bird, plummeting, pinwheeling from the hole Jerry had just made in its right wing. An albatross, looking as preposterous as a biplane on the deck of the *Albacore Four*.

People claim that so many things are bad luck. Black cats and broken mirrors and sidewalk cracks. What you probably don't know is that it's also bad luck to kill an albatross. And why would you? You are presumably not a sailor, and you've likely never seen an albatross, and even if you have, you probably hadn't anything against it personally and so you managed not to kill it. Unless it was an accident. But in general terms it is terrifically easy not to kill an albatross—you're probably not killing one right now.

The point is that you may not have known it's bad luck to kill an albatross, but Jerry the sailor knew. He knew this very well.

The usual custom in this sort of situation is to wear the albatross around your neck for a while, but instead Jerry scooped it up and, glancing about, rushed it belowdecks to one of the freezer holds, where he hid it inside a first aid cooler. Then he rejoined his crewmates and remarked loudly what a nice, birdless day it was outside.

When the *Albacore Four* was destroyed by lightning, Jerry found the first aid cooler useful to hold on to as he kicked for shore. On land, he found a buyer for his well-preserved and mostly intact albatross carcass, and bought

a fresh suit of clothes, and landed a new job, and was killed a week later in an unrelated pumpkin-catapulting incident.

The albatross was freeze-dried and resold to the New Jersey Museum of Natural History, where it was displayed with a plaque that failed to mention that it contained any pixies. A week later it was stolen by mistake.

"How will I know which one is the eagle?" the thief asked, fidgeting outside the museum.

"Aw," Haskoll answered. "And to think people say there's no such thing as a stupid question. Good for you!"

"Sorry, but not everybody's a . . . a bird doctor or whatever."

"You sure you're up for this, big guy? I bet I can find another hobo at the bus station who's willing."

"If you got the two hundred dollars, I'll get your bird. Just don't want to grab the wrong one . . ."

Haskoll smiled. "It's easy. You bring me the biggest bird they have, okay?"

"'Kay," the thief breathed. Then he headed across the quiet street to the rear of the museum.

When Haskoll saw him again at the meeting place in the parking garage, he was carrying an albatross and a pelican.

The albatross had been freeze-dried with its wings extended, and it caught the air like a kite as the thief ran.

"There wasn't any eagle, boss!" the thief said. "I swear!

There was a little sign that *said* eagle, but it was in front of another sign? And that one said 'exhibit removed for cleaning.'"

"And so you just grabbed every other bird you could carry," Haskoll replied. "What a go-getter you've turned out to be. You gonna make me an eagle out of spare parts now?"

The thief waggled the albatross in front of him, and it was one of the singular experiences of Haskoll's life. There's really nothing like having a dead albatross waved in your face.

"'The sign said this bird has the biggest wings!" said the thief. "Bigger than the eagle, maybe? I thought it might be just as good."

"So why the pelican?" said Haskoll.

The thief was giving Haskoll a look now, a look that said, *Man, why NOT the pelican?*

Haskoll sighed and glanced down, and that's when he noticed that the small chunk of iron on the tether around his neck was glowing. Faintly, sure, but there was definitely a glow. The little nugget was a coldstone, a lump of meteoric iron that gave off pink and purple sparks when it was near magic. Only now it was glowing black. *No, that's not right*, thought Haskoll. *Nothing can glow black.* Still, it was making a color he'd possibly never seen before.

Haskoll was part changeling, and like all changelings

he had a natural talent for seeing elves and magical creatures. He worked for a hunter named Papa who liked to shoot such creatures. But Papa was not a changeling and had to take Haskoll's word for it that his trophy room was filled with the heads of fairy-tale beasts, and not just empty wooden plaques.

Recently Haskoll had been contacted by a private collector who wanted to pay him good money to steal Papa's griffin head and replace it with just such an empty plaque. Haskoll had planned to give this collector an ordinary eagle head instead, and keep both the griffin and the money. Now he needed a new plan.

"I can give you a hundred for the both of them," he told the thief. "Minus fifty to pay the pelican disposal fee. So that's fifty, total."

The thief sighed and nodded. Haskoll paid him and waited until he was out of sight, then left the pelican on top of a Subaru.

He had to wait a week before he met his secret buyer, a week he'd originally intended to spend gussying up the eagle head. He'd only spoken to the collector on the phone, so the man's appearance was a bit of a shock.

"Mister . . . Mister Smith?" Haskoll said when the tall, thin man arrived.

"Mister Haskoll," the man replied. "Is there something wrong?"

"Sorry, it's just . . . you look *exactly* like Prince Charles. Of England?"

"I get that a lot." The man smiled. And of course he couldn't be Prince Charles. He didn't even have an English accent. "Do you have something for me?"

Haskoll exhaled. "I . . . didn't get the griffin head. I thought about it, and I just couldn't steal from Papa, you know? But I have something else that might interest you."

He produced the albatross from the tarp he'd wrapped it in, and set it on the table between them.

"A seagull," said Mr. Smith. "I don't think this is quite the prize you think it is."

"It's an albatross," said Haskoll. "But look at this." He pulled the coldstone over his head and held it at arm's length. Except now it was glowing quite pink. Pink *and* black, actually, as if the colors were fighting each other. "That isn't what it—" Haskoll began to add. Then he narrowed his eyes at Mr. Smith. "What *are* you?"

Mr. Smith stood, smiled, and then his skin split and fell away like laundry. Underneath were two goblins, one standing atop the other's shoulders. They were wearing little suits.

"Misters Pigg and Poke," said the goblin on top as he hopped to the floor.

"Conductin' a test of your loyalty," said the other.

Haskoll stood. "A test? For who? Did Papa set all this up?" It didn't seem possible—he just didn't give the old man that much credit.

"For our current employer," said the first goblin. "A very important lady from a good family. She prizes loyalty, you see."

"And yet she's able to make an exception and work with goblins," Haskoll said. "I think that kind of flexibility is really great."

"Oh, but Our Lady is righteous, don't you know."

Haskoll understood. You could always fool the righteous.

"You've shown loyalty to this Papa," said the second goblin with a conspicuous wink. "And yet also a willingness to work with other . . . interested parties. Our Lady would like to hire you, on retainer."

"Hire me to do what?"

"Maybe nothing. Maybe she'll never call on you at all. But for fifty thousand dollars, you will be at her beck and call. Much like we are."

Haskoll thought. "It's gotta be fifty thousand in *real money*. American money, capiche? No fairy gold, no enchanted bills. I don't wanna open my safe one day and find it full of bark or whatever."

The first goblin stood atop the other's shoulders again, and they grew a new Prince Charles skin. They shook Haskoll's hand.

"We'll take the albatross," they said with one voice. "And in return, a little gift."

They reached into their suit coat and removed a gun. Haskoll tensed, but then they turned the pistol and offered it to him, handle first. Haskoll took it.

"An enchanted weapon," said the goblins. "It never runs out of bullets."

"Sweet."

"And here's something for free," said the goblins. "A foretelling."

Haskoll looked up from the gun and frowned. "You mean, like . . . my fortune?"

"All the Fay get little glimpses of the future, though we never know quite when to expect them. But we had a peek just now when we shook your hand."

Haskoll shifted from foot to foot. "Good stuff, I'm sure?"

The goblin Prince Charles smiled. There was possibly something not quite perfect about the disguise—the smile was wider than it should have been.

"Something big is coming your way," said Charles in one of the goblin's voices.

"Soon," he added, in the other's. "Something *very* big. It's going to drop right in your lap."

Haskoll grinned and peppered them with questions about this big something, but they insisted that it should be a surprise. So he thanked them, and they left with the albatross.

It was the middle of the night. Pigg and Poke liked this world, with its nights and days. The other Fay could talk all they wanted about the perfection of twilight, but a goblin's rightful place was in the dark.

The Goodco factory was staffed at night by a skeleton crew, so it was easy for the goblins to find a quiet spot where they could tear the albatross apart.

"How now?" they addressed the pixie at the heart of the mess.

Prince Fi, still immobile, stared up at this poor counterfeit of a human face, searching for any trace of compassion.

"You know, I do believe it's the last of King Denzil's

boys," said the man in a goblin's voice.

"Right as usual, Mister Pigg," he answered himself in another.

Fi screamed in his mind.

"You know, I do think Our Lady Nimue would be pleased to meet you."

"She'd certainly thank us for making introductions, Mister Pigg."

"She would at that, Mister Poke. She would."

"We *could* set up a meet and greet."

"We *could*."

The goblins paused.

"Or we could just throw His Tininess into a cereal box and let the gods sort him out."

So that's what they did.

A Puftees box, of course. He was found by one giant girl and sold to another, who took him home and introduced him to a trunk full of princesses.

CHAPTER 8

"—Oh, Princess Barbie, I love you. Please honor me with a kiss."

"—But what will my father say?"

"—He won't mind at all 'cause I slayed the Dorkmonster, and now he must give me your hand. Kiss me, I love you so."

But I don't *love her,* thought Prince Fi as the tall blonde pressed close. *I* don't *even know her. Not that Barbie doesn't possess many . . . agreeable qualities, but—*

The giant knocked Fi's face against Barbie's and made kissy noises.

—*Mwah mwah mwah.*

The poor woman, he thought as he looked into Barbie's rapidly advancing and retreating eyes. *To be disgraced in this way. Were both our curses lifted, I might make an honest woman of her—if only she weren't three times my height.*

"—We shall be married in the springtime, in the Castle Fun playset."

It had been impossible to tell how long he'd spent in the darkness inside the fish, inside the bird, inside the museum. But now Fi could see that he'd traveled to a world with a sun that still rose and set, and he hit upon the idea of counting the days by composing a sentence. A sentence in his mind, one word each night.

At the end of the first day he chose the word *I* to remind himself that he was a man and not a toy. But by the end of the second and third days he'd written

I, Prince Fi,

and now you must realize that he had truly begun to despair. In three days he might have written "I will escape," or even "I am sad," and still you would have understood that the prince was hopeful, because these were complete sentences. And to complete a sentence would have meant that he felt the witch's magic wearing thin. But instead he wrote

I, Prince Fi,

and those commas were the commas of the hopeless. Each was a dark teardrop from a single *i*.

The giant girl, who he'd gathered was named Polly, carried him everywhere. Her accent was strange, but he soon came to understand her when she held her face close and whispered to him every asinine thought.

"I think I saw a little man in our house yesterday," she told him once. "Dressed in red. Well, not so little, I guess. Bigger than you." She lowered her voice even further. "I see lots of weird things. Even more now that we've moved here to Goodborough. When I was little I told Mom about them, but she always said they were my imagination, so I stopped telling her."

On the morning that Polly told him they were going to a commercial shoot with her father, he'd written

I, Prince Fi, decree that the Giant Girl is enemy to all pixies, and I hate her, and

And, and, and. It felt pointless to continue.

Fi was in the inside pocket of Polly's coat when she and her father were seized by the camera crew at the Goodco factory. He didn't see Polly's dad struggle free and punch a gaffer. He didn't see the Lady of the Lake step out from the shadows, and speak their names, and immobilize them with a spell. But he felt the spell wash over him. Frozen by pixie magic, he was now unfrozen by Fay. He felt his joints creak and come to life. With the mildly enchanted sword Carpet Nail, he ruined the lining of Polly's coat and slid free of her pocket.

It was nearly as dark in this room as it had been in Polly's coat. He gave his eyes a moment to warm up with the rest of his body, and adjust. They were alone in here—Fi, Polly, and her father. Fi climbed down Polly's leg and onto the floor. The humans were still frozen, and tied up to boot. That seemed unsporting. He could just leave them now, make his escape, find his brothers . . . or he could cut through the ropes and give them a fighting chance if the spell wore off.

"You know the rest," Fi told Polly in the back of the truck. "I severed your bonds, and you regained your mobility while I searched for a way out of the room. I didn't do it for you. I did it because you had been frozen by Fay magic, so you could only be an enemy of the Fay. And my people have ever struggled against the Fay."

Polly was faintly snuffling. "I've said I'm sorry," she whispered. "I've said it a million times."

"Some transgressions are beyond apology."

"We're stopping," said John. "I think we're here."

They were let out of the back by Biggs. The truck was in the middle of a vast parking lot in front of a shopping center. They'd arranged to meet John's friend here.

"Now to find Sir Richard," he said, hopping down to the asphalt in a hat and sunglasses.

"How are we supposed to find one knight in all this?" said Scott, scanning the parking lot.

"He'll be the only one on a horse," Erno suggested.

"I shall stay in the lorry," Fi announced, and slid down from Polly's head. Polly shuffled off to the edge of the cargo bay with everyone else. Then she turned.

"You think you're Prince Charming," she told Fi. "You think you're so good. But good people forgive mistakes. You're not even *trying* to forgive me," she said, wiping her eyes. When they were clear, she added, "You can sit on someone else's head from now on." Then she jumped to the ground, and Biggs pulled the steel door down between them.

CHAPTER 9

Harvey stood with his hands in his pockets while Mick scoured the field of clover at the edge of the parking lot on his hands and knees. Finchbriton hopped about looking for food, and the clearly amnesiac unicat stalked Finchbriton.

Mick glanced up at Harvey. "Little help?"

"Help?" said Harvey. "As if the courtly leprechaun Ferguth Ór needth my help finding a four-leaf clover. I wouldn't inthult you."

Finchbriton found a bug and cooked it a little bit before eating it. The brief reappearance of blue flame jogged the cat's memory, and it slunk off in another direction.

Mick tried to see what the rabbit-man was looking at, and his gaze paused on the big black town car parked in an empty part of the lot. Biggs stood stiffly beside it. Inside the car, John, Merle, and the kids were trying to convince Sir Richard Starkey that the world was in danger.

● ◐ ★

"Sooo . . . ," said Sir Richard. "All these invisible fairies are going to take over the world?"

The others wished he wouldn't keep putting it like that. Scott glanced at Emily. Emily shared a look with John. Scott and Erno and Emily and Merle were all a little cramped in this limousine seat, sitting backward, facing John and Polly and Sir Richard. They'd hired the limo to collect the famous drummer at his home in London and bring him here, and it was the biggest car they could get without renting another party bus.

Sir Richard was bearded, bald, wearing tinted glasses that made it hard to read his face. His hands were burled with thick gold rings, and he clacked these together.

"They'll only be invisible if they want to be," John explained. "Which they probably won't. It's like a . . . pride thing. Or something."

"But those fairy friends you mentioned . . . they were both invisible?" said Sir Richard.

Scott felt the conversation slipping away. "Mick—" he said. "That's the leprechaun—Mick is out of glamour."

"Out of glamour."

"Out of . . . magic. So he can't turn visible. And the rabbit-man is just a jerk," Scott added under his breath.

"Why can't Sir Richard see them anyway?" Erno

whispered to Merle. "He's a knight."

"Yeah, but he's not a changeling like Scott and Polly and John. Or an invasion baby like me."

"So he's magic enough to slay a dragon but not magic enough to see fairies?"

Merle shrugged.

"You couldn't see Mick and Harvey," John explained to Richard. "So they left to look for four-leaf clovers."

"Four-leaf clovers," repeated Sir Richard. Scott thought he could tell how badly things were going based entirely on how often Sir Richard repeated things.

John nodded. "Apparently we need them for a . . . thingy."

"Potion," said Erno.

"Potion," said Sir Richard.

"Come to think of it," said John, "we should have asked the finch to stay. Everyone sees the finch, for some reason."

"I saw that," Sir Richard agreed, brightening. "I saw it earlier."

"It breathes fire," Erno told him. This was followed by kind of a longish silence.

"Maybe one of us should fetch Fi," said Scott.

"No," Polly flatly answered.

"And so the cereal company . . . ," said Richard.

"Which is run by a fairy queen," John interjected.

". . . is rubbing out Knights Bachelor because we can kill dragons?"

Emily leaned forward and handed Sir Richard a piece of paper. He flinched as if expecting it to fold itself into something dangerous.

"This is a list of Knights Bachelor who have died in the last five years," Emily lectured, "categorized according to cause of death. Note the high number of accidents and sudden declines in health. Knights Bachelor have been seven times more likely to die during this period than an average Englishman of similar age."

Sir Richard studied the list, and his eyebrows lifted.

"I know it's a lot to swallow, Richard," John added.

Sir Richard frowned. "Your behavior has been so . . . uncharacteristic lately. I've seen the news."

"That isn't me. That Reggie Dwight is an impostor. These people will all corroborate that I've only just returned to England this morning."

Everyone nodded.

Sir Richard frowned and sucked on one of his rings.

"You don't have to believe all of it, Sir Richard," said Scott. "But . . . you're not safe. You need to believe that."

Richard thought for a moment. "Well. I guess it can't hurt to go away for a while."

"There you are." John smiled.

"What are you lot going to do?"

"John's going to trade places with the fake Reggie so he can meet with the queen and expose her," said Erno. "She's a fake, too."

Scott sucked air through his teeth. He wouldn't personally have volunteered this information.

"I see," said Sir Richard. The car was fidgety for a moment.

"The whole world will know what's going on," stressed John. "Soon. I swear. I just need you to trust me, Richard."

"I do." Sir Richard smiled and slapped his knees. "God help me, I do. But if it turns out you're wrong, I'm going to tell everyone I haven't seen you since the Grammys."

John laughed, and a pall lifted. "If I'm wrong, you can claim we've never even met."

Everyone smiled. Even Emily smiled. "So," Erno said. "You're a famous drummer."

Sir Richard beamed. "I was with the Quarrymen, a lifetime ago. You've heard our music?"

"No," Erno admitted.

Mick watched the car doors open, and everyone get out. He couldn't tell if Harvey had been looking at the car. He didn't know what the pooka was looking at.

Mick squinted back across the field of clover for a minute, then sighed.

"Why don't yeh go ahead an' insult me, Harv," he said.

Harvey slapped his hand over his eyes, bent over, and plucked a sprig at random. "Here ya go," he said.

Mick stared at the four-leafed clover for a moment, then put it in his pocket.

CHAPTER 10

A makeup girl cried on the London set of *Salamander Hamilton and the Three Ghosts of Christmas*. A production assistant cleaned what appeared to be vomit off what appeared to be Winston Churchill. Reggie Dwight loudly explained how neither thing was directly his fault. The assistant director sighed to the second assistant director. "Forty-three takes and his scene *still* isn't in the can," she said. "*And* he's supposed to record something for the soundtrack this afternoon."

The goblins dressed as Reggie Dwight faked a tantrum and locked themselves in his trailer for two hours, just so they could shed their Reggie skin and breathe awhile. One goblin napped while the other insulted people on the internet. When time came to return to the studio, they hid away their old skin with the others and grew a new one—you couldn't reuse them. If anyone decided to look inside the trailer's back closet they were going to wish they hadn't.

The goblins dressed as Reggie Dwight ate three sandwiches from the catering table, more quickly than Reggie was really able, so when they choked they did it in an entertaining way. Because they were entertainers. Afterward they got into a shoving match with an assistant who tried to give them what they later learned was the Heimlich maneuver. The goblins dressed as Reggie Dwight asked the assistant's forgiveness with a hug that went on just long enough to be uncomfortable. Then they went into the recording booth with pickle on their chin to see how long it would take someone to tell them.

At the piano, the goblins dressed as Reggie Dwight announced that they would not be performing "The Little Drummer Boy," as previously discussed, but would instead sing a new song they had themselves composed only that morning during toilet time. The assembled assistants and sound engineers all looked at one another and shrugged. It actually made a sound, so many people shrugging. Goblin Reggie played a chord and sang,

"I didn't mean . . ."

He closed his eyes and leaned into the next chord.

"I didn't mean to punch the queen."

The assistants and sound engineers looked at one another a little more pointedly.

> *"I didn't plan to greet Her Grace 'n'*
> *Sit for lunch 'n' punch her face in.*
> *Such a scene.*
> *I didn't mean to punch the queen."*

Goblin Reggie sighed wistfully.

> *"I didn't mean to spook the duke.*
> *Oh, whoah whoah WHOAH . . .*
> *I didn't mean to spook the duke.*
> *I guess I should have thought of that*
> *before I swung the cricket bat.*
> *It was a fluke.*
> *I didn't mean to spook the duke."*

Between that verse and the next, there was a ninety-second whistling solo. Then,

> *"Oooooh,*
> *I didn't mean to grope the pope—"*

"Uh, Reggie?" coughed some human in the sound booth. "Reggie? Hi. I think maybe that's enough for today."

The goblins thanked everyone for their good work and stepped into their private car. "Won't be back tomorrow, though!" they called. "Have a secret meeting! An ecret-say eeting-may with the Queen of England-way! Okay, bye-bye."

"Home, sir?" asked the driver.

"Yes, Jeeves," they told the driver, whose name was Michaels. "I'm going to fill a big bath and soak in it until my skin puckers and falls off."

"Sir," Michaels answered. He drove them to Reggie's home in St. John's Wood in the north of London. The gate opened onto a three-story stone house surrounded by trees, and Michaels edged the car up the drive.

"You should join me, Jeeves," said goblin Reggie. "It's a big bathtub."

"Thank you, sir, no."

The goblins dismissed Michaels and let themselves into the dark, empty house. They pulled the door shut behind them and paused. Centuries of being the things that creep in darkness had given them some insight into unlit houses. The darkness here was most certainly alive.

They could sense it without knowing just exactly what it was, and for a moment it made them afraid. They smiled.

"So *that's* what that feels like," they said, just before they were jumped from all sides.

CHAPTER 11

"JACKIE IS A PUNK! JUDY IS A RUNT! THEY BOTH WENT DOWN TO BERLIN, JOINED THE ICE CAPADES! AND OH I DON'T KNOW WHY! OH I DON'T KNOW WHY! PERHAPS THEY'LL DIIIIIEE, OH YEAH! PERHAPS THEY'LL DIE!" sang the goblin Reggie Dwight, tied to a banister. "THIRD VERSE! DIFFERENT FROM THE FIRST! JACKIE IS A PUNK! JUDY IS A RUNT—"

"Can't we gag them?" asked John, his fingers in his ears.

"They're two goblins inna suit," said Mick. "The singin' isn't even technic'ly comin' from their mouth."

"Well, then can we at least make them stop looking like me while they do it?"

"That we can," Mick answered, and trotted off toward the kitchen.

Polly came to a stop near her father. "This is a nice

house," she said. She'd spent the last ten minutes running all over it with Erno. "He has this big cabinet full of gold records and awards and things in the bathroom," she told Scott.

"VERSE EIGHT! I AM REALLY GREAT! JACKIE IS A PUNK—"

"In the bathroom?"

John smiled sheepishly. "So I can display them while pretending I don't care if they're displayed or not."

"Uh-huh," Scott said, turning to wince at his father's duplicate. The goblins were bound to the iron staircase with iron chains festooned with horseshoes. Biggs kept them under close watch. Prince Fi menaced them with his sword, for all the good it did. Scott didn't know the song the goblins were singing, but he doubted it had as many verses as they were currently claiming.

"VERSE TWELVE! WORD THAT RHYMES WITH TWELVE! REGGIE IS A—"

Mick returned from the kitchen with a pot of tea. "Helped myself," he told John. "Hope yeh don't mind."

"Of course not. Why . . . ?"

"Yeh'll see." Mick lifted the lid of the pot and dropped a four-leaf clover and a little yellow primrose into the steaming tea and swished it around. "Hey, fellas," he said to the goblin Reggie. "Yis want a cuppa?"

"NONE FOR ME, THANKS."

"Biggsie?"

Biggs took the teapot from Mick and opened the goblin Reggie's jaw like a change purse. The goblins gargled and growled. Then Biggs poured a stream of scalding tea down the passable replica they'd made of Reggie's throat.

They sputtered. They cursed in dead languages. Then they shuddered and rattled and their Reggie skin peeled like a banana.

"Yeesh," said Merle.

"That's what we're going to do to the queen?" said Scott.

"She's not the queen," said Emily from her corner of the sofa. "And if she is, it'll just be tea with some yard clippings in it."

The goblins, now laid bare, tried to wriggle out of their chains. Biggs pulled them tighter. One goblin sat atop the other's shoulders. They were wearing familiar little suits.

"This isn't Pigg and Poke, is it?" said Scott.

"The same." Pigg grinned.

"Cretinous hobgoblins!"

"Yis two really get around," said Mick. "Who's 'mpersonatin' the queen, then?"

"Misters Katt and Bagg," said Poke. "Took over for us after we got demoted to permanent Reggie duty."

"And where're yis supposed t' meet wi' them? Where

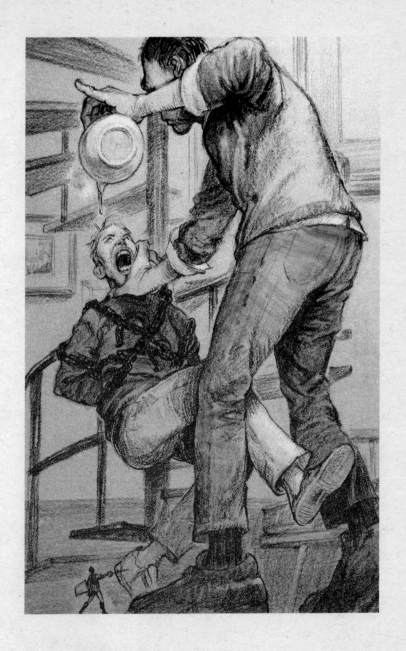

was fake Reggie gonna meet wi' the fake queen?"

"Ah, you know about that, eh?" said Pigg.

"They're clever, Mister Pigg," said Poke. "There's no gettin' around it."

"The royals're sending a car tomorrow mornin'," said Pigg. "Location TBD, though I unnerstand it'll probably be the British Museum."

"They're being awfully helpful all the sudden," said Emily.

"Maybe it's the horseshoes and clovers and such," said Poke. "*Makin'* us help."

"Or maybe we're secretly wonderful people," said Pigg.

"Everyone except Biggs, upstairs," Emily ordered. She started up the spiral staircase past the goblins, and the others dutifully followed. Finally the goblins were left alone with Biggs. They jiggled their chains.

"Left behind." Poke smiled sadly at Biggs. "They don't trust you."

"Trust me to do muh job," Biggs replied, staring over their heads.

"What's your job, big feller?" sighed Pigg.

"Peel your skins again if yuh try to 'scape."

And now the goblins were still.

"Our group should leave right away for Somerset," Scott whispered as soon as they were upstairs. "It'll take a couple hours just to get there, and we're not even sure what we're looking for exactly. Apart from the Queen of England."

"The Freemen files definitely didn't say anything specific except that she's being held in Avalon?" Merle asked Emily. She closed her eyes.

"I . . . I don't think so."

"You don't think so?"

Emily scrunched up her face. "I don't remember! Why are you asking me? Ask the owl! I told him everything I learned."

Archimedes turned his head and whistled, and Merle looked at his watch.

"'In a secure location in Avalon,'" he read. "I guess that's all the Freemen knew."

They reviewed their plans for the next day, such as they were, and separated. Scott, Merle, and Mick left for Somerset in the poppadum truck. Erno scooched up to Emily with Mr. Wilson's poem.

"Wanna work on this?"

"I just want to go to bed," she replied, and no wonder—she looked tired. "You know that kind of headache where it feels like someone's rummaging through your brain?"

". . . Nnnnno."

"Good night, Erno."

She left him alone in an odd little room that didn't look

like it got much use. It was snugly fitted with furniture that was better to look at than sit in, and shelves lined with matching spines of the sort of classics of Western literature that you could buy by the yard. He reread the poem:

> The new year has a week to wait till waking.
> The water's almost frozen in the well.
> The hours of the day
> pass swiftly by, then drift away,
> and yet there's nothing, less than nothing left to tell.
>
> Soon the final days are numbered, then forgotten,
> and the new year's hardly worth the time it's taken.
> By degrees the hourglass reckons
> all the minutes, all the seconds,
> and the next year still has weeks to wait to waken.

The unicat brushed up against his shins, stabbing him lightly in the leg.

"The new year has a week to wait," he told it. "Christmas Eve is a week before the end of the year. I wonder if that's important." In the margins he wrote *Christmas, Xmas, eve, 12/24.* "I guess it's about winter? Or time? Half the words are about either time or temperature."

He puzzled over the poem as the house slept around him.

CHAPTER 12

"Tired," said Merle, hunched over the wheel of the poppadum truck.

"I'd drive if I could," said Mick.

"You could teach me," Scott offered. He felt wired. "It's left brake, right accelerator, right?"

"Maybe you should just concentrate on keeping me awake."

"Tell us more about the good ol' days," said Mick. "The good ol' days that haven't happened yet, in your case. If yeh stop talkin' we'll give yeh a shove."

"Well . . . ," Merle began, hesitant, feeling his way back into the story. "I kept working on the time-travel question. I knew I could send things like Archimedes to the future, maybe even people to the future, but travel to the past seemed really impossible."

"You weren't sure you could send people to the

future?" asked Scott.

"I hadn't tried it yet."

Scott huffed. "I would have tried it right away."

"Would you?" Merle asked, turning. "Are you sure? You'd really be in a hurry to be the first human in all creation to try that, to have all your atoms taken apart and put back together again?"

Scott saw his point.

"Besides, I wasn't prepared to explain to everyone why I'd disappeared for a whole year. But word must have gotten out about my little trick with Archie, and soon the Fay showed up to ruin everything, like they always do. No offense, Mick."

"None taken, ugly."

"I'd just gone outside for some fresh air," Merle began, "when I got the feeling I was being watched."

He'd just gone outside for a smoke break, actually— arguably the exact opposite of fresh air—but like all former smokers he was ashamed to admit this in the presence of children. He was pacing the strip of sidewalk between the physics building and the tennis courts when a chill raised the hairs on the back of his neck.

Maybe it was because he was an invasion baby—a human born in the year the elves came, when magic swept like hurricanes over the earth—that he could sense something was wrong. Maybe, he'd think later, it was because one of the Fay *wanted* him to know. Whatever. He tossed his cigarette under his heel and walked swiftly back into the building.

Merle worked in a secure wing—the college had put locks on all the doors after some laptops and a bike had been stolen, years ago—but he cursed these locks now, even as he heard them click behind him. Put a keyed lock on a door, and one of the Fay might still get through it if you're careless, if you neglect to *make certain* you've shut it tight behind you. But these doors had combination locks. And a fairy's guesses were nothing if not lucky. Merle still had his hand on the knob when the door's small window filled with the face of Captain Conor of the Trooping Fairies of Oberon. There were more elves behind him, and Conor looked at Merle, then at the keypad below.

Merle turned, stumbled, raced down the hall shouting, "Archimedes! Octagon!" The mechanical owl met him at the door of his lab with the golden octagon, the time machine, in its claws. They turned the corner toward the wing's only other entrance and saw that here too was a group of elves, just on the other side of the door, patiently punching lucky guesses into the keypad. They'd get it right, and soon.

"Archie," Merle gasped, turning to the owl flapping in place beside him. "Calculate a time jump for both of us.

For both me and you." The owl whistled back, and Merle checked his watch. It said DURATION?

Distantly, from around the corner, Merle heard the click of a door.

"One year," he said. "No! Wait! They might think of that, come wait for me. A hundred years! No, that's nothing to an elf."

Archimedes whistled again. The sound of light footfalls tapped down to them from the far door. The nearest door clicked, and the elves pushed through.

"Five hundred years," he whispered to Archie. "Execute as soon as you've done the math," he added, and grasped the underside of the octagon so that he and the owl were holding it together.

Three elves stopped close on his left; another three turned the corner on his right. Conor was at the front of these.

"Put the device down, Merle," said Conor in that creepy voice he had. "Oberon himself requests an audience."

"*That's* kinda desperate, isn't it?" said Merle. "Collecting an audience at sword point? Must be a pretty bad show."

Five elves cocked their slings, aimed sharp flint missiles at Merle's head.

"Is Queen Titania gonna let him be the ventriloquist this time, or is he still the—"

Merle and Archimedes winked out of existence.

"—dummy," Merle finished, five hundred years in the future. Then he commenced falling.

The math of a five-hundred-year jump was, it turned out, tricky. He hadn't reappeared in his lab or even on solid ground. He found himself, instead, crashing downward through a canopy of leaves, then another, then grasping hold of a lean branch that bowed, snapped, and deposited him roughly on the forest floor. Archimedes fluttered down to meet him.

Mick punched Merle in the arm.

"Ow! Why?"

"Yeh hadn't said anythin' for a bit," said Mick. "Thought yeh needed perkin' up."

"I was thinking!"

"So where did you end up?" asked Scott.

"Near as I can tell, Costa Rica somewhere. I don't know for sure because I discover at this point that there don't seem to be any satellites for Archie to sync up with. But that's fine, I think. Five hundred years have passed, technology is probably so different now that Archie can't recognize it, and vice versa. So I nearly kill myself hiking out of the forest, living off fruit and rainwater, dreaming about my new plan, which is this: I find some future person here who's invented time travel to the past, and I use it to go back and save my parents and the whole world. I dream about this plan, even though I know there's something fundamentally wrong with it."

"What?"

"That if time travel to the past were ever really possible, then the past would be lousy with time travelers. But it wasn't. Nobody from my time had ever met a time traveler from the future, so what does that say?"

"Maybe . . . ," said Scott, not yet ready to give up on the possibility. "Maybe all the time travelers were really secret about it," he said, though he had to admit that didn't seem very likely.

"Well, whatever, it's a moot point. Because I spend the next six months traveling the earth, and I never meet another person."

"Not one?" said Mick. "Not even a fairy?"

"Not even a mouse. Not a creature was stirring. I find canned food, I find a bicycle, but everywhere it's empty towns, overgrown cities. I've jumped too far, and something terrible's happened."

"Jeez," said Scott. Immediately he wished he'd said something a little more profound.

"Yeah. Well. Eventually I can't take the loneliness anymore, so I ask Archie to jump us again—so far into the future that the earth itself will be dead and gone. Just to be on the safe side I settle on twice the age of the whole universe—twenty-eight billion years—and tell Archie to flip the switch. And he does, and we reappear in a cage in medieval England."

● ○ ★

Again the peasant rattled the wooden cage, which shook the wagon, which prompted the soldier who wasn't driving to turn and glare.

"Ignore him," said the driver.

"Please please *please* let me go," pleaded the peasant.

"We're under oath to bring you to King Vortigern," said the soldier.

The peasant pressed against the wooden slats. "When I said I never had a father, I didn't mean I *never* had a father. I meant I never *knew* my father. He died before I was born."

"Listen," said the soldier. "In good sooth? I believe thee. Of course I believe thee. But we're going to sacrifice thee anyway. We have to look busy."

"Look, what's this all about?"

The soldier turned entirely around and addressed the peasant. "King Vortigern has a tower that keeps falling down. His wise men tell him he needs the blood of a boy born without a father, to mix with the mortar. Thou wantest my opinion? I think the wise men just sayeth things like this when they don't know the answer."

"Verily," said the driver.

"Perchance they tellest the king he needs ice in August or a serpent hatched from a cockerel's egg or some similarly impossible nonsense. And the king tells us to go chase after phantoms. So fine—we get some fresh air and no one can ever check up on the so-called wise men."

The wagon creaked along the Roman road, in the north of Wales, toward Dinas Emrys, the Castle Ambrosius. Or what would be the Castle Ambrosius, if it didn't keep falling over.

"So . . . so let me go," urged the prisoner, "if it won't make any difference. You could change your mind and give me my liberty."

The soldier frowned, clearly confused. "So . . . thou proposest we take one who hast drawn the lot of sacrificial lamb and . . . just raise him above his station? Like a promotion?"

"I wasn't a sacrificial lamb this morning," argued the prisoner. "I was a peasant."

"Thou wert always a lamb," said the soldier as he shook his head and turned his eyes back to the road. "Thou just didst not know it. If Fortuna or . . . society or what have thee marks thee for death, then thou art a dead man. It's not our place to argue."

"Wait now," said the driver. "Are you saying there's no upward mobility? None at all? Does not the babe become a boy? Is not the boy promoted to a man? The squire to a knight? A knight to a . . . a . . ."

"Aha!" said the soldier. "You see, you've stepped in your own snare. Does the knight become a king? No. The

143

greatest knight will stay a knight, and the king will pass his crown to his own son, worthless though he may be. And is not the babe just a young boy? Is not the boy a young man? There's no upward mobility here, my friend. Each only comes of age and assumes the role he was born to."

The prisoner listened, and scratched his bottom. Then there was a kind of popping behind him, and he turned to see another man in the cage, holding an owl.

"Marry!" shouted the peasant. "Look here! Fortuna has sent you another lamb, to bleed in my place! A man with an owl! And is the owl not Fortuna's favorite?"

The soldiers turned to look. "Thou'rt thinking of Minerva," one said, but they both seemed pretty impressed with the new mystery prisoner.

The man with the owl staggered, looked around him with wild eyes. "Where am I?" he muttered. "When . . . when am I? How did I get here?"

"You see?" said the peasant, hurling himself against the front of the cage. "How he questioneth, like unto a child! How he gazeth with the eyes of a newborn babe!"

"This is impossible," Merle murmured. "Twenty-eight billion years into the future, and I'm standing in a donkey cart."

"What rubbish he gibbers! Surely he was born just now from the ether, a man without a father! Conjured from nothing to meet King Vortigern's swift justice!"

"Quiet," said Merle, remembering his Slumbro Mini. He flicked it at the peasant, who fell snoring in a heap in the straw. "Wait. Did that guy just say King Vortigern?"

The soldier in the front of the wagon was still a little dumbfounded, but he nodded. "That's where we're taking thee. To Dinas Emrys. We'll probably sacrifice both of ye, just to be safe."

"Dinas Emrys," repeated Merle, taking a seat. "King Vortigern. I know this story. All right, I got nothing else to do. I'll meet your king."

CHAPTER 13

They drove the wagon, and Merle with it, off the Roman road and over a rough path cut through the trees. Then straight through a narrow river and up an embankment that had been cleared of anything growing. Gray stones lay in ragged piles around the barest hints of castle walls.

"Ho there!" called a mason to the soldiers. "You've strange chickens in that coop!"

"Not chickens," answered the driver. "Lambs."

The mason frowned, then seemed to understand. He dropped his head as they passed. "Lord Vortigern is in the west pavilion," he said soberly.

Beneath a large peaked tent was Vortigern, a big man with a big red beard, dressed in furs and with an unfussy gold circlet atop his head. He strode out to meet the wagon and looked delighted by its contents.

"Two!" bellowed the king. "I' faith, that's good work, lads!"

One of the soldiers bowed and immediately set about managing expectations. "My liege. The sleeping one claims now that he hath a father, but that he didst know him not."

"Fine, fine, we'll kill him anyway. And the other?"

"I am Merle Lynn!" announced Merle, standing up in the cage, trying both to look and sound imposing. "And I wish to speak with these wise men who would have my blood!"

"God's teeth! I doubt they'll like *that*. If thou wert the wise men, wouldst thou want to meet the lambs? I wouldn't."

"This one just appeared in the cage," the soldier explained. "We didn't even have to catch him."

Vortigern grinned expansively, shot the grin around the hillock for a bit. "Well, that sounds promising! You have to admit! The wise men might have hit the bull's-eye on this one. And he has a bird! Cute."

"Lord Vortigern," Merle said, undeterred. "I know what you must do to make your tower stand."

"I bet thou dost. I bet thou dost. And I bet—I'm just guessing, now—but I bet thou thinkest it *doesn't* require bleeding thou dry and mixing thy blood in the mortar? I'm right, aren't I. String them up!"

Merle tensed and gripped his Slumbro tight as the cage was set upon by soldiers and laborers. The peasant beside him finally woke.

"Mwuh?" said the peasant as he raised his head.

"Still in the cage," Merle told him. "Still going to die."

"AAAH! No!"

"Stay behind me," said Merle, but the peasant didn't obey, and when the cage was opened he was grabbed roughly by a half-dozen hands. Merle waved his wand, and the peasant and two soldiers fell asleep.

"That keeps happening," said the driver.

Vortigern eyed the wand. "He must be a sorcerer."

"Yes!" said Merle. "A powerful sorcerer! So you'd better—"

"Aha! That's why his blood's so good for making

148

buildings out of!" Vortigern concluded. "Magic blood!"

The soldiers and laborers all nodded at one another, saying, "Oh yeah, magic blood."

"Nuts," said Merle. He backed away from the door of the cage and was surprised when a pair of arms grabbed him through the bars from behind. Startled, he dropped his Slumbro, and the strong arms of the laborers held him fast.

"Many thanks for putting our lamb to sleep, great sorcerer," said Vortigern. "So much less thrashing and dolorous lamentation if he sleepeth. Now: we only built the one truss for the sacrificial bleeding, so I'm afraid thou wilt have to wait."

They were dragging the sleeping peasant toward a wooden frame built over a cauldron. Soon they'd hoist him up on it and cut his throat, Merle supposed, and then his own turn would come.

He promised himself he'd think about it some more when he was no longer under threat of imminent death, but for now Merle figured one of three things had happened: that he'd strained the forces of time and space so considerably during his last jump that he'd gone backward instead of forward somehow; that he'd maybe (and this seemed too fantastic) jumped past the end of the universe and into a virtually identical new one; or that he'd really jumped into oblivion, as expected, and was dying and this was all some crazy dream he was having as his brain ran out of oxygen.

Still—if it was a crazy dream, it was one he'd read about a hundred times.

"Our blood won't do anything!" he shouted, struggling against the clutches of the king's men. "Your wise men can't even tell you why your tower falls! How can they know the solution if they don't understand the problem?"

"Quit your bleating, lamb," said one of the men.

"And I suppose thou knowest why my tower falls, sorcerer?" asked the king.

"I do. I do. Set that man free and I'll tell you, and if I'm wrong you can still sacrifice me."

They'd tied the peasant's ankles and were just beginning to hoist him up on the frame. King Vortigern chewed his lip.

"My . . . blood's probably really magical right now," Merle added. "I've been eating a lot of unicorn and stuff."

The king thought this over, then shrugged theatrically and ordered the peasant be released. They cut him free, and he continued to snore beside the cauldron. Then all eyes were on Merle, and the men let him go. He snatched up his Slumbro and crammed it into his jeans pocket before speaking.

"Beneath this hill lies a hidden pool. And in that pool two dragons fight—one dragon's red, the other's white." He hadn't meant to rhyme just then, but he figured it was all to the good. He stepped down from the cage to lead them to the secret tunnel beneath the hill, then realized he hadn't a clue where it was.

"Archie," he whispered. "Assume this hill is Dinas Emrys in Wales, United Kingdom. Do any geological records mention a cave entrance?"

Archie sent a map to Merle's watch face, and he led the king and his men to a gap in the rocks, shrouded by moss. The others lit torches; Merle lit the flashlight on his key chain.

"What rare light that burns without heat!" Vortigern said of the flashlight.

"Thanks," said Merle. "I got it free for opening a checking account."

They descended into the hillside, through a narrow passage, each hunched and a little fearful beneath the suffocating patience of the earth. There was a breeze against their faces, rising from below, and here and there thin roots breached the rock walls like hairs, like they were plunging into the cavernous nostril of some sleeping giant. The nostril rumbled, as if snoring.

"There," said Merle, worried he'd lose his audience.

"See? The dragons fight, and their fighting shakes the earth. The red dragon represents—"

Merle stopped short, realizing he'd just stepped into a large open chamber. It should have been dark, but the space was lit dimly by some source he couldn't identify. It was a huge, damp vault, enclosing a dark pool. And that pool was turbid and foaming with the struggle of two magnificent dragons.

Merle had known what to expect, and still he could only stare, stupid and gaping, at the creatures. Dragons. One white, one red. Each the size of an elephant, slick as a fish, tightly built with coiled, ropy muscles and a whiplashing neck, like lightning made flesh. He'd never seen a dragon. He'd heard of the colossal pink one that had terrorized the world before he was born, of course, but it spent most of its time in Ireland or someplace.

The dragons, mercifully, couldn't seem to care less about Merle and King Vortigern and his men. The men had all fallen silent, watching. The white dragon was dominant, trying to bite the red on its nape and hold it down. They crashed together into the deep of the pool, and again the earth rumbled.

"Um . . . so. The red dragon represents the Britons," said Merle to whoever might be listening. "The white one represents the Saxons. The Saxons have the upper hand

now, but one day soon, the red dragon will rise up and prevail."

"Why'd you tell them that?" asked Scott. "It's kind of a weird thing to say."

Merle shrugged. "I have no idea. But the books said that's what I said, so that's what I said."

"But . . . wait. If the books say you said it, but you only said it *because* the books say you said it, then—"

"I'm either too tired or not tired enough to have that kind of conversation right now," Merle told him. They were winding through a cramped little maze of a town, and Merle added, "We should be close now."

"We won't know we're *really* close until we see water," said Mick. "Avalon is an island."

"Yeah," Scott agreed. "When I saw it with my . . . salmon sight, on the cruise ship, it was definitely wet. Swampy."

Merle checked the map again, but let it be. "Anyway, there's one more thing to tell. Eventually Vortigern and his men leave, and while I'm standing there watching the dragons, an elf steps out of the shadows. A real *familiar* elf."

He was one of those regal, Tolkienesque elves that made you feel fat and unlovely. Six-five, lean, sloe eyed, with short green mossy hair.

"You're name's Conor," Merle said.

The elf frowned almost imperceptibly. "My name is Mossblossom."

"Yick. I can see why you changed that."

"King Vortigern called you Merlin," said the elf.

"That's what he called me, yeah."

"You know much, Merlin. My Lady of the Lake will be curious about you."

Merle didn't know what to say to that. He winced at the dragons—the white had finally succeeded in subduing the red, and now the waters calmed. "They're . . . they're not actually fighting, are they?"

"Not fighting, no."

Merle coughed. "I think maybe I'll give them some privacy," he said, turning to go. "You coming?"

"Alas, I am . . . chaperone to this congress. By order of my Lady."

"Good luck with that," Merle said as he left.

"I hope we meet again, Merlin of Ambrosius," said the elf.

Merlin didn't look back. "I don't," he said through his teeth.

"This is it," Merle said now, in the truck. "We're right on top of it." They'd passed through the town and emerged at the foot of a tall hill. Taller than Dinas Emrys had been.

Merle, Scott, and Mick got out and stood around the poppadum truck in the dark, in the quiet little town of Glastonbury, in Somerset, in the west of England.

"Well," said Mick. "*This* doesn't look right."

CHAPTER 14

It was only when John looked in on him hours later that Erno realized the night had passed and he had quite possibly fallen asleep with his eyes open, half focused on the bleak and bleary poem. The unicat was curled in his lap.

"Up already?" asked John. "Polly's still conked out. Your sister, too."

Erno rubbed his eyes. "Good. Good, she needs the sleep."

The small square window was an ocean-bottom blue. It was very early. John was wearing a three-piece gray gabardine suit with a pink tie and handkerchief.

"Don't know when this so-called car is coming for me," he explained. "Must be ready."

Erno stood, upsetting the cat, and followed John downstairs.

Biggs was standing in one corner of the front room, asleep. Prince Fi paced back and forth like a sentry in front of the goblins, who seemed to be engaged in talk of good ol' Pretannica with Harvey.

"Jutht thurprized we didn't know each other already," Harvey told Pigg and Poke. "Uth havin' the thame uncle and all."

"We're nearly brothers, when it comes down to it," said Pigg.

"A pooka's more goblin than elf, so they say," added Poke.

Harvey nodded. "Thatth true."

Just then a tinny rendition of "For Those About to Rock (We Salute You)" started playing from somewhere. Everyone but the goblins looked around.

"Is that a phone?" asked Erno.

"Not one of mine," said John.

"It is, actually," said Pigg, tilting his head toward the folds of Reggie skin hanging down around him.

"It's the mobile we stole off you at the Goodco factory last year," Poke added, smiling apologetically.

"You changed the ringtone," John said, aghast. As if this was the final straw, the ultimate indignity. Not the identity theft and character assassination so much as the ringtone. He set about the distasteful task of rifling through the pockets of a full-length Halloween costume of himself and found the phone.

"Hello?"

"That's it today?" said the voice on the other end. "Just hello? No 'Queenpunchers Anonymous' or 'You have reached Reggie's House of Fruit' or whatever?"

John winced at Erno. "It's early," he said.

"That it is. Car's out back."

"I'm on my way."

The sun was up, and Merle, Mick, and Scott had driven in and around Glastonbury and the surrounding countryside twice; asked for directions three times; breakfasted in the truck; and made mildly personal comments to one another on the subjects of eating habits, driving ability, age, height, and all-around usefulness. Scott made the mistake of mentioning that in books about magic villains and world saving, there was always a main character who died, and they had a spirited discussion about which of them, if any, it would be. Or if any of them even qualified as a main character. Then they didn't say anything for a long time.

Finally, in unspoken agreement, they gave up.

They were sitting now in a pretty garden on the edge of a stone ring around a two-thousand-year-old hole in the ground called the Chalice Well. It was apparently one of Glastonbury's chief attractions, purportedly the last

resting place of the Holy Grail.

"This mission of ours," said Mick. "'Twas always doomed, wasn't it? That's why they sent the likes of us?"

"It was a long shot," Merle admitted. "Assuming this place was the mythical Avalon, we didn't even know where to begin looking for the queen."

Scott could just barely see Glastonbury Tor from here, a sharp hill with a church on it that rose up from the surrounding plains. This hill had been an island back when the area was flooded, but the lady at the Chalice Well admissions gate said it hadn't been *that* flooded for a while.

"So when the Freemen's files said Avalon, do you think they meant somewhere else?" asked Scott. "When I saw the queen with my salmon sight, she was hard to focus on."

"Is that definitely what we're callin' it?" said Mick. "Your 'salmon sight'? I vote for somethin' else."

They'd driven all night for nothing and were all a little grumpy. Scott read aloud from the visitor's brochure again, just because he knew it annoyed Mick.

"'The interlocking circles on the well cover represent the inner and outer worlds, a symbol known as the Vesica Piscis. A sword bisects these two circles, possibly referring to the legendary Excalibur, sword of King Arthur, who is believed by some to be buried nearby.'"

"Please shut it," said Mick.

Scott put the brochure away. Merle appeared to have nodded off.

"Maybe I should check in at home," Scott said, dialing one of the new disposable cell phones they all had now.

"Hi," said Polly on the second ring.

"Glastonbury's a bust, maybe," Scott told her. "It doesn't look like Avalon. What's going on there?"

"Dad left awhile ago. Erno and Biggs are working on the puzzle poem with Archie the owl. Erno wants to thank Merle again for leaving Archie."

"What about Emily?"

"She's sleeping in. Hold on, Erno wants to know how you're doing." Scott listened to Polly explain to Erno that they hadn't found the queen, that Avalon didn't even look like Avalon. Then there was a pause. "Um, Scott?"

"What?"

"The goblins overheard me talking," said Polly, "and one of them, I think Pigg . . . no, maybe that's Poke. Which one's the ugly one?"

Scott didn't know how to answer that question. "Does it matter?"

"I guess not. One of them just said, 'Course they didn't find Her Majesty. She's in the *other* Avalon.'"

Scott felt suddenly more tired than he could have thought possible. "You're kidding."

"I'm not, but maybe they are?"

"No, it makes sense, actually—I bet they're telling the truth." Scott sighed. "I think they kind of like telling the truth if they know it isn't gonna make your life any easier. The queen is in Pretannica," he said, and Mick groaned. "How are we going to get to Pretannica?!"

"I dunno," said Polly. "Maybe Mr. Wilson's poem is a clue?"

"That'd be nice. Can you put Erno on?"

"Just a sec."

Erno took the phone. "Hey."

"Hey. What have you worked out so far?"

"Well," said Erno, and Scott could hear papers rustling. "Practically all the lines are about time or temperature. It has the words year, week, frozen, hours, day, degrees, minutes, sec—"

There was silence on the line for a bit. "Seconds?" finished Scott.

"Yeah, hold on," said Erno. "Saying those words out loud got me thinking. Degrees, minutes, and seconds. What does that sound like to you?"

Scott thought. "I dunno. Two words about time and one about temperature?"

"No. No. I think I just figured something out. I was always kind of into military history, and maps and stuff."

"Okay."

"So coordinates of latitude and longitude are written out in degrees, minutes, and seconds. Like a specific point on the globe might be written as minus fifty-three degrees, ten minutes, eighteen seconds latitude; twelve degrees, twenty-three minutes, five seconds longitude."

"So do you think the poem tells you a point on a map?" asked Scott.

" . . . Maybe. I wonder—" There was a faint noise on the line, like a shout from far away. "What was that? Hold on."

Scott hummed to himself until Erno returned.

"Man," said Erno. "Emily is, like, shouting in her sleep. It's hilarious. She must be having a dream."

"What's she saying?"

"I couldn't make out any words. You coming back?"

"I guess so, when Merle wakes up."

"Hope your dad's doing better than you guys."

"He'd almost have to be."

CHAPTER 15

That was not strictly true.

He was an actor, John told himself as he exited through the back door of his house; a good actor, and today he was not John Doe. He wasn't even Reggie Dwight—he was two awful little monsters in a suit, ready to take tea with a pantomime queen.

The car that waited for John outside his home in St. John's Wood was an ordinary black London cab, but it had an extraordinary driver. He was a black-suited, hard-headed man with stubbly black hair you could strike a match on, and so large and powerfully built that it seemed the car must have been manufactured around him. *Soon he'd have to leave the shell of it behind for another, larger one,* thought John, *like a hermit crab.*

"Lads," greeted the driver as John got in the back.

"So what was decided?" asked John. "British Museum?"

The driver frowned. Not that John could see his face, but he'd swear you could hear this man frown. "You weren't supposed to know that yet."

Oh, thought John. "Well, I have my ways."

"I?"

Shoot shoot shoot. "Yes, I. Mister Pigg, speaking. Mister Poke hasn't got my ways, you understand. He's got his own ways."

"That I do, Mister Pigg," John added.

"Right," said the driver with another frown, and the sound that made. Sort of a meat-tenderizing sound. Anyway, the moment had passed. John was supposed to get the driver to confirm the location of the meet, then make a quick sign through the rear windshield to Erno, who was watching from a window. But he'd gotten flustered and forgotten, and now they were blocks away.

It was early, and traffic was light. When they were near the museum, John asked, "So where are we setting up? Reading Room?"

"Look," said the driver, craning his neck. "You didn't tell anyone, did you?"

"Only our grocer. And the lady who does our hair. And this nice bloke from the *Daily Telegraph*, what was his name?"

"Funny. You're funny. Never have I known such a funny pair of goblins."

They pulled up Great Russell Street to the museum grounds and were waved through gold-tipped gates that would normally turn away all automobiles. They came to their final stop right in front of the building's columned facade. John's door was opened for him, and he stepped out to be frisked by police officers. They didn't find him to be carrying a weapon, even though he was.

The museum wasn't yet open, so everyone here was attached to the queen in some way. John wondered how many of them were in on the joke—how many of them knew the queen wasn't the queen, that John wasn't John. There was a distinct lack of winks and knowing smiles, so he was inclined to think most of them were legit. Then a prissy and pucker-mouthed little man who looked like he was sucking on boredom itself came alongside him.

"I thought I'd talked you both into the navy-blue check," he whispered.

"Be happy we're wearing pants," said John. Who was this man? Was he a Freeman? Was he even human?

"At least you had the good sense to wear pink," the prissy man conceded. He was wearing pink himself—an ascot and a small carnation. John scanned the crowd—there were maybe only ten others wearing some little blush of color, including one police officer with a breast cancer awareness pin.

The Great Court of the British Museum was vast,

clean, a gleaming blue-white at this time of the morning. A round, bright, modern structure with tall, evenly spaced windows like a zoetrope stood in its center, boxed in by more classical peaks and pillars and sheltered beneath a curvilinear lattice of metal and glass. A wide walkway clasped its staircase arms around the zoetrope, tapering down to rest its cold hands on either side of a door that led into the old Reading Room. This room was currently showing an exhibit of reliquaries, which, if John understood correctly, was a collection of the body parts of famous dead religious people. But they weren't going into the Reading Room.

Between the staircases, a blue backdrop had been erected, and in front of that, a table and tea set. He thought this place had the sort of symbolism the royals liked—a bit of old, a bit of new, a place of learning where he and the queen would supposedly come to a better understanding of each other blah blah blah. He took his place at the table and immediately started working out escape routes.

"Where are Katt and Bagg?" whispered John, hoping he'd gotten the other goblins' names right.

"First you, then the press are called, then the Goblin Queen makes her royal entrance."

"We hate waiting," said John.

● ○ ★

The new year has a week to wait till waking, thought Erno with an atlas across his lap. *Could that mean December twenty-fourth, then, or maybe twenty-fifth? Or . . . or, if there's a week until the new year, then that means fifty-one weeks have passed.* He checked the atlas. Assuming that the first number in the poem would be the first number of the coordinates, then fifty-one degrees latitude was far enough north of the equator to possibly be in England. *Or Canada or Germany or about five other countries*, he thought. Still, it was a nice coincidence.

The water's almost frozen in the well. "Archie?" Erno said, and the owl turned. "What temperature does water freeze at?" He read the answer off Merle's watch. *Thirty-two degrees Fahrenheit, or zero degrees Celsius. So if water's almost freezing, it would be thirty-three. Or one.* Again, fifty-one degrees, thirty-three minutes latitude could keep him in England, and Erno started feeling the thrill of discovery.

Within a half-hour, John was told the press had assembled outside the Great Court, waiting to be let in. He checked his phone and found the more traditional news outlets predicting a staged and uneventful reconciliation, while the tabloids speculated wildly about fresh queen punchings and royal retaliations. One newspaper was calling the event the "Tussle on Great Russell."

The table was real wood beneath the tablecloth, some expensive antique. The china teacups looked as delicate as fingernails. There was a small creamer of milk and a bowl filled with perfect sugar cubes. Somewhere, someone was making the tea. The whole tableau glowed under powerful lights. This kind of ridiculous stagecraft, this was his world—Reggie's world, really. He could do this.

Now the press was let into the Great Court and began immediately to snap pictures and pepper John with questions. They were kept at a distance, and he smiled and waved back and pretended not to hear them. A servant (who was *not* wearing pink, John noted) came with a bone china teapot on a silver tray and placed it in the center of the table. John took the lid off the teapot, under the pretense of smelling the tea, and slipped a four-leaf clover and a primrose unnoticed into the brew.

"Please don't touch the service, sir," said the servant.

"Sorry."

Erno rubbed his palms into his eyes and tried to focus on something apart from his sister mumbling in her sleep in the next room.

> *The hours of the day*
> *pass swiftly by, then drift away . . .*

171

Twenty-four hours in the day, obviously, thought Erno, and he wrote 24 beside 51 and 33.

and yet there's nothing, less than nothing left to tell.

Here he stumbled, until remembering that a coordinate could be positive or negative. Negative latitude meant it was south of the equator. Negative longitude was west of the prime meridian. *So less than nothing is negative one, maybe? Or even negative zero.* The way Mr. Wilson had repeated the word "nothing" made Erno think the latter was more likely.

More muttering from Emily, and then a sustained hiss. Erno would check on her. He'd do it right after he'd finished the poem.

Polly sat downstairs with Biggs and the goblins and Harvey, ripping paper, ripping, specifically, the pages of an '80s magazine she'd assumed was so old it was disposable. She would have panicked if you'd told her it was actually an expensive collector's item, but it wouldn't matter in the long run—everything in the house was going to burn soon anyway.

Conversation had vanished, replaced by one of those clock-ticking kinds of silences, a savagely quiet kind of thickness, and Polly was just rolling her bits of paper into pellets to throw at the goblins when they turned to her and spoke.

"Nothing to do, eh?" said Pigg.

"No secret mission, like the others," said Poke.

"Quiet," said Biggs.

"Eh . . . ," said Harvey. "Why don't you leave thith one alone, boyth. She'th all right."

"All right?" said Pigg.

"All *right?*" said Poke.

"She's our captor."

"Our rightful mark."

"We have our natures to consider."

"It's a big house, you know."

"She *could* sit somewhere else."

"Okay, okay," said Harvey with a shrug and a be-my-guest wave of his arms.

Polly looked squarely at the goblins. "So your question was, why no secret mission for me?"

"That's right."

"I'm only *seven.*"

Pigg nodded. "That's what your Prince Fi said. 'Just a little girl,' he told your brother last night, in passing."

Polly gasped. "He said that?"

"Pixies're like humans that way," said Poke. "Don't respect children like the Fay do. Queen Nimue, you know—she wants to build an *army* of children."

"Don't listen," said Biggs.

"The big lug's right," said Pigg. "Don't listen to us."

"Forget we brought it up."

"I mean, even if she *could* win Fi's respect—"

"It's not possible, Mr. Pigg. I hope you aren't suggestin' what I think you're suggestin'—"

"Oh, I agree, Mr. Poke. We could show her, and it'd be *amazing*, but still it wouldn't melt Fi's cold, cold heart."

Polly tightened her fists. "You don't know him. You're wrong about him."

"I'd like to be wrong," said Poke. "I would."

"And stop talking about me like I'm not in the room," said Polly, getting to her feet. "Grown-ups always do that, and I hate it!"

"An' well you should."

"You know what else I hate?"

"Tell us, tell us."

"I hate TV shows where the character *knows* the bad guy's trying to trick her into setting him free, but still all he has to do is say *one kinda true upsetting thing* and she's all like, 'You're wrong! I'm gonna unlock your handcuffs and prove it to you!'"

The room fell silent again, and Biggs smiled at her. She took her seat.

Harvey snorted. "Ah, the girl took you to thchool, ladth," he said. Then Polly allowed herself a little smile, too.

The goblins just stared, their chains hanging limply around them.

"Not scared of monsters anymore, you know," Polly added. "Or the dark. I haven't been scared of any of that since I was little."

Poke let his attention drift to the empty fireplace, feigning disinterest. But Pigg continued to watch Polly, and said, "You invented the darkness, you know. You humans. Filled it with stories of bogeymen and bridge trolls and sharp little hands snatching children in the night."

Polly narrowed her eyes. "That's not right. You Fay, you *are* those things. You *do* steal children. Mick told me."

"Yes," said Poke, turning.

"Oh yes," said Pigg.

"But only because we were invited."

"Only because you let us in."

John shifted in his seat and eyed a plate of shortbread on the table. He hadn't eaten any breakfast. Finally the queen herself appeared from behind a blind, wearing a pink dress, pearls, and a diamond brooch. John stood, bowed at the neck, and they sat down together as the cameras flashed.

"They can't hear us if we talk quietlike," said the Goblin Queen in a gruff, sailorly sort of voice. "There ain't no microphones."

John pretended to celebrate this by saying a rude word.

"Thassa spirit. Just lie back an' thinka England, an' it'll all be over soon."

John was fairly certain he was supposed to wait for the queen herself to pour. He was her guest here. He calmed himself by studying the queen's diamond brooch and discovered that what he'd mistaken for an abstract design was actually a giraffe throwing up a smaller giraffe.

"Where'd you get that?"

"Had it made."

Finally the Goblin Queen asked if John took milk, and when he said no she lifted the teapot and filled his cup, then her own. John didn't want any sugar either, so the queen helped herself to two lumps and stirred.

"I suppose you've both grasped the comedy a' this sitiation," said the queen. "It was *you* two what got punched, when you were 'personatin' Her Majesty. An' now it's *you* apologizin' t' us!"

"Misters Katt and Bagg," said John, "always with such a fascinatin' analysis of the facts. Except we're *not* apologizin' to you lot, we're tellin' you to shut your gobs and drink your tea."

"Heh," said the queen with an unladylike leer, and she took up her teacup and pressed it to her lips. Then a man, the same man who'd brought the tea, rushed from the blind and came to a stop by her side. This man gave John

a queer look, then leaned close to the Goblin Queen and whispered something in her ear. She lowered the teacup, the tea untouched. Then she gave John a bit of a queer look herself.

Soon the final days are numbered, then forgotten, read Erno, and he thought, *If there's a week left until new year, then there must be seven days.*

and the new year's hardly worth the time it's taken.

So it's the new year now? All right.

*By degrees the hourglass reckons
all the minutes, all the seconds . . .*

He was pretty sure this bit was just there to get him thinking about coordinates.

and the next year still has weeks to wait to waken.

So if it's the new year, then the next year has . . . fifty-two weeks to wait?

He looked at the notes he'd been taking. They read 51, 33, 24, -0, 7, 52.

He felt iffy about it but asked Archimedes to show him

exactly where fifty-one degrees, thirty-three minutes, twenty-four seconds latitude; minus zero degrees, seven minutes, fifty-two seconds longitude would be on a map. And the owl sent him an answer, and it was a north London house three miles away.

Only three miles. He could hit it with a rock from here. No, he couldn't. But still! This had to be the answer—and he'd found it without any help from Emily, he thought, with a rush of pride. Then, as if rebuking him, Emily shouted in her sleep from the next room.

Polly came up the stairs. "It sounded like Emily yelled real words this time," she said.

"Yeah . . . it did," Erno agreed, and he shifted himself closer to the bedroom door. They were both silent, waiting, and then it came.

"St. John's Wood!" shouted Emily in a mumbly dream speech. "We're in St. John's Wood!"

"Ohhh," said Erno. "That can't be good."

CHAPTER 16

The queen had sent her servant away, and now she stared at John with a little smile. John sipped his own tea, just to show it wasn't poisoned or anything, but the queen went on considering him for another dreadful minute. He thought even the reporters collectively sensed something was amiss. They had the reverent hush of sports fans watching to see if a ball thrown from half-court and backward was going to go in the basket or not.

"There's a wonderful story from the Hebrew Bible," said the queen in a queenly voice. John thought it could only be a bad sign that the goblins were using a queenly voice. "The Gileadites had defeated the Ephraimites in battle, and the surviving Ephraimites were trying to cross the River Jordan back into their homeland. Do you know the story?"

John coughed. "Don't think so," he answered.

"The Gileadites stopped every man crossing the River

Jordan and asked, 'Are you an Ephraimite?' But of course no one answered yes. So the Gileadites told every man, 'Say the word 'shibboleth.''"

There was a pause. John said, "What is—"

"It's a Hebrew word for a part of a plant or something. The meaning isn't important," said the Goblin Queen. "What's important is that the Ephraimites had no *sh* sound in their dialect, while the Gileadites did. You see?"

"So—"

"So any man who said '*si*bboleth' was killed. Say it with me: shibboleth."

John breathed. "Shibboleth," he repeated.

"Say it with both your voices," said the queen.

The Great Court was crushingly silent. Gather enough quiet in one place, in a big enough room, and John thought it could almost kill a man. It almost killed him now.

"Say it," said the queen. "Say shibboleth with both your voices at once, and I'll drink my tea and smile for the cameras and we'll all go home to our plum house-sitting jobs."

John was momentarily stuck for an ad lib.

"Sir Richard!" called the queen. And from behind one of the blinds came Sir Richard Starkey, drummer for the Quarrymen. This had the effect of really warming up the reporters. They shouted and surged against the velvet rope, a seething mass of nonsense.

"I'm sorry, Reggie," said Sir Richard. "I had to tell. You need help, you and your friends."

John rose sharply, and his chair clattered to the floor behind him. "You were always a mediocre drummer, Richard!" he said, pointing.

"Oh, look here, now—"

"You didn't even play on *The Pennyfarthing Policemen Ride Again*! It was a studio drummer!"

Speaking of policemen, several were now advancing on John. He sighed.

"I'm about to do something stupid, lads," he said.

"We sort of figured," said an officer.

"I wasn't," said John, grabbing the teapot, "speaking to you." Then something unexpected happened.

For weeks the world would buzz over the mystery of this unexpected thing, and the things that would follow. Television news cameras these days catch a lot of detail, and those at the British Museum appeared to show Reggie Dwight unfurl his arm with a flourish, and a small bird fly from his sleeve. One of the reporters went, "Oooh." Then the bird started breathing fire, and John punched the queen again.

She tumbled backward onto her royal bum. "THE QUEEN IS AN IMPOSTOR!" John shouted. It appeared to everyone present that he was about to pour hot tea on Her Majesty's face, but a couple of fearless staffers managed to avoid Finchbriton's canopy of fire and grabbed hold of his arms. John struggled, they held him fast, but then each in turn yelped in pain and lost their hold, retreating to nurse fresh cuts on their hands and arms. And the news cameras may or may not have captured the likeness of a four-inch-tall man with a sword, clinging to John's suit coat.

John turned, teapot still in hand, but by now the Goblin Queen had scrambled to safety. "Finchbriton!" he shouted. "Right flanking screen execute!"

They'd worked out some plans in advance. But John wasn't certain how much the bird had understood until now, when it fluttered to the right of the Reading Room and laid down a wide screen of perfectly smoky fire while John ran behind.

"I think today went really well," John said as he ran.

"Is this sarcasm?" asked Fi. "My family didn't believe in sarcasm."

Behind the Reading Room and through the Great Court there was another exhibition space, dimly lit, that was dominated by a large stone moai statue from Easter Island. For a moment John thought this moai moved. But no, it was just the seven-foot-tall figure of his cab driver stepping out from behind it. The brute cracked his knuckles and grinned.

"Good," said John, "our ride's here."

Fi said, "Once again—"

"Sarcasm, yes."

Finchbriton was all too occupied keeping the queen's guard out of the hall. Fi said, "Coin toss! Execute!" and John threw him high in the air. The driver arched his neck to watch Fi's trajectory, and it occurred to John that he was still holding a teapot. So he hit the driver with it. It shattered against the big man's jaw, and hot tea got on everything, including John's hand. He winced from the pain of the strike and the scalding liquid, but the driver howled. By now Fi had landed on the man's shoulder, and he proceeded to stab him in the eardrum before he was shaken off. He hit the floor hard, and John ducked to scoop him up.

"You okay?"

"I am fine. We pixies are a hardy lot."

"Finchbriton!"

The driver, meanwhile, was taking the tea pretty badly. His face was cut up, but now it also seemed to be bubbling, steaming. The big man spat liquid, hunched over, and with a wrenching squelch, transformed suddenly into the Incredible Hulk.

Or something like that. He doubled in size, his black suit opening like a time-lapse blossom and then hanging limply in ragged petals all around him. The ridge of his brow had thickened and his skin had lost all color. He

swung a massive arm and cracked the moai in half.

John goggled. "What?"

"Ogre," said Fi.

"Only grab what you can carry!" shouted Erno, who carried the unicat. "We have to go now!"

Biggs was holding six suitcases, and Emily. She was still asleep. No one seemed to be able to wake her.

"Why?" said Polly as she rushed around, grabbing things, new things, things that didn't make sense. Stuff from John's house that she'd never even seen before yesterday. "Just 'cause Emily shouted in her sleep?"

"She shouted our *location*," said Erno. "She told me she's been dreaming for weeks about her mother or . . . *someone* trying to find her. What if it's Nimue, sneaking into her head?"

"How will Dad and everyone know how to find us?"

"Everyone still has the new cell phones. We'll have to call them, tell them where we're going."

"Where *are* we going?"

"Can't say right now; the goblins might hear."

"WHAT?" Pigg shouted from downstairs.

"Keep trying to wake Emily," Erno told Biggs. "We can't have her talking in her sleep anymore."

They dragged their belongings down the stairs, and Erno dialed Scott.

"How'd you get through?" griped Scott. "I've been trying you, but the network's been overloaded."

"Why?" said Erno. "What's happened?"

"Haven't you been watching the queen's tea?"

"We couldn't figure out how to work your dad's TV. What?"

"We saw it on at a gas station. John's in trouble. We're coming back."

"Well, don't come here. I don't think it's safe anymore. I'm texting everyone a new address."

John's new phone rang, and then chimed to report a text, but he ignored it because he was being chased by an ogre. It chased him down the steps to the street, it chased him northeast toward the parkland of Russell Square. It might have overtaken him already if its broken eardrum hadn't been sending bad signals to its limbs and brain, causing it to stagger at times and jostle tour buses. Londoners screamed and ran from the sight of the monster; cars swerved. The only nice thing about being chased by an ogre was that the sight of it caused the policemen who were *also* supposed to be chasing you to pull back a bit and think about what they wanted out of life.

The ogre found a motorcycle and threw it at John. "Duck!" shouted Fi, who was clinging to John's collar and watching his back. John obeyed without question, and the bike skimmed his head and skipped against the pavement some fifteen feet distant, searing a blackened path toward the square. It broke down a section of iron fence John had been worried about jumping, so that was all right.

"So what do you know about ogres?" asked John.

"Dim-witted when angry," said Fi. "But also less sensitive to pain."

The park was teeming with people, strollers, little dogs off the leash.

"RUN!" John shouted to everyone around him.

"Is that Reggie Dwight?" said someone.

By his watch, the ogre should have crashed into the park already, but a quick glance told him it wasn't behind them anymore. Had it given up the chase? Or was it calming down, starting to think? John heard distant screams.

"Are you Reggie Dwight?" asked a man with a stroller. "My wife just called, said you punched the queen."

"Everyone knows that, mate," said another man.

"No, I mean, he punched her this morning. *Again*."

"Pull the other one."

"No, it's true."

"Finchbriton!" called John. "Where are you? Can you make these people run like I asked?"

The finch swooped down and drew a fiery little swoosh in the air.

"Thank you," said John as the men retreated. "Oh, look

at that! Perfect!" He'd spied a couple of teenagers facing off near the center of the park, wearing glasses and chain-mail armor and wielding longswords.

"Hi!" shouted John, approaching the kids. "Hello. Fancy selling me one of those swords? Say, a hundred pounds?"

"Are you Reggie Dwight?"

Then a moped sailed through the trees, crashing to the ground right where John and the boy would have been standing if John hadn't heaved them both out of the way.

The teens cursed and ran off as fast as their complicated outfits would allow, and John noticed with some satisfaction that the one had dropped his sword when tackled. John stooped to retrieve it, and it was only for this reason that he avoided getting flattened by a second moped.

Now the ogre came plowing through the trees, bellowing and holding a third moped over its head. John's phone rang and went to voice mail. He readied his sword, and Finchbriton set the moped alight so that the beast dropped it on itself. Then the little bird let loose with an inferno that engulfed the ogre itself, transforming the monster into a crackling blue blazing nightmare. And still it advanced, oblivious. Finchbriton sputtered, his flame spent, and barely made it back to John's shoulder.

"Tell your daughter . . . ," said Prince Fi. "Tell her I rode in a pocket."

"Come now," said John. "You know neither one of us is going to see Polly again."

The ogre slammed his fiery fist down, and John rolled to the right, came up with his sleeve smoldering. He struck the ogre's arm with his sword.

"I don't think this thing is even sharpened," he muttered. Then he ducked another swing from the ogre and plunged the sword tip into its belly. Sharpened or no, the blade went in, but then the monster turned and yanked the weapon from John's hand. John's phone rang again.

"Perhaps we should answer?" said Fi.

John took off running and called the number back. The ogre followed, dizzy and half blind from the smoke of his own burning flesh.

"Dad!" said Scott. "I've been calling."

John was shocked into silence for a moment, and so was Scott. He'd said *Dad*. But it didn't seem like the time to discuss it.

"I know," John answered. "Sorry. Been busy."

"Are you still near the museum? We're circling Russell Square right now in the poppadum truck."

"That's terribly good news. Meet me at the northeast corner."

He pushed through a wild hedgerow and emerged at the corner of the square, but the truck hadn't arrived yet.

And now he found he was right against another of those pointy iron fences he hadn't wanted to vault before. He set about gingerly climbing over it.

"Hurry, man!" said Fi. Finchbriton chirruped.

Then there was a great rustle behind him, and he turned to see the ogre break through the bushes. It swayed, lurched, a smelly black cinder. It raised both arms and roared in horrid victory. A frozen moment followed. Then it pitched forward, falling on its face and driving the longsword deep into its gut. And then it was still.

The truck pulled up, and John stumbled over the fence to meet it. The back opened, and Scott put out his hand.

"Punched the queen again, didn't you?"

"To be fair, this was an entirely different queen."

When he thought they were far enough away, when he heard distant sirens, Erno allowed himself a glance back. There was a dark tower of smoke rising up from where he thought John's house should be.

Emily was half awake, squinting foggily over Biggs's shoulder. "No surprise," the big man said. "Like t' burn things." Erno agreed—he remembered what the Freemen had done to Biggs's treehouse—but he was thinking of the goblins. So was Harvey.

"We should have let them go," said the rabbit-man.

CHAPTER 17

The new address, the one Erno had found, was on a sunny little street called St. George, in Islington, in the north of London. It was lined with friendly trees and tall row houses. They'd all made it here, and they'd all converged quite naturally on this particular house without even checking the address—it was like one rotten fang among a set of otherwise fine teeth. A neglectful gray, with scabby wood and pockmarked masonry. A tiny yard that somehow gave the impression of being both dead and overgrown at the same time. A garden where all the troublemaker plants came to smoke.

They'd converged on this house because they all felt, without realizing it consciously, that they belonged in a place like this. They were home. They stood in front of their new home now, exposed and unsure how to proceed. It wasn't even noon.

"Why is there a big sign that says TOILET?" asked Erno.

"Because you can't read," Emily answered. "It says TO LET."

"Oh, right. Why is there a big sign that says TO—"

"It means for rent. The house is for rent."

There was a phone number at the bottom of the sign. On a whim, Erno dialed it. After a moment, he held the phone to Emily. "Listen."

It was a voice-box message from the building's owner. He was on holiday, it said, wasn't showing the property right now, but leave your name and number, etc.

"It's . . . Dad," said Emily. "It's Mr. Wilson."

"Really?" said Scott.

"Then this is definitely th' place," said Mick.

"Whatever place this is," said John.

They continued to stare at it and didn't notice the little girl approaching from behind until Finchbriton twittered.

"'S haunted," the girl said, her tone letting them know that haunted houses bored her personally, but she thought maybe these nice people with their bird and cat might be interested.

"It does look pretty scary, doesn't it?" John turned and said, smiling.

"These squatters?" said the girl. "Were squatting in it. That means they were living there for free. And one

of them? Turned into a stag. So the other squatters ran out screaming, 'HE TURNED INTO A BLOODY GREAT STAG,' and no one's been in since."

Everyone mulled this over.

"Haunted," the girl concluded. "I can't play right now. My mum's making curry. I'd invite you, but I'm not allowed to talk to strangers. What's a ghost's favorite fruit?"

"Is it booberries?" asked John.

"Specterines?" said Merle.

"It depends on the ghost. Okay, bye."

They watched her cross the street.

"That girl was weird," said Polly.

"You were exactly like her not two years ago," Scott replied.

Emily was studying the house. "Are you guys all thinking what I'm thinking?" she said.

"Yes," said Scott, nodding. *There's a fairy in there, turning people into animals.*

"There's a rift in that house that leads to Pretannica, the magical Britain," Emily finished.

Scott looked at the others. "Wait—is that what we were all thinking?"

"I wasn't really thinking anything," said Erno.

"I was thinking of my brothers," said Fi.

"I was thinking about that chip shop we pathed back

by the tube thtation," said Harvey. "Could anyone elthe go for thome chipth right now?"

Emily looked exasperated. "When someone makes the Crossing, they have to trade places with another living thing of similar size on the other side, remember? Some squatter got a trip to Pretannica, and a stag ended up here. C'mon." She strode right up to the house, stepped onto the porch, and pushed through the door.

The building was broken up into single-room flats and zippered up the middle by a staircase so out of plumb it was nearly a ramp.

"Nobody try going upstairs," said Merle.

The ground floor had two flats, a bathroom, a kitchen, and a door to the basement. The ceilings were clouded over with water stains. The electricity was off, but John showed them little coin-slot boxes in each room that could be paid with pound coins to turn it on, as if the whole house was a grim nickelodeon. They got the juice flowing in the kitchen, which flustered an anxious, naked lightbulb in the ceiling and set the refrigerator to jittering back and forth between the cabinets like a bumper car. There was a single sheet of paper stuck to the fridge with a pie-shaped magnet, and the vibrations sent it skating across the surface of the freezer door until Erno unstuck it and gave it a looking over.

Emily, meanwhile, was blithely leading everyone into

the basement. The door opened onto a creaky but serviceable set of stairs and a pull chain that wasn't attached to any actual lightbulb. And now Emily hesitated at the edge of the dense blackness. "Here," said Merle as he lit his flashlight. The cold spill of it fell on an old stone wall, a concrete slab floor, the flinch of a cricket, other bugs, lots of bugs—and then horns, hooves, bones.

"Gah! Skeleton horse!" said Scott before he could stop himself. There was a polite pause.

Emily said, "I think it's the stag—"

"Okay, yeah. I got it."

It was almost entirely skeletonized. The lower jaw had nearly fallen away and gave it a look that was more or less completely terrifying. Its ribs had come loose and were set like kindling on the floor. Something slick and dark twisted in the kindling.

"Ooh, careful there," said John. "That looks like a black adder." The snake coiled itself into a question mark, a formal written request to be left alone.

Further investigation of the basement would reveal a lot more bugs, some food wrappers, and another skeleton (they'd eventually agree on badger), but the real discovery was a large cabinet against the wall opposite the stairs.

It was tall and plain, shabby really, with symmetrical doors. They opened these carefully to find that the back and floor of the cabinet had been removed, and a small octagon was drawn in chalk just behind it on the wall. Emily waved at it.

"Ta-da, the rift. He put a wardrobe in front of it," she added, smirking. "I guess that was his idea of a joke."

"I wonder if the rift's open," said Merle.

"It's open," said Scott.

Most of the rest turned to look at him. Not Polly and John, though. They were still staring at the octagonal rift as well, tilting their heads and squinching up their eyes.

"It's kinda . . . glimmery," said Polly.

"It looks like oil on water," said John.

Emily frowned at the chalk octagon. Because she could still only hear and not see the Fay among them, she said "Mick, Harvey, are you down here? Can you see what they're talking about?"

"Nope," said Harvey.

"No," said Mick. "Maybe it's 'cause they've fairy blood, but they were born here? They're of both worlds."

"The rift's bigger than the octagon Mr. Wilson drew," said Scott. "Like, four times bigger. Mick could walk right through it."

"It's growing," said Emily. "Probably gets bigger and bigger toward May Day." She grinned. "Who wants to go to Pretannica?"

CHAPTER 18

Scott slept through the afternoon in one of the musty ground floor apartments and awoke to find plans crackling all around the house. They'd gotten the lights working in the basement, which didn't really do the basement any favors appearance-wise, and had moved the wardrobe aside. The rift was noticeably larger even than it had been before Scott went to sleep. In the corner now was a stack of metal cages, ropes, stakes, and bags and bags of animal feed.

Scott eyed the cages blearily. "For the . . . snake?" But the snake was still coiled in its little tepee of ribs.

"We seem to have a working arrangement with the snake," said Emily. "Just don't put any part of yourself near his mouth; he's poisonous. No. The cages are for whatever comes through the rift."

Scott thought. "Because . . ."

"Because some of us are going through there, and when we do, it'll only be because something else happens to be on the other side. Hopefully it'll be an animal, and we can capture that animal and keep it here in the basement to swap it back for our team when they're ready to be extracted."

"When our team is ready to be *extracted?*"

Emily shrugged. "Your dad is big on this kind of talk."

"But then . . . ," said Scott. "What if the thing that comes through isn't an animal? What if it's a Pretannican human, or an elf?" *Or an ogre? Or a dragon?*

"At this point our plan is mostly hoping it won't be."

Scott glanced at the snake again. "Do you think that thing is from Pretannica? Maybe it isn't even a regular snake. Maybe it's magic or, like, an enchanted prince."

Polly walked up as he said this. "You should definitely kiss it," she said.

"Ha ha. Shut up. Speaking of enchanted princes—"

Just then Fi surfaced from Polly's jacket pocket. "Well met, Scott," he said.

"Oh. Oh, hey, Fi. I didn't think you liked pockets."

"It's been brought to my attention recently that I should try new things," said the prince.

Mick hopped down the stairs with two walkie-talkies. "Got 'em," he said. "We ready to do this?"

"Ready if you are," said Emily.

"Wait," Scott said to Mick. "Are you going to Pretannica right now? And a walkie-talkie? That's never going to work, is it?"

Emily took one of the walkie-talkies from Mick. "We know it will, thanks to your mom's research. Remember? She said so in an email."

"Asking her all those scientific questions was your idea," Scott reminded Emily. "I was mostly skimming to make sure she hadn't been kidnapped by Freemen."

"Well," said Emily. "Her research showed that all wavelengths of the electromagnetic spectrum bounced back from the rift in Antarctica except radio waves."

Mick got in position where the octagon was drawn and said, "This abou' right, kids?"

Scott narrowed his eyes. The shimmering octagon was transposed over and around and through Mick—he couldn't believe the elf couldn't feel it. "Step just a hair to your left. That's good."

"So now what?" said Polly. "We just wait for something Mick's size to wander by on the other side?"

"That's right."

Polly fidgeted. "That sounds like it'll take forever. I'm gonna get a snack."

"No, Polly, please stay," said Emily. "We may need help with whatever comes across."

Mick looked anxious but excited. "Goin' home,"

he muttered. "Never thought I'd see it. Scott? If . . . if somethin' bad happens an' I can't get back, don't yeh cry. Livin' ou' my days in a doomed world won't be so bad if it's home."

"You . . . you don't mean that."

"I'm Irish. We all think we're doomed anyway."

It would have been a good exit line, but the truth was they had to wait another fifteen minutes before anything happened. But then it happened. Polly gasped, so Scott knew she saw it, too. He didn't think Mick and Emily realized anything was going on. Mick's shape grew dark, flat, and then it joined with another shape, something sharp eared and bushy tailed and quadrupedal. Behind Scott, the adder hissed. Then Mick was gone, and a fox was in the basement instead.

It crouched low and darted off to a corner as Polly made a grab for it. Scott took a cage from the stack and tried to help her, but the little fox was everywhere, its claws ticking on the hard floor—up and down the stairs, nearly bitten by the adder, U-turning around Emily, who so far hadn't even gotten up from where she was sitting.

"Come in, Mick," she said into the walkie-talkie. "Are you there? Over."

The radio crackled. "It's IRELAND!" said Mick. "I'd know it wi' my eyes closed. An' the *glamour*! Sweet Danu, the glamour. I'm gettin' fluthered on it. Um, over."

"Hmm," said Emily to the others as they scrambled around her. "If it leads to Ireland, then the snake can't be from the rift. There are no snakes in Ireland, you know." The fox turned, an orange firecracker, and the Doe kids turned too, their sneakers scuffing, Scott accidentally whanging Polly with the metal cage. "I bet a lot of little Pretannican rodents and things trade places with all the bugs down here, and the adder just realized this basement made for easy hunting." Emily spoke into the radio. "Mick, it's going to be a minute before we extract you, we have a rogue fox situation in the basement. Over."

"No rush. Over."

"Now that I think about it," Emily told Scott and Polly and Fi, who had just managed to maybe corner the thrumming little fox with the cage and a jacket, "we should have started out with Mick already in the cage. Then the fox would have just popped up in there. I'm sorry, I've been so distracted."

Finally they coaxed the animal into the hutch, and everyone seemed relieved, fox included. They put it back in position over the rift.

"Mick, fox is in the henhouse. Over."

"Is that a code yeh just made up to mean it's back on the rift? Over."

"Yes. Over."

Maybe thirty seconds passed, and then the fox's form

went dark, and was conjoined with Mick's, and then it was just the leprechaun in the cage, looking sort of magnificent.

"Get me out of this thing," he said, smiling.

"Mick!" said Emily, jumping to her feet. "I can see you! Is that really what you look like?"

"More wrinkled than I recall," said Fi.

Scott opened the cage door, so Mick tossed him a tip—a gold coin, almost worn smooth, the faintest portrait of a bearded king on its obverse side, a dragon on the other.

"Where'd you get this?" asked Scott.

"Found it," said Mick. He was grinning from ear to ear. "An' for the lady," he added, and handed Emily something small and green.

A four-leaf clover.

CHAPTER 19

Scott had slept in the afternoon, and so wasn't tired at night. And that was good—someone had to watch Emily. Erno was certain that she'd somehow told Nimue and Goodco their location in her dreams, and she couldn't really assure them that this wasn't the case. Scott was to watch her and try to wake her at the first sign of any disturbance in her sleep.

"But it's not Nimue I keep dreaming of, it's my mom," she told Scott as she crawled into bed. She had tired eyes. Old eyes. "Why isn't he just here? Dad. Mr. Wilson, I mean. He could just be here, waiting for us. He could just tell us things, instead of leaving us stupid games. You know Erno thinks the thing that was on the refrigerator is another clue? I'm too angry to look at it."

"He's helping us, at least, in his own way," said Scott, taking a chair.

"I wonder if he's still taking it. The Milk. I mean, I know it was messing me up, but Scott! I'm getting dumber!"

Scott winced. "I'm not sure you are—"

"I think I am. I don't know. I can't say anything for sure without doing some tests. But I think one thing's clear: I'm not going to get any smarter."

Scott smiled. "I wouldn't worry—you're smart enough already."

But Emily looked at him squarely, soberly. "No. Think about what I'm saying." She blinked her red eyes. "You don't realize it maybe, but you're always discovering new doors and stepping into bigger worlds. Bigger and better worlds, with more doors to open. As long as you keep learning, your world gets bigger. Mine's just shrinking, now."

Scott hesitated until he was sure of his answer. "You got a bigger world than I'm ever going to, though. You got that."

"And I got to visit, and now I have to come back to the basement."

Scott looked at his hands.

"Help me fall asleep," said Emily. "Tell me a story."

"I don't know any stories."

"Please."

"You know who has good stories? Merle. I mean, he was the *wizard of King Arthur's court.* Merle!"

Merle poked his head in. "What's up?"

"Tell me a story," said Emily. "About the sword in the stone."

"Yeah, no kidding," said Scott. "Was that real?"

"Sure," said Merle. "Sort of."

"So . . . nobody but Arthur could pull the sword out? Was it a Fay spell? Or was it really a sign from God that Arthur was rightful king of England or . . ."

Merle was smirking. "It was magnets."

They stared.

"Maybe I should begin a little earlier," said Merle. "I told you about Vortigern, Scott, and the whole tower-and-dragons debacle. That gave me a bit of a reputation as a wise guy. So maybe you know that King Uther Pendragon was Arthur's father."

Scott made a sour face. He didn't like this story. King Uther squabbles with the Duke of Tintagel, and invites the duke to his castle. During the visit, Uther falls madly in love with the duke's wife, Igraine. The duke and Igraine flee, so later Uther gets Merlin to disguise him as the duke while his forces are fighting the real duke on the battlefield. Igraine thinks Uther is her husband, and they spend a night together, the same night her actual husband is killed in battle. After Igraine learns her husband has been killed, she wonders who that fake duke was, but she keeps the whole thing to herself, and when Uther proposes marriage, she says yes. Months later she gives birth to Arthur and tells her husband that the son belongs to a mystery man who looked like the duke, and Uther says, "Surprise! It was me," and everyone's happy. Then they give up Arthur to Merlin, because that was the deal. It was an all-around gross story.

"Calm down," said Merle. "I know you've read the books, but it didn't turn out like that. Of course, *I* had read the books too, so when Uther's man Sir Ulfius comes to me wanting help with his king's love life, I'll admit I didn't know what to do. I think, *If I don't help Uther, then Arthur is never born,* and that's a tragedy. But this is a terrible thing to do to Igraine. So I tell Uther I can help, not knowing what I'm going to do right up until the night itself. And that night King Uther is drinking a lot of wine 'cause he's nervous, and Sir Ulfius is drinking a lot of wine, and I'm trying to come up with a way to disguise us all and make this work, maybe something with fake mustaches, and finally I panic and put everybody to sleep."

Scott frowned. "Then what?"

"Then nothing. I rode them back to the castle, and when they woke up the next morning I told them the plan had gone off perfectly."

"What?"

"I saw the look of doubt on Uther's face, right, but I explained that people shape-shifted by the spell I used might experience a little memory loss. After that he looked happy, and if Uther was happy, there was no way Ulfius was going to argue. But in the back of my mind I feel a little weird, because I didn't do my duty. Arthur would never be born. Then nine months later Arthur was born."

"How?"

"Arthur was the duke's son. He was *always* the duke's son. But Uther says to Igraine, 'I know how your son was really conceived—on the night your late husband was killed, a man with his likeness came to you.' And Igraine was like, 'Uh, no, that never happened,' but Uther insisted and said, 'Fear not! For I was that man, ensorcelled to resemble the duke! Ha ha!'

"So Igraine's probably like, 'He thinks this is his son? Okay, great! Awesome. He's an idiot, but whatever.' Because Igraine was probably expecting Uther would just have the baby killed. Son of your enemy, and you don't want to look weak, right?"

"And they gave baby Arthur to you?" said Emily softly.

"Yeah. That was the deal the books said I made, so that was the deal I made, and like I said, I think Igraine was just thrilled not to have any of her family members murdered. She married her daughters Elaine and Morgause off to rich guys, and put her youngest, Morgan, in a nunnery, all at Uther's request."

"Morgan—that's Morgan le Fay, the sorceress, right?" asked Scott.

"Yeah. I realize now she must have been a changeling. I mean, not a changeling like you and Polly and your dad, who're mostly human with a little drop of fairy in you. I mean an Old World fairy, swapped in the cradle, who doesn't realize she's not really human—that kind of changeling. Anyway, you wanted to know about the sword in the stone."

"Yeah."

"Yeah."

"So I take baby Arthur away to this really nice knight I know, Sir Ector, who's recently had a son of his own. And Sir Ector and his wife raise Arthur, and I sort of help teach the boy things I think he needs to know. And I really grow to love this boy. He's a great kid. In another age he'd have made a great scientist.

"But during this time King Uther gets sick and dies, and England kind of falls apart a little. Everyone's vying to be the guy who takes over and rules as the new king, because Uther didn't leave any heirs. So I do what I'm supposed to, and I tell the Archbishop of Canterbury to demand that all the lords and gentlemen come to London at Christmastime, upon pain of cursing—"

"Upon pain of cursing?" said Scott.

"You like that? I thought that was a nice touch. I have him demand they all come upon pain of cursing and promise that God will show by some miracle who should be rightful king of the realm."

"But . . . ," said Emily.

"You see the hitch, right?" Merle smiled.

"Arthur *wasn't* the rightful king of England," Emily mumbled. "He was the duke's son."

"So I knew I couldn't depend on any miracles, and I had to make my own," said Merle. "I had a big hunk of marble carved, and an anvil stuck in it, and a deep groove cut in the anvil. Took forever. And I had a sword made by an illiterate swordsmith, with words written in gold that said WHOSO PULLETH OUT THIS SWORD OF THIS STONE AND ANVIL, IS RIGHTWISE KING BORN OF ALL ENGLAND. Cost me every penny I had.

"But the genius part," said Merle, really puffing himself up, "was the magnets made out of fairy gold. I suppose you both know that you can make a magnet with a coil of electric current around a nail or whatever."

"Yeah, we did that in science class," said Scott. He felt suddenly weary, wondering if he'd ever get back to doing anything so simple as electrocuting a nail.

"So I managed to scrape together a little bit of fairy gold," said Merle, "and with that I could make a battery to hide inside the stone and anvil. I had to hide my watch in there too, but then I could use Archie to transmit a signal and turn the battery's current on and off. Stick the sword in the stone, run the current through the anvil, and suddenly the strongest man in England couldn't pull it back out. Cut the power, and my tante could do it."

Emily smiled.

"Maybe you kids know the rest. No one could pull out the sword, so they put together a big jousting tournament so everyone can stick around and keep trying. And Arthur's foster brother, Kay, forgets his sword back at the inn, so Arthur, being his squire, runs back for it. But the inn is locked, empty, everyone is at the tournament. So Arthur takes the sword out of the stone, easy as anything, and brings it to Kay. 'How did you come by this?' everyone wants to know. And he tells them, and they're all, OMG!"

"Don't say OMG," said Scott.

"Hey! I can say slang. I haven't even been born yet—technically I'm younger than you."

"Sorry."

"Anyway, he tells them and they kneel down to him

and he's crowned King of England. That's the really short version, anyway."

Scott huffed. "You could have made *anyone* King of England. You could have made yourself."

"Yeah, but I don't like hats."

Scott looked over to see what Emily thought of all this, only to find she'd fallen asleep. He watched her anxiously, but her breathing was gentle and easy, her face finally untroubled.

Now seemed as good a time as any to ask Merle something that had been bothering him. He felt like everyone had been dancing around it. He leaned close and lowered his voice and said, "Mick told me that the Gloria that separated the worlds . . . he said it happened right after Arthur and his son battled each other, when they supposedly died. And that's when you and Arthur traveled to the future, right? So—"

"No."

"I didn't even say it yet—"

"You were gonna say that maybe it was us and our time machines that cracked reality in half? Separated the worlds? That maybe I'm responsible?"

Scott squirmed a bit.

"Well, honestly . . . ," said Merle. "I started wondering about that too, ever since getting mixed up with you bunch. But I've checked and rechecked the math. Emily's checked it, too. There was *nothing in my designs that could have caused this to happen.* I swear. It's some kind of crazy coincidence. I'm sure we'll learn the truth soon enough."

"Yeah. I'm sure we'll learn the truth soon enough."

CHAPTER 20

"I think everybody should have a copy of this," Emily said to all the others, seated on folding chairs in the dank basement. She passed them a stack of pages she'd made up at a local copy shop. They each unrolled their papers to find maps of Great Britain. "They're maps of Pretannica, courtesy of the Freemen and their big filing cabinet," Emily added. "Maps with rifts. That circle around the British Isles is the current edge of the universe, according to the Freemen. Everything beyond that doesn't exist. Those of you going through the rift should try not to get too close to the edge, or it's my understanding that you'll stop existing, too."

"What's this world map for down here?" asked Scott.

"That shows the locations of stable or semi-stable rifts in our world that Goodco knows about. Notice all the little dots around New Jersey."

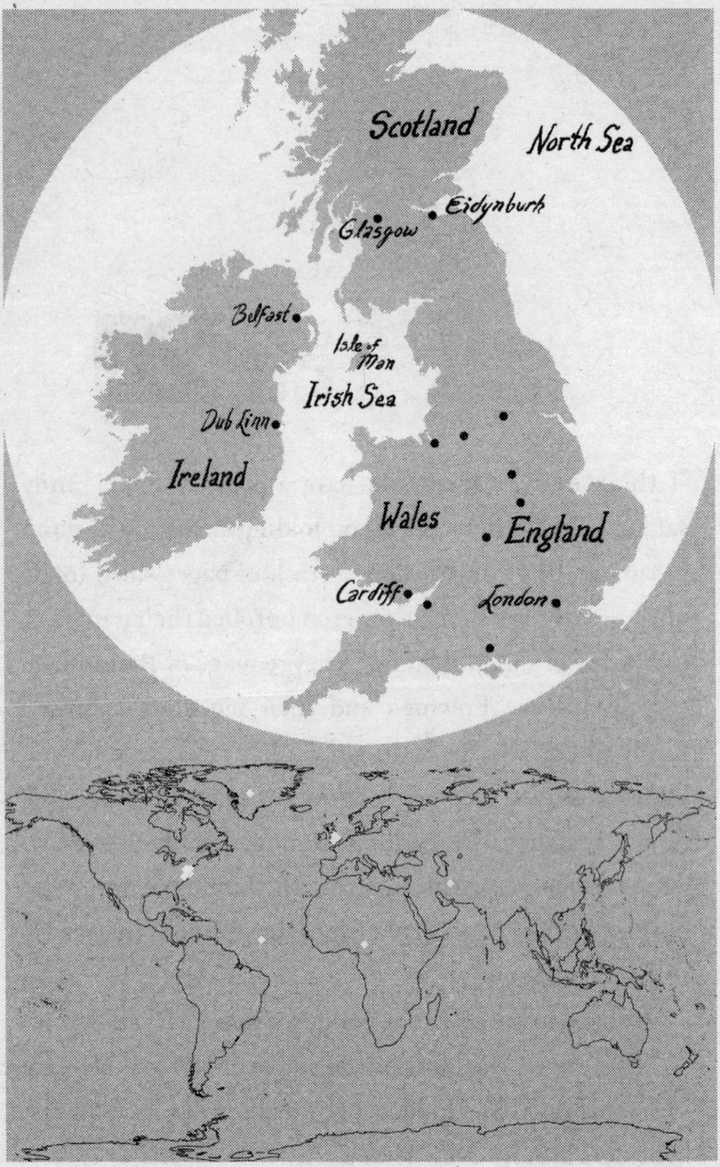

Scotland
North Sea
Eidynburh
Glasgow
Belfast
Isle of Man
Irish Sea
Dub Linn
Ireland
Wales
England
Cardiff
London

"Why so many around New Jersey?" said Polly.

"So," said Emily. "A little primer: rifts open up on Earth all the time. Most of them are unstable, only open for a moment, and nothing goes through them, so nobody notices. They're attracted to magic, so mostly they pop up in places where there's a little bit of magical buildup, which pretty much means any city where Goodco's built a factory. Magic is everywhere in Pretannica, so the openings on the Pretannica side are totally random. Point is that at any time a rift could open up in Pretannica so large that you could lead all the armies of the Fay through it at once, but you could never plan your day around it."

"But some rifts aren't unstable," said Merle.

"Right. They stay open for a few weeks, getting bigger, then smaller again around May Day and November Day. Some are even open all the time. Goodco knows about a lot of these, and as you can see on your maps, they're exactly where you'd expect—Goodborough, Slough, towns where there's a Goodco cereal factory. Though there's still a certain amount of randomness. For example, the great big rift in Antarctica that Scott's mom characterized, or that one in Iran."

"There's a rift in . . . Chad?" said Erno. "Is that a country? I thought it was just the name of that eighth grader with the missing earlobe."

"Anyway," said Emily, "all the stable rifts Goodco

knows about are really small, too small for even Mick to get through. Or else they're big but at the bottom of the ocean."

Fi was looking at his map. "I was sent through a rift and found myself in the Atlantic Ocean, near this rift you've marked here. Yet I was near the surface, not at the bottom."

"Yeah, it must have been a different one. You've said this pixie witch of yours had four stable rifts? Nimue would kill for those. She could start the invasion tomorrow. Well. I think John has a report."

John stood up and Emily sat down. "As you know, after the British Museum incident, I sent out a press release through Archimedes to all the news outlets, explaining our position. Of course most of the chatter on the internet is that I'm, er . . . crazy."

"Crazy talented," said Polly.

"No, just the regular kind. But serious journalists are devoting a lot of time to analyzing that footage from the museum and trying to prove that there weren't a fire-breathing finch and a tiny man there, and they can't. So that's all to the good. And people are asking questions, and Goodco has had to release an official statement, so I'm going to send out another missive and try to keep the ball rolling."

"Good," said Emily. "Well—"

"I have something," said Erno.

Emily's shoulders fell. "Is this about the thing from the refrigerator? It's not a clue."

"It definitely belonged to Mr. Wilson—"

"I'm not saying it didn't, but he didn't write it—it's just some page from an old handbook."

It was, specifically, a page torn from the 1921 Young Freeman's Handbook, and it began midsentence.

YOUNG FREEMAN'S HANDBOOK 1921

all know that the Sickle and the Spoon was developed from the vesica piscis, an ancient Christian symbol shown in some medieval traditions to be bisected by the sword Caliburn, or Excalibur.

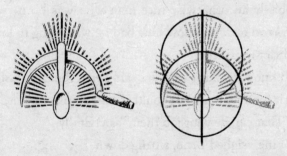

The enterprising young Freeman can draft his own Sickle and Spoon with everyday objects he'll find around the home or temple. Dr. Octopodes Bray (K. o. t. R.) has invented an ingenious method that requires no compass but may be accomplished with a straight edge and by tracing the circumference of any cup, plate, or pie tin.

Once the circle has been traced, the first and most important step is to determine its center.

That was all it said. The opposite side was just an etching of Dr. Octopodes Bray, Knight of the Round, probably an otherwise nice man who was born twenty years too early to know how bad he was going to look in a Hitler mustache.

"I know he didn't write it," said Erno, "but he must have left it for a reason. We should at least think about it."

"That can be your job then," said Emily.

"Fine," sighed Erno, sitting down.

"Anyone else?"

Scott stood up. "I want to go to Pretannica."

John turned. "You do? I don't know how I feel about that—"

"Oh, come on. You can't really be pulling the fatherly 'It's too dangerous' thing on me at this point, can you?"

"I'll be happy to have 'im," said Mick. "He's good in a scrape. We may need all the help we can get, savin' the queen."

"Except I don't want to go after the queen," Scott said. "I want to visit the fairies."

"What?" said Emily.

"*What?*" said John. Out of the corner of Scott's eye, he saw Harvey prick up his ears and start frantically scrawling on the back of his map.

"Like a . . . diplomatic mission," said Scott. "If they're all going to invade, it's because Nimue's been feeding them lies all these years. Lies like that the humans are responsible for their world dying. I'll go visit the High Queen . . . Titania, right? And plead our case. Maybe I can just prevent the whole invasion and get everybody talking instead."

"No," said John. "No way. It's too dangerous." And when Scott gave him a look, he added, "Yes, I *am* pulling that. I am pulling exactly that."

"Hold on now," said Mick. "This could actually work. Scott's part fairy, so he has ev'ry right to request an audience wi' the queen. An' if I go with 'im, an' demand his safety as a member o' the queen's court? Then none can harm 'im. Them's the rules."

"I'll go too," said Polly. "Please? I wanna go."

John sighed. "I can't imagine how I'll explain this to your mother next year if something goes wrong."

"Yeah." Merle coughed. "*This* is the part you'll be at a loss to explain."

"Okay," said Emily. "Scott and Polly and Mick and Finchbriton go to the court of Titania. John and Merle rescue the Queen of England. My current projections show this rift is never going to get big enough for Biggs, so he stays here and takes care of whatever animals come through. I keep studying the rift, Erno studies . . . that piece of paper. You all get walkie-talkies souped up by Merle with fairy batteries, thanks to that gold coin Mick found. Fi?"

"I will protect Polly."

"Ooh, better not, mate," said Mick. "You know I like yeh, but a pixie in the court of the Fay? That's an insult, that is."

Fi sighed. "I will go with the men, then."

"Happy to have you," said John.

Emily called to the rabbit-man, who was still writing. "And what are you going to do, Harvey?"

"Nuthin'."

"Right. I guess that's it, then. Let's all make ready."

There was the scuffle and squeak of chairs as class was dismissed.

"Maybe this is a stupid idea," Scott said to Mick. He had half expected everyone to talk him out of it, and now he felt like he was sitting on the edge of a cliff while all his friends said, *Go on, then, jump the motorcycle.*

"Prob'ly. But it speaks well of yeh that you're the first to think of tryin' it."

Harvey made a beeline for Scott and unfolded his map to show a scribble of handwritten notes. "I've made a litht of thingth you do that offend me."

"Oh good."

"One: you turn your clotheth inthide out."

"What?" said Scott. "When have I done that?"

"When you took off your thocks that one time."

"Yeh should listen to this," said Mick. "Harv an' I have been in your world awhile, so these kinds of things don't bother us so much anymore. But the fairies o' Pretannica will have certain hang-ups. The same fairies you're meant to impress."

"Fine," said Scott. "What else?"

"Two," said Harvey. "No ringing bellth."

"Bells? Why would I ring a bell?"

"Tho don't, then."

"Three," interrupted Mick. "Try not to give or receive any gifts. Or food or drink."

"Got it. If they try to give me anything, I won't take it."

"Oh, you'll *have* to take it," said Mick. "Only thing worse than gettin' a gift from the Good Folk is not acceptin' one when it's offered. Yeh want to end up belching flowers the rest o' your life? Just try not to get offered anything."

"How am I supposed to do that?" Scott squeaked. This list was making him nervous.

"If it seems like any fairy's abou' to give yeh somethin', change the subject. Create a diversion."

"Like what?"

"*Don't ring any bellth!*"

"Try singin' somethin'," Mick suggested. "They'll like that. Just don't be surprised if yeh start up a whole big musical number, like in a Disney movie. That can happen."

"It's contagiouth."

"Like a yawn."

"Remember . . . ," said Harvey. "Remember when Jack Muthtard thtarted up with that thong and danthe about thinging and danthing?"

"Do I." Mick groaned. "Hard to know how to end something like that. Eventually everyone's singin' abou' how we can't stop singin', an' we'd be doin' it still if the Milesians hadn't invaded."

"I'm going to lie down," said Scott.

COMMERCIAL BREAK

CHIP
Ah, this is the life!

SPARKLE
The sun, the sand...

PIP
And the frootycrisp
flavor of Puftees!™

CHIP
Blueberry blue!

SPARKLE
Raspberry red!

PIP
And new crispity
Purplegrape!™ Now with
Intellijuice™, the magic
juice that makes you
smarter!

KID ONE
Look, there they are!

KID TWO
Real pixies!

SPARKLE
Oh no! Giants!

KID THREE
Grab the pixies!

CHIP
Why grab pixies?
Why not grab the
delicious taste of
crispy froot?

PIP
Part of this
complete breakfast!

KID ONE
Mmmm! Puftees!™
With new Purplegrape!™

SPARKLE
We'll always outsmart
those kids as long as
we have Puftees!™

KID TWO
You can't fool us
anymore, pixies!

KID THREE
New Intellijuice™
has made us smarter!

CHIP
Aw, blueberries! Outsmarted
by our own pixie magic!

ANNOUNCER
Only YOU can help the pixie
brothers escape from the
jars of giants! Find out
how inside every box of
new, improved Puftees!™

CHAPTER 21

Then the big day came. Everyone was in a tizzy. Polly sat in the kitchen and tried to breathe calmly as the ship tipped around her. A cartoon was playing quietly on the tablet computer, a cartoon in which ordinary kids defeated the forces of darkness in extraordinary ways. Fi sat cross-legged on the table.

"So that's the plan," Polly whispered.

"An ignoble plan," said Fi. "Surely we can do better. We've made promises—"

Just then the cartoon broke for a commercial. Three blue-skinned cartoon pixies were relaxing on a beach.

Polly and Fi watched in silence. Fi's tiny eyes reflected the flickering screen dimly, like distant stars.

John appeared in the doorway. "Did that just say there's Intellijuice in the Puftees now? That's bad news."

Neither Polly nor Fi answered.

"There are already reports of smarter kids, better test scores," John added. "Have you heard? The news is reporting it like it's all a joke, but a mob bought every last Goodco box from a grocer's in Chelsea."

The cartoon children crunched spoonfuls of cereal while the pixies tiptoed away.

John clucked his tongue. "Does anyone really *want* a grape-flavored cereal? You know what kind of fruit people never put on their corn flakes? Grapes."

The commercial ended with a final image of the pixie brothers under glass. "Only *YOU* can help the pixie brothers escape from the jars of giants," it said.

"Oh," John added then, and cleared his throat. "Um. I'll bet that makes you think about your . . . I'm sorry, Fi, I forgot."

Fi stood and turned to Polly. "All right," he said quietly. Then he slid down a chair leg and went off toward the basement.

Polly clicked off the cartoon. John looked adrift until Scott squeezed past him through the door.

"Hey! Did anyone tell you the latest?" John asked Scott as they both tried to move and eat their way through the kitchen. "The Goblin Queen got some questions about the British Museum event this morning and got so flustered she hissed at the minister of health!"

Scott smiled. "Nice to think about *them* being on the

defensive for a change," he said. "Maybe if they think their plan is falling apart, the Fay will be willing to talk to me."

"Yes. Yes, break a leg with that. Really."

"Yeah, you . . . you too," Scott answered. Then they stared at each other a moment, having lost all momentum. Finally Scott turned and retreated down the basement steps. Polly followed him.

Mick and Finchbriton were already in Pretannica. So now they had a Pretannican mouse, who was burrowing in the wood chips of a little plastic hutch inside the wardrobe. And another fox (or maybe the same fox) was crouching in the corner of one of their wire cages, with Biggs unsuccessfully trying to feed it. Polly made kissy noises at it. Merle was down here too, apparently in conversation with Prince Fi. Emily was in radio contact with the leprechaun.

"I bought some sheep from a certain Robert Shepherd nearby," said Mick through the radio. "Over."

"With what money? Over."

"Found some more fairy gold. Over."

"That's unethical," Emily groused. "Fairy money is an illusion. Over."

"Isn't all money technic'ly an illusion? Over."

"Oh, whatever. Just get them back here. Emily out. Biggs? We're going to have sheep."

"Yuh," said Biggs, and he commenced to pounding

232

metal stakes into the mortar of the walls and floor. The adder swayed along with the hammer blows.

Polly lost interest in the fox and crossed to the stairs.

"Don't go far," said Emily. "You leave soon."

"I know." She climbed and met Erno in the kitchen. "Where are you headed?" she asked him. He shrugged.

"Emily wants my help with animal wrangling or something. I dunno."

"Do you wish you were going to Pretannica?"

"Does it matter?" asked Erno, looking out the kitchen window, which only faced an alley. "John and Merle and Fi don't want kids along on their mission, you can tell. And I don't have any fairy blood, so I'm not allowed in Queen Titania's clubhouse."

"Emily's got Biggs for the animals, though," Polly said. "Why aren't you working on that clue? That's important."

Erno scoffed. "You're the only one who thinks so."

"Yeah, but it *has* to be, right? That Mr. Wilson left *so little* in this house. Just a couple chairs and a wardrobe and a jar of Nutella and *that piece of paper*."

"*I know!*" said Erno. "Thank you! Finally!"

They stared at each other a moment.

"You know what? I *am* going to work on the clue," said Erno. "Tell Emily I'm in the back bedroom if she really needs me."

"Okay." Polly followed him out into the stairwell,

watched him shut himself up inside the back bedroom, then arched her neck to look up at the gap in the ceiling. A little aspect of the second floor could be seen at the top of the ruinous stairs. It wasn't going to be the easiest throw, but she was the athletic one in the family. She took Harvey's cell phone from her pocket, squared her shot, and threw—a perfect sky hook, something the WNBA was going to be interested in if she ever got her growth spurt. Then she sauntered back to the basement.

Everyone was accounted for except Erno—and Harvey, who wasn't really expected to show anyway.

"So how are we doing this?" said John as he got into place near the octagon. "Everyone at once?"

"Should work," said Emily. "The rift's wide enough. It's held at the same diameter for three days now. I calculate you have as much as two months in Pretannica before it gets too small for the tallest of you to return, but let's not test that unless we have to, okay? Get home quickly."

"Guys?" said Merle. "Fi has something to say." He held up the little prince on his palm. Fi cleared his throat.

"I am sorry, my compatriots," he said, "but I have decided not to go to Pretannica. I believe I am honor bound instead to make inquiries into the fortunes of my brothers."

The basement was silent.

"Oh," said Scott. "Right. Sorry, Fi, we've been so

wrapped up in saving the queen—"

"There shall be no need for apologies among brothers-in-arms," said Fi. "Truly the welfare of your English queen is paramount. She can knight a thousand soldiers to slay the Great Dragon. But I think I can no longer serve you well when my heart is cut in twain. Merlin, please set me down."

Merle put Fi on the floor, and the pixie strode proudly, if slowly, across the basement floor.

"Good speech, right?" Polly whispered to Emily, next to her. Fi got to the stairs and paused.

"Merlin, please help me up the stairs."

Merle helped him up the stairs.

"Can't beat a prince for a good speech," Polly agreed with herself.

With Fi gone, Scott, Polly, John, and Merle arranged themselves in the rift and waited. Merle handed Archimedes off to Emily.

"Take care of him," he said.

They were dressed warmly, with backpacks, radios, Swiss Army knives, canteens, water purification tablets, and plastic flare guns. John had his sword. Emily got back on the radio.

"Mick, how far out are you? Over."

"'Bout ten minutes. Over."

"This is it," said John. After a moment no one had

confirmed or denied this, so he said it again.

"You mentioned something on the cruise ship," Scott murmured to John. "About how actors want to be loved and are afraid of rejection. That's why you never visited, all those years. Isn't it. You were afraid we'd reject you."

John pulled his lips back into a thin smile, a sad smile, and he raised his head as if to nod. But then his head just sagged.

"No."

Scott frowned. "No?"

"Not at first, no. That wasn't it." John stared at his shoes. "I want to be honest with you kids, and . . . honesty isn't always easy."

Scott and Polly watched him as he gathered his thoughts.

"Your mom and I weren't really happy anymore, but I wanted to stay together for your sakes. Then I went off on a film shoot and came home to find your mom had left, and had taken you with her.

"I called your grandparents. I called all our friends. And no one could tell me where you'd gone. But then I had to leave on a press junket, and on another trip after that, and . . . I stopped looking. I figured your mom would get in touch eventually, when she was ready, and so I went off and played movie star for a while. It was kind of a relief, really: knowing I could have fun, be famous, and that it wasn't my fault. *She* was the one who'd left."

"Didn't you ever think of us?" asked Polly, in a voice that made you want to lift her up, carry *her* around in your pocket.

"All the time. But maybe I'd be leaving on a world tour so I'd think, *Well, obviously I shouldn't call just now.* Then there'd be another film shoot looming, and I'd say, 'Well, of course *now* isn't the right time for a visit.' And somehow seven years slipped away."

Scott discovered he was making fists. It was startling. He abruptly unclenched and shook out his fingers, no less alarmed than if his hands had changed to werewolves.

"And now by this time," said John, "by this time I really *was* afraid. Afraid I couldn't blame everything on anyone but myself anymore, afraid you wouldn't want to see me. I'm trying to be better, I *want* to be better. I want to be here. Not . . . not necessarily in this basement especially, but . . . you know. Here. With you. But even if it's harder, even if it doesn't make you feel any friendlier toward me, I still think you both deserve honesty."

"Honesty," Polly repeated flatly. Scott thought maybe she felt the way he did, like this honesty was something they hadn't asked for, like it was an unwanted gift they had to pretend to appreciate while the Christmas music was still playing.

"Anyway," said John. "So. Pretannica. This is it."

"This is it," said Merle. "Good luck, everybody."

"Saying good luck is unlucky," said John.

Meanwhile, Polly fiddled with something in her pocket. She knew she could count on Biggs to hear it first. After Harvey, he had the best ears.

"Phone," said Biggs.

"Phone?" said Emily. "I don't hear it." They were all silent and still, and then they could all hear it, a phone ringing faintly, somewhere in the house. "That's one of our special rings. But everyone's here, except for Harvey."

"And except for Erno," said Scott.

"Erno," said Emily. "Where's Erno? Oh, geez, Biggs, could you get that phone?"

Biggs left the basement, followed the noise out into the stairwell, and determined without question that the ringing was coming from the second floor. To say that he grimaced at the ramshackle staircase would be an overappraisal of his talents for expression, but he frowned on the inside. Then he took his first, hesitant step.

"I should tell Mick to wait," said Emily. "I don't want to try to corral four sheep by myself."

Then the pounding started. Someone was knocking, knocking hard, on the front door of the house. Emily flinched, looked forward and back. She spoke into the radio. "Mick? Don't get the sheep in position till I give the word. Copy."

"Ten-four."

"Hold on," said Emily, and she ran up the stairs as the pounding came harder and faster.

Polly turned to her father. "I don't want to go to Pretannica anymore," she said.

"You don't? Why not?"

"I'm . . . I'm scared. I didn't want to admit it, but—"

"No, no, that's okay, Polly," said John, smiling. "Really, I'm relieved. I mean, I know you're a very capable seven-year-old, but—"

"I'll go help Biggs and Emily," Polly said, and she rushed up the stairs, spooked the unicat, and took out her walkie-talkie, the one she would have taken with her to Pretannica. She switched it to Mick's channel.

"Mick, we're back on," she said in her best Emily voice. "Sheep in place. Over."

"Copy that."

Then Polly climbed up onto the kitchen counter, opened the window, dropped down into the alley, and shut the window behind her.

Inside the house, Emily was at her wits' end. The moment she'd get to the door, the knocking would stop. She'd peer out through the narrow windows beside it and see nothing, no one. Then she'd turn, and the knocking would start again. Meanwhile, Biggs had managed to answer the upstairs phone (hang-up, blocked) and was trying to get down again without collapsing the staircase. Erno stormed out from the back bedroom.

"Do you all mind? Some of us are *trying* to decipher a *clue*!"

Sometime later the three of them descended back into the basement to find the black adder being menaced by three of the thickest sheep in two worlds.

"Woah," said Emily. "Mick must have gotten the sheep too close. And there's only three? Mick?" she said into the radio.

"I'm here. Over."

"Did everyone make it? Over."

"Everyone made it. Your knocking stop? Over."

Emily listened. It *had* stopped. "Yeah."

"Maybe that little lass was right an' the house *is* haunted. Over."

Emily went to press the radio button, then stopped. "I'm not going to dignify that with a response."

Outside, Polly met up with Prince Fi and Harvey.

"You were right," Polly said to Harvey. "That was easy."

"People like uth can alwayth manipulate otherth," said Harvey. "We can get them to do what we want."

"So is that what you're doing?" said Polly. "To all of us?"

"Naw, not me."

Polly studied him. "Why not?"

"Haven't figured out what I want, yet."

Fi was watching the both of them and signaled to be lifted into Polly's pocket. "There is nothing about this I like," he said. "The deceit. The danger for Polly. I am without honor."

"I'll be a big help to you. I'm even a bit stronger than you."

"It's not strength of body that's required. It's strength of mind, and of character. Which, I must admit," Fi conceded, "you have showed in great measure if I ignore today's escapades."

They walked off toward the tube station.

"What I did today," said Polly. "Was it bad?"

"It was not good," said Fi.

"It wath fine," said Harvey. "Ath long ath you had good reathonth. And didn't enjoy it. You have to try not to enjoy it."

After another block he added, "Not that I didn't enjoy knocking on Emily's cage a bit. Little prith."

CHAPTER 22

Pretannica.

"What . . . what color is everything?" Scott asked Mick.

"'S green."

"Are you sure?" This was the green of camera ads and television commercials for other televisions.

Pretannica.

The trees were brawny, titanic hosts for ivy and velvety moss, shade for fern and flower and fungus. *Oh, man, the fungus,* thought Scott. All prehistoric shapes and back-of-the-refrigerator colors. He thought maybe one mushroom in particular had called him a name when he passed.

But more than any particular sight was the smell, the air, the everything of the place. The *otherworldliness* of it. The magic, the glamour. *Pretannica!* He could see his father was caught up in it too, so could it be the fairyness

of them both that was tuned to this trill, this connection?

"I feel like," he said, struggling to put it into words, "like my fingers have to sneeze. I feel like . . ."

"Running through the hills and twirling like a nun in a movie," finished John.

"That isn't what I was going to say."

Merle was watching them. "I have no idea what you guys are on about. I'm okay with that."

They'd emerged from the rift in a tangled glen, tearing through shrubbery and scattering field mice in every direction. There was no way to get your bearings in a land with no sun, no moon, no stars, but Mick assured them they were in Ireland, in the forests near Killarney. Close to his old mound, in fact. The sky was a Prussian blue above, warming to pumpkin orange at the horizons. Everything seemed brighter than it should have. As if the whole world might be faintly luminous, like a dying glow stick.

"All right, enough gawkin'," said Mick. He addressed Merle and John. "Unless yis have plans to the contrary, England is that way, an' may the road rise to meet yeh. If Scott has no objections, I'd like to stop off at my old mound an' see if anyone's been waterin' my plants. Finchbriton?"

The little bird chirruped.

"I love yeh like the ugly son I never had, but I wan' yeh

to consider goin' with John an' Merle here. They have the more dangerous mission an' could use a real powerhouse like you. Of course Scott an' I'd be delighted to have your company—all your little stories, your thoughts on love an' life an' so forth."

Finchbriton seemed to consider the options, then he tweeted his decision and flew to John's shoulder.

"Oh, thank goodness," said Merle. "You know my Slumbro doesn't even work on the Fay."

John was lingering, like he wanted to be knighted just for refusing to lie. Honesty wasn't all *that* hard.

"So, bye," Scott said finally.

John nodded, taking his medicine.

They all said their good-byes and parted. Scott and Mick pressed through the woods—Mick easily, gracefully, Scott as if he were being pranked constantly by a spiteful slapstick universe. He tripped on roots, stumbled over logs, was poked by thickets, had his face raked by brambles.

"It's just up ahead," said Mick. "The ol' mound. An' when I say mound, I'm not bein' modest—'s a mound. But inside it was as cozy as your mother's handbag. Here we are."

They arrived at a small clearing and a mound of earth ringed by small mushrooms. Atop the mound was a weathered and whitewashed wooden cross. Mick stared quizzically at the cross.

"Well, that's new. I hope you won't be offended when I tell yeh it has no place on a leprechaun's domicile."

"There's something tied to it," said Scott, and he climbed up, wondering too late if it was bad manners to just hike up another man's house like this. At the base of the cross was a pair of very old, shriveled baby shoes. They'd probably been calfskin or something similar, but now they were hard and dry as raisins.

"Well, Monday Tuesday an' Wednesday—it's you, Finchfather. Isn't it," said a voice, and they turned to see a man in the nearby trees. He wasn't a tall man, but he nonetheless appeared to be a sprightly, smartly dressed human.

Mick squinted. "Lusmore? By my baby teeth, it *is* you. Older, sure, but still alive, after all these years."

"It's thanks to all that fairy food an' drink I ate, plus all the gifts the Good Folk gave me," said Lusmore.

Scott gave Mick what he hoped was an appropriately what-the-heck? look.

"Exception that proves the rule," said Mick.

"How have you been, Finchfather?" asked Lusmore. "*Where* have you been? Is it true there's another Ireland out there, beyond the veil?"

"I'm going by Mick these days. This here's Scott, a changeling friend o' mine." Lusmore bowed. "An' there *is* another Ireland, an we're hopin' to speak with Her Majesty the High Queen abou' that. Yeh know where she can be found presently?"

Lusmore smiled. "Just so happens I do. It'll be nice to do yeh a favor, after all your people did for me."

"Oh, come now—we only paid yeh in kind for improvin' on that song we all had stuck in our heads. What's the story here?" Mick asked, hitching his thumb toward the cross atop his mound.

Lusmore gave the cross a sad smile. "The day you disappeared, she arrived. Just a wee babby, no aul' wan to care for her. The Good Folk tried to take her in, make a changeling of her, but yeh know how it is. Sometimes they don't thrive. They gave her a Christian burial, as they thought proper for one such as she."

"Baby Ann," whispered Mick. "Poor lass."

"Aye."

They took a moment. But then old Lusmore stepped up the mound.

"If yeh want to catch up to your queen, we'll have to move fast," he said. "Now Mick, yeh're lookin' as glamourous as the Lord's haircut, so I'll bet if yeh rummage through your things yeh'll happen to find two oilskin sacks just big enough for you an' your friend. 'Cause that's what yeh're going to need."

CHAPTER 23

It turned out Mick did have two such sacks in his mound, not to mention a fresh red tracksuit, which didn't even make any sense. They took the sacks and followed Lusmore through the wilderness.

"Hustle now," he said. "Not much time."

Their movement stirred all manner of creatures— unseen, but they rustled the underbrush. High above, the trees groaned and clicked, clicked, clicked, as if speaking to one another in their own language,

"Have ta admit," said Mick, "things have changed in the last hunnerd an' fifty years. The forests seem more built up, wilder."

"A lot has changed, an that's the truth," said Lusmore, and Scott thought he heard a grim note in the man's voice. "Now, while we walk we'll be lookin' for a particular plant. Weedy-lookin' thing, with little white flowers and

249

fleshy leaves. Try not to touch any others."

"Any other whats?" asked Scott.

"Plants. Here's a helpful little song: Leaves o' one, turn an' run. Leaves o' two, not for you. Leaves o' three, leave it be. Leaves o' four, instant death. We used to have a better rhyme for that, but too many little ones were dying for the sake o' poetry. Leaves o' five—"

"And why are we looking for this plant?" asked Scott, trying to hold his arms as close as he could to his body.

"Right. So abou' sixty years ago Titania grew tired of moving her whole entourage from one castle to another all the time, season after season, so she asked the sorceress Queen Morgan le Fay to enchant the Tower o' London. She moved herself an' her whole retinue inside, an' now it just disappears from one place and pops up in the next, quick as yeh like."

"The whole thing?"

"Every last brick. Well, the whole White Tower, anyway. Ah! Here we are!"

Lusmore took a small knife from his belt and carefully cut a cluster of weeds free of the earth. Each had a spray of tiny white flowers. He handed them to Mick and Scott.

"Don't let the young one put these in his mouth."

Mick gave Scott a stern look, and Scott rolled his eyes. "So," he said, "the Tower of London is nearby?"

"*Was* nearby. She was just off the peninsula this

mornin', inspectin' the boundaries of the Gloria Wall. Now she's up in Dub Linn."

"All respect, Lusmore," said Mick, "but this helps us how? Dublin is two hundred miles away."

"Follow me into this meadow, an' all will be revealed."

Scott was noticing the first signs of a path, and a tall, rough stone, standing upright, with symbols carved into its face. An octagon and a moon. After another twenty feet, there was another on the opposite side of the path, with a moon and two stars. Then they broke through a hedge and into a meadow, and there stood three ravens the size of cement trucks.

"Woah," said Scott, taking a step back.

"Gentlemen," said Lusmore, "the famous ravens of the Tower of London!"

The meadow narrowed to a wide stone wall, the ruins of some old fortress. Here and there were more standing stones, like jagged fingers reaching out of the earth. They also bore carvings of spirals, moons, octagons, stars, a crude dragon with outstretched wings. One prominent stone showed two overlapping circles, bisected by a sharp line. Mincing among these stones were the three blue-black birds, their nightmare feet pulling up tufts of grass and soil. Their beaks were clacking like gunshots. One of them watched Scott and Mick and Lusmore with its glassy black eye, followed them with brisk movements of its head.

"The famous what of what?" Scott whispered.

"The Tower o' London has always been famous for its ravens," said Mick. "For its *perfectly ordinary-sized ravens*," he added, glancing at Lusmore. "What's the story?"

"You know how spellcastin' can be," said Lusmore. "Unintended consequences. The ravens got caught in the edge o' Morgan's spell, became a part of it. Now yeh can't separate 'em. The ravens don't disappear along with the tower, but as soon as it's gone they pick up an' follow it. It's uncanny, but they always know where to find it."

Scott watched a fourth raven, just beyond the ruins of the stone wall, amble into view.

"Poor things have gotten fat an' stupid on all the magic they've been soakin' up over the years, though. They can only fly a short bit before they're knackered."

"So we capture one and ride it to Queen Titania's court," said Scott.

That wasn't the plan, but Lusmore made sure to let them know that he thought it was adorable.

Lusmore explained the actual plan, explained that people did it all the time, which was how Scott and Mick came to be hopping into the middle of a meadow, covered head to toe in oilskin sacks, while the Irishman shouted

252

to them from the trees that they needed to wiggle their bums more.

"I can't see," said Scott.

"That's probably for the best, don't yeh think?" asked Mick.

"You two are the most unappetizin' grubs I ever did see!" Lusmore called to them, distantly. "Wiggle it! Wiggle it!"

"Maybe this isn't any kind of plan at all," said Scott. "Maybe this is just a joke he plays on out-of-towners."

Then it happened. Scott couldn't see anything, but he was certain he was swallowed whole by a giant raven. He felt the lacquered black coffin of a beak snap around him with a thunderclap. He tipped up and slid back, and felt himself being forced in fits and starts down the creature's esophagus, then dropped down with a little splash into what science class had told him must be the stomach. A few seconds later he heard another splash beside him.

"Mick?"

"Yep."

Scott sighed and tried to breathe through his mouth.

"I'm glad we ended up inside the same bird."

"Aye."

It wasn't long before the flock took flight, and Scott sloshed around, trying to touch the oilskin sack as little as possible, doing his best to stay dry. He knew the sack was supposed to be waterproof, but he'd owned enough supposedly waterproof raincoats to know that the rain always won in the end. He tried to think about what he was going to say to Titania. Public speaking wasn't really his thing. He'd always hated oral reports in school.

Twice the ravens landed and rested, and took to the air again. Lusmore had instructed them that they wouldn't be at the tower until all the ravens cawed at once.

"Mick?"

"Yeah, lad?"

"I'm in a bird."

"I as well, boyo."

He listened to the raven's heartbeat for a while.

"Mick?"

"Still here."

"I'm supposed to be in the sixth grade."

"I know yeh are, son."

"I thought maybe everyone'd forgotten."

Finally they landed for the last time, and heard their raven crow, and the muffled croaks of six or seven other ravens join in chorus. That was the signal. Scott opened his Swiss Army knife and cut the tiniest slit he could in his sack, then pushed the plant with the little white flowers through the slit, into the raven's stomach. It took a second, but the stomach convulsed like a waterbed.

Here we go, thought Scott.

The raven pitched its neck out, *huck huck huck*, and then Mick and Scott spilled to the lawn in front of the Tower of London. Scott finished cutting open his sack and stepped out, hoping for a James-Bond-emerging-from-his-scuba-suit-in-full-tuxedo kind of impression, even though he had to admit it probably didn't look like that at all. Mick did the same. The raven left the scene out of general embarrassment.

They ran, just to get away from the birds, hugging the wall of the castle. It was gleaming even in the twilight of Pretannica, dripping whitewash. It wasn't a huge castle by any means, and Scott and Mick had quickly turned a corner and then another before pausing to calm their nerves.

Scott looked up at the White Tower. "We made it," he said with a swell of pride.

A strange voice said, "Aye, you did, recreants; now who are you?"

CHAPTER 24

Biggs finished sewing Emily a little lab coat covered with pockets, and he made her model it for him while he tried to whistle (couldn't) and clapped arrhythmically. She filled these pockets with all kinds of scientific equipment and devices—an oscilloscope, a laser pointer, concave and convex mirrors, spider-web bolometers for the measurement of the cosmic microwave background radiation; that sort of thing. One pocket alone held something fanciful and unscientific—the shamrock Mick had found in Pretannica—and this was to remind her that there might be limits to what she could learn through science. Even though she didn't really believe this. Even though she currently suspected that "magic" was just another kind of science, with rules she didn't understand yet.

The sheep minced about on their tethers. The adder

257

slithered around, possibly reasserting the borders of its narrowing territory. They'd all really disrupted the good thing the snake had going in this basement, and Emily wondered if it had eaten even once since their crew moved in. She felt sorry for it, but interested, too—the adder had hissed right before anyone or anything passed through the rift. As if it could see what Scott had seen—the shapes of both travelers merging, darkly, into one shape before they traded places. Emily never saw anything of the sort. To her, Mick would just be standing there one moment, and then the next, a fox. Or four humans, and then, the next moment, three sheep.

Not that she'd actually been in the room for that one. She hadn't actually *seen* it.

She'd been so certain that four humans would require four sheep. She thought as she sat down in front of the rift with Archimedes. *Maybe because Scott and Polly were smaller . . . ?*

"Oh, good," said Erno as he came down the stairs. "Biggs made you a mad scientist costume."

Emily stiffened. "*I'm not mad.*"

Erno shuffled his feet. "I know. It was just—"

"You mean because of Mr. Wilson? Because he's crazy, and we were both taking the Milk? Is that what you were thinking?"

"Hey," said Erno, with his hands up. "You know I don't usually start thinking until I'm done talking."

Emily watched him tensely for a moment, then she sagged. "Sorry," she said, barely.

"What's up with you?" said Erno. "You've been chewing on my head for days."

"I'm not mad at you. I'm mad at Dad. Mr. Wilson."

"Well, I'm mad at him too," said Erno.

"Yeah, but you've been mad at him for years. You're better at it. Plus I'm mad that he's a coward, that he's hiding . . . I mean, yes, it's great he was obviously gathering all this secret information all these years and keeping it from Goodco, great that he's feeding it to us, but now he's letting a bunch of kids do all the dangerous stuff for him while he . . . nibbles chocolates in Switzerland or whatever."

"Why Switzerland?"

"That's where *I'd* go. And then I could tour the Large Hadron Collider near Geneva—"

"Is this why you hate me working on his new clue so much?" asked Erno.

Emily sighed. "Probably. I just don't even want to hear about it. I'm angry at a piece of paper. Proof I'm getting stupider."

One of the sheep made a sheep noise, which was just

the sound effect for a statement like that. Emily frowned at the sheep.

"Stupider or not, I swear I can still count," she said. "Four people needed four sheep. Someone didn't go through the rift."

Polly, Fi, and Harvey got to the Goodco factory in Slough easily enough after Harvey stole a taxicab.

"Itth not thtealing," the pooka explained. "They're public automobileth. Don't you thee them everywhere, those boxy black thingth? You take a free one, you leave it when you're finished for the next perthon. It'th a British thing."

Polly didn't feel like she was in a position to argue. After she'd learned they drove on the wrong side of the road here, she was prepared to believe anything.

Now they lay on their stomachs on a knoll at the edge of the Goodco parking lot, watching the entrance. Polly wished they had binoculars. And costumes.

"Okay," said Polly. "We sneak in, we find the pixies, we sneak out. Easy."

Nobody made any motion to do anything in particular.

"Might not even be in there anymore," Harvey offered. "Rumor wath alwayth that Goodco put pixthie in the Pufteeth."

"*Harvey!*"

"Jutht a little bit of pixthie, mind you, ground up. Pixthie dutht."

"You are a vulgar and hateful beast," Fi murmured.

The little hill was silent and chilly for a minute.

"The Goodco factory back home had groups of schoolkids going in and out a million times a day," Polly grumbled. "If only there was something like that, I could sneak in at the back."

Fi said, "I expect one of my size could enter quite easily alone."

"But then?" said Polly. "And please please please don't take this the wrong way? But you might have to climb some stairs. Or see what's on the top of a counter."

"Forsooth."

"And I'm worried about Harvey, too," said Polly. "I know he's invisible mostly, but they probably have some kind of fairy detection system."

"Oh, there wath never any chanth I wath going in there," Harvey answered.

Polly thought.

"All right. We're going for broke," she decided, not because there wasn't time to plan but more because she was seven years old and impatient. "Forget sneakiness. They're gonna take us right inside themselves."

● ○ ★

And that was how Polly came to walk right past the man at the front desk in the lobby of the U.K. headquarters of Goodco, trying to summon real tears to her eyes. She thought of Grandma Peggy. And when that didn't work, she remembered the giraffe at the zoo that died because a volunteer accidentally fed it oleander. At this she sniffed and felt her eyes well up. *Sorry, Grandma Peggy,* she thought.

The front-desk man got up to follow her, as she expected him to. He bent at the waist and rested his hands on his knees, his face immediately coloring from the effort. "Um, hello? Little girl? I'm sorry, can I help you? Are you looking for someone?" He was an older man, a grandfatherly type, just the sort Polly thought she could handle. He looked like he didn't get a lot of unaccompanied children through here, which was fine.

She turned, and the sweet, earnest look on his face was the perfect thing to really get her tears flowing. "It was supposed to be a secret," she bawled.

"What was, love?" said the guard, glancing over his shoulder, trying to watch his desk and be a hero at the same time.

"My dad couldn't find anyone to babysit me, so my dad's new girlfriend brought me into work here and said don't touch anything and don't go anywhere, but I just wanted to look around and now? I got lost and I can't find my way back." She sucked a snotty breath. She hoped nobody was taping this.

The man relaxed his shoulders and smiled. "That's fine. Just tell me your . . . da's girlfriend's name, then, and I'll have her come get you—"

"NO! No, she said if anyone saw me I couldn't say who brought me or she'd get in trouble, she works in some secret part."

"Well, I think you'd better tell me now—"

"I won't. She'll get mad. Don't make me."

The guard straightened, steadied himself, gathered his features together to regroup.

"I don't know the name of her department," Polly offered, because things weren't moving along as quickly as she would have liked, "but she says it's the one 'with all the bloody pixies.'"

"Bloody pixies . . . ," the man repeated foggily. This obviously wasn't ringing any bells, but at least it suggested a course of action. "You just come back to my desk here, while I call Ms. Aleister. She'll know where to take you." He made the call.

"Ms. Aleister, this is Henry at the front. Yes, ma'am, I do think it's important. I have a little girl here who came in with one of the employees, and now she's lost. No ma'am, she won't say which one. No ma'am, she won't say which department, but she says it's the one with the

264

'bloody pixies'? Does that mean anything to you?"

Henry the guard flinched and turned off his earpiece. "She said she'd be right down. So." He offered Polly a little brown lump of something from a bag. "Would you like one of my candy lozenges? They taste like horehound."

CHAPTER 25

"Wow, look at it," said John. "Just look at it!"

"Stop telling me to look at it," said Merle. He paused to push some nettles away from his face. "I get it. Pretannica is very pretty. I imagine your slight elfishness is making it all extra sparkly for you."

"How do you know where we're going, by the way? Emily said compasses won't work here, and there aren't any stars or sun to navigate by."

"I'm mostly just heading toward that gap in the trees. Finchbriton, can you fly up high, tell me if there's a lake in that direction? Lough Leane ought to be near here."

"Lough Leane?"

"Really big lake."

Finchbriton scouted up above the trees and returned a minute later, alighting on a low branch before the men.

266

He twittered back his report, and John and Merle stared at him.

"I've just realized I have no idea what that means," said Merle.

"Mick always seems to kind of understand him," said John.

"Mick has known him for a thousand years."

Finchbriton lowed kind of an annoyed whistle and flew to another branch farther along the same path.

"I think that means we're doing all right," said Merle. "Follow the bird."

A light rain began to fall. Just as John was about to remark that this seemed unusual, as there were nothing but the thinnest whispers of clouds in the sky, he noticed that it did not appear to be raining at all a hundred feet ahead of them, nor a hundred feet behind.

"Hard not to take that personally," he muttered, and pulled his hood up. The trail, if indeed they were even on a trail, dipped into a deeply ferny patch surrounded by young trees. "So . . . we're hiking to this big lake . . . why? I think England is technically in the opposite direction."

"I'm hoping for a shortcut," said Merle, hunching up his shoulders against the rain. "Something the Lady of the Lake told me once, back when we were friendly, or pretending to be friendly. She said, 'All lakes are one lake in my kingdom.' She could sink beneath the waves of one lake and break the surface of another, a hundred miles away. In no time at all."

John waited politely for Merle to explain why this was relevant, but the old man started whistling, so he found it necessary to reopen the conversation.

"Okay, what?"

"We're gonna try to travel from one lake directly to another, in Avalon," said Merle. "Use Nimue's magic against her. Nice, huh?"

Finchbriton chirped something that sounded ruffled and complicated.

"I think I agree with that, even if I couldn't understand the words," said John. "None of us are spellcasters like Nimue. It can't be as easy as just dunking your head underwater and saying, 'Avalon, please,' like a taxi. Can it?"

The bird whistled his agreement.

"Look—I have some small idea of what we might find at Lough Leane," said Merle. "But if I'm wrong, it's only a few miles out of our way. A few extra miles never killed anybody."

"The miles won't," whispered a voice from the underbrush, "but the Hairy Men might, yeh thick idjits! Hide!"

John ducked slightly to look for the source of this new voice and felt a smooth stone whiz past his ear. It shattered against a nearby boulder and resounded like a firecracker. This was followed by a screech, a monkey-house kind of sound.

John pulled his backpack up over his head. "Under the boulders! Quickly!"

He and Merle and Finchbriton dove for cover as the air filled with stones and shrieks, an angry rain, and little hairy men made themselves visible on the high limbs of trees. They were all lean and wild maned, bearded and bigmouthed, maybe eighteen inches tall and wearing only the poor memories of outfits. They chattered to one another in their own language and hurled stone after stone from little leather slings. All around were thuds and cracks.

John slid under one particular boulder, only to find it occupied.

"Oi!" said a small (but nonetheless obviously human) man. "Get your own!"

"Oh, excellent," said a nearby voice, a woman's. "They have gotten the Hairy Men to resume slinging their stones. I was just wondering to meself, *Have they any more stones?* And now, happily, I have my answer."

"Merle!" said John. "Finchbriton! You all right?"

"Not dead," said Merle from beneath a nearby boulder. Finchbriton whistled.

"Your mate there's under a rock," the small man told

269

John. "Why don't yeh go share wi' him?"

Stones ricocheted off the ground and struck John's side—not terribly hard, but he expected he'd bruise. "There's room for us both," he said, just as the forest grew quiet. "They've stopped. Is that good or bad?"

"Probably just pausin' to gather more stones," said the woman. "They can keep this up long as yeh like."

"Where are you?" called John.

"In the shrubbery, under a shield."

"You have a shield . . . ," John said to himself.

The rain was letting up already, but still it was trickling down into the crevices beneath the boulders where they hid and pooling in uncomfortable places.

Merle was peering out from his hiding spot. "Are those . . . maybe this is a stupid question, but are those *brownies?*"

"Course they're brownies! Hairy Men!" said the woman. "What've I been sayin'?"

One of the stone-collecting brownies, on the ground, approached John's boulder and slung a little spear down off its back. It bared its thick teeth and leaned forward, gave John and his roommate a good look at its fierce face, its flea-peppered mane of yellow dreads.

"EEEEEEEEEK," it said. "Wuh-WEEEEEEEEEK!" Then it commenced to trying to poke some part of John that John wasn't covering with his backpack. Other brownies gathered to watch and holler encouragement.

John anticipated one of the brownie's lunges and grabbed the spear himself, wrenching it from the hairy little man's grip. "HA!" he said. Then he spun it around and started poking back.

"*REEEEEEEEEEEEK!*" the brownie answered, and retreated to a safe distance with its fellows. Then they started hurling rocks again.

"Oh!" said the small man. "Ow! Beautiful!" John wriggled between the man and the barrage, tried to block as much of it as he could. Then there was a whistling, and a burst of blue flame surged past them, sending the brownies hooting and scrambling for the trees. Before long the rain of stones began again, but from above.

"Thank you, Finchbriton!" called John. "You stay under cover, though! I know you're a small target, but just one hit and you're done for! Merle! I don't suppose your wand—"

"Works on this bunch? Nope, like I said—only humans."

"Right. I'm going to try something. Madam? Hello?"

"Are yeh talking to me?" asked the woman in the bushes.

"I was," said John. He paused. "Is there anyone *else* hiding nearby?"

"Just me an' my husband an' my babby."

"Your baby is here? Where is it?"

"Oh, toddlin' 'round about someplace SHE'S RIGHT HERE WI' ME, WHERE DO YEH THINK SHE IS?"

"All right, all right," said John. "Um. Well. That makes this next part harder to ask, but . . . can I borrow your shield?"

"So it wasn't so hard when yeh thought yeh were just askin' for the only means o' protection from a helpless woman, is that right?"

"I will get you to shelter with your husband. But I'll need your shield to fight the Hairy Men."

"Let 'im have it," said the husband. "The Hairy Men won't be satisfied till they've killed a human. Maybe after this one's dead they'll bugger off."

"That's some beautiful gratitude, right there," said Merle from his rock. "If I had a pen I'd write that down."

"Finchbriton!" called John. "A little cover?"

So another plume of especially smoky fire issued forth, and when the brownies paused in their barrage to watch, John ran just behind it and into the bushes. There he found a slight young woman curled up under a battered metal shield painted with a weathered and fading image of a chickadee. She clutched what was perhaps a six-month-old baby to her chest. The baby, apparently used to this sort of thing, was fast asleep.

John huddled down beside them both.

"Hullo," he said. "I'm John."

"Clara Tanner. Oo, yeh're a nice-lookin' one."

"Soon to be dead, though!" her husband reminded her from his rock. "Terrible shame."

"Ready?" asked John, and Clara nodded. "Finchbriton?"

The finch sent out another screen of fire and smoke. But the brownies, despite their mook behavior and monkey chatter, weren't entirely stupid. When they saw the flames again, they rained missiles down even harder, and John did his best to protect what the shield could not as he brought mother and baby back underneath the far side of the boulder. They were nearly home when a stone creased his temple.

"AAH! SSSSS!" he hissed, and pushed all three of them to safety. They curled close in the mud and moss. Clara examined the cut.

"Oo, it's a bleeder—head wounds always are—but yeh'll be all right. Here." She touched at it tenderly, then removed her scarf and tied it around John's forehead.

"Do I look like a pirate?"

"I don't know what that is."

"Enough pillow talk!" said the husband. "Why, I'd almost think yeh're stallin'! Do yeh want to go die or don't yeh?"

"You sure about this?" called Merle.

"Never ask me if I'm sure about anything! Finchbriton! Want to come along?"

John launched into the fray, sword drawn, with Finchbriton clinging to his jacket front behind the chickadee shield. Stones clanged noisily off it.

The brownies were concentrated in two trees—a lean-trunked one rather close to John and a taller, stouter one farther away. He aimed his shield at the far tree and hugged close to the leaner one, even using it for cover and frustrating the Hairy Men up above. With John standing almost directly below them, the tree's own thick head of branches got in the way of many of their stones, and the brownies in the lowest branches were now in danger from wayward shots flying across the gully.

There was a lot of angry chatter. A couple brownies threatened to drop down on top of them until Finchbriton sent hot little balloons up at each, and they retreated, singed and barking.

John wasn't sure he could even swing his sword at a brownie—they looked too human, despite everything. But he did start hacking at the trunk of the tree, intending to topple the whole business. The brownies gibbered and yelped. The tree quivered. The tree quivered more than it should have, maybe.

The tree, possibly tired of being hacked at and pelted with stones and filled with tiny hairy people, sprang to life. John leaped away, and Finchbriton flew free. The tree snapped a root from the earth like a tentacle and gave John an uppercut that he only partially managed to absorb with the chickadee shield. He landed hard on his back and looked up to see a spindly fist of branches swinging down at him. He rolled and turned, just as he had done on the set of *Galileo's Revenge*, and carved a few twig-fingers from the fist. Then Finchbriton fluttered in and set the rest ablaze.

The tree pulled back, creaking and groaning, and shook itself like a dog, joggling the some twenty Hairy Men still camped in its branches. Then it plucked one of these Hairy Men free like an apple and chucked it at John.

"WAAAAH!" The brownie whanged off John's shield and landed in a wad a few feet away, then crawled off. After a moment the tree found another brownie and did it again.

"WAAAAH!" *(whang)*

"Stop that!" said John.

"WAAAAAAH!" *(whang)*

The tree hadn't forgotten that the other brownies in the far tree had been pelting it with stones, so it started flinging Hairy Men at them, too. Soon all the brownies were decamping quickly, some of them simply falling straight into the underbrush, and scattering in all directions.

The tree had a few more roots up now and was trying to get ambulatory. Finchbriton set another woody arm alight, which the tree tried to smother in the ferns.

At this John leaped forward and finished the job he'd started—he chopped the trunk from its root system, then went about pruning whatever moved until the tree finally collapsed in the ditch and was still.

John's arms fell limply to his sides. He was dripping sweat.

"Well," he breathed as Finchbriton perched close to his ear. "That was just the *worst*."

Another tree across the gully, seeing what had happened to the first one, uprooted itself and ran off into the bushes.

"Yeh've saved us!" said Clara, and she ran to John, still holding the baby. "This is Mab. My worthless husband is Alfie Skinner."

John pulled his hood back, shook hands with Alfie.

"We were takin' furs in our donkey cart to Agora," said Alfie. "They killed our donkey, chased us down here."

Merle had emerged and stepped over to a brownie that was lying on its back among the ferns. He poked it with his boot.

"Wuuuuuh," moaned the brownie, and it took a halfhearted swipe at Merle with its hand. "Wuh."

"Yeh can keep the shield," said Clara, bouncing the

baby, which had now, just *now*, awakened and started to cry. "I know it isn't much, but it was my da's. I painted that chickadee on it when I was a girl."

"Thank you. It's a good shield."

"I don't believe it," said Merle now as he joined them. "Brownies! They used to be the gentlest of the Fay. Clean-cut, hardworking. They lived in human homes! Did chores for the humans at night when no one was looking."

Clara pulled baby Mab away from Merle a bit and made a face. "Mister, maybe yeh're older than yeh look, but my *granddad* told me stories abou' the Hairy Men." She spat on the ground. "Only help they offer roun' the house is givin' folks fewer mouths to feed."

Merle raised his hands. "Hey, I didn't mean anything by it. Things are just . . . different here than I expected. I'm from very far away."

Clara squinted. "Mister, there's no such place."

John thought it best to interject. "It's probably unsafe to hang about, isn't it? Perhaps we can walk together as far as Lough Leane?"

At the sound of his voice Clara beamed again, and John thought he saw Alfie roll his eyes. "We'll tell everyone what yeh did for us here," she said. "Oo, an' I'll be so proud to tell them yeh're carryin' my da's shield. Folks might even start callin' yeh the Chickadee!"

"It would be all right if they didn't call me that."

CHAPTER 26

Scott and Mick turned to see a dark-skinned, black-haired teen, holding a bow and arrow at the ready. A company of four other beautiful youths were behind him, each with a stylish and richly appointed outfit, each with his own favored weapon. They were the boy band of assassins.

Mick stepped forward. "Well met, young blood. Your reputation precedes you—I believe yeh are Dhanu, most favored changeling of our High Queen—"

"And charged as captain of her Changeling Guard."
   (said Dhanu.)
"Alas, I asked you two for your own names,
Sirrah, Sir Runt. I'm freshly vers'd in mine."

Mick looked snookered. "Right. Sorry. I go by Mick,

an' . . . um, I am a full an' trusty member of the Seelie Court, leprechaun in good standing, Crest of Ór. As such, I request safe conduct for myself an' my compatriot here, Scott, a changeling from parts distant."

At this Dhanu took renewed interest in Scott.

"An' Scott an' I both crave audience with our High Queen, as is the right of all with Fay blood, at least once in our happy lives. I'll be obliged, of course, to furnish my True Name whensoever—"

Dhanu, his bow relaxed, raised a hand and stepped uncomfortably close to Scott.

"You cannot be but human. What fairy
Nursery tended this, such fusty fruit?"

"Come now," said Mick, "He—"

"Speaks, yes? If not to me, how to a queen?"

"I was born to humans," said Scott. "I was raised by humans. But my dad and I have fairy blood."

Dhanu looked Scott up and down at this and curled his lip.

"You have but drops of fairy blood in you,
And smell as like the inside of a crow."

As insults go, this was so close to accurate that Scott thought it would be petty to tell him it had been a raven.

"I'm . . . pretty ordinary," he agreed. He looked at these changelings, carrying themselves with red-carpet grace. He thought he was right in assuming they were all human, but a lifetime of fostering in the fairy court had given them a kind of ageless glamour. Still, they were human, and he was not—not entirely. "You need us in a way, don't you," he added, realizing something. "Us ordinary ones. Without us, someone else would have to be ordinary."

Dhanu glowered at him a moment. Then his eyes changed. They didn't soften, exactly, but they looked like a pair of eyes Scott might be able to work with. Like he and one of the popular kids had been grouped together on a science fair project and it would all be over soon. Dhanu turned without a word and motioned for Mick and Scott to follow.

"He's kind of hard to talk to," whispered Scott.

"Man, it's this courtly speech," said Mick. "I don't think I can pull it off anymore. It's been too long, an' I was never very good at it anyway." He pointed at Scott. "Don't yeh even try it. Jes' be polite, an' don't put on any airs."

They walked along the castle wall. Scott liked the

Tower of London. This was the castle a child would design: a white stone box, buttoned with arched windows, topped by a toothy parapet, braced at each corner by a tall tower. It lacked only a drawbridge and a moat. They passed an ogre diligently whitewashing one side with brush and bucket.

Then they turned a final corner, and Scott saw where the Fay had concentrated their improvements. The front facade of the Tower was whitewashed like the rest, but the gaps between every stone sprouted mushrooms, wild rose, clover and foxglove and bluebells and ivy. And here and there the fungi and flowers themselves had been trained to form signs and symbols: the now-familiar stars and moons and octagons that Scott could not help but see rendered in marshmallow and floating in milk. Cracks in the masonry had begun to form—nature was having its way. Eventually the elves would tear down their own castle for beauty.

There was still no drawbridge, no moat, but the main castle doors here were twenty feet off the ground. And emblazoned on these doors was another symbol, of two overlapping circles or spheres, split in two by a line.

"I've been seeing that a lot lately," said Scott.

"*It came to fair Titania in dreams,*" answered Dhanu.

Towering giants stood to either side of these doors,

stripped tree trunks in the grips of their long bare limbs, their belts hung with the tackle of their villainous, storybook lives—skulls, knives, the spine and rib cage of something or other, a lot of iron horseshoes that had been twisted together on chains. Scott thought the Fay weren't supposed to like iron; but then he thought it might be like a tongue piercing—something unpleasant the big kids did to show what they were capable of.

He caught his breath. He supposed the only way up to that door was to have one of these bald-headed, snaggletoothed giants lift you up to it, and he suddenly felt a depth of sympathy for Fi that never would have occurred to him otherwise. But instead Dhanu whistled, and stout vines grew down from the castle door, weaving and intertwining so that when they'd reached the ground they'd formed a grand staircase. Roses bloomed as they climbed.

"'S that you, Cuhullin?" Mick asked the giant on the left when they were at the level of his waist. "How's the wife?"

The giant didn't answer.

"Ah, sometimes I think the Old Mother should have given giants a set o' ears on their ankles," Mick said. "I asked—"

"Not supposed to speak to you, Finchfather," said Cuhullin.

Mick frowned. "Not supposed to speak on the job, or not supposed to speak to me person'ly?"

Still the giant didn't answer.

The doors were open. Dhanu said,

> "So now the stage is set, and it is seen
> How churl and chaff assay to sway a queen."

CHAPTER 27

Near the lake John and Merle parted company with Clara and Alfie and Mab.

"Fare thee well, Chickadee," said Clara with a girlish smile.

John couldn't help twitching a little. "We're definitely calling me that, then?" he asked.

"Chickadee is another name for Titmouse," said Merle. "We could call you Titmouse."

"Chickadee's fine," said John.

They watched the little family disappear, then proceeded down to the water's edge. When Merle saw movement, they paused and concealed themselves behind a copse of trees. Finchbriton hopped nervously back and forth on John's shoulder.

Mermaids.

"Ah," whispered Merle. "If only I were fifty years younger."

"Seriously?" murmured John. He squinted to see better, but he didn't think it helped.

Lough Leane was vast and electric blue, reflecting the dwindling light of the sky above. Down past the rushes the lake met the land, and there were a handful of low, wide stones lapped smooth by water. Lounging on these stones were the mermaids.

John supposed they might be pretty. But like so many things that are meant to be seen in the water, they looked stringy and colorless when out of it. Like seaweed drying on a beach. Their top halves were pasty and bare apart from whatever their lanky hair covered. Their bottom halves looked like low tide. There was a distinct pet-store sort of smell wafting up from the lake.

One thing that really surprised him: nearly all of them were wearing hats. Red silk pointed caps. Those that weren't had red silk capes. A few had both.

"Merrows," said Merle. "A sort of Irish mermaid. With so much of the seas disappeared here, I was hoping they might be hanging out in the lakes. The females are all honeys but the males are all hideously ugly, so they tend to be partial to human men. I'd been thinking we'd have to steal a couple of their caps, but the way that Clara was going goo-goo for you reminded me that I'm traveling with *People* magazine's Sexiest Man Alive for 2010."

"I'm embarrassed for you that you know that. And what about these caps?"

"Don't ask me why, but without one of those caps or capes they can't dive beneath the water. But if we get a couple of them, we can go *SHOOM!* down to the bottom of the lake like rockets. Once we're at the bottom I'm pretty sure we'll find a door, a door that'll take us to any lake we want. So how about sweet-talking those gals out of a coupla hats?"

John sighed and prepared. He couldn't merely be a man who wanted some hats. He needed to be a man who loved fish women. He had to believe this. If he loved them, they would love him. They would *want* to give him their hats. He massaged his temples and searched his past for any and all fish affection he could think of. He'd had a goldfish as a boy, that was something, wasn't it? He'd always enjoyed films about people helping whales be free. As a teenager he'd practically *lived* on fish and chips.

"What are you doing?" asked Merle.

"I'm getting into character!" John answered through gritted teeth. "Okay, fine. Fine. Okay. Here I go."

He breathed and stepped down the mucky bank.

The merrow women flinched, and one moved as if to dive into the water. But John walked with his arms wide, hands open, his face a beatific Get Well Soon card to the universe.

"What treasures!" he said, and beamed them a smile that could be seen from space. "What treasures have washed ashore! And here I thought one had to dive to find pearls."

The merrows exchanged glances. None of them said anything in return, but neither did they swim away, even as John drew slowly closer. One smiled, shyly. A second even giggled. All of them began to fuss in some way with their hair, pushing it back behind their webbed ears or combing it with their clamshell fingernails.

"Ladies." John went down on one knee in the mud and bowed his head. Then he raised it slightly, looked up at each of them with lifted brow, did that thing where his jaw muscles clenched just a little like he had to bite down to keep from crying for joy to the heavens and so forth. All the stuff he'd perfected the year he'd done the Australian soap opera. Now the merrows were all grinning, and one of them made sort of a dolphin noise.

"What . . . what is your name, landsman?" asked one of the merrows.

"I am John. I travel with my elderly and mute and also unfortunately simpleminded father, who rests not far off. And you are of course right to call me a landsman, though I long to explore the beauty of the deep waters

of the lakes of the world."

"*Aw,*" said another merrow.

He wasn't using contractions all of a sudden, thought John. Why wasn't he using contractions? "Is it beautiful, beneath the waves? Tell me, please, so that I may describe it to my brainless and often gassy father."

"Hey!" came a faint shout from the trees. The merrows craned their necks to look until John did sort of a puckery thing with his lips and got them to refocus. So they told him about the inky blue beauty of their home, the easy rhythms of the water weeds and grasses, the corals and sponges that had tumbled in centuries ago, afire with magic they'd absorbed from the Gloria Wall. They told him of the sea monster in Scotland that never left its cave because it didn't believe in itself. They described the silver schools of fish that moved like one body and arranged themselves, just twice a year, into arcane symbols that none could decipher. They told him which fish they thought were stuck up and which ones could be really popular if they weren't always camouflaging themselves all the time.

John listened patiently, nodding, hoping one of the merrows would get around to suggesting what he wanted, all on her own. And indeed, eventually one said, "You know, I have a spare cap in my grotto. I could make a gift of it to you—then you could see these splendors with your own eyes!" She gasped as if she'd surprised herself.

John pretended to really perk up at this. Could he really? One of the merrows with both cap and cape pointed out that *she* really only needed one or the other, so she could give John the hat right off her head. A small squabble erupted over who would give him what. In the midst of this, he sighed heavily and turned all their heads.

"What is it?" said a merrow. "What ails you?"

"Oh . . . just . . . any experience beneath the waves would be a hollow one if I could not share it with my halfwit father, who is not long for this world."

So it was quickly decided that John would be given not one but *two* caps, and also an enchanted comb made from a conch shell. When pressed, the merrow who'd given the comb admitted that it wasn't so much *magic* as it was merely the only thing she'd had on her person at the moment, but John thanked her extravagantly anyway. Then he brought Merle out ("Oh, he's just as you described," said one merrow), and they took up places by the water.

"Where's Finchbriton?" whispered John.

"Zippered up inside my bag."

"Are these bags waterproof?"

"'Bout to find out. But he's in the ziplock with the flare gun."

"We'd better hurry, then."

John blew kisses to the merrows, which they made a great show of pretending to catch in their webbed hands and then devour, noisily. It was disturbing.

The men put on their caps. "So what do we do, exactly?" asked John.

"Okay, I think . . . I think this door, if there is a door, will be right in the middle of the lake," said Merle. "So I think we have to, like, dive in, and if we *think* about the middle of the bottom of the lake, then I think the caps will take us there. And then we find the door, and I think we have to *think* about where we want it to take us, and then we open it and *bam*! We're there."

"Do you know what word I noticed a lot of in that plan?"

"Relax. What do people say in your movies? 'It'll work. It *has* to.' Plans always work after the character says that."

"Do we have to hold our breath with the caps on?"

"Better hold it just to be safe."

"On three?"

One, two, three, and then they breathed, and dove.

CHAPTER 28

John's head surfaced first, then Merle's. Each gasped for air, then Merle scrambled up this new shore as quickly as his old joints would allow and unzipped his bag, then the ziplock. Finchbriton fluttered out, drowsily. He landed a few feet away and fluffed himself.

They looked at the marsh around them, the shroud of mist, the bandy-rooted and bare-limbed trees like the taut-skinned mummies of things that had tried to struggle free from the mire. Frogs chirped and croaked. The air smelled like rotten apples.

"Avalon," said John. "Mick said this place was supposed to be nice."

The plan with the caps had worked better than it had any right to. As soon as they'd hit water their bodies had been whisked downward, spiraling through a flurry of bubbles, to the bottom of the lake. The whole trip took all of two seconds, and that was fine—had it been slower, or had there been fewer bubbles, John and Merle might have been aware of all the colossal eels, or the one merrow who was as large as a submarine, or the fish with the pincushion teeth, or even the moment when their trajectory actually took them *through* the coils of a sea serpent and past its jagged jaws.

But they'd had no idea. They reached bottom, squinted about through the murk for an exit while entirely failing to notice the octoclops barreling down on them, swam over to a pearly door set into a tall stone amidst the weeds, and stepped through, thinking, *Avalon*.

"Well," said Merle, looking at Avalon now. "I haven't been *here* in a long time. Not properly."

They scuttled up to a felled tree and crouched in among the roots. John couldn't help looking at most trees a little suspiciously ever since one had tried to kill him, so a dead specimen like this was sort of a comfort.

He wondered if it was the gloom of this place or merely the fact that the two of them were dripping swamp water that made Merle shiver just then.

"First time I came to Avalon was also the first time I met Nimue, actually," the old man said as he twisted around to survey the island, the sweep of the hill dotted here and there by stones and caves. Dreary as it was, at least he could get his bearings. The place he'd visited in

Somerset back on earth had barely looked anything like this. "It was one of Arthur's early misadventures. He'd gotten himself wounded and his sword broken fighting this enormous knight named Pellinore."

"This was before Arthur was king?"

"Nah, he was king already."

"Why was he fighting Pellinore, then?" asked John.

"Oh, the usual. I don't remember the specifics. A squire or a damsel rushes into the great hall of the king to tattle on some bad knight who's knocking down other knights and taking their lunch money. So the king . . . does what? Tries him in court? 'Course not. One guy goes out to beat him up. Maybe kill him. No talking, no trying to reason with anyone. Just the juvenile belief that the guy who gets beaten somehow lost the argument. Whoever wins the fight is right, and whoever's right wins the fight. I tried to point out that whoever wins the fight might just be lucky or do more push-ups than the other guy, but I never got a lot of traction with that.

"Anyway, the first guy Arthur sends to fight Pellinore doesn't do so hot, so Arthur sneaks off to fight Pellinore himself. And does pretty well, but eventually he's going to die if I don't rush in and put Pellinore to sleep."

"And no one ever thinks to send, like, a posse out?" asks John. "A proper police arrest?"

"Please. It was like high school with swords. All the

cool kids, the rich kids, sitting at the big round cool kids' table. Acting like the serfs don't exist. Racing around, playing chicken with spears. Every one of them with some tragic, heroic opinion of himself. It was the adolescence of man."

"Was it really as bad as all that?" said John. "Didn't Arthur bring law and order to England or something?"

"Oh, sure, mostly. It was *much* worse before Arthur came along. Arthur practically invented chivalry. Honor, and protection of the weak. Each noble knight must be willing to lay down his life in service to those less fortunate than himself. Funny how they still managed to almost completely ignore all the farmers and poor people, though."

On all the island there was only one footpath that looked well worn, and it led up to a vault of granite that protected a shaft into the hillside. Merle and John and Finchbriton scrambled closer and staked it out over the edge of a shelf of stones.

"So what does Pellinore and all this have to do with Nimue and Avalon?" whispered John.

"Well, I take Arthur away to heal up at an abbey, and remember, his sword is broken. So I know this is the time in the story where I take him to a particular lake and a particular lady offers him a new one."

"Oh, right."

● ○ ★

They traveled, Arthur and Merlin, like pilgrims to the lake of Avalon. It looked much sweeter then, but no less mysterious. Mists still hung low and thick as carded wool, but these were often spun by sunlight into brightly colored tissue that robed the island like a fine mantle.

And in the water they saw a milk-white arm, around which was wrapped the band of a scabbard, and the hand of which held the finest sword ever forged by man or fairy.

Arthur inhaled sharply. "I would give my kingdom for such a sword," he said.

"Jeez," said Merle. "Keep your voice down. Somebody might hold you to that."

"The sword Excalibur," spoke someone new, and they found they'd been joined on the shore by a stunning young woman with hair like a moonless sky. It seemed to

please her that this hair be still, but that her pallid gown sailed and slipped on a breeze that touched no other nearby thing. "Do you like it?"

"I like it very well," Arthur answered, "and I would bring much worship to the Isle of Avalon, were I allowed to wield it in your name."

"Hmm," said Nimue, and she poked out her lip. "But if I give you my sword, I'm left just a lake with an empty arm in it. You see my predicament."

"I vow I shall return it to this lake before I die, lady."

"See that you do," said the Lady of the Lake, and just then a small boat drifted to shore through the mists.

While it took Arthur to the arm and Excalibur, Merle stayed with the lady and looked her over. Unless he'd misread the stories, this was the woman who would one day pretend to be his girlfriend and trap him in a cave under the earth. Well, she was a looker, so he could think of worse things.

"Your name's Nimue, right?"

"And you are Merlin," said Nimue. "I've been following your career for some time."

"I'm flattered. So what's your game here? Giving Arthur a free sword? And I know you've been raising Lancelot, and that you're gonna send him to be one of Arthur's knights. His *greatest* knight, a good man, and yet more than anything, it's Lance that's going to end up tearing the kingdom apart."

"Ah, yes," Nimue purred. "This fantastic gift you have for foresight. We Fay get the odd flash now and then, you know—but nothing like this talent of yours. You really must tell me one day how you accomplish it. You *must.*"

Arthur was just now returning with sword and scabbard, trying to look solemn and dignified when you could tell what he really wanted to do was swing his new toy around and stab trees. And it was best that they get out of there before Merle said something stupid. He never had learned how to talk to girls. They bowed and said their good-byes, and turned toward Camelot.

"So, uh . . . which do you like better?" Merle asked Arthur later. "The sword or its scabbard?"

The young king examined them both. The scabbard was golden, inlaid with silver and stones. Very nice. But the sword was magnificent. "The sword," said Arthur.

"You should like the scabbard, actually. 'Cause anyone who wears it will never bleed, no matter how badly he's cut."

Arthur was impressed. "The sword cleaves, the scabbard protects."

"Yeah. Really—don't lose the scabbard," Merle told him, knowing he would, knowing that story was already written.

John and Merle and Finchbriton dashed to the vaulted entrance of the mine. They couldn't hear anything, couldn't see any signs of life, so there was nothing for it but to plunge downward. The shaft was dimly lit, though there were no visible sources of light. The tunnel was wide enough for four men to walk abreast, and only about seven feet tall, which was itself a kind of relief—the low ceiling really cut down on the variety of Fay that could be coming and going through here.

At the end the tunnel forked, and they heard a sharp voice approaching from the right, so they ducked into the tunnel on the left. They watched as a scarlet-cloaked and hooded woman emerged, flanked by tiny figures in robes, and continued up the main corridor to the cave entrance.

". . . *you* try to tell the largest dragon in all the isles what she can and can't eat. I say, 'Saxbriton, do you want to stay *cooped up* in this mountain till *YOU DIE*, or do you want to slim down to whale weight and go conquer the universe?' Stupid!"

"MAH," said one of the little robed people.

"Right. Whatever. Anyway, she's an angel for two or three weeks and then she gets depressed and eats a whole orphanage."

When these Fay were out of earshot, John and Merle and Finchbriton stole into the tunnel from which they'd come and followed it into a small chamber made up like a proper bedroom. Oil lamps, chairs with poufy cushions, a lion tapestry on one wall. And asleep on a bed in the center of the room, the Queen of England.

"Huh," said Merle.

"Huh," John agreed. "So. Did you think she was going to look like *that*?"

CHAPTER 29

Scott could see the elves trying to size him up as he passed through the wide hall—who was this stranger with the leprechaun, in the company of Titania's most favorite? Was he changeling or human? They'd appraise his clothes, his glamour (or lack of it), and have a flustered little moment of panic. Had they miscalculated? Was boring the new interesting? Were they all to look like smelly highwaymen now? No, they dismissed their fear finally with a wave. The boy was just some charity case.

"*Is that the Finchfather?*" said one, a tall elf whose hairline grew birch-wood saplings. He and his compatriot kept pace with the party as it walked.

> "*Methinks it is.*
> *Must this one then beside him be the finch?*"

"Does yonder one resemble selfsame finch?"

"Well, sure I am 'tis not impossible.
Perhaps in time a finch becomes a boy.
Forsooth a finch was not a finch at first—
But does the bird resemble then the egg?
Do crops bear semblance to the excrement
From which they bloom? What majesty might grow
up from the filth that presently walks past!"

The elves enjoyed their joke and shared it with whomever would listen.

"Jester tryouts today?" Mick grumbled.

Scott leaned over to Mick. "Did the tall one just call me poop?"

He wondered if it was magic or just nerves that made this hallway seem longer on the inside than it looked on the outside. They passed winged sprites that flitted about like hummingbirds; dwarfs and gnomes; Scandinavian trolls like bent tubers, massive and shaggy with roots; a rail-thin Hindu who kept his head in a birdcage and fed it apple; a woman made entirely of flowers and leaves that reminded Scott of something awful Emily had done to a Freeman a few months ago; a fairy who was like a well-dressed man with the head of a goat; another Scott would have liked to have called a well-dressed goat with

the head of a man, though in fairness it was really more of a fawn; a column of smoke that Scott assumed was a column of smoke until Dhanu paused to bow to it before passing. Each of these persons and others gave the impression of having had nothing to talk about for the last thousand years, so they seemed glad to see Mick and Scott happen by.

Then Scott and Mick and their changeling escorts reached a pair of intricately carved doors that opened on their own, bleeding light, and they stepped inside the throne room of the High Queen of the Fay.

It was like a chapel, a cathedral, with a dark colonnade to the right and left that shined at the edges, outlining every column and arch. A runner of white marble divided the room up the middle like a spill of cream, and a throng of fairy courtiers stood to either side of it, against the walls, like at certain middle-school dances Scott had been to. It parted ways with a typical middle-school dance crowd due to the sheer number of swords and axes everyone seemed to be carrying.

It reminded him, actually, of every throne room scene of every movie he'd ever watched, where you wondered just what everybody had been doing *before* the strangers came in. Talking quietly? Waiting in line to sit on the queen's lap? Whatever it was, they'd all stopped it in favor of staring silently at Scott and Mick, judging them so scathingly that Scott thought it might set his hair on fire.

But honestly, the first thing Scott saw upon entering, before the axes even, was Titania.

Her throne was a crescent of columns at the end of that spill of cream, framed by rich tapestries and embellished with a carving of a dragon biting a lion on the neck. Atop the crescent was an alabaster dish, and she sat lightly on that dish like a pearl on an oyster.

There was nothing about Titania that was not unnerving.

Her skin was nearly as white as the marble, with a blush of pink at the cheeks, the eyes, the lips, the knees. Her limbs were a touch too long, slightly too slender, and arranged just so out of the confectionery folds of her prom dress. The whole of her body was just too large to be human, but that struck Scott as a whim—she might awake tomorrow with the proportions of a doll, or eat something for supper that disagreed with her and swell up like Alice.

She lowered her head, gave Scott full view of her high-browed face with its strange mix of vixen and child.

Dhanu bowed low. Mick did, too, so Scott followed suit. Then the changeling said to everyone assembled,

> *"Behold her grace, my gift and godmother:*
> *Our kingdom dies for love of this, its queen."*

He turned to Titania.

"*The fickle stars have quit for jealousy;*
The hidden moon retires to gaze at you."

Titania smiled faintly and fanned her fingers at him, an "Oh, *you*," sort of gesture. Dhanu continued.

"*I bring today two children of the Fay—*
Two wan'dring sons I've sworn will see no harm
By compact with the changelings of the guard."

Dhanu stepped aside, and suddenly it seemed like Scott and Mick's turn to speak. Scott thought he understood how to handle this Titania: talk fancy and kiss her butt. He just needed to *want* her attention. He just had to want to be the golden boy (that's how Mick had put it once), and whatever natural glamour he possessed would rise up to the surface. He had more glamour than Dhanu. His *dad* was a *movie star*. He could do this.

"Your Majesty, High Queen Titania," he said. "I would speak with thee about a great—"

Mick elbowed him in the shin. The peanut gallery tittered. Titania herself inclined her head a matter of degrees, a minuscule gesture that made Scott want to crawl into his own pocket. What had he done?

"I *said* no puttin' on airs," whispered Mick.

Titania spoke, with a voice that sounded like something musical turning inside your head.

> *They laugh at phantoms; ghosts; a word misheard.*
> *They thought you called us 'thee,' but that's absurd.*
> *Or are you now our lord? We had not known—*
> *How thrilling! Let us help you to your throne.*"

Scott could have *sworn* words like "thee" and "thou" were fancy talk. He'd have to ask Mick about it later. And was Titania seriously rhyming? He glanced around, but it didn't seem to be bothering anybody else.

Then a little elf maid approached and tried to offer Scott a glass of cordial, and he was forced to sing "Froggie Went a-Courtin'" until she went away again.

The hall felt chilly. Scott sighed and bowed once more at Titania.

"I'm not your lord. It . . . looks like I'm your jester," he told her, remembering what Mick said earlier. "I'm sorry. I come from a very different place, and I don't think that's the last mistake I'm going to make. But I mean no offense, High Queen."

Mick gave him a smile and a nod before Titania answered.

> *"Well said—our changeling cousin knows his place.*
> *Return you to your thoughts, and plead your case."*

This rhyming—it was like talking to someone who has food on her chin. Scott could barely concentrate on what she was saying.

"Um. I want to . . . I want . . ." Scott breathed. "I've heard rumors of a fairy invasion of Earth. I think you've been told maybe that humans split our world off from all the magic and the Fay on purpose, so I've come here to tell you it isn't true. I know people say Merle . . . Merlin is responsible for the split, for the Gloria, but we don't think that's true either."

The Fay murmured at this. Scoffed.

"He was really worried it was all his fault, honestly," Scott insisted. "But . . . well, I know him, actually, and we've investigated it and this whole thing's a big misunderstanding."

> *"Of course! The fault is ours for being blind.*
> *When man in ancient times behav'd unkind*
> *And stole from us the lands we'd held above*
> *How could we doubt he played but games of love?"*

"Um—"

"And absence made your hearts grow ever ripe!
You slandered us with fables, tales, and tripe—
How mystical we were! How fierce and fine!
Yet tame to hide our flame and keep in line."

Scott shifted from foot to foot. "With . . . with respect, I think humans have changed a lot since then."

"How true—once fate deprived you of the elves,
You humans turned your swords upon yourselves.
How swiftly did you newly fantasize
Of tribes to conquer, then romanticize.
Our Nimue has told me of the wars
O'er Africans, red Indians, and Moors?
You cast us each like actors in the parts
Of all the best and worst in thine own hearts."

Scott thought this might be kind of an oversimplification, but he didn't want to debate history with a woman who had lived through most of it. And *she* got to say thine! How come *he* didn't get to say things like thine? Whatever.

"You're definitely not wrong," he said. "Humans are bad at dealing with things they don't understand. So we tell stories. That's what humans do, is tell stories. I think it's what we do instead of magic."

More murmuring around the hall, but a good kind of murmuring. Thoughtful.

"But I also think . . . in the centuries since we've lost real magic, and the Fay . . . I think we've gone a little crazy. I mean, glamour used to only mean a kind of fairy magic, I guess, but now humans look for glamour wherever they can get it. We look for magic in movies and clothes and stuff, and in believing that certain people can have a kind of glamour. My dad's one of these kinds of people. We treat them like they're more than human, but they're not, so they always let us down."

The room was quiet, really quiet. He thought Titania was ever so slowly leaning forward.

"If the Fay come to Earth," Scott told her, "they won't have to invade. We'll worship you anyway. I'm sure of it. There are already a dozen magazines in every supermarket checkout lane waiting to do it, a hundred cable shows, a thousand websites. Maybe . . . maybe you don't know what those things are, but . . . won't it be better if you don't have to rule us? Won't it be better if we just give you our love?"

> "And does my new young friend not understand?
> We cannot simply stride from land to land.
> For ev'ry elf that parts this shrinking sphere,
> Some wretched soul must cross from there to here."

"You could trade places with animals!" Scott suggested. "Cows or sheep or something that would be happy to live out its life grazing in a place as beautiful as this."

But here he'd hit a nerve. The elves began to grumble, to make remarks behind their hands. Apparently they found this idea distasteful.

"Or people!" Scott added quickly. "There are seven billion humans on Earth. How many elves and humans here, a few hundred thousand?" He glanced at Mick, and the leprechaun bobbed his head back and forth, then nodded. "They could totally find enough on Earth who would be willing to trade places. You know, just for the adventure of it. Humans do stupid things all the time for adventure; you have no idea. They have this thing called bungee jumping?"

Mick nudged him. "Stay focused," he whispered.

"Well, anyway, humans are short-lived. They'd die naturally anyway before this world disappeared forever."

Scott took a half step forward. What did they call this on lawyer shows? Closing arguments? He thought Titania might even be smiling a little.

"I know about the Fay's famous sense of honor. I don't believe they want to push a whole species down because of the mistakes of the past. You're right that we tell stories about you. Over the years those stories have only gotten . . . kinder, and sweeter. They all have happy endings now. Let's . . . let's write a happy ending together."

That last bit made him want to throw up a little, but he thought it was probably what was called for. Mick gave him a sock in the leg, and when Scott looked down the little man was smiling up at him.

Titania was smiling, too. She was unquestionably smiling.

> *"I must commend you, boy—you've had your say*
> *And honored both your people and the Fay.*
> *And now will I confess I've played a trick:*
> *I know of all your treasons, Scott and Mick."*

"Uh." Scott felt his heartbeat in his stomach. The throne room was suddenly small. Was everyone closer than they'd been a second ago?

"Okay," whispered Mick. "We're banished. We get out quick, get as far away as we can."

Titania glared at Scott now.

> *"You're but a stranger here, so I'll concede*
> *Your plots have not the bite to make me bleed.*
> *But Mick—"*

Here Scott thought he could hear Mick rasping beside him. The little man's eyes might have been damp.

"—the fabled father of the finch.
If fairy folk have hearts, mine feels thy pinch.
And so we'd quite agreed before you came
To strike you from our court and curse your name.
'Twas foolish to surrender to my power—
You had no claim to safety in this tower."

Dhanu gasped and surged forward.

"And why was I not told? I must protest!
Upon my honor was their safety pledged."

Titania clasped her hands together, all girlish smiles
again.

"A necessary falsehood, pet of mine.
I longed to hear this plaything mewl and whine.
Such fun in one so young! Such grace and poise!"

Her fingers tightened.

"A crime, in time I always break my toys."

And the Fay, and those swords, and those axes,
advanced from all sides.

CHAPTER 30

Ms. Aleister walked Polly down halls, elevators, through complicated-looking systems that analyzed retinal patterns and fingerprints and spit for some reason. She waltzed her past all the best security money could buy, and only because she was under the impression that Polly had already been wherever she was being taken.

Ms. Aleister looked like a pretty velociraptor. Her heels sounded against the tile like a raptor's hind claw, *click click*. Ms. Aleister was explaining that little girls sometimes let their imaginations run away with them, that their eyes can play tricks, that what Polly no doubt *thought* she'd seen in Sensitive Research Area Alpha was not what it looked like.

Polly gave Ms. Aleister a dopey smile. "I know that already—daddy's new girlfriend told me it was all special effects, like in the movies."

"Exactly! Daddy's new girlfriend. What did you say her name was?"

"I'll point her out when we get there."

"See that you do. 'Special effects.' Your father's a lucky man—what a smart lady! Too bad she's soon to be unemployed."

"My dad has enough money for all of us."

"And what does he do?"

"Rocket-car test pilot."

"Uh-*huh*."

They reached Sensitive Research Area Alpha, which was in a wing labeled MICROFICHE ARCHIVE 1940–1959 and plastered with notices that it was shortly to be fumigated for earwigs. To pass through this door, Ms. Aleister had to press her hand against a little mirror on the wall. A green light flashed above the door, then a red.

"C'mon," said the woman, "you too. Fairy detector. You must have done it this morning."

Polly edged forward. Was she enough of a changeling to set this off? "Didn't realize I had to do it every time."

"That's why it's a security system, and not a hand stamp. This isn't the county fun fair."

Polly put her fingers, then her palm against the cold glass. She felt a buzz. All was silent for a moment.

"Got a slight blip off you," said Ms. Aleister. "Very faint. That's odd."

"Daddy's girlfriend said it's been doing that all week."

Polly concentrated and tried to push the fairyness down inside her. She imagined she was Scott—staying home on Halloween; doing sudoku puzzles; eating lunch alone in the library.

The lights above the door flashed green, and the door clicked open.

Inside was a wide and vaulted octagonal room lit up with a branching system of radial florescent tubes like a neon snowflake. There was a small team of researchers (three women, two men) who paused and looked up at the unexpected visitors. There were cases and refrigerators holding vials and samples of chemicals, work stations and computers and miles and miles of cables. And against one wall, cages holding a royal-looking elf and a manticore.

The former was easy to recognize: tall and lean and stately, even as it sat forlornly on the concrete floor in a hospital gown. A foxlike face with large and tapered ears and ginger hair. The latter was something Polly would have to ask about later—she didn't know what a manticore was. But the caged thing had a scorpion's tail on a wasted lion's body, with a nearly human face, and a disconcertingly wide mouth so packed with teeth they were growing in sideways.

Next to the manticore's cage there was a massive, windowless reinforced steel vault painted to say DANGER:

RONOPOLISK. Something huge kept whanging against the door from the inside.

In one corner was a small tank filled with a thick pink liquid. Milk-7. Interesting.

But most interesting was the table near the center of the room, the table with the yellow plastic hamster cage and the Habitrail, because inside this were three pixies.

One prince paced a rut through the wood chips. Another was shirtless, his tunic drying over a tunnel entrance. There were plastic tunnels to three separate sleeping quarters, and dishes of food and water. There was even a hamster wheel, and the last of the princes was running it. Which seemed kind of demeaning to Polly, but she supposed they had to keep fit somehow. It came to her suddenly that they had to go to the bathroom somewhere too, and she looked away quickly before she found it.

"All right," said Ms. Aleister, arms akimbo. "Who's responsible for this kid?"

Of course nobody volunteered anything. They glanced at one another, trying to decipher the situation. Maybe this was a surprise team-building exercise.

"Come on, come on. The longer you string this out, the worse it'll be for you."

Polly moved closer to these people in lab coats, under the pretext of giving them a closer look at her. But what she was really doing was getting closer to that hamster cage.

"I don't understand, ma'am," said one of the scientists as he watched Polly. "Is she a test subject?"

"Oh, for heaven's sake, shut *up*," said Ms. Aleister. And while she had everyone's attention like that for a moment, Polly stretched out her sleeve and released Prince Fi onto the table with his brothers. Then she walked swiftly away. "Girl!" Ms. Aleister continued. "Anni . . . Ann . . . What was your name again?"

"Anastasia de la Taco."

"Just point to your daddy's girlfriend so we can fire her and leave."

"What's this?" Polly asked, picking up the first thing she could get ahold of. Which turned out to be a beaker, and Ms. Aleister told her so. "I can make it stay over my mouth," Polly said, and she held it there with suction.

"Little girl—"

"How many things can I stick to my face?" Polly tested her question by circling the lab, snatching objects at random and affixing them, or trying to affix them, to her cheeks and forehead. A metal washer. Litmus paper. A cell phone, a test tube, a public-radio coffee mug. Some clattered to the floor, or even broke. "My mom says I have 'combination skin.'"

The manticore seemed to chuckle, gruffly.

"Seize the girl," said Ms. Aleister, and you could sort of tell it wasn't the first time she'd said it.

Polly had maneuvered her way to the Milk-7 tank, however, and as the scientists moved on her, she spun the spigot. The goopy pink stuff spilled out onto the floor.

"Pretty!" she squealed. "Strawberry! Food fight!" Then she kicked a spray of the Milk at the advancing researchers. They recoiled as if vampires before holy water. Then Polly moved to an adjacent refrigerator and grabbed a test tube of something yellow. "Ooh, what's this?"

"It's an antidote for children who've grown extra fingers and toes," said a scientist. "Please put it down."

Polly poured the liquid into the pink milk. "What do yellow and pink make?" she asked, then frowned. The answer, apparently, was lightning.

Now the adults were really panicking. A jet of steam rose from where Polly had mixed the chemicals, and some kind of detector started beeping. Ceiling sprinklers activated, and the lights in the room turned red. Everyone rushed for the door as a serious-looking barricade began to slide down in front of it.

"Girl!" shouted Ms. Aleister. "Hurry!"

But Polly made no attempt to escape the room. The emergency door slid into place with a thump and a hiss, and now there was two inches of steel between her and the adults, apart from a little window bricked up with

Plexiglas. They stared at her through the little window, the scientists and Ms. Aleister, shouting silently. Polly found some tape and covered it over with a piece of notebook paper.

Before long Polly found a set of keys, and when the elf was free he kissed Polly's hand while struggling to keep his gown closed in the back. He thanked her graciously while Fi heaved open a hatch on the hamster cage and lowered a string of rubber bands down to his brothers.

The elf appeared to be about to say something as Polly tried key after key in the lock of the manticore's cage, but he checked himself. He nonetheless urged her not to release the ronopolisk.

"I would sooner face a cockatrice, a basilisk, and a catoblepas all at once than fight one ronopolisk," he insisted.

"You're making up words," Polly told him. The door of the manticore's cage clicked open, and the devil beast rubbed against Polly's shoulder as it passed.

"Human girl," it purred. "Though I am hungry, I shan't eat you." He said it like it was a pretty big compliment.

"Thanks."

The sprinklers were cleansing the room and sending the toxic mess down a drain in the middle. The manticore hunched and looked as miserable as any wet cat. Fi introduced Polly to his brothers.

"Denzil, Fo, and Fee, this is the Lady Polly Esther Doe." The princes bowed deeply.

"This was a gallant rescue, brother, Lady Polly," said Denzil, the oldest. "But I fear while we pixies might clinch our escape, those larger than we are doomed."

"I will be proud to die fighting," said the elf, "and will relish destroying as much of this infernal apothecary as I can."

But Fi was watching Polly, and Polly was peering at the refrigerator where she had found the yellow test tube.

"You are thinking," said Fi. "You are hatching plans. I know this because my stomach hurts."

"Goodco did all kinds of weird experiments on kids, I hear," said Polly. "That's what made Biggs big and hairy—some chemical they invented. But he said something once, when we were on the cruise—he said the chemical didn't make everyone big and hairy, just the boys."

"So it did not work on the girls," said Fi.

"No," said Polly, "it made them *smaller*."

"That does not follow. Just because—"

"That's why I'm going to drink some of the same chemical Biggs drank, and I'll get to be the size of a pixie!"

The sprinklers had stopped. The red light had extinguished. Polly crossed back to the fridge.

"You cannot do this!" Fi insisted. "I believe it to be

dangerous." But Fi was trapped on a counter, far from Polly. "Brothers," he said, "help me."

Polly heaved the fridge open again and began pushing around little racks of test tubes. "Emily is always going on about how Goodco doesn't know about any big rifts," she said. "Right? Except that one in Antarctica, but nothing ever goes in or out of it. They don't know where it connects to in Pretannica. That's why the rift in Mr. Wilson's house is so special—regular-sized people can go through it. But if Goodco can't usually send regular-sized people through rifts, then how'd they get the Queen of England through?"

"Nimue forced *her* way through," Fi reminded her. "With witchcraft."

"Yeah, and it nearly killed her, it was so hard. So of *course* they shrank the queen down to tiny size to get her through one of the small rifts. Duh." Polly uncorked a vial of something clear and fizzy.

"Please remember, if you drink the potion that grows finger and toes, that you've already flushed the antidote," says Fi.

Polly swallowed a bit of the liquid. Just a bit. It didn't have a flavor, per se. It tasted a little like the smell of a new raincoat? Or like anger? It was hard to explain. Anyway, she otherwise tried to report that nothing had happened, but nothing happened. She'd entirely lost her voice.

"A most heartrending tragedy," said Fee.

Polly scrambled for an antidote and swallowed something blue, and her voice returned—albeit hoarse and squeaky like she'd been sucking helium and screaming.

The emergency gate was starting to come up. *I need more time!* Polly squealed.

Fi sighed and asked elf and manticore to take him and his brothers to the gate. The manticore and elf braced their hands and paws on metal handles and strained to keep it closed, while Fi jabbed with his sword at any hands that appeared under the gate from the other side.

"An elf and pixies and a manticore fighting as brothers," said the elf. "What a rare death."

"A good death," growled the manticore. "I am old. I had cubs I will never again see. I am ready to die with blood in my teeth."

Polly twisted every sample around in its container, trying to make sense of their labels. "Just another minute!" she squawked.

The elf smirked down at Fi. "Who gives the orders here, pigsie? She is but a human girl."

"Yet see what she has done today," Fi answered. "Is she not something?"

"Fi!" Polly shouted. "I drank another one and

something went pop! Can you look?" She hiked up her shirt in the back.

"You have tiny wings."

"I HAVE TINY WINGS? I wonder if I can flap them! Are they moving now? What about now? I don't know which muscles to push."

"We'll find you the antidote," says Fi.

"No we won't. Oh, listen! My voice is going back down."

"Polly, hurry!"

"She is *something*," said the elf.

"The pixies have a story," Fi continued. "You would not know it. But we say that the Spirit, the Spirit that made all things, and who separated good from evil, is reborn from time to time into a mortal person. And that this person cannot help but be remarkable. Remarkable, but not necessarily good."

"An old story," Denzil agreed as heavy-heeled footsteps thundered up to the gate. "The mortal Spirit must decide, as each of us does in turn, what is right and what is wrong. And in this way good and evil is redefined, and the world remade. But the story says the Spirit is born into a pixie, brother."

Fo said, "You don't think this girl is—"

Fi shook his head, and laughed, and speared a scientist's hand. "I think it's a story. You know I do not hold with such things, brothers. If anything, I think we might all be born with a little Spirit in us, pixie and human and elf alike, and we are each the bumbling makers of our own folly. But still and all, the girl—she might be remarkable, might she not?"

"Everyone?" said Polly. They turned to see a two-foot-tall girl, blanketed by her own clothes. "I found it, didn't I? Just a little bit more."

Fi and his brothers rushed to her as she sipped a little bit more of the liquid she'd found. When they'd traipsed through folds of pants and jacket, they found a pixie-sized seven-year-old, pulling a vastly oversized shirt around her. Fi passed her his topcoat, and she ducked down under the shirt collar with it. When she came up again, they saw that it made a fine little dress.

The elf and manticore were tiring. The gate was coming up by inches.

"I wish we could help you more," Polly told them.

"You've done more than you know," said the elf. "You're a changeling, aren't you, girl? A little agent of sacred chaos. I am your servant."

"Then you might lift us to that air vent," said Fi. "We are ready to leave."

"We're all going to leave this place," growled the manticore. "We are all of us going to leave this place, one way or another."

CHAPTER 31

Merle and John stood in the velvety bedroom chamber, over the tiny canopy bed in which slept the tiny Queen of England. She wore a tiny nightgown. They'd fashioned her a tiny pair of slippers.

"No wonder they made the queen on the Clobbers box look like Mick," said Merle. "They're the same height."

"She looks good otherwise though, right?" asked John. "Well rested."

"I bet they've had her asleep ever since she came here. An enchanted sleep."

John massaged his jaw. "Do you think we have to kiss her?"

"I don't think there's any 'we' about it. Knight of the Realm, seems like your duty."

"I'm . . . going to try the forehead first and work my way inward," said John. He leaned in.

"Now if you feel yourself about to punch her," said Merle, "just step back and count to ten."

"Shh."

John kissed her little forehead and straightened again. Nothing happened immediately, so he was just thinking, *All right, cheek then,* when she woke and trained her eyes on his.

"You're that pop star we knighted," she said creakily. Her throat was probably pretty dry. "I thought you were too young, but my advisers thought it would be good for public relations. You appear rather larger than I remember."

"We have a lot to explain to you, Your Majesty," said John. "And not a lot of time. But first and foremost, it is fundamentally important that you get inside this backpack."

Scott and Mick sat on the cold floor of a little bell-shaped cell high above the ground. There was nothing for light but a single cross-slit hole in the wall and a tiny torchlit window in the door. Just enough to see the occasional dim shape that you'd mistaken for a stone suddenly lift itself up from its torpor, shuffle a few inches, and die.

"Prison sucks," said Scott. "They make it look like fun on TV, but it secretly sucks."

"Try to at least have a sense o' pride abou' it," said

Mick. "Yeh're a prisoner o' the *Tower o' London*. There's none more famous jail."

"Alcatraz."

"No sense o' history," Mick grumbled.

In a way, Scott did not so much mind the dim light—it concealed his red eyes. In the darkness Scott wished to be comforted. He wanted, not to put too fine a point on it, his mommy. He would never admit as much to Mick, however, so instead he said, "Eleven months until Mom comes back."

"So 'tis."

"No matter . . . no matter what happened, whether we won or lost, I thought at least I'd be there when she reappeared. But now maybe—"

"We'll be there, lad. Somehow. I always escape my cages, 'ventually."

"You know," said Scott, "in Arthurian stories they got thrown in cells like this all the time. Arthur and Lancelot and the rest."

"How'd *they* get out?"

"Pretty girls would let them out in exchange for favors, mostly."

They watched the window of the cell door as if that might be some damsel's cue, but none was forthcoming.

"You ever hear Merle tell about how he got out of his prison under the earth?" asked Scott. "The one all the stories say Nimue put him in?"

"Don't think so."

"He knew she was gonna do it, and he knew he couldn't really stop her from doing whatever she wanted. So he found a cave on Avalon with a tunnel he could dig out that led far away, and had a back door. And one day, when he and Nimue were still acting all smoochy, they went by this cave, and he told her, 'Oh no! I'm getting a vision that I'm doomed to die in that cave! But how could anything bad happen to me on Avalon?'"

"Heh." Mick chuckled. "Smart man. Nimue wouldn't want to spoil the story."

"Right. So she 'trapped' him right where he wanted, and he could work on his second time machine, the one for Arthur, in peace."

They fell silent. After a few minutes of this, Scott decided there may be nothing quieter than two people not talking to each other in a dark room in a tower they can't leave. If they weren't careful, they might just forget how to speak altogether, and the decades would pass without notice, and Scott would be dead ten years before Mick mentioned, *"Yeh've been awful quiet."*

"He gets a weird look on his face sometimes when he talks about the old days," said Scott. "Merle, I mean."

"I'll bet he does do."

"He almost even talks like he and Nimue cared for each

other a little bit. But how could he like her? She's awful."

Mick said, "Ah, love she's a python/she'll pull yeh in snug/an' yeh'll die with a sigh/'cause yeh think it's a hug."

"Did you just make that up?"

"Aye."

"I'm gonna let my mom give me the boy-girl talk, if that's okay with you."

"Aye."

"Thing is, maybe Nimue actually cared for Merle a little too? 'Cause he asked her for a final favor before she sealed him in, and she actually did it. It starts out as one of those Arthur-in-prison stories, actually."

"Any useful tips?"

"Mmm . . . no."

"Well, tell it anyway."

"Okay, you know Morgan le Fay hated her half-brother Arthur, right?"

"Hoo, yeah. Pretty li'l changeling, but she was always barking."

"Well, she manages to snare Arthur in this enchantment while he's out hunting. He wakes up, doesn't understand what's happened, but he's in the dungeon of this real nasty knight named Damas.

"Damas is feuding with his brother, Ontzlake, and needs a champion to do his fighting for him because he's

334

a coward. So a pretty girl comes to the prison—"

"Natcherly."

"—and tells Arthur that Damas will let him go if he fights Ontzlake's champion. So Arthur agrees, and Morgan le Fay, pretending to be the good sister, sends him his sword Excalibur and its scabbard. But they're both fakes. She sends the real ones to Ontzlake's champion, Sir Accolon.

"The day comes, and everybody's gathered to watch. Arthur and Accolon both fight bravely, and both score a lot of hits. But Accolon can't bleed because he has the magic scabbard, and meanwhile his sword is the best in the world. Arthur's sword actually *breaks*. But still he won't fall, though he knows there's been some trick. And now Nimue comes and stands at the edge of the crowd, watching."

If there is one thing on which the old stories agree, it's that Nimue did not act right away. She waited and watched as Accolon and Arthur landed still more blows. But only Arthur's wounds bled, and the lawn was dark with his blood. Near to Nimue, a seated woman remarked that it was a wonder the swordless knight could still stand. No one knew who either man was— they wore helmets.

"Fools, both," Nimue muttered, though whether she meant Merlin and Arthur, or Arthur and Accolon, or Merlin and *Nimue*, was a secret she was keeping even from herself.

She didn't kill Merlin. She would never kill, not like that mad Morgan. Now *there's* a girl she should have left at the nunnery—still barely more than a spoiled child, and getting ever harder to control. But no—she didn't kill Merlin. She left his fate to the gods. And to story! The stories that clung to that man, like the stink of every mess he'd ever stepped in. Such a man would have another chapter, surely.

She'd trapped him to protect her interests. The interests of her people.

But oh, his last request, that she rush here and save Arthur. Naturally. And humans say the *Fay* are overdramatic.

Nimue sighed. *"Fine,"* she said, and waved her hand just as Accolon was about to shamefully slay the weaponless king. The fact that her timing made for the best possible story was not lost on her. By her magic arts, the sword Excalibur fell from Accolon's grasp and landed near Arthur. The young king seized it, and attacked. Nimue didn't stick around for the ending.

After he'd gotten his sword, Arthur snatched back the scabbard. He ceased to bleed, and now Accolon was suddenly bleeding profusely. The contest was over soon, though both men were sorely wounded. Accolon died shortly thereafter.

Arthur was taken to an abbey to heal, where he slept with Excalibur in his arms. But he was careless with the scabbard.

Morgan le Fay stole into the abbey while Arthur slept. Not daring to touch the sword, she snapped up the scabbard and rushed back to her horse. Arthur woke and pursued her with his men, but she ran her horse dead from exhaustion, then alit on the tip of a sawtoothed cliff over the sea. She held the scabbard aloft, and for a moment it was edged with fire against the setting sun. "So sorry, *brother,*" she hissed through clenched teeth as her hair blew ragged around her. "Brother. Brother brother *brother.*" She could hear horses approaching as she threw the scabbard off the cliff into the sea. Then she turned herself to stone.

"He lost the scabbard," repeated Scott. "If he'd kept it, maybe things would . . . I don't know . . . would have turned out different."

"Yeah," said Mick. "Like maybe he never would have gotten in Merle's time machine in the first place, an' the worlds wouldna' have split."

Scott shook his head. "Merle says the time machines didn't cause the split."

"I know what he says. An' I know he needs to believe it. But I don't believe it."

"I wouldn't believe a bit of this," said the Queen of England to Merle and John, "if it weren't for the fire-breathing finch. Nothing better to convince you that you're trapped in a Harry Potter novel than a fire-breathing finch."

"We're not out of the woods yet, Your Majesty," said Merle. "Better keep our voices down."

She shifted in the backpack, unused to keeping her balance while being borne along by a man three times her size. "I shan't argue. But if my continued imprisonment is so important to the . . . fairies' plans, one might expect them to have me a shade better guarded."

"I don't think they believed it possible that anyone from Earth would make it to this world, much less to this cave," said John. Still, he was pretty pleased himself with how well things were going. Then they reached the mouth of the cavern and heard an intake of breath behind them.

They turned. The woman in the scarlet cloak had appeared at the bottom of the passage, and she pulled down her hood to reveal a frizzy mushroom of red curly locks. She was a ginger, a wild-haired, half-feral woman-child.

"Oh, shoot," Merle muttered. "That's Morgan le Fay."

"MEN!" she screamed. "MEN OF ADAM! TAKING THE PRIZE!"

Her scream raked down the corridor like nails on chalkboard, rattling shale loose from the walls and ceiling.

John and Merle stumbled, ears ringing, down the hills of Avalon. Morgan shrieked once more behind them, a keening, birdlike noise. And now the Hairy Men were pouring like roaches from every cave, every hole in the ground, scurrying in clusters, long lines, converging on the interlopers. And all of them appeared to have slings and stones.

"Their caps!" screeched Morgan. "Merrow caps! Don't let them get to the water!" She chanted behind them and swung her arm like she was throwing an imaginary fastball. And where that invisible pitch would have landed, the earth heaved with a seismic belch, flinging John and Merle to the ground in a shower of sod and tossing brownies everywhere.

"She's not one of those killing-is-dishonorable Fay, is she?" John groaned.

In a moment they were completely surrounded. Which was, ironically, the only thing keeping them alive, since the brownies were reluctant to sling stones when they were all facing one another.

"I always suspected I'd die like this," said the queen.

Merle started. "Really?"

"No. Not really. That was something we in Britain call 'humour.'"

"What do you think, Finchbriton?" said John.

The bird winged his way forward and burned them a path through the crowd. The brownies eeked and howled.

"Forget what I've told you!" screamed Morgan. "KILL

THEM ALL! KILL EVEN THE *QUEEN* RATHER THAN LET HER ESCAPE!"

Stones came down, thudding, clanging, cracking against larger stones. John did his best to cover them with the chickadee shield as he brought up the rear. Merle was shouting something about knowing where he was going.

"Oh," Merle said now. "Whoops."

"Whoops *what?*"

"This is . . . my old cave," said Merle, pointing to a pile of boulders. "The one I was, you know, trapped in. I thought we could hide in it, use the old back door. But of course it's collapsed."

They ducked behind a cairn of stones. The brownies' bullets chipped away at the edges of it. The water's brink was maybe a hundred yards away. John tried to remember his better track-and-field times from school.

"Think we can make it?" he asked.

"No, I do not," came the queen's muffled voice in answer. "Don't let's be reckless."

"Well, they're afraid to get too close because of Finchbriton, but there's nothing to keep them from circling around and firing on us from all sides."

In fact, that seemed to occur to the brownies as well. They were starting to skirt a wide perimeter around the stone bunker. Merle dug into his sack and produced his flare gun. He shot a couple flares to either side, and they landed near the advancing brownies, who backed immediately away. The flares didn't burn long on their own, but while they did, they made an odd green light that the Hairy Men could plainly see wasn't natural.

"Well done," said John. "They think we have some kind of magic. Magic ammo. But how long is that going to last?"

Sometime after the flares burned out, the brownies resumed their hesitant advance, so Merle gave them another couple of flares to look at. After that they seemed content to hunker down and sling stones.

Every now and then, some patch of earth exploded. As if Morgan was blindly casting about, not caring who or what she killed.

Another stone landed near them, which was nothing special in and of itself, except that this one was on fire. So was the next. They made the grass smolder and give off a dark smoke.

"Fantastic," said John. "*They* have magic ammo now. Fire ammo."

More flaming stones fell all around. One bounced off the boulders and into Merle's lap, and he hooted, pitched it off quickly, and then sucked on his fingers.

"Is that what magic smells like?" asked the queen. "Smells of paraffin."

Merle peeked over the boulders. "She's right," he said.

"It's not magic—they've got a big vat of kerosene. They're dipping the bullets in it and lighting 'em on fire. Heh. Bet they'd rather not get a flare in it. Get ready to run."

John heard the Hairy Men chattering and a petulant voice joining them from afar.

"Well, I'm here *now*. Morgan le Fay doesn't run for you or anyone."

"Better zip into the sack, Your Majesty," said John. "You too, Finchbriton. When I say so, hold your breath."

"CHILDREN OF ADAM!" Morgan screeched, closer now. "I'M COMING TO RECLAIM THE PRIZE!"

John stole a look and instantly regretted it. Now he'd have the picture of furious Morgan—face like a gash, tramping across the pockmarked and smoldering island while a petrified rain thumped around her—to take to his grave with him.

"Hold on," said Merle. He shot a flare. "Missed."

Morgan sneered at the flare but didn't break stride.

"Missed again," Merle said a second later.

"Give me your flare gun," he told John after firing a third time. "I'm out."

John handed Merle his gun, but as he shifted around, a sling bullet grazed his shoulder.

"YEEEEAAH!"

"Missed again. Are you okay?"

"Erg. *Fine*. Do you want me to do that for you?"

Just then Merle fired a final flare, and it landed in the vat. The kerosene ignited, sending up a bright FOOSH of flame. The Hairy Men scattered, wailing and covering their eyes, and Merle and John raced to the bank and dove beneath the water.

CHAPTER 32

Emily couldn't sleep. She sat up, listened to the old mattress springs bray and creak. Erno was supposed to be watching her, making certain her sleep wasn't disturbed, but there he was, snoring in the chair by the bed. She reached out to where Archie perched on the headboard, and he stepped down onto her arm. Then she tiptoed out of the room and shut the door behind her. She might as well get some work done.

Scott couldn't sleep. He wondered how many hours straight he'd been awake now, in this prison cell. Twenty-four? Thirty?

"How long do you think we've been in here?" he asked Mick.

"Six hours, maybe."

"Six—that's all? Are you sure?"

"No, I amn't sure. I didn't bring my Rolex. Is it important?"

"Well, I was thinking of scratching marks into the wall, to count the days, but . . . never mind," said Scott. "It's not like we'll ever be able to count them anyway without a sun or moon. What makes this world work, anyway? Where's the light coming from? What makes the plants grow? What keeps it going?"

A voice said,

> *"What keeps our kingdom going, glowing on?*
> *Suspense—suspense and stubborn expectation.*
> *A wish to witness how the story ends."*

Scott squinted at the silhouetted face in the door's window. "Beautiful damsel?"

"Nah," said Mick, "it's just Dhanu."

> *"What fools you were to come and court the courtly,"*

the changeling said through the door.

> *"More fool was I to lend you my good name.*
> *What covenant could you have hoped to gain?*
> *The mission of the Fay is right and just.*
> *It must be just—for if their cause were not?*
> *For lack of glamour's blush they'd wilt and waste."*

347

"Thassa crock," Mick said cheerily. "We've gotten it all turned around, we Fay. I think we used to tell ourselves we needed to be good, to be honorable, an' that the glamour was our reward. Now 's our barometer. If we still have our glamour, then we're sure we *must* be good, no matter how heinous we've become. I think yeh know what I mean."

Dhanu watched them for a moment.

> "*It was* my *honor pledged,* mine *on the line*
> *When conduct safe I promised in the court.*"

"I know," said Scott. "I'm sorry."
Dhanu smirked.

> "*And now apology, from you to me.*
> *From jailed to jailer; that is passing strange.*
> *For all your folly, still I'm fain to think*
> *You spoke with honest valor in the court.*"

Scott and Mick were silent.

> "*If I arrange your swift release, will first*
> *You swear what you foretold will come to pass?*
> *The Fay, all Fay, led safely to your world?*
> *Admired and living free among your kind?*"

348

"Sure," said Mick. "That's what he thinks. That's what we both think."

> *"He made predictions all his own in court,*
> *So now I'll have his answer for myself."*

Scott opened his mouth to reassure Dhanu as well, and it would have been easy, so easy to lie. Instead he grimaced as he realized he was about to be honest. It really wasn't all that simple after all. What do you know.

"No."

Mick turned his head. "Lad?"

". . . No," Scott told Dhanu. "I won't promise that. It wouldn't be right. I think that's what will happen . . . mostly . . . but I can't make any guarantees. I'm just a kid—I don't have any power in my world."

"*Scott,*" said Mick.

You couldn't read Dhanu's dim face there, in that small frame in the door, but when he spoke again it seemed to be with greater urgency.

> *"I trust you grasp the pact I'm offering?*
> *An oath, mere words, and then I'll set you free."*

"Sorry, Mick," Scott breathed. He turned to Dhanu. "Yeah, I understood you the first time. Thanks, but . . . I guess I'll have to stay in here."

Dhanu studied him, then turned and motioned to someone who must have been standing with him there, in the hall. There was a jangling, and the bolt slid free of the lock. The door opened, and Scott and Mick scrambled to their feet.

Dhanu was accompanied by another changeling Scott recognized from before. This second teen had Scott's backpack. Now Scott could just see Dhanu's face in the blue light of the cross-shaped window, and he was smiling. Sort of a rueful smile.

> *"Our horses wait in secret down below.*
> *Now softly, and attend to what I say.*
> *And if your drop of fairy blood bestows*
> *A drop of fairy grace, do use it now."*

Scott was stunned. "Thank you."

"I think you'll be a king among your kind," said Dhanu.

"Nah," said Scott, shrugging uncomfortably. "I'm thinking maybe a lawyer."

CHAPTER 33

"If you were truly Merlin," said the queen, "then I think you have much to answer for. All that I-know-the-terrible-future-but-I'm-going-to-let-it-happen-anyway business."

"Oh." Merle laughed. "*That.*"

Merle and John were still dripping wet, though Her Majesty and Finchbriton had remained relatively dry inside the backpack. They walked back through the southwest of Ireland, toward the rift, on their guard but otherwise enjoying a rare moment of triumph.

"Putting aside the tragedy of Lancelot and Guinevere," said the queen, "you must have known that Arthur would have a bastard son who would grow up to oppose him."

"Mordred," Merle agreed, nodding. "So why didn't I stop it? I actually tried. I did. Just like I got Arthur born by doing everything wrong, I got Mordred born by doing everything right. All the old accounts agreed that Mordred's mom was Morgause, so I never left her and Arthur alone together for even a second. Sure, some newer versions of the legends said Mordred's mom was Morgan le *Fay*, but I knew that was just because modern writers think Morgan's a fun villain and they wanted to make the stories simpler by getting rid of characters. Right? So I'm watching Morgause like a hawk, and meanwhile Arthur and Morgan le Fay are sneaking out the back together."

The queen pursed her lips but said nothing. John said it for her. "Arthur and that . . . wild child?"

"She had a more alluring glamour back then, I swear. And actually ran a comb through her hair every now and then. So Mordred was born after all, but I was there to meet Arthur on the battlefield of Camlann. Arthur killed his son, but Mordred got Arthur pretty bad, too. The books all say that four queens took him off to Avalon to rest and heal, but I guess that's just 'cause no one was around to know the truth. It was actually me."

Merle drove his skittish horse and cart through the field of the dead, a hundred thousand men, looking for movement that was not some crow or snake in the grass. Quiet as an anvil. Only the dry curses of scavengers creaking under a leaden sky.

When his horse quailed and wouldn't go any farther, Merle got down and walked, slipping occasionally on things he didn't care to identify, looking for that extraordinary sword and the Pendragon device on a shield, looking for his friend.

He found Arthur breathing shallowly on the ground next to the body of his son. He pressed on the king's wound until the bleeding stopped, mostly, and dressed it with fresh linen.

"Merlin," said Arthur, fluttering his papery eyelids. He looked so much older than Merle remembered, so much older than his years. "So I've died, then. Is this heaven or hell?"

"What a thing to say. I've missed you too."

"What are you doing now?"

"I am trying," Merle grunted, "to drag you back . . . to

my cart. The books said Lucan . . . and Bedivere would be hanging around to help?" *(Cough.)* "But I guess they just made that up?"

After the better part of a sweat-soaked hour, Merle had Arthur in the wagon, and they were away. Merle had to keep nudging Arthur to keep him awake.

"Whither we travel?" asked the king after one of these proddings.

"Avalon."

"Good. I shall return the sword Excalibur to the lake and fulfill my vow."

"Mmm . . . yeeeah. Why don't you hold on to that, actually," said Merle. "You're gonna need it where we're going, and I don't intend to let you die."

"Old friend," said Arthur. "My wound is mortal."

"Let's let twenty-first century medicine decide what's mortal and what isn't. You'll be amazed how different the doctors are from the ones you have here. Like, do you know what they'll almost never put on an open wound? Moss. And they're gonna wash their hands and everything. You'll feel like a king. The Once and Future King."

He snuck them both through the back door tunnel to his secret cave, explaining all the while that there was a new kingdom, another world that needed his help more than any other. They were going there. Inside the cave Arthur found Archimedes, and some work benches, crude tools, copper and tin wire, pipes. The time machine Merlin had built for him was a hundred times larger than his own and would have looked to the modern eye more like plumbing than science. But to the medieval man, plumbing *was* science, and Arthur was much impressed. Merlin told the king that he must place himself within a large octagonal ring, surrounded by batteries of fairy gold.

"You can sit," said Merle.

"I will stand." Arthur was barely on his feet, but he raised Excalibur, pointed it before him as if ready to cleave his way into the next millennium.

Merle and Archie gripped their little octagon. "Okay, Archie," said Merle. "Sync us up and do the math. Then jump."

Arthur's machine rattled and hummed. And glowed. There was a lot more light than Merle expected. Especially from Arthur's trembling sword. Excalibur was incandescent.

Then there was a *pop*, and Merle and Archie were in New Jersey.

Alone.

He'd tumbled to the grass, so now Merle rose near the edge of a park, squinted at a boulevard of row homes just visible through the trees. The breeze was in his face, a summer breeze. He smelled . . . marshmallows.

"Arthur?" asked Merle, looking all around him, but nothing. The legendary king was legendary once more.

Scott clung, stiff fingered, to the galloping pony, Mick in his backpack, with Dhanu and the Changeling Guard riding alongside. The forest was a panic of log-jumping, low-hanging boughs, grasping branches, and the ever-changing kaleidoscope of dappled twilight that pinholed through the trees. This was a truly excellent pony and didn't seem to need steering or even the slightest encouragement from Scott, which was good—after his initial order of "Giddyap," he'd entirely exhausted his horsemanship.

Dhanu caught Scott's eye and nodded. The other changelings looked grim. Their treachery hadn't escaped notice for long, and they had a battalion of the Trooping Fairies of Oberon on their tails.

"'Why don't you go with John and *Merle*, Finchbriton,' says Mick," Scott grumbled. "'We shouldn't have any need for you.'"

"Oh, enough already," said Mick.

Arrows whizzed by. Small ones, like the elves only wanted to murder them a little bit. One lodged itself into a flowering elder, and Mick got a look at it as they passed.

"Ooh, did yeh see the craftsmanship on that arrow? Sure to be poisoned, too, that was. 'S like they're tryin' to kill us with the good silverware."

"Neat."

Dhanu drew his horse near and called out over the thunder of hoofbeats.

> *"We'll scatter at the border of the shire.*
> *Perhaps my guard will draw off their pursuit."*

Scott nodded, grateful. The changelings, all the changelings, would probably never be welcome back in fairy society again. What would happen to them?

> *"The horse you ride is fairy bred, and bright,"*

Dhanu added.

> *"Just tell her where you'd go, and she'll abide."*

Before Scott or Mick could say a proper word of thanks, Dhanu had reined his horse away, and less than a minute later they could neither see nor hear the Changeling Guard anymore. They must have crossed the county line, and now they were on their own.

After a time Scott felt Mick twist around in the backpack and lean into Scott's ear. "Good news an' bad news," said the leprechaun.

"What's the good news?" asked Scott as another arrow whistled by.

"We have us just two pursuers."

"And the bad news?"

"It's the same news."

They were dogged pursuers, these last two, and better riders. They gained ground. Mick ducked into the backpack and popped up, facing backward, with a flare gun. He fired a flare, and it cut a spectral laser trail through the blue wood. The elves forked to avoid it, then came back together again, losing a little ground as they did so. Mick reloaded and played this card again and again until they couldn't see their hunters anymore.

Scott smelled water. The trees were thinning out ahead, too—they were coming up on a river. "We can't keep this up," he said. "Hold on. I'm going to try something."

"Can I maybe have a little more explanation than that?"

Scott arched forward and spoke into the horse's ear. He hoped it understood.

It wasn't an especially wide river—that was good. They careened down the bank and plowed into the water, sending a heavy swell to either side. Then, of course, their mythologically nimble horse became suddenly sluggish as she surged against the water and the current.

"Come on, come on," Scott whispered, terrified the elves would catch up while they were so exposed.

Then, when they were halfway across the river, Scott fell sideways off the pony's back and let the current take him. He and Mick took breaths and went under. They could hear the water being breached as their pony emerged on the far bank and galloped on. They heard the disturbance, underwater, as the elven riders entered the river a few seconds later, and crossed, and then were gone.

Scott and Mick surfaced, gasped, and swam to shore, panting.

"What . . . what did yeh say to the pony?" asked Mick.

"Told it to keep running without us, fast as it could. Wonder how long the elves'll follow before they realize they aren't chasing anyone?"

CHAPTER 34

In the basement, Emily was conducting an experiment with Archimedes, and a lead box with slits in it, and some photosensitive paper, and a spoon. She looked at the spoon. Why did she need a spoon? The answer was she didn't, and she set it aside, quietly, so as not to wake the house.

In the basement, Emily returned to her experiment with Archimedes, and a lead box with slits in it, and some photosensitive paper, and she needed the spoon for ice cream. *That's* why. Her research would lead to a heretofore unimagined flavor of ice cream, with tiny rifts in it. And brownie bits, maybe.

In the basement, Emily was nodding off.

"Don't fall asleep—you know it's dangerous," says a voice.

Emily looks up, dimly. "Oh, it's *you*," she says. She

smiles. "You found me."

Her mother is beautiful. She'd forgotten how beautiful. Tall and raven haired, like a storybook queen. Her mother leans in close, asks what she's working on.

"A rift! A stable rift! A really big one," Emily tells her mother.

Her mother is silent for a long time. "You don't say," she breathes.

"I've learned so much about them," says Emily. She's excited to be talking about it.

"I'm so silly," says her mother. "I don't remember exactly where we are. Is it London?"

"Did you know that each rift is a pair of tiny white holes with a black hole in the center? Is that not crazy? And there's no time displacement. Also I think I've discovered a new elementary subatomic particle I'm calling the Emilyon."

"The house we're in, dear. It's in London?"

"Yes, London." Emily winces. There is a sound, like a ringing in her ears, but it isn't a ringing. The sound goes *shhhhhhhhhhhhhhhhhhhhhhhhhhhhhhhh*. "Can you hear that?"

"I hear nothing. What part of London?"

Shhhhhhhhhhhhhhhhhhhhhhhhhhhhhh, goes the sound.

"Is . . . Islington. That snake . . . do you see that snake there? It could see something coming through the rift just before it happened. There's no reason a reptile should

362

be able to do that naturally, but it *has* been eating a lot of mice from Pretannica—I think that has to be the explanation."

"Pretannica?"

"That's . . . what we call the world on the other side." Emily's face is suddenly hot. Her forehead is damp.

Shhhhhhhhhhhhhhhhhhhhhhhhhh.

"Is this . . . ," she asks, ". . . is this real life?"

"Of course, silly mouse. Now where in Islington, do you think?"

Don't.

"On a . . . on a street called St. George, which is funny, because *he* slew a dragon, and we have to slay a dragon, too—"

"Very good, Emily," says her mother. "Stop talking. There we are. Now come upstairs."

Don't.

Emily doesn't want to disobey her mother, who looks familiar, like someone she's seen before, doesn't she? Emily can't remember. She's sweating through her nightdress to the white lab coat Biggs made her.

She ascends to the kitchen. The woman with the coal-black hair is already standing in the center of the room like a bent needle.

"Look there on the counter," says the woman.

Emily looks. It's a knife.

"It's a knife," the woman agrees, nodding, though Emily hasn't said this aloud. "Why don't you pick it up?"

In Erno's dream, there was a dog that could say Erno's name. In fact, all it seemed to be able to say was "Erno, Emily, Biggs, come in—over." It wasn't much of a vocabulary, but still Erno expected the dog would make him rich, somehow. He was going to name it Walkie-Talkie because dogs like going for walkies and also this dog could talkie. He was just trying to remember why this name seemed so familiar when he woke with a start and realized Merle had been shouting through the radio for five minutes.

"Sorry. Sorry," said Erno. "Was asleep. Um, over."

"Don't worry about it," Merle answered. "But hey! Good news! John and I got the queen, and we're on our way. So ready two sheep and the fox—we'll have to get something else to swap for Mick later. Over."

"We got a rabbit at a pet shop," said Erno groggily. Then, "Hold on. Emily should be here. Shoot, I fell asleep while I was supposed to be watching Emily."

Just then Scott came in on the same channel. "Are you guys there?" he asked. "We need you to get the rift ready soon. Mick and I are coming back."

"How did it go with the elves?" asked John. "Did you make your case?"

Scott thought before answering. "It went pretty bad.

But I told the truth, and I'm glad I told the truth." He hoped he was being understood. "You know what I'm saying?"

After a pause John said, "I know what you're saying."

Scott smiled. "But yeah, otherwise I made our case pretty horribly."

"The Fay are sendin' us some pointed comments," said Mick. "Some sharp retorts. Some barbed replies."

"That's Mick's way of explaining that they were shooting arrows at us," said Scott. "When he gets a lot of glamour in him he's like a bad poet or something."

"Guys, I'll get Biggs up and get the animals ready, but first I have to find Emily," said Erno. "I screwed up." Erno rose and crossed to the door, turned the handle. But it wouldn't budge. "I can't open the door," Erno said into the radio. "Guys, something's going on—I can't leave my room."

Emily is in a different room, and she's looking at Biggs there, sleeping. He sleeps standing up. He says he's done it that way for a long time. Emily can't remember how she got here. She can't remember climbing up onto the desk. She's holding a knife.

"It would be so much better if all your friends were gone," her mother is saying. "Then it could be just you and me. None of these weird characters about. They would hurt me if they could, you know. Do you love me?"

Emily loves her *so* much. She's crying, silently. Her mother was gone, but now she's come back. That makes sense, doesn't it?

No.

"I would never kill another living thing myself," her mother is saying. "It goes against everything I believe in, you must understand that. And I would never ask another person to kill for me. But then I don't know how *you* feel about it, this idea of killing. I don't want to make up your mind for you. You do love me, *don't you.*"

No. No.

But Emily nods, her breath coming loose with each jerk of her head.

"He seems like a sound sleeper, but still," says the beautiful black-haired woman. "Can't have him thrashing about. Is that a ratchet strap I see in your right pocket? You might secure it around his ankles."

Emily reaches a shaking hand to the lower right pocket of her lab coat.

No. Upper pocket. Upper pocket, says the voice in her head. The *other* voice in her head. The one that sounds an awful lot like herself.

"The strap isn't *in* the upper pocket," says Emily.

"What's that, dear?" says the mother woman.

No, it isn't. Is it.

Frowning, Emily reaches, trembling, into the upper

366

right pocket of her coat and feels something small, delicate, like a tiny flower. She curls her fingers around it, and the sun shines inside her mind.

She pulled it out and looked at it, this tiny delicate thing. The four-leaf clover Mick gave her. Dainty little spell breaker. Emily breathed deeply, powerfully, and stepped from the desk to the bed, to the floor. Past the woman with the pitch-black hair, who suddenly looked altogether more familiar.

"Dear, what are you doing?"

"I want to show you something. It's really cool. I'll kill Biggs later."

She walked back through the kitchen with the knife and stepped down the basement stairs. The sheep shifted at her approach. They never seemed to sleep. She walked right up to the adder, which shimmied back and coiled. Before she could give herself time to really think about what she was doing, she snapped her hand down and seized the snake at its tail, using the blunt edge of her knife to keep it from striking her.

"If you wanted to show me the adder, darling," said Nimue, "I've seen it already."

"You've seen it, I suppose, because you're looking through my eyes? Is that how this works? I know you're not really here. You're in my mind." *Listen,* she thought. *I can speak to you without speaking.*

Nimue didn't say anything for a long time. Meanwhile Emily was holding the struggling snake near the rift.

"I don't need to be there," said Nimue. "My men will be there soon."

Emily put the shamrock in her mouth and swallowed it. That would keep her hands free. Then she removed her radio from another pocket and opened a channel.

"I know your men are coming," she said, and everyone heard it. Erno, Scott, John, Mick, and Merle. "I know I blew it, told you where we are."

"RUN, EMILY!" shouted Erno into his radio, but he was shouting to a locked and empty room. Emily still had the channel engaged.

"I've told you where we are and given you a rift. Let me tell you a little bit about your new rift, then," said Emily. "First of all? You were . . . you were right about something. Magic split from the world when Merle and Arthur left for the future. I'm sorry, Merle, it's true."

In Pretannica, Merle sat heavily on a nearby stone.

"I've been studying the energy from the rift, and I'm a hundred percent certain," said Emily. She looked at Nimue, or rather the illusion of her by the stairs. "He didn't do it on purpose. He didn't want it to be true, and it wasn't entirely his fault. There was some kind of interference. Some big, magical hoo-ha. It confused me, because I was sure that if Merle's time machines were

368

responsible, then the bubble . . . well, never mind about the bubble."

In his room, Erno sat down, stood up again. "That's *it*," he said. "The bubble. Finding the centers of circles."

"Anyway," Emily continued into the radio, "you found the remains of Merle's time machine, and it taught you how to make magic milking machines, is that right? That's how you've been stealing glamour all these years, storing it in batteries so that you can overload yourself and tear the rifts open, start your invasion, even if it kills you? But now . . . *now* you think it's going to be easy. Now I've given you a big stable rift, so you think it won't come to that."

"It seems it won't," said Nimue. She was letting herself sound smug. "You have to learn to admit when you've lost, dear. It's a part of growing up."

"Oh, please," she said to Nimue, and to everyone else on the radio. "I know we've lost. All we've managed to do so far is slow you down a little. Delay the release of a cereal. Waste some of that magic you've been saving. I mean, who ever really thought John was going to slay a dragon? No offense, John, if you're listening."

"None taken," John said weakly into his radio.

"But you know something?" said Emily "Aha! There! Look!"

The snake had suddenly recoiled back upon itself and struck, seemingly at nothing. Its crisp and startling mouth

clenched around something invisible but clearly there.

"See? It's caught something. The adder can see it before we do. Do you know that in the instant before two creatures trade places, they're actually a single mass? One interdimensional being? What do you think happens when that interdimensional being swallows itself in the middle of a rift?" said Emily. "I'm asking because I'd love your opinion—I'm honestly only about ninety-five percent sure."

The snake engulfed the mouse on the other side, and the rift shrank. Emily couldn't see that, but she could see the brick wall contract as if squeezed by an invisible fist.

"NO!" Nimue screamed in Emily's mind. "NO NO NO!"

"Sorry," Emily whispered to the snake, to the mouse. Then she set free the animals they had in cages, and cut the sheep's tethers with her knife, and tried to shoo them all up the basement stairs.

Emily breathed heavily. Now the ceiling seemed to be crumbling. The floor was buckling and moving in toward the collapsing rift like the tide. She ran up the stairs behind the animals. "Wake Biggs!" she told Archimedes.

"Little *witch*!" said Nimue. "Do you know what I'm going to do to you and your friends?"

"Nothing bad, I'm sure," said Emily, turning her back on Nimue, or on the idea of Nimue. "It would go against everything you believe in."

Erno came tumbling out of his room with the unicat, Nimue's influence suddenly broken. He was already packed. "What's going on? Are they really coming?"

"They're really coming. Help me get my things. And these animals out the front door."

"I'm going to win," said Nimue in her mind.

Emily sighed, exasperated. "I *know* you're going to win. Of *course* you're going to win. It's just not going to be *easy*. You're going to have to *die*. Now let me ask you something," said Emily. "Seriously. Was this really your plan? To make someone super-intelligent and then TURN HER AGAINST YOU? How did you think *that* was going to work out?"

There wasn't any answer. But still Emily knew she wasn't alone.

"You," she said. "You paper doll. You nothing. You're not my fairy godmother, you soft-witted figment." Emily breathed. "NOW GET OUT OF MY HEAD!"

She was alone. She could feel it.

Finally Biggs was awake, confused and pajama clad, and they left—not out the front door, but up the rotted staircase to the roof, then in Biggs's arms across the rooftops of London just as the white vans pulled up.

Across the street from the house, a little girl was up late (as she was most nights) filming the haunted house with an old camcorder, just in case something interesting happened. So she captured it when the front door opened and something small like a rabbit hopped out, followed by a fox. Followed by three sheep, which fumbled right and left and smack into one another like a comedy trio before cantering off in separate directions. Then a squad of white vans screeched to a stop in front of the haunted house, and the little girl saw what might have been movement up at the roofline. It was hard to say. Men in black outfits and helmets and guns rushed from the vans toward the building, which sort of flinched, as if they'd startled it. The men stopped short, looked at one another. Then the building crumpled like a soda can, flicking bits of brick and mortar every which way, cracking helmets. The men retreated as the whole haunted house collapsed into a super-dense lump and sank beneath the earth.

The little girl watched this, wide-eyed. It wasn't exactly what she'd been expecting, but still she whispered, "I knew it," because she'd been waiting to whisper that for a long time.

The following evening she tried to show the video to her dad, but her brother had erased it to record himself burping the alphabet. "He already showed me," her dad told her. "As soon as I got home. Say, did you notice your haunted house is gone?"

CHAPTER 35

Tiny Polly and the pixie brothers found Harvey, right where they left him.

"Thomething'th different about you," he said when he saw Polly. "Ith that a new dreth?"

"Harvey," said Polly, "this is Fee, Fo, and Denzil. Your Not-So-Highnesses, this is the pooka Harvey."

They exchanged uncomfortable handshakes.

"We were afraid you'd have run into trouble, since we were gone so long," said Polly.

"No. No trouble. Should we go?"

Harvey was quiet on the way back to the house. He hunched over the steering wheel and paid a lot more attention to the road than usual. But then the brothers were doing most of the talking—sharing the details of their misadventures, their failed attempts to rescue Morenwyn.

"Fi said that Fray said that Morenwyn likes him," Polly announced.

"I . . . do not remember saying that."

"You did."

"Nonsense," said Fo. "Anyone at court would tell you she found me most handsome and Denzil the best conversationalist."

"She would want me," said Fee, "if only I wasn't the youngest."

"Or perhaps she does not want any of us, my brothers," said Denzil. "We have to accept it: fair Morenwyn does not wish to be saved. We cannot make her change."

"That'th exactly it," Harvey said, suddenly animated. "You've put your tiny finger right on it. Can't save everyone. Can't change anybody. Gotta play the cardth you're dealt."

"I don't believe that's what I intended—"

"You know, when I wath a captive of Goodco mythelf . . . I remember the day the guardth brought me the firtht box of Honey Frothted Thnox. Fresh off the line, they told me."

Harvey ran a red light, but Polly didn't say anything.

"They pointed at the Thnox Rabbit in hith shirt and tie, jutht like the clotheth they'd drethed *me* in, and thaid, 'Look. You're trademarked. You belong to *uth*, now.'"

Polly crawled up to the front. "Did something happen

376

while we were inside the factory?" she asked.

"Courth not. What could have happened?"

Nobody spoke again until they pulled up St. George Road.

"Weird," Harvey said, leaning over the wheel. "Could've thworn there wath a building here when we left."

"I can't believe it," said Merle, in Pretannica. "All my fault. I mean . . . I was afraid it was true, but then the kid didn't used to believe it, and she was so scary smart. . . ."

Finchbriton hopped to Merle's shoulder, nipped his ear in what was presumably an affectionate way.

"She said there was something else that caused it," said John. "Some 'magical hoo-ha.'"

"We don't lose ourselves to self-pity," said the queen. "We keep calm and carry on. If this rift has been closed, then how are we to get home?"

"I can't believe it," said Mick. "Emily marooned us. We're doomed."

"No," said Scott. "No, she wouldn't do that," he added, convincing himself. "She did the right thing. She kept the rift from Nimue." Scott fiddled with the walkie-talkie. "I think this thing is dead—whatever happened when the rift collapsed must've fried the batteries. Not only can

I not reach Biggs and the Utzes, I can't reach John and Merle, either."

They had a moment to themselves right now, but Mick was sure the elves would be good trackers. They had to keep moving.

"Don' know what we're gonna do," said Mick. "We might find a rift close to May Day that's big enough for me, but I'm not leavin' without yeh."

Scott smiled at him. Then he thought. "But that's not true, is it? Emily knew we had other options. I'll see my mom again, and Polly. And my dad. We can visit Fi's pixie witch! She has rifts. Big ones. We can talk her into letting us use one."

"Yeah, that's good. She sounded like a real nice lady."

"We just have to get to the Isle of Man," Scott continued. "How hard can that be?"

"Have yeh ever heard of anythin' good comin' of a person sayin', 'How hard can that be?'"

"Sorry."

Polly and the brothers and Harvey sat in the car in utter silence for several minutes, staring at the house-sized hole in the neighborhood.

"I do not understand," Fee said finally. "We are looking at what, exactly?"

"A house that used to be there," whispered Polly.

"A mysterious absence that knells like a bell in our hearts," said Fi.

"Yeah," said Polly. Then she noticed a bit of movement—a dash of white. "Is . . . is that an owl at the end of the street? Harvey, drive to the end of the street."

Harvey complied, and at the end of the street they spotted Archimedes sitting in a willow tree. "Roll down the window!" said Polly. And when Harvey did, the owl glided down from its perch and into the car. Fi's brothers scattered everywhere. Denzil came up hooting.

"He's not a real owl," Polly told him. "Look! He has Merle's watch." Polly struggled with the hugeness of it, and read the face. "Emily says she figured out that I didn't go to Pretannica. Well, course she did. And Erno and Emily and Biggs are okay! They just had to make the building vanish, is all, and now the . . . the rift is gone."

Polly and Fi looked at each other.

"It also says that John and Merle rescued the queen, but they're still in Pretannica and that Scott and Mick are too, and that Scott and Mick are on the run from elves. Oh *no*. Scott's in trouble and he can't get home!"

The car was respectfully quiet.

"There's also . . . there's also this stuff about that thing Erno was working on, but I don't get it. Stuff about finding the centers of circles, and about how the circles

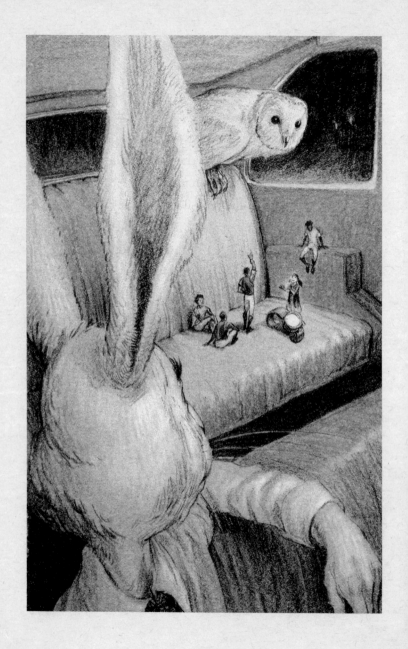

don't match, and . . ." Polly's eyes were welling up.

"Hey now," said Harvey. "People like uth, we don't cry—"

"Well . . . well . . . *sorry!*" Polly seethed, tears streaming. She turned from the others, pressed her hands against her hot face. "I guess . . . I'm not a person like us then! 'Cause I can cry if I FEEL LIKE IT for my brother who's gonna get killed and *I'll never never see him again—*"

"*Impossible!*" Fi roared, and there was such panache to it that Polly was startled out of her misery. "You are *Polly Esther Doe!* Rescuing brothers is what you do! The witch Fray has doors that lead home, and we will help Scott and Mick to use them! Our size is our strength! There are any number of rifts we may use! We go to Pretannica!"

Polly sniffed. "We do?"

"Harvey! Will you take us to one of the small rifts on Emily's map?"

Harvey stared, then shrugged. "Yeahshure."

Fi turned to the other pixies. "Brothers! Will you join us?"

The princes glanced at one another. Then Denzil stepped forward and gave Fi his hand. "I will go, brother. To the isle of Lady Fray and the lovely Morenwyn." Fee and Fo joined their hands as well.

"To Pretannica," said Fo.

"To Morenwyn," said Fee.

Polly wiped her eyes and smirked. "You'll get to see Morenwyn too," she told Fi.

Fi took a knee, and then grasped her hand.

"Ah, dear Polly—little sister—*you* are my love."

Polly blushed.

"Now. Shall we go?"

"Let's go."

They went.

PENGUIN BOOKS

BUST

Bust

*How the Courts Have Exposed the Rotten Heart
of the Irish Economy*

DEARBHAIL McDONALD

PENGUIN BOOKS

PENGUIN BOOKS

Published by the Penguin Group
Penguin Books Ltd, 80 Strand, London WC2R ORL, England
Penguin Group (USA) Inc., 375 Hudson Street, New York, New York 10014, USA
Penguin Group (Canada), 90 Eglinton Avenue East, Suite 700, Toronto, Ontario, Canada M4P 2Y3
(a division of Pearson Penguin Canada Inc.)
Penguin Ireland, 25 St Stephen's Green, Dublin 2, Ireland
(a division of Penguin Books Ltd)
Penguin Group (Australia), 250 Camberwell Road,
Camberwell, Victoria 3124, Australia (a division of Pearson Australia Group Pty Ltd)
Penguin Books India Pvt Ltd, 11 Community Centre, Panchsheel Park,
New Delhi – 110 017, India
Penguin Group (NZ), 67 Apollo Drive, Rosedale, Auckland 0632, New Zealand
(a division of Pearson New Zealand Ltd)
Penguin Books (South Africa) (Pty) Ltd, 24 Sturdee Avenue, Rosebank, Johannesburg 2196, South Africa

Penguin Books Ltd, Registered Offices: 80 Strand, London WC2R ORL, England

www.penguin.com

First published by Penguin Ireland 2010
Published in Penguin Books 2011

1

Copyright © Dearbhail McDonald, 2010
All rights reserved

The moral right of the author has been asserted

Typeset by Palimpsest Book Production Limited, Falkirk, Stirlingshire
Printed in England by Clays Ltd, St Ives plc

ISBN: 978-0-141-04922-9

www.greenpenguin.co.uk

To my twin, Aoife

Contents

Prologue

Thursday, 19 February 2009

In hindsight, it wasn't the smartest thing I have ever done in my journalism career: travelling alone, on a hunch, to the Algarve to spend time with a man I had never met – a man who refused to tell me his real name and gave me no details about his background.

'Seamus' had phoned me to talk about Michael Lynn, the rogue solicitor who had fled Ireland with a bench warrant and an €80 million mortgage fraud trailing in his wake in December 2007. The drawback was that Seamus, whoever he was, refused to give me any substantial details over the phone and would only speak to me if I travelled to Portugal to meet him.

February 2009 was a bad time to be asking for time off from the newsroom. The country was in utter turmoil: the government had just nationalized Anglo Irish Bank, and it had emerged that Anglo had lent €300 million to ten clients to buy out 10 per cent of its shares held through contracts for difference by the troubled billionaire Sean Quinn in a desperate bid to prevent the share price from collapsing.

On 10 February it had emerged that Irish Life and Permanent had engaged in a swap of deposits worth €7 billion each in order to allow Anglo to make its year-end accounts look better during the dark days of September 2008.

When I asked my editor at the *Irish Independent*, Gerry O'Regan, if I could go to Portugal to check out a vague story on Michael Lynn – who seemed like old news by this stage

— he sighed and laughed, saying: 'Whatever it takes to get him out of your system.' My news editor, Shane Doran, also thought the brief trip would help me draw a line under almost two years of writing obsessively about Lynn.

I had broken the Michael Lynn story on 13 October 2007, in a piece about a high-profile but as yet unnamed solicitor who specialized in property law and had engaged in an alleged mortgage fraud involving four banks and worth €30 million.

I didn't know the half of it: it would later emerge that the true figure was more than €80 million and that Lynn had taken mortgages on false pretences from nearly every bank that operated in the country.

Everyone in Ireland can remember a moment when it suddenly became clear to them that the boom was over.

For one solicitor in a high-profile law firm, it was when he was met with a friendly greeting in a lift by a partner who worked in the property section of the firm. For almost a decade property lawyers, riding high on the crest of an insane housing boom, had little time for lesser mortals working in more mundane areas of law. Having been ignored for years by the property gurus, the solicitor interpreted this sudden change of heart as an ominous sign that all was not well in the housing game.

For another lawyer, it was when a colleague popped his head around the door of his office and casually inquired what would happen, from a legal perspective, if there was a run on a bank.

For me the moment of truth occurred as I was travelling back to Dublin on a train from Belfast the morning our story about Lynn appeared, when I was inundated with calls and texts from legal contacts asking me if the unidentified lawyer was one of a number of names they subsequently volunteered. By the time the train crossed the border at Newry, I had taken down the names of fifteen solicitors who their colleagues suspected were guilty of mortgage fraud. Not one of them was Michael Lynn.

When I travelled to Faro sixteen months later to meet 'Seamus', I had no intention of looking for Michael Lynn, although it was known that he was in the Algarve.

What I did not know was that he was on the lookout for me.

My luggage took an age to emerge on to the carousel, and consequently Faro airport was all but abandoned by the time I emerged and met 'Seamus'. I learned his real name – which I agreed not to publish – when we exchanged passports to confirm our identities. I knew from previous research that he was working as a consultant on Costa de Cabanas, Lynn's flagship housing development in the Algarve.

Seamus had insisted on meeting me personally at the airport and driving me to my hotel. As we walked to his jeep, I could not avoid the feeling that this was not a good set-up: no one knew where I was or who I was with, and I knew nothing about this man or whose side he was on.

Sitting in the jeep and cursing my own stupidity for not having better personal security arrangements in place, I was just about to thank Seamus for his kind offer and head back to the terminal when I heard raised voices from behind, including the phrase: 'I cannot fucking believe this.'

I looked in the rear-view mirror and there was Michael Lynn, wearing an orange T-shirt, shorts and a mile-wide sneer.

The two men kicked off into an almighty row, Seamus repeatedly asking Lynn to leave.

Convinced now that Seamus was in cahoots with Lynn, I got out and headed back towards the terminal. As Lynn headed in that direction too, Seamus implored me to give him the benefit of the doubt. It soon became apparent that Seamus was as freaked out by Lynn's advent as I was.

Seamus, who is suing Lynn through the Portuguese employment law courts, reassured me that he had not had contact with Lynn, whose nickname in the Algarve is 'La Cucaracha' – the cockroach – for months.

I was hard to convince and in the near-empty parking lot – from which Lynn had seemingly disappeared – I accused Seamus of enticing me out to Portugal on Lynn's behalf; he assured me repeatedly that he had not. Eventually Seamus and I made a tentative agreement to drive to my hotel before making any further decisions.

It was then that Lynn reappeared, sauntering back to the jeep from the terminal.

He paused and eyeballed Seamus and me before swaggering away. The confrontation, as far as we could tell, had been designed by Lynn to let us know that Lynn knew we had made contact, knew where we were.

Later that evening, after a long and illuminating day in Seamus's company, another contact and I drove past Lynn's gated home in Tavira. As we were leaving the estate, another car appeared from nowhere and escorted ours down on to the freeway, where we were trailed for a while.

We both presumed that the escort was part of Lynn's security detail, and my contact begged me to consider staying in another hotel. I didn't, but I got in touch with a member of the Gardaí back in Dublin to tell him where I was staying. Just in case.

Seamus and I laugh now about the fracas in Faro, but the trail of destruction wreaked by Michael Lynn is no laughing matter.

★

Michael Lynn isn't the biggest villain in Ireland's economic meltdown, but he was the first of many actors who took centre stage at the Four Courts when Ireland's runaway property boom ground to a halt three years ago.

Throughout our history the courts have held up a mirror to Irish society, reflecting who we are and where we have been. And in their own way the courts, in particular the fast-track Commercial Court presided over by Mr Justice Peter Kelly and his High Court colleagues, have been writing the first draft of the demise of the Celtic Tiger.

It is, of necessity, an imperfect and incomplete draft, but the tales emanating from the courts have shone an extraordinary light on the way we have lived in the past fifteen years.

The stories told in this book, many of them still unfolding, are just the first in a series of reports from the front line of our extraordinary journey from boom to bust.

1. The Rogues

Michael Lynn was losing it. Again.

'I'll tell you one thing, in terms of style I may lack it sometimes but, by fuck, if I have something to say to somebody they will know where they stand,' the solicitor railed at Robert Lee, his project manager for Cabanas, an apartment complex he was developing in the Portuguese Algarve. Lee had just told Lynn there had been a minor earthquake in the Algarve, but it was Lynn's anger that was hitting the upper end of the Richter scale because Cabanas, his flagship development, cash cow and ticket to the stars, was plagued by incomplete sales, bounced cheques and poor marketing.

It was February 2007 and Lynn, the swashbuckling solicitor turned property developer, was holding one of his daily 'pulse' meetings with his lieutenants when he lost the rag.

'My message to you is a clear one,' he admonished Lee. 'Before you start to throw the stones, look very carefully inside your glasshouse.'

Through his KenDar Holdings, the parent company of a labyrinth of firms, Lynn was planning, in his own way, to conquer the world. He envisaged offering an entire catalogue of trans-jurisdictional financial services to reap profits for KenDar: domestic and overseas mortgages, pensions, equity release schemes and life insurance products in multiple languages. KenDar would be a one-stop international property shop where customers would invest in numerous financial products that would feed into one massive 'commission matrix' for the ambitious Mayo man.

The products were not just aimed at 'buckaleiros', Lynn's term of endearment for small-time investors at home in Ireland; in time he envisaged that his empire would grow to such an extent that institutional investors would also back KenDar.

He planned to ape the success of the 2003 Special Olympics in Ireland by twinning Irish towns and villages with his apartments in Slovakia, Hungary, Bulgaria and Portugal; and he was making plans to bring the buckaleiros to Brazil. He stalked Eastern Europe in search of car dealerships, shopping centres and luxury hotels.

In February 2007, as he lambasted his lieutenants over what he saw as their failure to fast-track his ambitious plans, they did not know that their boss had just embarked upon a frenzied personal borrowing spree that would see his dreams turn to dust.

'Bring. Him. Before me. At 2 p.m. sharp,' thundered Judge Richard Johnson.

Barely containing his anger, the President of the High Court spat each word out with deliberate emphasis, sparking a panicked exodus as barristers and bankers fled Court 6 in the Four Courts in search of Him.

Him was Michael Lynn. The date was 12 December 2007. Starting at 11 a.m., Johnson's registrar had quietly called for an appearance by or on behalf of Lynn, but Lynn was not there.

The Law Society, the ruling body for solicitors, had begun to investigate Lynn's practice in September of that year. Within weeks, the practice had been shut down and the Law Society secured a court order freezing his bank accounts. Just before details of the Society's investigation and freezing orders in relation to an as-yet-unnamed solicitor were revealed by the *Irish Independent* on 13 October, Lynn sought refuge from his legal and financial woes by travelling to the Algarve, the European hub of his empire. The next day the *Sunday Independent* named Lynn as the solicitor at the centre of the probe and the Law Society moved to have the case heard in public after securing its initial court orders during a private hearing.

Lynn returned home from Portugal to face the music in October, as more details of the Law Society investigation were revealed in the High Court; but when the Society tried to cross-examine him in December about a series of property deals involving multiple bank loans drawn down on individual properties, he fled the country with a bench warrant for his arrest trailing in his wake.

The Society took these drastic steps having discovered that Lynn had used his clients' money to fund his opulent lifestyle and had taken out multiple mortgages from banks on the same properties. Lynn had managed the multiple mortgage gambit by means of an abuse of a legal device called a solicitor's undertaking. As a general rule, banks do not allow mortgage funds to be drawn down until the borrowing is secured: no deeds, no loans. The first legal charge over a property, backed by necessary documentation such as title deeds, is a bank's security in the event of a default by the borrower. For many years the closing of a property transaction involved three parties – the bank, the seller and the buyer – and the process required much duplication. This resulted in extra costs for borrowers, as the bank's legal fees for carrying out due diligence on the transaction were inevitably passed on to the buyer.

During the 1980s the Irish government introduced new rules – known as the Boland regulations – aimed at making property conveyancing simpler and cheaper. They allowed banks and solicitors to bypass the three-way closing rule and the need for independent checks and balances to secure title when mortgaging residential property. Now, instead of banks insisting on title deeds being exchanged or lodged before they issued a mortgage cheque or bank draft for a house purchase, as was the norm in pre-Boland times, they relied on an undertaking or written assurance by the buyer's solicitor to make sure that the deed or title of the property had been verified and that the transaction could go ahead.

The solicitor's undertaking is essentially a promise to ensure that the deeds will be lodged and that the property is not already mortgaged or suffering from any defect that would affect the bank's title and security. Based on the undertaking, the bank releases the funds and the deal proceeds. The premise underlying the mechanism of the solicitor's undertaking was that a legal professional, an officer of the court, could be trusted to carry out such transactions without producing title deeds and other vital documents before a bank authorized the drawing down of mortgage funds. Trust was critical, as there is no central or electronic register of undertakings and conveyancing transactions that would enable a bank to check if there were any previous charges against properties before they released mortgage funds.

Used legitimately, as most were, solicitors' undertakings were one of the lubricants that greased the wheels of Ireland's residential and commercial property boom. The device was never intended to be used by solicitors to fast-track their own borrowings or to act on their own behalf – or that of family and friends – when buying property. But Lynn, in violation of his own profession's codes and of the law, used the mechanism to take multiple loans against single properties, unbeknownst to the lenders involved.

*

As it became apparent on 12 December that Lynn was not present in the Four Courts – in a farcical hearing attended by more than 100 lawyers representing banks that had been duped by the solicitor – his legal team, the second set of lawyers to represent him in as many months, asked Judge Johnson to discharge them from the case. Shane Murphy, the Senior Counsel representing the Law Society, asked Judge Johnson for a brief recess to figure out what to do.

Eventually, as news of Lynn's disappearance spread like wildfire through the Law Library, the Law Society asked Judge Johnson to have Lynn arrested.

At 2 p.m., Lynn's name was called and was greeted by another silence.

Judge Johnson issued a bench warrant for Lynn's arrest, but it was too late: Lynn was already on the run.

It was no accident that the first high-profile legal drama arising from Ireland's ruinous property frenzy should have centred on a member of the legal profession. The boom years saw an unprecedented surge in the numbers of young people training to become solicitors and barristers, and property transactions represented an increasingly bounteous source of income for them. In 1998 there were fewer than 5,000 solicitors on the roll in Ireland; by 2010 there were more than 12,000. There were just 356 trainee solicitors in 2002; in 2008 the Law Society churned out 777 newly qualified solicitors. The growth of the Law Library was even more prolific: the number of practising barristers rose from 1,112 in 1998 to almost 2,500 in 2010.

One of the main attractions of the profession was money. Revenue Commissioners data from 2002, studied by the Competition Authority, showed that the average income of lawyers in 2002 was €164,023. The median income – a more reliable indicator of the sort of money most lawyers actually took home – was €92,280.

From this healthy starting point – at roughly the moment when an economic boom driven by productivity and exports transformed into one driven by property speculation – the earnings of lawyers involved in commercial and property law skyrocketed. It had been feared that the creation of the Personal Injuries Assessment Board in 2003 would spell death for many solicitors and barristers who relied on personal injury litigation to sustain their practices, but the booming property market led to an explosion in new practice areas. Equity partners in some of Ireland's top law firms were taking home in excess of €1 million a year at the height of the property frenzy.

What first distinguished Michael Lynn from his contemporaries, even in this heady atmosphere, was his meteoric rise to a standard of living well beyond that enjoyed by the vast majority of solicitors plying an honest trade in house sales, wills, family law and personal injury actions. Those who attended Trinity College Dublin with Michael Lynn from 1987 to 1991 could not believe the wealth amassed by the easy-going young man who put himself through his early years of practice by singing at weddings with Marc Roberts, the one-time Eurovision contestant.

It seemed too good to be true. And it was.

Born in 1969, the youngest of seven children of the late Hugh Gerard Lynn and his wife Angela, Lynn grew up on the family's 100-acre farm in Crossmolina, Co. Mayo, at the edge of Lough Conn. After he qualified as a solicitor, Lynn took up an apprenticeship with a Dublin firm, Moran and Ryan, dotting the i's and crossing the t's on residential and commercial property transactions. Moran and Ryan also specialized in European and international property law and acted for property buyers and sellers in Ireland and in foreign climes, grounding Lynn with experience in the nuts and bolts of overseas property law.

The young solicitor surprised many of his contemporaries when he opened up his own one-man practice in the late 1990s in Blanchardstown, west Dublin. He specialized in conveyancing and property, and won huge business from developers and builders.

Lynn was simultaneously revered and feared by staff.

'He could blow up at the slightest thing,' said one former employee. 'One day you could be facing the sack and the next day he would charm the pants off you as if nothing had happened at all. He had a split personality.'

Lynn dipped his toes into the recruitment business in 2000, investing in three companies and joining forces with businesswoman Kate Ryan. He sold his interest in the firms to Ryan in 2003 and, impressed by the money his clients were making, abandoned recruitment in favour of property speculation just as the Irish property boom was shifting into an even higher gear.

With John Riordan, a well-known Dublin developer, he created KenDar Holdings. The company got off to a modest start, building apartments in Carrick-on-Shannon in Co. Leitrim, but KenDar moved to a different level when it snapped up a site in June 2003 in Cabanas, a picturesque village that lies to the east of Faro on the Algarve, for €5 million. KenDar planned a development of almost 300 apartments and houses in three separate phases.

Rui Costa, the Portugal and AC Milan midfielder, fronted a high-profile marketing campaign for the Algarve development, named Costa de Cabanas. Lynn saw a huge value in using sports icons to promote KenDar, and in 2004 Ray Houghton, the former Ireland soccer international, led a small army of GAA veterans in Croke Park to promote the company, which by then was embarking on a spree of acquisitions in Slovakia, Hungary, Bulgaria and Romania.

Lynn revealed in an interview in May 2005 the rationale behind their endorsement of his ventures.

'People who have brought sport on to a higher level have a huge ability to achieve in business,' he said. 'People identify with their sporting heroes, who are often the local guys who have proudly represented their community and would be as trustworthy in business as they were on the pitch.'

Phase one of Costa de Cabanas was a resounding success. Lynn's development promised to fulfil the dreams of hundreds of small-time investors who sought a quick return that could pay for their children's education or build a nest egg for retirement. Lynn's investors were not major players in the property market. They were, for the most part, ordinary punters, many of whom remortgaged or released equity from their homes to put down €30,000 deposits on apartments retailing at up to €300,000.

Lynn, a passionate GAA man, sourced much of the €12.1 million KenDar Holdings took in deposits for the first phase of seventy-six Cabanas apartments through GAA contacts, and he enlisted leading lights in the movement, including former Galway hurler Joe Connolly and former Mayo footballer Willie Joe Padden, to act as selling agents. Such was Lynn's confidence that he bought out Riordan's equity share in KenDar in 2005 and the pair parted ways.

Lynn scored a massive coup in 2006 when KenDar collaborated with the *Sunday Business Post* and RTÉ's *Late Late Show* to give away a €105,000 penthouse apartment in the Bulgarian ski resort Bansko. It was the biggest prize ever given away on national television in Ireland. Lynn personally whisked the married couple to the resort to maximize the publicity.

Lynn displayed all the trappings of his new-found wealth. He lived in a home in St Alban's Park off Sydney Parade in Sandymount, the upmarket Dublin 4 suburb, drove a Range Rover and had an account with the private jet company NetJets. In April 2006 he staged an ostentatious reception at Dromoland Castle in Co. Clare to celebrate his wedding to Bríd Murphy, a nurse from Tulla in the same county. In January 2007 the pair made their biggest statement to the world that they had arrived, buying Glenlion House, a stone pile on a 4.75-acre site with its own private beach on Howth Head, for €5.5 million.

What the rest of the world did not know was that Lynn took out at least three mortgages, worth a total of nearly €12 million, on Glenlion. He drew down a loan from Irish Nationwide Building Society (INBS) on 4 April and another from Bank of Scotland (Ireland) on 20 April. Four days later, he drew down a third mortgage from ACCBank.

It remains a mystery why Lynn embarked on the fraudulent borrowing binge. In early 2007 the credit crunch had not yet hit; and while things were slowing down in the property market, the crash was still not envisaged. Indeed, his borrowing spree was possible only because the banks were still lending freely, and evidently judged Lynn's financial position to be strong enough to sustain the taking of huge borrowings against the purchase of a multimillion-euro house.

In late February Lynn called a meeting with key staff, including solicitor Fiona McAleenan, at his law firm, Michael Lynn and Company, to conduct an overview of the firm's domestic and overseas property law files as well as general litigation cases. At the time, Michael Lynn and Company, later rebranded as Capel Law when the legal firm moved to plush offices in the city centre, had nearly 1,000 sets of deeds in its possession, a measure of the volume of property transactions it was involved in. Many of its foreign property deals were handled by a stand-alone firm called Overseas Property Law. Money flowed between KenDar and the law firms, even though they were separate legal entities.

As well as abusing the legal undertakings system to draw down multiple loans against the same transaction, he also used his clients' accounts in his legal practice to fund his property deals.

There are two kinds of account in a legal firm: the office or practice account, which is a normal business account, and the client account, into which funds belonging to clients are paid for purposes such as the deposit for a house or a compensation payment. The funds in the client account belong to the client and not the solicitor. Under no circumstances should a deficit arise in the client account, and under no circumstances should a solicitor use it as a slush fund for his own purposes – which is precisely what Lynn did with millions of euros belonging to his clients.

The existence of a deficit in a client account is one of the most common warning signs that cause solicitors to be investigated by the Law Society. Solicitors sometimes dip into their client account to prevent another account, usually the practice account, from going into the red; this sort of 'teeming and lading' is usually a short-term expedient. Michael Lynn's use of his client account was different: for him it was a source of funds for personal use, and he forged documents and used elaborate methods to deceive the Law Society whenever it came to scrutinize his dealings.

By the time Lynn's colleague Fiona McAleenan reported him to the Law Society, Lynn was in control of 154 bank accounts in ten different countries and a portfolio of 148 properties stretching from Dublin to mainland Europe, Dubai and China.

Had it not been for Fiona McAleenan, Lynn's frauds may have gone undetected for much longer than they did. The married mother of seven, who lives in Co. Meath, worked as a solicitor in Lynn's firm from November 2004 until September 2007, when she blew the whistle.

On 10 September 2007 McAleenan contacted the Law Society when she became aware that Lynn had drawn down €7 million from Ulster Bank, a withdrawal that was not recorded in the practice account. The Society instructed her to resign her position immediately. Within days it began to investigate Lynn's law firm, where it discovered Lynn's practice of making multiple solicitor's undertakings in relation to a single property and his misuse of client funds.

Alarm bells ought to have been ringing about Lynn's practice long before Fiona McAleenan blew the whistle.

Had the banks checked Lynn's credit profile they would have seen that it was deemed 'risky' by Businesspro, the credit bureau and debt reporting agency that assesses risk according to court judgments issued against individuals and companies and tracks their record of repayment, if any, in its weekly debt publication, *Stubbs Gazette*. In May 2002, a High Court judgment for an unpaid debt of €7,061 was registered against Lynn, but he did not pay the debt until 2006. The debt was published in *Stubbs Gazette*. Banks routinely access Businesspro's database as part of their due diligence before issuing loans and, if they did check Lynn's profile, they chose to ignore the red flags about his credit history.

Lynn had come to the attention of the Law Society in June 2003, when his biggest client, property developer Brian Cunningham, and Cunningham's wife, Marian, claimed that Lynn had overcharged them when he acted for the Cunningham Group in the sale of the Finglas Shopping Centre on the north side of Dublin. The Cunninghams complained that Lynn had deducted fees of €817,747 from a sale deposit of €1.4 million, and the Law Society sent an investigating accountant into Lynn's practice in January 2004. Lynn gave the Society his full cooperation, handing over twenty-five document boxes of files covering his dealings with his client. He claimed that another Cunningham Group director had approved the fees, and the Law Society concluded that the complaint did not constitute grounds to warrant intervention.

Lynn was the subject of a second complaint when Bank of Ireland notified the Law Society in 2006 that he had failed to honour an undertaking on a property transaction – to produce title deeds to the bank – within the specified period of time. A similar complaint was lodged in April 2007 by the ICS building society, a subsidiary of Bank of Ireland, which had released mortgage funds on six properties in a housing estate in Carrick-on-Shannon but had also never received the certificate or the title of deeds as promised by Lynn in his solicitor's undertaking.

In April, May and June of that year the Law Society wrote to Lynn seeking an explanation for the failure to honour the undertakings, and on 14 September ICS wrote to the Society to find out what was happening with its query. Three weeks later the Law Society wrote to Lynn, warning that this time he would be brought before its complaints committee if he did not honour his undertakings.

This scrutiny did not cause Lynn to alter his behaviour. Between January and August 2007 he abused the undertakings system in order to borrow a total of €26 million, from at least seven banks, to fund KenDar's frenetic expansion.

The havoc he would later wreak was evident from his increasingly fraught 'pulse' meetings at KenDar and Capel Law in the early months of 2007, when he lost his temper with staff over the slow progress of his developments. They did not know that Lynn was engaged in a race against time. Nobody did.

To the outside observer, Lynn was in control of his vast enterprise. He was borrowing money, occasionally legitimately, in a free and easy credit environment, and abused the system because he could.

The banks were as much to blame. In a frenzied climate of slipping credit standards, they could not get enough of Lynn.

In December 2007, the sight of bankers rushing to the Four Courts to register their loans against Lynn sent alarm bells ringing, warning that perhaps the security for other property loans on those banks' books was fragile.

It was.

Within days of the revelations about Lynn's transactions, it emerged that another solicitor, Thomas Byrne, had racked up multimillion-euro debts – eventually reckoned at almost €60 million – by abusing the undertakings system and stealing from banks and clients.

From that point forward, Lynn and Byrne would be linked in the public mind as 'the rogue solicitors'. It was October 2007 – just weeks after the troubles of British bank Northern Rock came to a head and a global credit crunch began to be felt – and it would be some time yet before it was possible to view the cases of Lynn, Byrne and the parade of bent solicitors that followed them into the courts as one of the harbingers of Ireland's deep economic crisis.

As news of Lynn's dealings broke in the media, banks quietly began to review their own dealings with highly geared lawyers. Byrne – who, like Lynn, had crossed the line from acting for clients in property transactions to getting involved in property development himself – was one such lawyer. IIB, which had recently allowed Byrne to draw down €9 million to refinance property in James Street owned by his client and business partner John Kelly, conducted a trawl and discovered that twelve of the twenty properties offered by Byrne as security for the loan were already mortgaged to other banks.

On 18 October, five days after the Lynn story broke, IIB asked Byrne to fax through a letter to show that loans from another bank, Anglo Irish Bank, had been discharged. But Byrne never faxed the letter, prompting IIB to ask the Law Society to intervene.

By then the Law Society had also been contacted by Barbara Cooney, a solicitor in Byrne's firm, regarding two letters of undertaking on property loans provided to Byrne. Cooney said signatures which purported to be hers on letters of undertaking were not in fact hers.

On Monday 22 October the Law Society conducted an audit of Byrne's office. Byrne did not turn up to work that day, and within days IIB went to the High Court to secure freezing orders, fearing that their assets would be dissipated.

IIB was not the only worried bank. As the details of Byrne's financial transactions came to light, it emerged that eight banks were owed substantial sums by the solicitor. The Law Society was ordered to send its files on Byrne to the Garda fraud squad by Judge Peter Kelly, head of the Commercial Court.

Unlike Lynn, Byrne turned up for every court hearing relating to his case, a shadow of the man he once was. On one occasion he broke down crying in court as he told how his own mother's family home had been used as collateral in some of his multimillion-euro dealings.

Byrne told the court that he had acted as he did due to John Kelly's 'vampire-like demands for capital'. Byrne also claimed he had never received any profits from the ventures he and

Kelly were involved in. (Byrne and Kelly have sued each other over the affair; at the time of writing, the long-running case has yet to conclude in the High Court.)

As with Lynn, the victims of Byrne's fraud included small investors who had invested in his property developments. Among them was a consortium of Gardaí, including members of the Special Branch, who clubbed together to invest in a prime development site in Dublin, and couples who placed deposits on an apartment block Byrne planned to develop in Greenhills in his native Walkinstown.

And as with Lynn, there had been warning signs, dating back a number of years, that all was not well with Byrne's practice.

In 1996 a Dublin accountancy firm owed £1,083 by Byrne registered its debt in the District Court office as part of its efforts to secure payment. The following year the Collector General registered a £7,950 judgment against Byrne in the Circuit Court, but Byrne paid off only about half of the debt.

The Law Society first encountered problems with Byrne as far back as 2002 when it investigated his practice and, on foot of concerns about his client account, contacted the bank which held it. Following its investigation, the Law Society ordered that Byrne should not be the sole signatory of cheques on his client account. In May 2005 Byrne came to the attention of the Law Society again when Cathal McCarthy, the group chief legal officer of Irish Life and Permanent, complained that he had failed to honour an undertaking on a property transaction. The IL&P complaint, which was also reported to the Garda fraud squad, triggered a fuller review of Byrne's accounts.

This time Law Society officers discovered that there was a deficit of almost €1.7 million on his client account at the end of May 2005, and that Byrne was using his clients' money for his own purposes.

In December 2006 Byrne was hauled before the Solicitors Disciplinary Tribunal to address the deficit in his client account. Byrne was censured by the Disciplinary Tribunal, an independent body that investigates complaints against solicitors, usually after they have been reported to and investigated by the Law Society.

The Disciplinary Tribunal, composed of twenty solicitors and ten lay people, is answerable not to the Law Society but to the High Court, and usually handles the most serious complaints against solicitors. It has two choices when dealing with an errant solicitor. It can censure him and restrict his practice, imposing a maximum fine of €15,000, or it can make a recommendation to the President of the High Court for a greater punishment, up to and including removal from the solicitors' roll.

When Byrne appeared before the Tribunal in 2006 he was given a €15,000 fine and allowed to continue in practice, albeit with a huge black mark against his name. From time to time the Law Society appeals to the High Court against the perceived leniency of a disciplinary sanction, but Byrne's case did not give rise to such an appeal.

Byrne continued to practise until his practice was shut down in October 2007. By the time he was struck off the solicitors' roll in June 2008, his debts totalled €57 million and he waited for the day, long expected, that he would be arrested by Gardaí.

That day never came.

The frauds perpetrated by Michael Lynn and Thomas Byrne were symptomatic, in their size, type and modus operandi, of the Irish property frenzy of the early noughties; but there was nothing fundamentally novel about them.

Many solicitors, by the nature of their work, frequently handle large amounts of other people's money, and the scope for fraud is considerable. In 1993, a young solicitor called Elio Malocco was found guilty of fraud and forgery involving money that had been given to him to settle libel cases on behalf of the Irish Press newspaper group.

The attempt by the Law Society to strike off Malocco – one of the best-known faces in the legal profession and the husband of Jane de Valera, granddaughter of Éamon de Valera – was epic. The Irish Press first complained to the Law Society about Malocco in 1991, and in October of that year he fled the country. In 1993 he returned to Ireland and was convicted in the Circuit Court for his audacious fraud. He began a five-year prison sentence in 1995. A former colleague of Malocco's, Conor Killeen, was jailed for a year for going along with the fraud, but most of Killeen's sentence was later suspended.

Malocco served less than three years of his own prison sentence. By the time he was released in 1998, seven years had passed since the Irish Press's first complaint to the Law Society. But it would take another six years for Malocco to be struck off as the solicitor, a legal genius as well as a crook, challenged the procedures of the Solicitors Disciplinary Tribunal. The case eventually reached the Supreme Court, where Malocco finally lost in 2005.

As a result of Malocco's fraud, the Law Society paid almost €2.35 million from its compensation fund, the second-largest payout made by the fund to that point.

Since the disgrace of Lynn and Byrne in autumn 2007, a roll-call of dodgy solicitors has been hauled before the Solicitors Disciplinary Tribunal and into the courts, heaping shame on the legal profession and calling into question the efficacy of the Law Society's regulation of solicitors.

The solicitors' profession in Ireland, like other professions, is self-regulating. The vast majority of complaints regarding solicitors are received by the Law Society, which refers those it considers to be the most serious to the Disciplinary Tribunal. This regulatory role is in constant tension with the Law Society's other main purpose, that of representing solicitors' interests. In 2005, the Competition Authority heavily criticised self-regulation in the legal profession. 'The structure of self-regulation that governs the supply of legal services has few, if any, of the safeguards needed to protect customers from the inherent conflict of interest that arises with self-regulation,' it said.

Within months of the Competition Authority's salvo, the Law Society found itself at the centre of another storm when solicitors were accused of double-charging victims who had received compensation from the government for abuse they suffered in residential institutions. So the Society was already fighting a rearguard action to defend its regulatory function when the cases of Lynn and Byrne set in motion a series of events that flushed out a gallery of rogue solicitors, many of whom had already been picked up by the Law Society's radar for violating regulations. The Law Society toughened up its act, and a number of solicitors were sanctioned professionally and legally.

In 2008 Niall Colfer was struck off after stealing almost €1.6 million from up to 100 of his clients. Colfer, a Progressive Democrat party activist in the early 1990s, stole €700,000 from a property company, deducted money from a dead man's estate and did not pass on a €6,000 charity donation that had been stipulated in a will. Many of his victims were members of the Howth Yacht Club, in which he was a leading light. Colfer is, at the time of writing, the subject of a Garda fraud investigation.

Colm Murphy, a solicitor in Kenmare, Co. Kerry, had been disciplined by the Law Society eight times in ten years when, in July 2008, the Solicitors Disciplinary Tribunal found that he had pocketed £21,000 out of a £134,000 arbitration award to three brothers in 1995. Murphy had represented Joe, Patrick and John Arthur in several land deals in Kerry over a fifteen-year period, including the sale in 2005 of the most expensive piece of land sold in the county's history: 39.25 acres in Kenmare for €19.5 million.

The Disciplinary Tribunal referred Murphy to the High Court in 2008 after the Law Society accused him of fourteen counts of professional misconduct arising from a series of land deals: he was eventually found guilty on ten of the counts when the case moved to the High Court.

Murphy claimed that he had not engaged with a large number of complaints against him since 1999 because he was suffering from a mental disorder, and he lambasted the Law Society for the stress it had caused him during their long-running dispute with him. In an affidavit in 2008 he wrote: 'I confirm I have nothing but disdain and contempt for certain officers of the Law Society.'

The feeling was mutual. So frustrated was the Law Society over its failure to get Murphy to comply with various court orders they had secured against him, that they were forced at one stage to bring an application to have him committed to prison for disobeying the High Court.

The Law Society was not the only body losing patience with Murphy, and in June 2008 Judge Johnson, who oversaw the solicitors' roll, queried why the prison threat had not been carried out much earlier. 'I was given excuses which would have amazed theologians of a medieval nature in their dexterity and which would have even surprised three-card-trick men at Puck Fair in the manner they were applied,' said the judge.

Sean Acton and Michael McDarby from Ballinrobe, Co. Mayo, who overcharged accident victims through a fees scam, were allowed to continue practising despite repeated pleas by the Law Society that they were not fit to practise after 'driving a horse and cart' through solicitors' regulations. The Solicitors Disciplinary Tribunal denied the Society's request that it recommend to the High Court that they be struck off, instead fining them €25,000 each. In November 2008 the pair complained to Judge Johnson that the fines were unfair; Johnson's response was to quadruple the fines, saying he wanted to send out a message that dishonesty would not be tolerated in the legal profession.

Ciaran Callan was a solicitor in Rathfarnham, Co. Dublin, with a large conveyancing business: more than 85 per cent of the fees he generated for Callan and Co. came from buying and selling properties for his well-heeled clients. Callan, a former rugby player who had been the first coach of Leinster in the professional era, was immensely popular in rugby circles. As a lawyer he represented players who were charged with violent conduct on the pitch and he also served as a disciplinary commissioner for matches in the Heineken European Cup.

Callan, who had suffered from ill health in the months leading up to his practice being investigated in February and March 2007, had desperately tried to conceal a deficit in his client account by 'teeming and lading': concealing the loss of one client's money by replacing it with funds from another client. When the Law Society moved in to inspect his practice, it could not assess the true deficit as books of account had not been fully written up and there had been countless incidents of non-recording of payments.

Two years later, in July 2009, a forlorn-looking Callan turned up at the High Court and admitted several breaches of solicitors' regulations including failing to keep proper books and records, failing to register deeds and transferring money between accounts to conceal an underlying deficit that was eventually calculated at €1.9 million by the time Judge Johnson struck him off.

One inexplicable drama that emerged in the aftermath of Lynn and Byrne was the refusal by the High Court and Supreme Court to strike off two high-profile solicitors who had engaged in a massive tax scam.

Roger Greene and Sons was a small but prestigious Dublin law firm that had cornered a lucrative market representing health boards in childcare disputes. Its principals, Henry Colley and Colm Carroll, were the envy of other, larger Dublin-based firms that vied for this lucrative state business.

Colley came from a family that was steeped in law and politics. His father was George Colley, the late Fianna Fáil deputy leader and archrival of Charles Haughey, and his grandfather Harry was an old IRA veteran and a Fianna Fáil TD. Henry Colley, known to his friends as Harry, followed in his father's footsteps and qualified as a solicitor. His sister Anne also became a solicitor, and was elected a Progressive Democrat TD in 1987 but lost her seat two years later; she now chairs the Legal Aid Board and has served as vice chair of the Law Society's compensation fund committee, which compensates victims of dishonest and fraudulent solicitors.

The sudden transfer of much of Roger Greene and Sons' lucrative health board work to a rival firm in 2004 took Dublin's close-knit legal community by surprise. The reason did not become apparent to the wider public until early 2008, when the Law Society went to the High Court to seek to have the solicitors struck off the roll.

The Society, which investigates every solicitor's practice

at least once every five years, had stumbled across problems at Roger Greene and Sons during a random practice inspection in June 2003. Mary Devereux, a chartered accountant whose name strikes fear into the hearts of even the most compliant of solicitors, discovered a €197,000 deficit in Colley and Carroll's client account.

What worried her most at that point was the fact that client liabilities which were recorded as being due at December 2001 had seemingly disappeared. This prompted Devereux to embark on a painstaking quest to reconstruct the firm's accounts. At every step she was obstructed by Colley and Carroll, and finally she was forced, in 2004, to go to the High Court to seek orders against the solicitors.

Colley and Carroll had plenty to hide. What Devereux did not know when she began her investigation was that the solicitors had set up a secret account, hidden from the Law Society and the Revenue Commissioners, at Ulster Bank on O'Connell Street in Dublin, into which they placed millions of euros, mainly in professional fees, in a bid to evade tax. At one stage the secret fund had more than €41 million in it. Devereux also discovered breaches of solicitors' regulations, including the forging of practice accounts to mislead the Law Society into thinking that huge fees owing to barristers engaged by the firm had been paid when the fees had in fact been siphoned off into the secret slush fund. (Treating barristers in this way is not as difficult as it might seem. Unlike other professionals, barristers are not allowed to sue for non-payment of fees, and appeals to their ruling body, the Bar Council, to coerce solicitors into paying, are often fruitless.)

When the Law Society referred the case of Colley and Carroll to the Solicitors Disciplinary Tribunal in 2004, it expected an open and shut case that would result in the pair being struck off. But what happened next was staggering.

Henry Colley and Colm Carroll appeared before the Solicitors Disciplinary Tribunal in September 2006. Each hearing of the Tribunal is conducted by two solicitors and a lay person, and on this occasion the solicitor members of the Tribunal were Frank Daly, a former president of the Law Society, and Ian Scott, a partner in Arthur Cox. When they appeared before the adjudication team, Colley and Carroll confessed to more than fifty breaches of professional regulations, including deliberate non-compliance with the Tribunal and deliberately fiddling their accounts. Their chief plea in mitigation was that their scam was designed only to fool the tax man. They insisted that their clients and members of the public were not at risk. (This overlooked the damage done to the public interest by tax evasion, as well as the public interest in the health board cases in which the practice specialized.) The Tribunal recommended that they be suspended for twelve months, be allowed to practise only under the supervision of another solicitor for three years, and pay €50,000 each to the Law Society's compensation fund.

Two months later the Law Society, unhappy at the perceived lenience of the Tribunal's recommendations, brought an application to the High Court to have the two men struck off. Normally when such an application is brought before the President of the High Court, it is heard within a matter of weeks or months at most. But Colley and Carroll's case languished inexplicably in the High Court, and did not come before High Court Judge Liam McKechnie until February 2008, more than a year after the Law Society's motion to strike them out.

Senior Counsel Shane Murphy led the Law Society's challenge before Judge McKechnie. His case was concise: the men had set up secret accounts, withheld fees, operated hidden bank accounts and doctored their accounts in a deliberate bid to obstruct the Law Society. They deserved to be struck off if the public were to have any confidence in the regulation of solicitors.

Carroll's lawyer pleaded that striking off was a draconian penalty and laid great emphasis on the fact that no money was owed to the public. (Colley and Carroll had, by now, made a €7 million settlement with the Revenue Commissioners; Carroll had stopped practising law but Colley was still working in Roger Greene and Sons.)

Judge McKechnie delivered an immediate oral judgment in which he described Colley and Carroll's misconduct as orchestrated, deliberate and sustained; but, in a move which caught the Law Society off guard, he upheld the recommendation of the Disciplinary Tribunal and refused to strike the pair off. He stated that the men were in their fifties and were unlikely to reoffend. But the most critical factor in his decision not to strike Colley and Carroll off was the fact that their clients had not been left out of pocket and that the men were able to repay their debts. Had there been any shortfall, Judge McKechnie said, he would have struck them off.

The judge said he believed that his decision would help maintain public confidence in the legal profession and uphold the good name of the Law Society, but his decision had the opposite effect. It stuck in the craw of the public, and it puzzled solicitors who had seen many of their colleagues struck off for much lesser offences than a €32 million tax scam. It sent out a message that white-collar crime in general and tax fraud in particular was a gentlemen's affair. Colley and Carroll's settlement with the Revenue Commissioners meant that there would be no criminal investigation.

The treatment of Colley and Carroll stood in stark contrast to that of lesser mortals hauled before the criminal courts for fraud. People such as Joseph Sullivan, a Dublin father of one with a €50,000 gambling habit who received a three-year suspended sentence after he falsified work documents in order to transfer €36,000 to his own bank account. Or Karl Holmes, who made fraudulent tax repayment claims worth nearly €53,000 and was jailed for a year.

Former Bank of Ireland employee Susan Dowling was caught having made bogus expenses claims on behalf of companies affiliated to the bank and lodging the cheques into her personal and credit card accounts. She defrauded her employer of €103,000 over a five-year period. Dowling, who came from humble roots in Dublin's inner-city Basin Street area, had developed a serious cocaine addiction and was deeply in debt to a dealer.

By the time her case came before Dublin's Circuit Criminal Court, Gardaí revealed that they had agreed to speak to the social welfare department on Dowling's behalf after they discovered she lived in 'dire circumstances' during the fraud investigation. Despite this, Judge Katherine Delahunt said she had no option but to punish Dowling's 'wholesale deception' and sentenced her to twelve months in prison.

'There was no excuse or desperation for funds, it was simply to lead a high lifestyle,' said Judge Delahunt.

Cheryl Nielsen, a 42-year-old grandmother from Australia, defrauded her lover's company of €77,000 after he made the mistake of hiring her as his financial controller. She lodged stolen cheques directly to her account and cashed others through an unwitting boutique where she was spending €20,000 a year on luxury goods.

In the Circuit Court Judge Tony Hunt imposed a four-year prison sentence, and stipulated that Nielsen hand over the proceeds of her pension and savings account as compensation. Judge Hunt called it an 'unsophisticated crime' and said Nielsen had 'squandered the money on the high life'.

There were plenty of people, Carroll and Colley included, who squandered money on the high life, but the public was puzzled by the disparity in the way the legal system appeared to treat solicitors and lesser mortals.

After the McKechnie ruling the Law Society regrouped and, for the first time in its history, decided to appeal against a High Court refusal to strike a solicitor off.

Behind the scenes, the Society, under fierce pressure in the wake of the seemingly never-ending cascade of scandals, hoped that the Supreme Court could not close its eyes to the scale and implications of Colley and Carroll's fraud and would reverse, or at least significantly amend, Judge McKechnie's ruling.

When he appeared before a three-judge Supreme Court panel, led by Judge Hugh Geoghegan, Shane Murphy said that confidence in the legal profession was the most important consideration in deciding whether to strike off the two men. It did not matter, in this context, that 'nobody was out of pocket' as a result of their scam, said Murphy.

The Supreme Court's verdict, delivered in May 2009, was jaw-dropping: Colley and Carroll would not be struck off and the Disciplinary Tribunal's recommendation, upheld by Judge McKechnie, would stand.

The Supreme Court, which in principle considers only points of law on appeal but in practice can substitute its own verdict on the facts, barely considered the substantive case made by the Law Society, confining its deliberations to the narrow question of whether it was open to Judge McKechnie to arrive at the decision he did.

Judge Geoghegan made reassuring noises that the court did not condone Colley and Carroll's conduct and described as 'flagrant' the numerous breaches of solicitors' regulations by the pair. The Supreme Court was also unequivocal about the fact that the scheme operated by the duo was designed to evade tax. But it refused to reverse Judge McKechnie's verdict, saying it could only do so if, as a matter of law, his ruling was clearly incorrect. The Supreme Court found it was not.

The Supreme Court ruling has set the bar for expulsion impossibly high: if a €32 million tax scam does not constitute grounds for striking a solicitor off the professional roll, what does? And it arms delinquent lawyers with a stunning precedent to use when they are hauled before disciplinary committees or the courts for misconduct.

If only because, unlike solicitors, they do not handle clients' monies, barristers emerged largely untainted by the wave of legal corruption that broke starting in the autumn of 2007. But not wholly untainted.

Patrick Russell first appeared in the Four Courts as a state witness in the 2000 trial of Catherine Nevin for the murder of her husband. A former member of Sinn Féin who styled himself a business and property consultant, Russell had testified that Nevin wanted to buy her husband's share of Jack White's Inn. A year after the murder trial that had gripped the nation, Russell – a former business associate of ex-Taoiseach Albert Reynolds – qualified as a barrister and represented the late Fianna Fáil TD Liam Lawlor at the Flood Tribunal (which became the Mahon Tribunal).

Russell came to public attention again in 2006 when he was linked with an investigation into a Jersey-based company called Universal Management Consultants (UMC), in which Reynolds had a beneficial interest. The Mahon Tribunal was probing UMC's involvement in an attempted land purchase in north Dublin.

More trouble was brewing for Russell when an extraordinary

case involving a refrigeration company came before the Commercial Court in June 2008. The liquidator of Ardline Aircon Ltd brought an application to have Russell committed to prison for failing to tell the liquidator what he did with €635,000 the company gave him in 2007 to pay its tax bill.

Russell faxed apparent receipts for the money from the Revenue to Ardline and also got a person purporting to be a tax official to speak on the phone to the director of the company, who paid him €50,000 for his services. It later emerged that the money had never been passed on to the Revenue at all, and that the 'receipts' furnished to Ardline were bogus. Russell later confessed to his own legal team that he had actually put the 'tax' money into an account which contained not only his own funds but funds belonging to his property partners.

Russell, who had left the Law Library and stopped practising as a barrister when Ardline was placed into liquidation in 2007, was packed off to Mountjoy prison for a few hours in November 2008 for contempt of court and his behaviour was branded as 'disgraceful' by Judge Peter Kelly.

Russell was being investigated by the Professional Conduct Tribunal of the Bar Council, the representative body for barristers, when he left the Law Library, and he is now believed to be pursuing business interests in England.

The Benchers of the King's Inns, a panel of judges and senior lawyers, met in 2007 to discuss what to do with Russell, whose antics were bringing the profession into disrepute, but it did not disbar him. In fact, it has no formal record in its 469-year history of ever having disbarred a barrister. Finally, in December 2009, it introduced new rules that will allow it to receive complaints from the Bar Council, making it easier to strike off rogue barristers.

At the time of writing, alleged victims of Russell are being interviewed by members of the Garda fraud squad.

The Lynn and Byrne scandals had exposed major flaws in Ireland's land registry and conveyancing systems, but these flaws had been evident to some observers within the legal profession for some time. In August 2007, a few weeks before the Lynn and Byrne stories broke, Richard McDonnell, a solicitor from Ardee, Co. Louth, wrote to the Law Society warning of a 'conveyancing time bomb' that would cost the profession dear in terms of both insurance premiums and reputation.

McDonnell, an experienced conveyance practitioner, had examined huge numbers of titles that his office had received for existing and new properties and discovered that a significant proportion of them had not been scrutinized properly, if at all. The carelessness he witnessed in title, planning and building regulations documentation was staggering, with many contracts arriving with 'almost comically incomplete' or defective titles.

McDonnell blamed much of the sloppiness to the proliferation of one-stop conveyance firms that had mushroomed during the boom and offered fixed-price deals, undercutting the practices of traditional conveyancing solicitors who could not beat them on fees. He also blamed incessant and unreasonable demands by clients who wanted to buy or close the purchase of homes within days in a frenzied market.

'It is so unfair: people will, with equanimity, accept a three-month delay in delivery of their new car or an appointment with a medical consultant, but if their solicitor won't complete a purchase or sale within an absurdly short time, all hell breaks loose,' McDonnell told Mark McDermott, then editor of the *Gazette*, a bimonthly magazine issued to solicitors.

Colleagues had complained to McDonnell that they were under so much pressure that they did not even bother to read titles any more and instead just signed certificates of title and signed off on loan cheques to get clients off their backs.

The Law Society – which by now had raided Lynn's legal practice – published McDonnell's letter in full. Under the heading 'The title time bomb and the competition fuse' McDonnell made a timely prediction: 'The headlong rush to earn fees and attract clients by taking short cuts, which is no doubt making lots of money for some colleagues, will have grave repercussions for the future.'

And it did.

For two months after the Lynn and Byrne scandals broke, there was a nearly daily stampede by banks to the Commercial Court in a race to see who could secure judgments against the solicitors first.

Initially the banks solemnly agreed to pool whatever information they had about the pair, but they soon broke ranks and fled to the court presided over by tough-talking Judge Peter Kelly in hope of securing priority over each other.

As soon as the cases came before the Commercial Court, Judge Kelly dispatched the papers to the Garda fraud squad, thus sparking a major criminal investigation.

For his part, Judge Johnson, the President of the High Court, spent two years asking the banks that had lent money to Lynn and Byrne for information on bonuses paid to the employees who sanctioned loans to the struck-off solicitors, but the banks refused to divulge that information.

The banks had been defrauded on a massive scale, but none of them had made a complaint to Gardaí. They had every reason for wishing to confine the scandal to the civil courts: criminal proceedings would open up the appalling vista, from the banks' perspective, that their internal credit control and security procedures would be exposed through court actions.

Judge Kelly's intervention meant that that prospect is still a live one; but three years after the scandals broke, neither Lynn, Byrne nor any other rogue lawyer referred to Gardaí has been arrested, let alone charged or convicted.

Lynn, living in Tavira in the Algarve, has not returned to Ireland, but has turned up in various other countries. On 11 August 2009 he was arrested on foot of a European Arrest Warrant in Budapest and detained, but was released after the chronically under-resourced Garda fraud squad said they could not extradite him. Although Lynn faces more than 250 civil proceedings from banks and clients, he could not be extradited because there were no criminal proceedings against him. (The bench warrant for his arrest related only to a civil charge of contempt which Lynn argued was moot once he was struck off the solicitors' roll.) That Lynn has not yet been charged with criminal offences raises serious questions about the ability of the fraud squad to prosecute white-collar crime.

Coverage of the cases of Lynn, Byrne and other rogue solicitors understandably focused on the lawyers' own misconduct, but the conduct of the banks was arguably the bigger story by far. All six of the Irish banks whose liabilities were guaranteed by the Irish state in 2008, along with all the big foreign banks that lent against property, were hit by the undertakings scam. In their failure to exercise due diligence when issuing loans, they made it far too easy for solicitors to deceive them. While the losses associated with the rogues represent a minuscule proportion of the banks' overall losses, it is hard to avoid the conclusion that they all arose from the same root cause: a frenzied desire to inflate the size of property loan assets on their balance sheets.

This fact was not lost on High Court Judge Frank Clarke

when he delivered a key ruling on 1 June 2010 in a €7 million case brought by ACCBank against a solicitor who had acted for it in its dealings with a property developer. Opening his 65-page ruling Judge Clarke invoked Warren Buffett's oft-repeated remark that we only get to see who has been swimming without their togs on when the tide goes out. The judge urged the introduction of an electronic conveyancing scheme to minimize the risk of shoddy and shady property deals alike; and, although he found that ACC's solicitor had acted negligently towards the bank by failing to put in place proper security for the loans, he also pointed the finger of blame at Ireland's banking culture at the height of the boom.

The workings of that culture were exposed in an explosive but short-lived High Court action in November 2007 involving a senior employee at Irish Nationwide Building Society. Home loans manager Brian Fitzgibbon, a rising star at the building society, was earning more than €80,000 a year when he brought an application to injunct his employer from suspending him and subjecting him to disciplinary procedures. Fitzgibbon claimed that he was being made a scapegoat for the bank's €20 million exposure to Lynn and Byrne. The Tipperary-born banker said that he had twice declined loan applications from Byrne in November 2006 and April 2007 but that Michael Fingleton, the building society's chief executive, overrode his decisions. Fitzgibbon also claimed that at least one of the substantial loans to Michael Lynn – more than €4 million for Glenlion – was made directly on Fingleton's approval.

Fitzgibbon sat on Irish Nationwide's credit committee, which met to assess loan applications of more than €1 million. Fingleton was also a member of the committee, but Fitzgibbon claimed in a sworn statement submitted to court that Fingleton 'never' attended meetings and that the committee existed 'simply to satisfy the requirements of the Financial Regulator'. Fitzgibbon also stated that he was aware of a 'significant number of high-value loans which were personally approved by Fingleton without any recourse to compliance with the normal procedures'.

The case was admitted for full, plenary hearing because the court found that Fitzgibbon had established a strong, arguable case that Fingleton had allowed 'deviations from the society's written lending policies'. A full hearing beckoned, inviting further insights into Fingleton's management style; Irish Nationwide moved quickly to settle the case and Fitzgibbon was reinstated to his post by order of the High Court.

The overall legacy of the rogue solicitors is manifold.

In 2008, the Law Society paid out €9.64 million to compensate victims of fraudulent solicitors – more than 300 times the overall amount paid out by the fund in 2000. To date, more than €10 million has been paid to clients of Lynn and Byrne from the compensation fund. But perhaps the most damning statistics lay in the number of solicitors' cases that were referred to the High Court and inevitably made their way into the public domain. In 2006, as the property boom was hurtling towards its peak, just four solicitors were referred to the High Court. In 2009, the number of such cases was eighty-six.

The disintegration of Lynn and Byrne's empires, combined with the collapse in Irish property prices, also contributed to an unprecedented crisis in the legal insurance industry. Law firms struggled to secure cover for their practices and some small and medium-sized firms have seen their premiums double, treble and even quadruple since 2006.

Solicitors were obliged to almost double their level of insurance cover against potential negligence claims. The Law

Society, facing an avalanche of negligence claims against solicitors over their failure to comply with undertakings in commercial property transactions, also moved in November 2008 to introduce tougher regulations for legal practices, again driving up insurance costs.

The profession was plunged into a further crisis in July 2009 when the annual accounts of the Solicitors' Mutual Defence Fund, a not-for-profit insurer, revealed the shocking news that a bond into which it had invested €8.4 million of its reserves with stockbrokers Bloxham was worth almost nothing after its value collapsed by 97 per cent. The SMDF warned the Law Society that it would not be able to write indemnity business for the new insurance year unless it could guarantee repayment of a loan that it needed to plug the gap left by the failed bond. Following an emergency meeting in October 2009, the Law Society stepped in to prop up the fund by giving the guarantee.

Faced with the prospect of a market failure in legal insurance, Gerard Doherty, the Law Society's then president, wrote to his members arguing that in the absence of a bailout 'there would probably have been an enormous number of solicitors' firms unable to obtain PI [professional indemnity] insurance, with disastrous consequences both for the firms themselves and for their clients'. But many solicitors were angry that the Society – which had spent €22.4 million in 2006 to buy a 1.09-acre site beside its headquarters, the value of which was written down to €7 million less than three years later – had pressed ahead with the bailout without any consultation. Although the vast majority of firms were able to secure insurance by the year-end deadline, it is feared that many will be priced out of the market in the years ahead.

Another consequence of the bust for solicitors, unsurprisingly, was unemployment: by late 2009, there were more than 800 solicitors signing on for the dole. This prompted the Law Society to appoint its first-ever career development adviser to help solicitors find work or leave the profession altogether.

The saga of Michael Lynn and Thomas Byrne was more than just a tale about rogue solicitors: their stories were a microcosm of Ireland's boom and bust and a harbinger of things to come. As the storm clouds gathered over the duo's law firms in 2007, a hurricane was forming in the wider economy. Arguably, what saved the legal profession from further disgrace was the emergence of ever more colourful rogues and even greater scandals. The sins of the solicitors would soon be dwarfed by those of the bankers and developers.

2. The Strange Case of the GAA Hero and the Fianna Fáil Star

KILLALLY – On this, her Christening Day, big bros Odhran and Iarfhlaith announce with pride the birth of their baby sister, Béibhinn Maria Killally, on August 6, 2009. Mummy and Daddy, Naomi and Ger, are 'in the pink'!

When they announced the christening of their first baby daughter in the notices section of the *Irish Times* in December 2009, Mummy and Daddy Killally were not just in the pink. They were also hopelessly in the red.

Serendipity, Mummy's interior design business, had folded and Daddy, a one-time rising star in Fianna Fáil and former General Election running mate of Brian Cowen, was bankrupt, facing debts of more than €40 million and mired in a labyrinth of litigation.

Just a year earlier the Killallys had attended a meeting in the Four Courts to assess the prospect of defending a series of claims against Ger and his business partner, Richie Connor. Their Senior Counsel, John Gleeson – brother of Dermot Gleeson, the former Attorney General and ex-chairman of AIB, for whom he is often mistaken – had three pieces of advice to dispense to Ger Killally and Richie Connor.

Talk to these people.

Settle with them.

This could end up before the Director of Public Prosecutions.

The Killallys didn't flinch as Gleeson detailed the possible civil and criminal consequences of failing to honour the fiduciary duties owed by Killally and Connor to the business partners from whom they had concealed profits in a series of property deals. But Helen Connor, Richie's wife, almost collapsed. She staggered from the meeting room with the words 'prosecution' and 'fiduciary' ringing in her ears. The mother of three had never heard of fiduciary duties, the legal and moral responsibilities of company directors and parties involved in partnerships, but the prospect of a criminal prosecution hit her like a ton of bricks.

In 2007, Richie Connor's net worth had been estimated at €19 million, but for over a year the teacher turned property speculator had been borrowing from his local credit union and using his credit cards for day-to-day living expenses as his foray into the property market with Killally drew to a shuddering halt.

In the world of the GAA, Richie Connor is a hero.

The Walsh Island native holds three Leinster senior football championship medals, won an All Star in 1981, and captained rank outsiders Offaly to an unforgettable All-Ireland victory over Kerry in 1982. In September 2008 he fulfilled the dream of a lifetime when he was ratified as the new Offaly senior football manager. But within weeks he was making headlines for all the wrong reasons when it emerged that he and Killally were being sued by Frank Lawlor and Declan Guing, their partners in several land deals.

Less than six months later, he was no longer Offaly manager and was back teaching at Rath National School.

It was when managing Laois in the early 1990s, and serving as principal of Rath National School, that Connor was tempted into a new career. Businessman Paschal Phelan offered him a two-year contract as development manager with Master Pork, which was building a factory in Edenderry. Local opposition to the piggery was something that Phelan needed to subdue and Connor, whose name carried great currency owing to his GAA profile and extensive local contacts, was recruited to iron out any difficulties.

Connor did not particularly want to leave teaching, but the salary and the two-year time frame appealed to the young father, who soon relished the task of working with farmers, sourcing land for rearing pigs.

After several years with Master Pork, Connor, who was constantly adding to his impressive list of local and regional contacts through negotiating various land deals with farmers and their advisers, branched out into selling life insurance products for a range of major brokerages.

Connor did well as a broker for a number of years. Starting out as Midlands manager with insurer Prudential, he had then spent eight years working with New Ireland, one of Ireland's leading life assurance companies. Connor was then recruited by Canada Life, heading up their regional sales operation from Athlone; but he was made redundant in 2002 when the firm restructured its Irish operations.

The redundancy forced Connor to strike out on his own, just as Ireland's property boom was beginning to take off.

Connor's work as a broker had brought him into contact with Ger Killally, a young county councillor from Edenderry who was being tipped to become a Fianna Fáil TD for Laois–Offaly. Killally was an accountant who had himself branched out into auctioneering and was also moving into the mortgage and insurance markets. He was one of the leading lights in Ireland of ERA, the New York Stock Exchange-listed residential real estate brokerage, and was the go-to guy for anyone buying and selling homes in Edenderry.

Connor was impressed by the young man's vision and ferocious work ethic, but Ger Killally's political pedigree was his primary asset. He got his first taste of politics at the age of 16, when he served as a youth officer for Fianna Fáil's Rhode Cumann. He later founded a 70-strong Ógra Fianna Fáil branch at Portobello College in Dublin. He first ran in a General Election in 2002 and, although he failed to get elected, the highly successful campaign had blooded Killally and his supporters.

Even before his redundancy, Connor had contemplated setting up his own business as an insurance broker as he wanted to be his own master and there was plenty of business to chase. Killally, meanwhile, was at the height of his powers transacting a great number of property deals and working towards adding the letters TD after his name in the next General Election, when he would be running alongside the Minister for Finance and possible next Fianna Fáil Taoiseach.

As his auctioneering business grew, Killally's swashbuckling swagger and increasingly vulgar display of wealth annoyed some and amused others. He and his wife, Naomi, earned the moniker of 'Edenderry's Posh 'n' Becks' around this time when they invested in his and hers OY1 and OY2 registration plates for their cars, which they changed every year.

On the outskirts of Edenderry they built a nine-bedroomed faux-Gothic stone mansion, with more than 8,000 square feet of stables on an acre and a half of land to accommodate a collection of ponies and horses, with garages to house their classic car collection.

The boglands of north-east Offaly – not far from the Kildare border – fell within the ever-expanding Dublin commuter belt and a gold rush was on. Edenderry was, in local parlance, 'flying it'. Like Michael Lynn with his 'commission matrix', Killally envisioned a one-stop business offering support on every aspect of property transactions: mortgages, life insurance, the works.

He was big on ideas but lacked attention to detail. The idea behind the Mortgage Warehouse, the retail investment intermediary company he and Richie Connor set up, was that Killally would line up the leads and Connor would execute them. The men would split the business 50:50 and whatever they made would go jointly into the pot.

Connor was staggered by Killally's commitment to his politics. Killally would routinely phone Connor to inquire about the who, what, why, when and where of local funerals. It did not matter that Killally did not know the deceased. The quintessential Irish councillor would milk details from Connor about the dead person and then made sure he was there to shake hands and commiserate with mourners at the funeral.

The problem for Connor, as he told me during an interview at his home in Walsh Island, was that the Mortgage Warehouse was struggling in its early years, and it was his only source of income. Killally, by contrast, had his auctioneering income, and that business was going from strength to strength. He did extremely well out of Chancery Park, an upmarket housing estate developed in the town by Hugh McGill, a Fianna Fáil donor. The entire development sold off the plans over the course of a weekend.

Shortly after the Mortgage Warehouse was set up, Killally opened a second auctioneering office in Tullamore.

As 2004 drew to a close, Connor confided in Killally that he and Helen were tapping into their savings, including their children's education fund, to get by until the Mortgage Warehouse started to pay its own way. Killally, who in 2005 watched his wealth increase to staggering levels on foot of transacting land deals for others as well as himself, was sympathetic, and told his new business partner that the real money was in land. One night, when Connor was driving home to Walsh Island, he received a call from Killally, who offered him his first stake in a land deal.

'There's land outside Edenderry that can be bought for €1 million, but it is worth more than that,' Killally told Connor. 'Do you want in on the deal?'

Connor went home and spoke to Helen. He told her that for €25,000 they could take part in a four-way deal with Killally and two other businessmen, Frank Lawlor and Declan Guing, to buy 9.5 acres at Carrick Road, Edenderry. All he had to do was sign a cheque made payable to a solicitor in Tullamore, and sign some papers. Forgoing any legal advice, Connor went in on the deal.

Within six months, the plot of land at Carrick Road, bought at just over €1 million, had been sold for €3 million. After paying capital gains tax, Connor cleared a couple of hundred thousand euro.

The Connors could not believe their luck. Unbeknownst to themselves, they had just joined a club of amateur speculators – teachers, Gardaí, taxi drivers and other people of ordinary means who had no particular knowledge of or experience in the property business – who were getting rich as land prices surged by the week.

'We didn't think there was anything wrong,' Connor told me as we drove in April 2010 to his home in Walsh Island, the same road where Killally offered him an involvement in Carrick Road.

'People were flipping land, houses, everything. That was the culture of the time and I thought that the reason people were able to do this was that they recognized the value. We knew several auctioneers who were also involved in a lot of these deals. The desire on all our parts was to make money.'

Serious money.

Richie Connor's faith in Ger Killally was consolidated by the Carrick Road deal. Naomi and Ger were, he would say later, 'in a different league', but he enjoyed the young couple's company and marvelled at their own plans for their future.

Helen was just happy that the boys' education fund had been restored to good health. What she did not know was that within three years almost everything they had ever worked for would evaporate.

In late 2005 Killally urged Connor to get involved in the auctioneering side of the business to boost his income and, through the potential referrals from house and apartment sales, that of the Mortgage Warehouse. The two men then entered into a partnership as auctioneers, trading as ERA Gerard Killally Auctioneers incorporating Killally Connor and the Mortgage Warehouse, and operating from offices in Edenderry, Tullamore, Portarlington and Portlaoise.

Meanwhile, buoyed up by the success of the Carrick Road deal, Connor agreed to consider going in with Killally on the purchase of a site at Cappincur, just outside Tullamore, known as the Daingean Road lands.

The developer who owned the lands told one of Killally's agents that it could be bought for €5 million. Killally suggested to Connor that they buy the site and 'flip it on'. The developer was in a rush to sell and Killally was also in a rush to buy it and flip it on, not an unusual ambition at the time given the rate at which land values were increasing.

What happened next is not entirely clear, but it involved no small amount of cunning on Killally's behalf and is best explained by a sensational memo issued by the office of Miriam Kavanagh, who routinely acted for Killally, to her own solicitor, Robert Dore.

The memo was headed 'Off the Record', underlined and in bold. Kavanagh wrote:

What is happening here is as follows. Ger was buying this property with business partner Richard Connor at €5m from Mulligan Builders (Midlands) Ltd.

However he did not want his identity disclosed so we did up a declaration of trust for Cyril Keegan and Laurence Murphy who signed the contracts on his behalf under the guise of Daingean Road Builders (actually it was signed by Cyril but they are the two trustees). Ger was doing a sub sale to a company called BPMK for €6.5m but the sub sale has fallen through.

In order for Ger to satisfy the bank for the loan approval to continue the purchase, he has got an independent valuer at €6.5m and he needs to bring in another two partners.

He doesn't want the two new fellows to know that he had originally got it bought for €5m and is basically screwing them for another €1.5m.

The people Killally was 'basically screwing' were his friends, Declan Guing and Frank Lawlor, who formed a partnership with Connor and Killally to acquire the Daingean Road lands for €6.5 million oblivious to the fact that Connor and Killally already owned the land – at arm's length, via the trust arrangement with Cyril Keegan and Laurence Murphy.

'They were buying the land at €6.5 million, we were part of it,' says Connor. 'We were buying it off ourselves, [having bought it] at the other side for €5 million.' Connor says that while he never imagined that there was anything illegal about the secret profit he and Killally made on the deal, 'There was a tinge of, "Are we screwing the boys?"'

One of 'the boys' was Frank Lawlor.

A tyre distributor from Edenderry, Frank Lawlor had built up a modest yet healthy property portfolio but used every minute of his spare time building up the political profile of Ger Killally.

Killally had lots of acquaintances, but few people he could actually count on as genuine friends or confidants. Lawlor was an exception, and he in turn ranked Killally as one of his best friends. The two men became acquainted through Fianna Fáil and were often seen together at party political functions or on the canvass as Lawlor pressed flesh in a bid to get his friend into Leinster House.

'I stood behind him on everything, absolutely everything,' said Lawlor, now living in Shanghai, where he is trying to rebuild his life and repay some of the €35 million in debt that awaits him back home.

Lawlor is still at a loss as to where it all went wrong: he trusted Killally, his accountant as well as his friend and business partner, implicitly.

Such was the continuing escalation in property prices that the general expectation was that the Daingean Road lands, bought at €6.5 million by the partnership, could be flipped on for €9 million.

'That is the way things were,' recalls Connor. 'There was only one way land was going.'

During 2005 the Killally/Connor/Guing/Lawlor partnership also bought the 200-acre Downshire site at the back of the main street in Edenderry for €11.5 million. The deal was part-financed to the tune of €8 million by AIB, and although it was put together in the dying days of 2005, it was not completed until March 2006, shortly before the market started to turn.

As with the Daingean Road deal, the Downshire deal was not what it seemed. Unbeknownst to Guing and Lawlor, the actual vendors – their identities again concealed – were Killally and Connor, who had bought the land for €9.5 million from a company linked to Hugh McGill.

Oblivious to Killally and Connor's secret profit on the deal, Guing and Lawlor joined forces with their colleagues with the aim of developing a 109-bed hotel with restaurant, leisure centre, banqueting and conference centre on the Downshire site.

Privately, Helen and Richie Connor were beginning to get worried. On paper they were worth millions, but in reality their property investments, both personal and in the form of at least three other partnerships with Killally, were eating cash instead of generating it. Connor's activity in the sector was frenetic at this time. According to the Companies Registration Office he became a director of eleven companies, mostly related to property developments, in 2006 alone.

Despite the cash difficulties, and the deeper danger that the paper profit would turn into unmeetable debts should the market go sour, Connor continued to plough equity into new ventures. Nor did he decline to make the jump from land speculation to property development, as envisaged in the partnership to develop the hotel complex.

Dublin accountants and consultancy firm Horwath Barstow Charleton were drafted in to help prepare the bank financing, to conduct feasibility studies, and to provide tax and financial advice towards the Edenderry Plaza hotel development.

The partnership needed €16 million in bank funding, but HBC could only get a commitment for €8 million. By the time this unforeseen difficulty had been identified, work had already started on the hotel, as it needed to be 15 per cent complete by December 2006 in order to qualify for tax relief.

In November 2006 the four-man partnership put the Daingean Road lands up for auction, hoping for a nice profit on the €6.5 million they had paid – a profit that could help bridge the gap between what the bank was willing to lend towards the Edenderry Plaza hotel project and the €16 million needed.

The auction was widely publicized, but the land did not receive a single bid.

'I thought, Jesus, what is happening here?' Helen Connor told me during an interview at her home. What was happening, although it wasn't widely recognized at the time, was that the property boom had peaked.

Only a month earlier, Justice Minister and PD leader Michael McDowell had declared that the state did not need the massive level of funds generated by stamp duty on property transactions and promised reform of the unpopular tax. The intervention by McDowell, widely perceived as a pre-election gimmick, caused home buyers to hold off on purchases in anticipation of stamp-duty reform. Suddenly, the seemingly bottomless demand for new houses – of the sort being built at record rates on sites like Daingean Road – was shown to indeed have a bottom.

To apply for bank funding for the hotel development, each of the men in the partnership was required to obtain an independently verified Statement of Affairs. It was from this exercise that Connor learned that his net worth was €19 million. Killally was valued at more than €40 million, as was Lawlor. But these were meaningless figures; the market had turned, and there wasn't enough cash to develop the hotel. Lacking the expected profit from a Daingean Road sale, Richie and Helen Connor put the proceeds of their newly matured SSIAs straight into Edenderry Plaza. Soon the Connors were remortgaging a few apartments they owned, and Killally and Connor remortgaged their commercial premises in Portlaoise to meet the increasing cost of keeping the hotel development on track.

It did not stay on track, and in July 2007 Killally, Connor, Guing and Lawlor sought the appointment of a High Court examiner to devise and implement an investment programme for the project. By summer 2008, Richie Connor, the €19 million man, was living off loans from his local credit union, his day-to-day expenses covered by cash withdrawals on his credit card.

Frank Lawlor was struggling, too. In early August 2008 he picked up the phone to Hugh McGill, the developer who had been a key figure in Killally's rise to fame and fortune and who had sold part of his Downshire site to the Edenderry Plaza partnership.

Mindful of the men's difficulties, which by this time were well known in the locality, McGill asked Lawlor if the partnership was going to sell on the Downshire lands. Lawlor replied that they were unlikely to make any profit, given that they had paid BPMK – the company of which McGill was a director – €11.5 million for the site.

McGill told Lawlor that he was mistaken: BPMK had been paid €9.5 million and not €11.5 million for the Downshire lands.

Lawlor was staggered to hear this, and the revelation prompted him to conduct a review of all his dealings with Killally.

He asked McGill to fax him a copy of the sales advice notice which confirmed that BPKM had sold the Downshire lands for €9.5 million.

Lawlor rang Miriam Kavanagh, who had acted as solicitor for the Daingean Road and Downshire partnerships, and asked for a contract for sale of the Downshire lands.

He also engaged Dublin law firm LK Shields and sought a meeting with Miriam Kavanagh. At a meeting on 1 September 2008 at the Spa Hotel in Lucan, Kavanagh conceded that she had been aware of the initial sales to Connor and Killally that had preceded the sales to the Connor/Killally/Guing/Lawlor partnership. According to Lawlor's sworn statement recalling the meeting, Kavanagh claimed that when she told Killally that she could not act in each of the two transactions he was planning for the Daingean Road and Downshire lands, he advised her that another firm of solicitors 'would be seen to be acting for' the partnership in the initial purchases in each case.

Lawlor and the remaining investors complained that Kavanagh had been negligent in her duty towards the four-man partnership on the two purchases because she knew that Killally and Connor were making secret profits.

Four weeks later, Guing and Lawlor began proceedings against Killally and Connor in the Commercial Court claiming that the men had misrepresented the deals, had acted in breach of contract and had enriched themselves at the expense of their business partners.

The case also involved Adrian Daly, a farmer from Tullamore, who was not involved in the Daingean Road or Downshire deals but had invested in two later deals along with Killally, Connor, Lawlor and Guing in which it was alleged that the auctioneers had again made secret profits.

*

Within days of the opening legal moves, the Edenderry Plaza Hotel, which had been placed into examinership in July 2007, went bust.

The news could not have come at a worse time for Edenderry, which was reeling from the closure of Rationel Windows and the shower component manufacturer Sanirish, which between them employed more than 100 people in the town.

When the writs arrived, Killally and Connor initially thought that Daly, Guing and Lawlor had lodged their actions as a strategy to exact money from the pair on foot of deals that had gone horribly wrong for all. They also thought the action might be a prelude to professional-negligence claims against the firms of solicitors involved in the various deals. But John Gleeson's legal opinion, delivered in his initial meeting with his clients in the Four Courts, shattered any notions that the men were playing war games.

The Red Mass is an old tradition, first observed in Paris in 1245, which is still used to mark the beginning of a new legal year in places all over the world – including Ireland. Amid great pageantry and solemnity, the Holy Ghost is asked to bestow wisdom and morality upon the shoulders of the legal profession.

After the excesses of the Celtic Tiger, both virtues were badly needed in Ireland.

The Red Mass in this country is in fact two services, held at two different churches named for St Michan in the vicinity of the Four Courts: the Catholic church in Halston Street, and the Protestant church in Church Street.

At the Protestant service, Father Godfrey O'Donnell, the head of the Romanian Orthodox Church in Ireland, began his sermon on a sombre note.

'We seem to be living through the death throes of raw capitalism, please God, with its appalling greed, recklessness, lack of accountability and complete disregard for any ethical behaviour and the consequences of that for ordinary hard-working people's lives, especially the poor,' intoned the priest.

At the Catholic mass, Bishop of Ossory Seamus Freeman also referred to the financial crisis, telling the congregation – which included Chief Justice John Murray and Attorney General Paul Gallagher – that what the newspapers today call greed, St Paul called self-indulgence.

Assisting the Bishop, as they do each year, was a small group of lay lawyers who perform the duties that altar boys normally provide at Sunday Mass. Manning the incense was Peter Kelly, the High Court judge and head of the Commercial Court, who needed no lectures, legal or moral, about the near-biblical tide of recklessness and greed washing up at the door of the Four Courts.

When it was created as a division of the High Court in 2004, the Commercial Court was heralded as a no-nonsense forum where businesses could resolve large-scale disputes without enduring lengthy delays that could have catastrophic commercial consequences. It was the offspring of the stunning escalation in the scale of business during the boom years in Ireland; but, quite suddenly, it became the graveyard of the Celtic Tiger, where the bones of those who tried to ride what seemed like an eternal property-fuelled boom lie scattered. In years to come, historians, economists, psychologists and sociologists will try to wholly understand Ireland's extraordinary boom-to-bust cycle, but those seeking more immediate answers as to why and how the economy has tanked so spectacularly could do worse than spend a day or two in Judge Kelly's court.

Shortly before Killally and Connor entered Kelly's list, the judge warned that his court was being 'littered' with claims for specific performance of contracts, where one party in a contract asks a court to compel the other side to complete their side of the deal. The surge in such actions mostly related to the sale of development lands agreed in 2006 and 2007, when funding and bank borrowings were easy to come by and when – as we now know – asset prices were at an extraordinary peak from which they would soon fall dramatically. Day in, day out, would-be sellers of once-valuable lands hauled would-be buyers to court for performance of the contracts they could no longer afford to honour. In the early years of the Commercial Court, by contrast, most 'specific performance' disputes arose from transactions in which the participants were fighting over the spoils.

The arrival of Ger Killally on to Peter Kelly's stage marked the beginning of a pantomime season. It was Richie Connor's great misfortune that his choice of business partner was a serving Fianna Fáil politician. That Ger Killally was the former running mate of the sitting Taoiseach ensured that a dispute involving five Edenderry businessmen would become a sensation.

Daly, Guing and Lawlor accused Killally and Connor of making secret profits in relation to a total of four transactions. Judge Kelly admitted the cases on 20 October 2008.

Within weeks, Bank of Ireland had moved against Ger and Naomi Killally for the repayment of some €2.9 million in loans, €300,000 of which the couple disputed. The ink was barely dry on newspaper stories detailing the latest setback to afflict Edenderry's Posh 'n' Becks when Ger Killally's car careered off the road in Edenderry and Killally was brought to hospital. Then Killally scored a spectacular own goal when he took to the airwaves on his local radio station, Midlands 103, and complained that he was the innocent victim of a vindictive media. He apologized to the Taoiseach and to his family and friends, and then broke down on air. Party colleagues viewed the performance as pathetic.

The drama surrounding its bright young star became a problem for Fianna Fáil as every twist and turn in the tale was reported under headlines such as 'Cowen's Crony in Court' and 'Biffo Running Mate Sued'.

'There would be none of this if Brian [Cowen] wasn't from Offaly, no one would even know who I am,' Killally complained to the *Sunday Independent* in December 2008. He also staunchly defended his role in the deals. 'I didn't chase these investors; they came of their own free will,' he said. 'Everything was clear and above board. They [the plaintiffs] are not greenhorns, they did their due diligence, they are all professional business people with legal advisers. I have no case to answer.'

It was not just the legal actions by Daly, Guing and Lawlor that he was contending with. Killally was also hit by a lawsuit from a consortium of investors who claimed that he and others had made secret profits when the consortium bought 35 acres of land at the former briquette factory site in Mount Lucas. (This case is still before the courts.) When John Gleeson advised Killally to settle in advance of any hearing, Killally objected. Richie Connor, by contrast, recognized that what he and Killally had done was wrong, and when Judge Kelly directed that the two men provide sworn answers to interrogatories – specific questions by their former partners' lawyers to flesh out their defence – he knew the game was up.

In February, Killally and Connor admitted that they had

made secret profits on the Daingean and Downshire partnerships, but denied making any profits on the deals involving Adrian Daly.

Judge Kelly, who described the pair's conduct as unconscionable and dishonest, observed that the admissions had had to be 'wrung out of them' under threat of contempt proceedings. But he also distinguished between Connor, who had not tried to blame anyone else, and Killally, who claimed he had got legal advice to the effect that it was all right not to disclose the profits to his colleagues.

What the legal proceedings never fully illuminated was why Killally and Connor structured the Daingean Road and Downshire deals in the way that they did, or why they misled Lawlor and Guing. Was there a grand plan, or just a series of individual decisions that, collectively, brought about a disaster? Killally testified that, as a county councillor, he wanted to preserve his own privacy in his land dealings; but this does not explain his failure to tell the truth to his business partners. The mechanisms used in the Daingean Road and Downshire deals can be employed – quite legitimately – to avoid various kinds of tax, but no such rationale emerged in the legal proceedings. As Killally pointed out, Lawlor and Guing 'were experienced businessmen and were very satisfied to be involved in the transactions at the price negotiated with them'. The root of all the trouble, it seems, was not any particular element of the transactions, but the fact that Connor and Killally misrepresented the transactions to their business partners.

The admissions by the two were accompanied by an €8 million freezing order on their assets, so that they could not dissipate them or move them out of the country in order to frustrate a creditor's attempts to get a judgment. Judge Kelly amended the freezing order to allow Connor to be paid as a national school teacher, remarking that he should have stuck to the teaching job.

Connor resigned as Offaly football manager six days later, after just five weeks in the job, on foot of the withdrawal of nine players from the county panel - an action that seems to have had no direct connection to Connor's legal troubles.

The hardest part for the Connors was the adverse and never-ending media attention, but any hopes of that abating were dashed by another tearful performance in the High Court by Killally in March 2009. Seeking a relaxation of the freezing order to allow some funds to be released for day-to-day expenses, Killally broke down in front of Judge Kelly as he told how he needed €16,000 a month. This sum included €1,500 a month for electricity costs and €42,000 a year for health and life insurance policies for him and Naomi. In a pathetic display, he sobbed as he told the judge about burst pipes, problems with underfloor heating and other faults with his new mansion. He also talked about the expense of raising two small children, with another child on the way, and said that he was 'in between' cars, as his 2008 Audi Q7 SUV had been damaged in his recent accident and he could not afford to have it repaired.

'I'm here telling the truth, everything,' he said, revealing how his and Naomi's family were financially supporting them as they hurtled towards bankruptcy. But the request for €4,000 a week towards household expenses rang hollow when pictures of his 8,000-square-foot home were beamed into every other cash-strapped household in the country.

Judge Kelly told Killally to come to his senses and radically reduce his living standards. It particularly irked the judge that Killally had splashed out on the new Audi at a time when he was shutting down his businesses. Still, he varied the freezing order to allow Killally some living expenses and to receive any surplus rental income on several properties owned by him and

Naomi. The couple had borrowed €10.7 million to buy properties, including nine holiday homes in Tullamore and houses and shop units in Counties Laois, Westmeath and Dublin.

On 30 June 2009, Killally and Connor met Lawlor again in the Four Courts at a hearing to decide what damages they should pay for making secret profits on the Daingean Road and Downshire deals.

When Lawlor took to the witness stand, he fought back tears as he told Judge Brian McGovern that Ger Killally was his friend and that he had been dumbfounded to discover irregularities in the transactions. As Lawlor told of his joy at being present at Killally's children's christenings, Killally bowed his head in what appeared to be genuine grief.

Lawlor also told the court of how Ger Killally – who had been chairman of Offaly County Council at the time – had been able to tell him that a piece of land they planned to buy was to be rezoned in a matter of weeks, thus making the site more valuable.

Connor sat quietly in the back row, listening to Lawlor as the bells of the Angelus chimed at noon from the Catholic steeples of Dublin's north inner city.

Lawlor's quiet testimony about the men's friendship and its betrayal was a catalyst for a settlement, and over lunch the former business partners and their lawyers began negotiations, reaching a deal under which Killally agreed to a €15 million judgment against him and Connor accepted a judgment of €10 million. Both men also agreed to transfer their interests in the Daingean Road and Downshire lands to Guing and Lawlor.

Separate proceedings by Lawlor and Guing against the solicitor Miriam Kavanagh, who had acted for Killally and Connor and whom they claimed had failed to advise them

of the circumstances surrounding the deals, were withdrawn.

It was all over for Richie Connor, who insisted that his
lawyers read out a handwritten apology explaining his
actions.

'I got caught up in the mania of the property boom that
allowed temptation of easy gain to impair my judgment,' said
Connor.

He wasn't the only one.

3. The Glenageary Madoff

On 10 December 2008, Bernie Madoff broke the news to his sons Mark and Andrew that Bernard L. Madoff Investment Securities – in which both men were senior traders – was a massive Ponzi scheme. The fraud would eventually be valued at close to $65 billion: arguably the largest financial scam in US history. But the Madoffs were not the only family in New York trying to come to terms with a debilitating secret that morning.

Within hours of Madoff's confession, financier and investment manager Bernard Lambilliotte welcomed his brother-in-law, Breifne O'Brien, into his plush Manhattan home. Only a week earlier Lambilliotte, the Chief Investment Officer and managing director of London-based investment firm Ecofin, had advanced almost $1 million to O'Brien as part of a deposit to secure options on a host of properties in Dublin. In all, the Belgian, whose personal wealth was in excess of £100 million, had given the Irish investment adviser almost €2 million to invest in various Dublin property schemes.

Or so it seemed.

For weeks O'Brien had tried to keep Lambilliotte at bay, reassuring him that his funds were on deposit, earning a high rate of interest topped off with lucrative commission fees. But two days before the agreed 12 December deadline for the return of the monies, O'Brien turned up in New York and confessed to Lambilliotte that he had been living a big lie. For some fifteen years the 49-year-old, who sported a permanent tan from frequent holidays to exotic locations, had operated a Ponzi scheme that fed on the goodwill of his oldest friends and family members. Lambilliotte, who was married to O'Brien's sister Aoife, was told bluntly that there was no chance he could ever be repaid.

As news of Madoff's arrest, the day after he confessed to his sons, sent tremors throughout Wall Street and global investment markets, O'Brien returned to Dublin to quietly confront family members and friends who had given him money to invest. Before doing so, he conducted a SWOT analysis – an assessment of his strengths, weaknesses, opportunities and threats. Mr Justice Peter Kelly, head of Ireland's Commercial Court, was identified as a potential threat by O'Brien, presumably because of his tendency to refer suspicious commercial disputes to the Garda fraud squad.

On Friday 12 December, Madoff was charged with securities fraud. At Invergarry, his Victorian house in Glenageary, O'Brien started a round of phone calls to his best friends.

In pre-Christian times in Ireland, the Hill of Tara in Co. Meath was the coronation seat of Ireland's kings and queens. In the 1990s, when the Republic entered its golden Celtic Tiger era, the middle-class suburbs of south Co. Dublin became the sacred dwelling place of mere mortals who were transformed into demigods by the country's runaway property boom.

To the outside world, Breifne O'Brien and Fiona Nagle were the epitome of the Celtic Tiger generation: sophisticated, confident and well connected. In addition to Invergarry, the family home in Glenageary, the couple owned an apartment at Vico Road, Dalkey, arguably Ireland's most exalted address, and a villa in the Sandy Lane golf resort and luxury hotel complex in St James, Barbados. Nagle, a former receptionist at the global public relations firm Fleishman-Hillard Saunders, had gone on to run her own PR and event management company. The mother of five charged a minimum €2,500 for a private party for six, and managed parties and balls at home and abroad for Ireland's nouveaux riches.

The jewel in Nagle's crown was the annual Sinatra Ball in Dublin's Four Seasons Hotel, where her husband assumed the role of a suave Rat Pack playboy. The ball, which raised money for several charities, was one of the best-known high society events in the Irish social calendar, attracting Hollywood stars such as Aidan Quinn and Pierce Brosnan.

Even private family gatherings for O'Brien and Nagle were written up by the social diarists. For the christening of their son in 2005, they 'erected a marquee resembling a continental speakeasy club' in their back garden at Invergarry, according to the *Sunday Independent*. Two hundred friends, including Fianna Fáil TD and former Minister for Social and Family Affairs Mary Hanafin, attended the bash. RTÉ presenter Marty Whelan, celebrity chef Johnny Cooke and *VIP* publisher Michael O'Doherty were also present to raise a toast.

The following year, Nagle's style acumen was hailed in Ireland's fashion bible, *Image* magazine. Nagle talked about the high priests of couture whose designs languished in her closet, and revealed a weakness for diamond jewellery by Van Cleef & Arpels. 'My style is practical, but totally impractical after 8 p.m. I never stick to one designer – a few Chanel pieces always rise to the top of the pile,' she told the magazine. 'Roland Mouret makes me feel like a woman.'

Breifne O'Brien and Fiona Nagle, who had been living together since 2000, married in a quiet civil ceremony at Wicklow Registry Office in July 2007, following Nagle's divorce from estate agent Gerry Hoban, with whom she had two children. Two months later they entertained over 300 people at their wedding party at Carrigrohane Castle, O'Brien's family estate in Cork.

Breifne O'Brien didn't, according to those who attended Trinity College Dublin with him in the 1980s, possess a stunning intellect or a dazzling personality. 'He was nondescript, that is the amazing thing,' recalls one former college friend who declined the opportunity to invest in O'Brien's fund in later years. 'He was slightly posh and there was something permanently middle-aged about him even though he was only a student. He seemed a harmless fool. Had there been no boom, I would have expected to see Breifne living out his days in the civil service.'

But O'Brien was popular at Trinity, and made some friends who went on to do very well for themselves. After university, most of his friends emigrated, but O'Brien and his close friend Peter O'Reilly stayed at home in Ireland to try their hand as entrepreneurs.

O'Brien was an impressive self-starter, and he and O'Reilly surrounded themselves with experienced guides and mentors. In the early 1990s, O'Brien and O'Reilly sought advice from Evan Newell, a businessman from Rathgar in Dublin who had been involved in the launderette business for more than a decade before he began developing an interest in property investments.

Although he never invested in any of O'Brien's businesses, Newell was happy to dispense his advice and experience on business and entrepreneurship to the young man.

O'Brien's first venture was a highly successful launderette in Rathmines called Shirley's, for which Newell helped him source the property. Shortly afterwards O'Brien set up another launderette on the sprawling University College Dublin campus.

At the end of 1992, O'Brien and O'Reilly sought Newell's advice about opening a diner near O'Connell Bridge in the centre of Dublin. Newell ran up calculations for the two young men and told them the projections did not look encouraging; but they decided to forge ahead, turning to some of their school and college friends to co-invest on the project.

One friend who got the call was David O'Reilly. O'Reilly, a second cousin of Peter O'Reilly, had studied Economics and Social Science with O'Brien at Trinity. They met each other socially roughly once a year between 1984, when they graduated, and the early 1990s.

When David O'Reilly left Trinity, he embarked on a successful career in merchant banking in London that would ultimately see him headhunted to become the Managing Director of Bankers Trust, one of the world's premier foreign-exchange trading houses.

He was in London in 1992 working long hours at Bankers Trust when O'Brien and Peter O'Reilly told him they were putting together an investment consortium to develop the diner, Starvin' Marvin's.

The investment proposal coincided with David O'Reilly's transfer from London to New York to head up the New York operation of Bankers Trust. He visited the diner only once and, although he wasn't too impressed with the venture, he invested all the same.

He should have trusted his instincts: within twelve months of opening in 1993, the diner had gone bust. David O'Reilly lost his entire investment, but the men remained on friendly terms.

A year after the collapse of Starvin' Marvin's, O'Brien,

now styling himself as an investment adviser, rang David
O'Reilly in New York to offer him the opportunity to take
part in what he described as 'low risk' property investments.
By that time O'Brien was, by all accounts, doing well in his
own business life.

Between 1993 and 2008 O'Reilly invested in a number
of property deals with O'Brien, usually for sums ranging
from €200,000 to €500,000. Most of the property deals
related to options on land including houses, commercial
buildings and rights of way. An option on a property grants
a party the exclusive right to buy or sell the property within
a specified time at a set price. The option is usually secured
by the payment of a non-refundable fee to the owner of
the property.

The fee covers the opportunity cost incurred by the seller
in tying up his asset. The appeal of an option to the potential
buyer is that no one else can buy the asset during the period
of the option. If the buyer believes the value of the property
is going to rise, the option gives him the opportunity to
benefit from the price rise; it also gives him time to round up
the investment partners and bank funding needed to complete
the deal.

Because an option binds both would-be buyer and seller
into a legal contract, even for a short period, it is customary
for the seller to demand proof that the buyer is 'good for it',
by requiring him to demonstrate that he has enough money
to cover the option. This 'show me the money' stipulation
wards off time-wasters and those who cannot afford to exercise the option.

Over the fifteen-year period that David O'Reilly invested
with O'Brien, he believed that any money he gave O'Brien
was to show potential sellers of optioned property that he
'could call on substantial monies if required'. The financier

also believed that any money he gave O'Brien would be held in a bank account, and that the options would only be exercised if they could reap a profit. O'Reilly would later state in an affidavit that 'the returns promised were typically of the range of 0–15 per cent over and above what might then have been the rate available for monies on bank deposit' and that the time frame of the options in the transactions he undertook with O'Brien ranged from three to ten months.

David O'Reilly, who moved in 1995 to a New York hedge fund where he worked eighteen-hour days, was happy to reap the rewards of these investments while being relieved of all the bureaucracy of the deals, which were handled in Dublin by O'Brien. O'Reilly never sought to formalize any of their dealings: there were no contracts, no due diligence, no poring over the details. Such was the trust between the two that when O'Reilly's bank refused to finance his investment in one of O'Brien's proposals in 1998, after initially agreeing to do so, O'Reilly withdrew money out of another investment scheme run by the bank he worked for, even though this involved taking a major loss. O'Brien meanwhile invested in three companies on the advice of O'Reilly.

'People liked him, he was very genial and positive,' said one international lawyer who was involved in some property deals with O'Brien. 'You would not for one minute imagine that he was capable of ripping people off.'

By the time he returned to Ireland in 2003 to pursue new entrepreneurial endeavours, David O'Reilly's trust in O'Brien was complete. So he asked few questions when O'Brien approached him in September 2008 about part-financing an option on property located at Place Vendôme in Paris, one of Europe's most sought-after addresses and home to the Ritz hotel. O'Reilly transferred sums of $3 million and €1.6 million to O'Brien for the Paris option, expecting the repayment of his capital and accrued returns by 30 November 2008.

What he did not know was that his 'investment' had been siphoned off in its entirety to an account in Coutts, the exclusive private bank in London.

The Coutts recipient was Brian Reid, an Ulsterman whom O'Brien had befriended at Trinity, and who had gone on to become one of the most senior executives at Royal Bank of Scotland (RBS).

When O'Brien delivered his groom's speech at Carrigrohane Castle, he made a point of thanking those who – unbeknownst to his assembled guests – had bankrolled him for the last ten years.

He singled out David Bell for particular praise. Bell, 86, was the former taxing master of the High Court and one of the most respected lawyers in Dublin prior to his retirement. He was also the father of one of O'Brien's best friends, Paul Bell. O'Brien told his guests how he had often sought David Bell's counsel and how good David had been to him in the thirty years they had known each other.

O'Brien had got to know Paul Bell at Trinity. He also befriended Paul Bell's best friend from secondary school, Paul Galligan. Around Christmas 1997 Paul Bell spoke to his father about O'Brien, with whom Galligan had transacted some successful investment deals earlier that year.

Paul Bell, who had gone into banking in London, told his father that there could be a number of opportunities worth pursuing with the up-and-coming investment adviser. The Bells had just received funds from the voluntary liquidation of a company in which they had been shareholders.

In January 1998, David Bell had some of the money he had received from the liquidator on deposit in an account in

National Irish Bank (NIB). After the conversation he had with his son about the possibility of investing with O'Brien, he moved the money to an account opened in ICC Bank in Cork.

The account was opened in Paul Bell's name, but father and son agreed that the investment account would be maintained for the benefit of them both.

On 26 January 1998, O'Brien travelled to Silver Birches, David Bell's home in Dundrum, to discuss the maiden deal. O'Brien told Bell that he needed £200,000 urgently to support the continuation of a property option that he had with Edward Quinlan, a Cork businessman.

O'Brien claimed he already had £100,000, but needed £200,000 to seal the deal and that if he could demonstrate to Quinlan that he had access to the extra money, Quinlan might consider extending the option until April.

To reassure Bell, O'Brien told the elderly solicitor that if he lodged the £200,000, he would receive a letter from ICC showing the balance in the account. The arrangement was that all of the money lodged would stay in the ICC account, undisturbed, until April when the extended option for the purchase of Quinlan's property was completed. The plan then was to exercise the option at £300,000 and sell the property on to another party for £330,000, resulting in a £30,000 profit to be divided between O'Brien, Galligan and the Bells.

Everything seemed above board. When the £200,000 lodgement – of which £174,000 came from David Bell – was faxed to ICC Bank in January 1998, a bank official confirmed that there was an account in O'Brien's name, that there was credit in the account before the lodgement was made, and that the arrangement required the signed and witnessed permission of Paul Bell before any withdrawals were made. Following the initial transfer of the money, O'Brien regularly called to update David Bell on the deal, including reports of the overall balance in the account and interest earned.

On 9 April 1998, O'Brien called to see David Bell at his office in Dublin, accompanied by a £174,000 bank draft in favour of Paul Bell. He told the lawyer that the interest on the Bell family's contribution was in the process of being credited and he would furnish him with the details later.

O'Brien also told David Bell that there would be 'other opportunities', and it was agreed that Bell would not cash the £174,000 draft, but that O'Brien would use the sum to open a new account in the name of Paul Bell at the ICC bank in Cork.

There were always more options, new opportunities, and in May 1998 Paul Bell withdrew £55,000 savings from another bank account to help O'Brien tie down another option he was apparently negotiating.

In August 1998, O'Brien sought another £228,831 from the Bells to help him secure an option to buy 30 acres of land in Cork which, if bought at £21,000 an acre, could soar in value if rezoned.

In October 1998 O'Brien wrote a letter on the headed notepaper of Standard Laundry, in which he was a director, enclosing a copy of an ICC Bank statement showing that the balance on the Bells' account was £432,297.

Extraordinary as it seems, this appeared to reassure the Bell family, whose relationship with O'Brien was deepening, even though they had received very little by way of returns on their investments.

From 2000 David Bell, now in his late seventies, started working as O'Brien's solicitor on a series of deals. A year later, O'Brien told David Bell about an upcoming land deal involving Evan Newell, O'Brien's friend and business mentor. He said that he (O'Brien) was giving Newell advice on the rezoning of lands owned by Newell and that he had been offered an option to buy 3 acres of the lands at a price of €50,000 per acre. The Bells were invited to participate in the option and asked to part with another £231,000 for the privilege of doing so.

The Bells never saw the supposed Newell option agreement, which, David Bell would later remark, probably did not exist at all.

Two years after the deal was first mooted, David Bell transferred £231,000 to O'Brien, again in order to show that he could call on more money if he needed to.

The Newell option, had it truly existed, would have been utterly spectacular. O'Brien reported that after Newell's lands had been rezoned, the lands that were the subject of the option – originally 'struck' at €50,000 per acre – had been 'sold' for €1 million an acre. This meant that if the investors exercised their option to buy the land at €50,000 an acre, they would benefit from the onward sale of the land now valued at €1 million an acre.

In the year leading up to the collapse of his Ponzi scheme, O'Brien told David Bell that his funds were being retained by Newell's solicitors until certain tax matters that Newell was required to deal with were settled. He then told Bell, at a meeting, that there was potential for a further option on another 3 acres of Newell's land on which a shopping centre would be built. This option didn't require new money, said O'Brien. This ploy – claiming to place investors into a new option without additional funds being needed – was a signature O'Brien ruse to deflect attention when people expected the return of their capital. O'Brien then cited the new option as the reason for the delay in returning the Bells' funds. In all, the Bells were owed more than €750,000.

★

Evan Newell had no idea that his name was being used by O'Brien to dupe unsuspecting investors. Nor did he imagine he would be duped himself.

Newell rented office space to several companies of which O'Brien was a director, including an Irish incorporated entity known as Ecofin Services, which was linked to Bernard Lambilliotte's London-based Ecofin Financial Services Ltd, which managed somewhere in the region of £3 billion worth of funds. O'Brien never stopped talking about Lambilliotte's success, regaling Newell with tales of the financier's legendary decision to invest in Irish energy firm Aitricity before the company was sold for €2.2 billion in 2007. O'Brien claimed that he himself, through his affiliation with Lambilliotte, had 'made a killing' on Airtricity. Newell assumed that this, along with his launderettes and a new-found flair for property investing, was the source of the young man's vastly increasing wealth.

One spectacular deal stuck out in Newell's mind during this period. This deal involved a substantial holding in Cork owned by Edward Quinlan, which O'Brien bought with his father, Leo O'Brien. The property was subsequently sold, netting a €4 million profit.

Newell had no financial involvement with the deal but had discussed it in some detail at the time with Leo and Breifne O'Brien. He met with O'Brien at monthly intervals and typically the men would discuss the various ventures O'Brien was involved in: buying a shop in Harold's Cross, selling launderettes and an internet café, the purchase of another property in Cork and a small shopping centre in Monkstown. O'Brien's taxi companies in Blackrock and Dun Laoghaire were expanding, prompting O'Brien to terminate his rental agreement with Newell in December 2001 and move into his own premises. Later, Newell would state in court documents that he could not remember with sufficient clarity or confidence the detail of the various transactions O'Brien regaled him with or whether there was any substance to them at all.

It was ironic that, having known O'Brien for such a long period of time and without ever becoming financially involved with him, Newell was among the last of the investors to get sucked into his Ponzi scheme. Newell wasn't too pushed when, early in 2007, O'Brien invited him to join an investment consortium to acquire a shopping centre in Hamburg for over €100 million. Initially, he said no. But O'Brien persisted, indicating that he was in a position to obtain an option to buy the shopping centre.

After perusing what appeared to be a well-documented project, Newell agreed to invest and transferred €3.35 million to O'Brien on 8 June 2007 to fund an option to buy 75 per cent of the shopping centre in Hamburg. O'Brien agreed that the investment would be returned at Newell's discretion or when the consortium he was trying to put together was in a position to lodge funds to cover the option. Newell was not guaranteed any profit or return other than the standard deposit interest rate for the investment, which he thought was safe in a bank account. He later said, during the legal proceedings, that he advanced the money to O'Brien as a favour and did not need or expect any remuneration or payback over and above the standard bank deposit rate. As favours to friends go, even from someone who had done well through his own property investments, it was colossal.

By April 2008, Ireland's economy was in free fall. The property bubble had well and truly burst, and hedge funds had launched an attack on the shares of Anglo Irish Bank, the beloved lender of developers and speculators. Newell had not sought the return of his monies and O'Brien had other plans for the funds. He came back to Newell and told him that he had negotiated a new and improved deal on the shopping centre, this time including an option over an adjacent car park. The 'new' deal required a second transfer and, on 1 April, Newell sanctioned the release of a further €750,000.

On 7 November 2008 – when, unbeknownst to Newell, O'Brien was desperately trying to pay off other investors – Newell sank another €300,000 into the deal, believing that by tipping the total level of funding over the €4 million mark he would attract a better deposit rate.

The pair agreed that the transaction would now be completed and that the full capital and interest would be returned to him within the first two weeks in December. O'Brien even checked which Irish banks were offering the best deposit rates and opened two accounts in Newell's name – at Permanent TSB and Anglo – so his friend's investment could enjoy the fullest return.

Newell rang O'Brien on 8 December to ask again about his money. This time O'Brien told him that part of his money had been transferred in error to Lambilliotte's account in New York and he had to travel there to secure its return.

Newell patiently waited, but the funds never arrived.

Don Maher had known Breifne O'Brien for twenty-five years when their friendship, along with a €450,000 'investment', evaporated.

Maher first met O'Brien on a holiday in Greece in 1983, when both men were studying together at Trinity. The friendship endured and in recent years the men had gone on skiing holidays together. Don Maher had established his own highly successful chain of mobile phone shops before becoming CFO at Abbey PLC in the United Kingdom, and later director of Customer and Channel Management at

Vodafone Ireland, joining its board as an executive director in 2006.

By the early 2000s, O'Brien's extraordinary wealth was obvious, and Maher attributed this to a wildly profitable Cork property deal several years previously which, the businessman believed, had given him a war chest to speculate in a rising market ever since. As with Newell and other friends, O'Brien made much to Maher of his connection with Bernard Lambilliotte. He told Maher that he was an alternate director of Airtricity on the back of Lambilliotte's directorship, and that he had 'made a killing' on the sale of Airtricity because he had significant co-investment rights which he had happily executed. Such was the exclusive nature of O'Brien's scheme that Maher didn't even know that O'Brien invested other people's money.

In the autumn of 2008, just weeks before his Manhattan meltdown, O'Brien asked Maher to give him around €500,000 to secure an option on a property deal in Paris. He said he needed to show that he had €7 million, representing 10 per cent of the purchase price of the property, in order to be granted an exclusive option to buy it. O'Brien told Maher that he already had an agreement to sell the property on and would make a €7 million profit on the forward sale.

According to O'Brien, he already had €6.5 million; Maher's 'half bar' deposit would seal the deal. Maher was told that the money would never leave O'Brien's bank account. For his troubles, Maher would receive a 10 per cent return within four to eight weeks.

As far as Maher was concerned, he wasn't part of the Paris deal, only helping a friend make a lucrative investment and getting a handsome reward for doing so.

In early October, O'Brien sent Maher an email reporting that he had bought an option on the Paris property and

believed he could flip it on again at a profit to the under-
bidder on the original deal.

O'Brien assured Maher there was no risk. Maher gave
O'Brien another €450,000, expecting another 10 per cent
return within four to eight weeks.

There was no Paris option. And when O'Brien received
Maher's funds on 14 October, the money was sent directly
to the account of another of O'Brien's investors, Brian Reid,
in London.

The treatment of brothers Louis and Robert Dowley showed
Breifne O'Brien at his worst.

Louis Dowley had gone to secondary school with Paul
Galligan and was a close friend of Paul Bell. Like O'Brien,
he counted David Bell as a close friend and mentor. A
successful dairy farmer in Tipperary, he had known O'Brien
socially for more than twenty years when, in 2003, he and
his brother Robert decided to join their friends and invest
with Breifne.

Their maiden investment was as part of a syndicate to
secure a €5 million option on a shopping centre in the UK
that was under construction. Louis Dowley handed over
€530,000 drawn from his personal account, a farm account,
and from a company that he and his brother owned. In February 2004, in another one of O'Brien's signature ruses, he rang
Louis to say that the deal was progressing well, but one of
the 'co-investors' had to be bought out owing to a conflict
of interest. Louis was grateful to O'Brien for giving him first
refusal on the buyout and handed over another €250,000 to
O'Brien, inviting him to share half of the profit on the latest
investment as he had been 'good enough' to include him on
the buyout of the former co-investor's position.

In March 2004, O'Brien told Dowley that the profit on the

deal was €500,000 and that the brothers were about to receive their €65,000 share of the payout. But then O'Brien told Dowley that the €65,000 had mistakenly been lodged in a joint UK account drawn upon by O'Brien and the previous investor. The Dowleys did press O'Brien on the return of their profit, and when Louis contacted O'Brien he was told that it was 'only a matter of time' before a joint signature was arranged and the funds would be repatriated to Ireland.

The Dowleys were not deterred by the delayed return of the profits on their maiden deal and continued to invest in separate deals with O'Brien. On each occasion they advanced money to O'Brien, they received a letter recording any payment and correspondence detailing what they were owed or what was being held on their behalf. As with other investors, they were also reassured when O'Brien provided cheques to them for the capital sums invested on the understanding that they would not be cashed until the transaction was completed.

Sometimes the cheques were cashed in the normal way, but for the most part another new investment would be proposed by O'Brien – avoiding the need to present a cheque at all – and the investment would 'roll over' into the next deal.

Although it is clear in retrospect that it was folly to trust O'Brien, there are significant upsides to rollover arrangements, and it is not uncommon for investors across all asset classes to do so. Each time a deal rolls over, the value of the overall investment increases and investors can legitimately avoid paying tax, as they are taxed only when an asset is sold. Tax can thus be avoided for months and even years.

As with all rollovers, the key ingredient was confidence in the fund manager, which is essentially what O'Brien was – except the fund was fictitious.

O'Brien evidently mastered the art of gaining investors' trust and confidence and, crucially, maintaining it.

No sooner had the UK shopping centre deal concluded than O'Brien was on the phone to Louis Dowley touting an opportunity to secure an option on a site in Donnybrook. This option, he told the brothers, would cost €1.3 million, and he said there was pressure to complete. O'Brien claimed that Owen O'Callaghan, one of Ireland's most prolific developers, was prepared to pay an upside of 8 per cent if he bought it and would even pay 1 per cent of the purchase price just to look at the deal.

The Dowleys were impressed when, weeks after ponying up for the Donnybrook deal, they received €13,000, representing 1 per cent of the capital they had invested, plus an interest payment of €4,500.

In January 2005 the Dowleys invested €500,000 in an option on the National Toll Roads, but when nothing became of the NTR option the money was returned. Two months later, Louis Dowley invested €498,750 through Avonmere, one of O'Brien's laundry companies, almost half of which was used to buy shares in Sechilienne Sidec, a utility company that Ecofin was involved in. To buy the shares, Dowley transferred €250,000 to Ecofin Services, which had an account at the Permanent TSB branch in Blackrock, Co. Dublin. The ink was barely dry on the Avonmere deal when O'Brien invited the Dowleys to invest in the underwriting of linen shipments. These deals were transacted through O'Brien's company Standard Laundry Ltd. As with the property deals, it was all seemingly low risk. The Dowleys believed their funds would be held on deposit, and they would receive a 10 per cent return on their investment within four months of the linen arriving.

By the end of 2006 the Dowleys had in their possession cheques from O'Brien in the amount of €2.05 million which

– they believed – represented the monies owed to them from the linen deal, their capital, profit and interest that had accrued. O'Brien implored them not to cash the cheques, and they did not, as the linen shipment insurance deal 'rolled over' right into the first half of 2008.

In all, between property options and linen shipments, the Dowleys invested €4.2 million with O'Brien – and paid out more than €500,000 to the tax man in relation to their purported profits. But not one cent had gone to a legitimate deal.

The funds, O'Brien would later claim, had been used to pay off other 'investors', including David O'Reilly and Suzie Cruess O'Callaghan, an ex-girlfriend of O'Brien's. O'Brien used €1.3 million of the Dowleys' money to repay Brian Reid and more than €1.5 million to repay a loan from Abacus Treasury Nominees Ltd in Jersey. O'Brien also claimed that he used €250,000 to repay a loan from Finbarr Crotty, his insurance broker, and €200,000 to buy shares in Go Commercial Mortgages, a UK subprime mortgage lender established in 2005. He was a director and sole shareholder in the company. At its height, Go Business Mortgages, a subsidiary of Go Commercial Mortgages, which opened for business in 2007, was lending £20 million a month. In May 2008 it was placed into administration.

O'Brien had successfully operated a Ponzi scheme for almost fifteen years, but the house of cards began to tumble down during 2008, when he engaged in a fresh wave of bleeding 'investments' from his friends to meet the demands of older clients.

He extracted €1.25 million from the Dowleys in March and €750,000 from Newell in April. In May Bernard Lambilliotte gave him $1.845 million, and four weeks later the Dowleys invested another €1.2 million. By July the Dowleys were demanding reports on their positions from O'Brien. In August O'Brien dissolved his company Avonmere.

In September David O'Reilly handed over €3 million and €1.6 million for the glorious Place Vendôme option that never was. O'Reilly demanded that his funds be returned by November. Newell was also seeking his monies.

Certain investors, it seemed, had to be looked after over and above others. In November 2007, Lambilliotte, O'Brien's brother-in-law, had given O'Brien €1 million to secure options on investment properties in Dublin. In March 2008 Lambilliotte was paid in full by O'Brien, with a tidy €112,475 profit. In May 2008, he gave O'Brien $1,845,000 as part of a deposit O'Brien said was needed to secure options on investment properties in Sandyford, Dublin. On 12 September 2008 O'Brien gave Lambilliotte €119,975 as a partial profit.

The interim return kept his brother-in-law on side and on 2 December 2008, as O'Brien desperately tried to keep his scheme intact, Lambilliotte gave him another €780,597 after O'Brien claimed that NIB – where the property investment monies were apparently deposited – would pay 1 percentage point higher than the existing rate if the money remained there until 5 December.

O'Brien's biggest concern was Brian Reid, the RBS executive. More than £4 million was transferred to Reid in the two months leading up to December. On 6 December, in dire straits, O'Brien was still trying to tempt new investors at a lunch at the RDS in Dublin.

Four days later, he was on his knees in New York.

When Louis Dowley received a phone call from Breifne O'Brien on Friday 12 December, he and his brother Robert drove straight to O'Brien's house in Glenageary. They brought with them the €5 million worth of cheques that O'Brien had asked them not to cash until that date.

When the Dowleys arrived, O'Brien told the brothers that all their years of business dealings with him had been a fraud and a scam. They had been conned out of their money. The cheques were real, but there were no funds to back them.

The brothers noticed a contract note, from a stockbroking firm, sitting on O'Brien's kitchen table. The note showed a sale of shares in excess of €50,000. The Dowleys feared that O'Brien was secretly liquidating his assets and building up a slush fund to avoid paying them back. They immediately called their lawyer, Brian Quigley at McCann FitzGerald, one of Ireland's top law firms. The meeting lasted six hours.

The Dowleys told the Bells and other O'Brien investors that they were meeting Quigley again the next day. O'Brien, meanwhile, was trying to arrange a private meeting with Don Maher, but when he heard about the group that was convening at McCann FitzGerald he agreed to come and speak to them.

One by one on Saturday, the members of the group arrived: David Bell Jr, brother of Paul, who was representing the Bell family; the Dowleys, Don Maher, David O'Reilly and Evan Newell.

The group agreed that no matter how tempted they were, no punches would be thrown. Their nerves were fraught, but when O'Brien arrived he was as cool as ice. The Dowley brothers could not bear to be in the same room with him, and neither could Newell, who paced the corridors as the meeting took place. In addition to Quigley, Niall Powderly, a partner at McCann FitzGerald, was present, as was Paul Keenan, a former partner at accountancy firm BDO Simpson Xavier, whose presence was sought by some of the investors with a view to assisting with the task of finding out where the investors' funds had gone.

O'Brien, who did not have a solicitor with him at the meeting, took a seat beside Quigley and refused a glass of water. He was told that anything he said could be used in any subsequent legal proceedings. Quigley advised O'Brien that the group were about to seek a freezing order in the High Court to prevent O'Brien from reducing his assets or moving them out of the country.

O'Brien expressed his 'deep sorrow'. He was calm and did not show any distress. The conversation moved from general discussions about his operations to specific transactions and back to general matters again. He said that back in 1998, when he had sold the Cork property, he was in the clear. He could have paid off any outstanding debts. Instead, he had begun the cycle again, and had been living a lie for up to fifteen years. The investors' money had never been held in bank accounts in the manner stated or for the purpose claimed. He said there were more victims – by his own estimation, eleven people were owed anything between €16 million and €19 million. Their money had never been held in a bank account for any substantial period of time, or any longer than was necessary to move the funds elsewhere.

O'Brien detailed his modus operandi. He invented phony deals, sought money from an investor, and, when the time came to pay the investor back, he would try to convince him to reinvest in another fake deal. The pattern was all too painfully familiar to the shattered investors in the room.

O'Brien explained further that if he couldn't convince an investor to reinvest, he would seek out fresh blood to pay off the first investment. By his own account, using the lower €16 million figure, O'Brien guessed that he had used €4 million to fund his personal and family lifestyle, another

€4 million to buy properties, €4 million to keep his own business ventures afloat and €4 million to pay fictitious profits to other investors.

Turning to Quigley, he said that it was 'easy to pull the suckers in when the economy was booming'.

Some of those suckers were in the room. Some of them were among his best friends.

By lunchtime on Monday 15 December 2008, Breifne O'Brien's reputation was in shreds as Judge Peter Kelly – whose high ranking on O'Brien's SWOT list had been well merited – granted an order directing that O'Brien not reduce his assets below €20 million. At first, it might have been possible for an observer in the courtroom to believe that O'Brien was just another businessman gone bust; but any sympathy for O'Brien quickly evaporated when Quigley revealed in an affidavit what O'Brien had said about pulling the suckers in.

The court heard that in the preceding eight weeks alone, O'Brien had received €6 million from investors. Five million of that had gone to pay off Brian Reid, €600,000 to another investor. O'Brien couldn't account for the other €400,000. The fallout from the litigation was immediate. Within days O'Brien resigned from the boards of two high-profile property companies, Bulberry Properties and Hawridge Properties. Newspapers oozed with Schadenfreude. Renovation works continued at Invergarry, which was now under siege from reporters and photographers.

When the case came back before Judge Kelly in the New Year, a fuller picture of O'Brien's wealth emerged. O'Brien told the court about his properties on the Vico Road in Dalkey, Barbados and Sandyford. He also revealed that he had a 20 per cent share in three apartments under construction in the G Tower in Dubai and syndicated property investments in Berlin, Boston, Spain and Belize. In addition, he held commercial property in his own name in Monkstown, Sandyford, Reading and Paris.

O'Brien also revealed that his assets included art works valued at €50,000, a €70,000 Aston Martin, €2.2 million lodged in an investment fund for wealthy individuals operated by Anglo Irish Bank and 1.3 million shares in Maltese Holdings, a Jersey-registered company. One thing that was noteworthy about this was the fact that Maltese Holdings – which, along with another holding company controlled by O'Brien, had bought a car showroom in Munich with an €8 million loan from Anglo Irish Bank in December 2007 – was a subsidiary of two companies controlled by Bernard Lambilliotte.

Judge Kelly invited any others affected by O'Brien's scam to come forward, but few did. Many of the investors had good reason not to, either because they had got their money out before the whole scheme collapsed, or because they had not declared previous returns on their investments with O'Brien to the Revenue. Or perhaps they were simply embarrassed by the greed and stupidity that had fuelled their investments.

As the drama unfolded in Court 6, there was a wave of sympathy for Fiona Nagle, who was not implicated in the fraud in any way. Nagle indicated that she wanted to have the freezing order varied to release funds for her day-to-day expenses. The personal humiliation was made even more acute by the fact that her lavish lifestyle that had filled the society pages of newspapers and magazines during the boom times was now being regurgitated with a hostile spin by the same scribes who had lauded the couple in the first place.

But any sympathy that had accrued to Nagle evaporated

the following week when, in court papers, she asked Judge Kelly to release €4,000 a week – more than €200,000 a year – for her day-to-day expenses. It also emerged that she had instructed her legal team to withdraw the application if it were to be heard in open court. Nagle was forced into retreat when Judge Kelly refused an application by her barrister to hear the case in camera – with the media and public excluded – or to transfer the case to the family law division of the High Court, where secrecy was assured. Nagle's barrister Bernard Dunleavy quickly withdrew the application to relax the freezing order, and the costs of the brief but illuminating application were awarded against her. The €4,000-a-week request, which was exposed when Judge Kelly opened the relevant document in court, sent the media into a state of apoplexy, and even some of Nagle's sympathetic friends were stunned at the plea.

There was worse to come. Granting judgment for almost €13 million in November 2009 to Maher, the Dowleys, the Bells and Evan Newell, Judge Kelly compared O'Brien to Montague Tigg, the money-grabbing villain in the Charles Dickens' novel *Martin Chuzzlewit*. The judge gave O'Brien some credit for accepting responsibility and sparing his friends the trauma of a trial, but that wasn't enough to exculpate him: Judge Kelly directed that the court papers be sent to the National Bureau of Fraud Investigation to be examined by Gardaí.

The fraud squad referral prompted a change of tack by O'Brien. His contrition was now qualified: although he had confessed to his scam in the offices of McCann FitzGerald and had agreed to the €13 million judgment, he reserved his position in relation to the content of statements provided to the courts by his victims. He refused to incriminate himself.

Two new investors, who had been referred to O'Brien by

Peter O'Reilly, came forward to the courts seeking to recover almost €1 million they had invested with O'Brien. The proceedings by Barty O'Brien Ltd and Robert Dennison resulted in the value of the judgment jumping to €16 million. Even more worryingly for O'Brien, a cheque for €27,236 issued by him to Barty O'Brien from Avonmere in December had not only been dishonoured: Avonmere had been dissolved four months previously. In light of this, Judge Kelly invited the Office of the Director of Corporate Enforcement to investigate potential company law breaches.

As a chaotic January drew to a close, Bernard Lambilliotte became the tenth investor to sue O'Brien. At the meeting at McCann FitzGerald, O'Brien had pinned his hopes on accessing his brother-in-law's wealth to meet his debts, but now Lambilliotte was suing him for €1.8 million instead.

As her world fell apart, Fiona Nagle made a public appeal for privacy. In a letter to the editor of the *Sunday Independent*, which was published on the front page of the 22 February edition, she acknowledged that the media had to cover the court hearings but begged journalists to stop using 'ancillary references' to herself and her children.

'My request is not to suit myself but for my five children who are subjected to immense stress at a vulnerable age,' she wrote in her letter to the *Sunday Independent*. 'My primary concern is to protect my children and to look after their health and safety. If you can spare them this additional suffering, I would be most grateful.'

The plea fell on deaf ears in some quarters, with the *Sunday Independent* reporting that she was still driving her Audi Q7. Nagle also found herself in the spotlight when a District Court judge issued a warrant to bring her to court for non-payment of a parking fine. The warrant was subsequently withdrawn.

The next humiliation came at the annual Peter Mark VIP Style Awards in the Shelbourne Hotel when Michael O'Doherty – the publisher of *VIP* magazine – made a series of mischievous and unrepeatable comments about Breifne O'Brien. The Schadenfreude reached its zenith in July when the papers reported that O'Brien had driven to Heuston Station in Dublin to hand over his beloved Aston Martin DB7 to the County Sheriff. His art collection, meanwhile, was shipped off to Adam's auction rooms in Blackrock. The couple also had to deal with a raid by the Garda fraud squad at Invergarry.

Despite all the publicity and the freezing orders, O'Brien's victims struggled to recoup any money. Robert and Louis Dowley tried to execute their judgments in Britain, Paris and Barbados, where O'Brien had property. They also secured permanent charging orders against various shares owned by O'Brien, but the shares turned out to be worthless. Efforts to target his bank assets failed too, as banks exercised their right to offset O'Brien's assets against his debts.

By July, Nagle could no longer afford legal representation. She did not object to the Dowleys' application to secure orders against most of the shares but she pleaded with Judge Kelly in court documents to stay away from Blackrock Cabs, of which Nagle was a director and a 1 per cent shareholder. Now she claimed that 50 per cent of the company was held in trust for her. She said she had been working full time at the taxi firm since news of her husband's dealings broke and had been forced to turn to her mother for a €20,000 working capital loan. Nagle revealed that she was desperately trying to resolve a 'substantial' revenue debt owed by Blackrock Cabs.

In her personal life, Nagle was also struggling to come to terms with the breakdown of her marriage and revealed she had issued family law proceedings against O'Brien.

★

Bernard Madoff was four months into his 150-year jail term when Gardaí raided Invergarry. In stark contrast to the swift action by the US authorities, the wheels of justice were grinding slowly in Ireland.

The fraud squad embarked on a detailed trawl of O'Brien's web of corporate and personal bank accounts to try to trace where all the money had gone. It was a gargantuan task for a chronically understaffed and under-resourced unit already trying to deal with the panoply of investigations surrounding the demise of Anglo Irish Bank.

Why, Gardaí wondered, had O'Brien's banks missed the signs? Under money-laundering laws, banks are obliged to report suspect transactions and Gardaí were staggered by the vast sums of money entering and leaving O'Brien's bank accounts, of which he had close to a hundred.

At the time of writing, O'Brien has not been charged with any offence and investors are still being interviewed. If the Gardaí decide to move on O'Brien, they will have a twelve-hour opportunity to interrogate him before making a recommendation to the Director of Public Prosecutions or letting him go.

4. Up to Her Neck: The Case of Caroline McCann

There are some people who don't belong in a courtroom – people whose lives are chaotic, people too poor, too sick or too ignorant to engage on an equal footing with the stress, complexity and theatrics of adversarial hearings. And yet, one of the remarkable things about the canon of Ireland's landmark legal cases is that so many of them have been litigated by or on behalf of ordinary citizens and people on the margins of society; people with modest intellectual, social and economic resources and people with none at all.

Caroline McCann was one such citizen, and when she swore an oath before High Court Judge Mary Laffoy in May 2009 the 36-year-old unemployed mother of two probably could not grasp the significance of her groundbreaking challenge to the constitutionality of Ireland's Dickensian debtors' law regime, which had sent thousands of people to jail for the crime of being too poor. Barely literate, McCann could not even read the text of the Bible which she held in her trembling right hand as she took her place in the unfamiliar surroundings of a High Court witness box in the Four Courts in Dublin. Four months after her release from a psychiatric hospital, all she could think about was staying out of jail and making sure she was not taken away from her children, a threat she faced because she could not afford to repay the arrears on her credit union loan.

In May 2006 two Gardaí called to her mother's home in Mullaghmatt, a sprawling council estate on the outskirts of Monaghan town. The Gardaí told McCann they were there to take her to jail because she had disobeyed a court order to pay her credit union loan arrears in weekly instalments. Seeing her distress, they took pity on her and gave her a week's reprieve to get advice before they executed the committal warrant.

It was a small act of kindness and discretion that would lead to the striking down of the state's main legal apparatus for dealing with delinquent debtors.

Gardaí were regular visitors to the hard-pressed but mostly hard-working residents of Mullaghmatt, which was built in the early 1970s and, with its 300 mainly social housing units, is home to more than 1,200 people. When the Troubles escalated close to the border town, Mullaghmatt became a sanctuary for many fleeing the conflict in Northern Ireland. Almost thirty years later, Mullaghmatt was home to hundreds trying to flee the effects of the recession as residents were hauled before the District Court in Monaghan and threatened with prison over their failure to pay their credit union loans.

Such were the levels of indebtedness on the estate that when Caroline McCann testified in the High Court before Judge Laffoy at least four other residents had initiated legal cases to prevent their imprisonment with the help of the Northside Community Law Centre (NCLC).

How Caroline McCann — an unemployed single mother with a history of mental illness — was able to accrue a debt of €18,063.09 from Monaghan Credit Union in the first place was a great mystery — a mystery that was never solved during the course of her epic court case.

What we do know is that Caroline McCann had left school at the age of 14 with no formal qualifications and was one of nine children whose parents, members of the Travelling community, had settled in Monaghan town. She was an alcoholic with hardly any record of employment: she had once worked picking mushrooms on a farm, but the work was sporadic – a week on here, three weeks off there – and it lasted less than two years. Because of her poor education, her mental health difficulties and raising her two children, she never worked again.

Like many credit union borrowers, McCann's borrowings were initially small, but she quickly fell into arrears and raised new loans in order to pay off previous arrears.

When Gardaí called to her door in May 2006 to execute a committal warrant to jail her for failing to pay an instalment order made by Monaghan District Court in favour of the credit union, her only income was a €208 weekly one-parent family allowance and €65.35 in child benefit payments. Living with her two sons in a local authority house in Mullaghmatt, she was later forced to move in with her mother, also a local authority tenant on the estate, when her mental health deteriorated and she gradually lost control of her finances. McCann gave her mother €150 a week from her social welfare and by her own admission used much of her massive credit union loan to support her alcohol dependency. When her baby daughter died, McCann couldn't afford to pay for the funeral and turned to Monaghan Credit Union; the credit union obliged, but eventually forbearance gave way to frustration.

Monaghan Credit Union first wrote to Caroline McCann on foot of her falling into arrears in January 2000, and it sent numerous subsequent requests for payment to her. On three occasions in 2001 it warned her in correspondence that it intended to refer her account for legal action. It wrote periodically to her in 2002, and twice during that year credit union officers conducted house calls, all to no avail.

In August 2003, the credit union upped the ante, issuing a letter of demand seeking payment of the loan and warning it would bring legal action. In October of that year, Monaghan Credit Union obtained judgment for the entire loan at the Circuit Court in Monaghan town.

McCann was summoned to court but did not turn up and the judgment was granted in her absence without her being legally represented and without a judge being able to fully examine her means and assess her ability to repay.

The lender applied in January 2004 to the District Court in Monaghan for an instalment order, under which the court would decide how much had to be paid back in regular instalments. A summons was served on McCann advising her of the move, but because she didn't turn up in court for this instalment hearing either, the judge had to make a decision as to what she should pay without hearing evidence about what, if anything, she could pay.

In her absence the District Court directed that McCann begin to tackle her mammoth debt by paying off some €5,685.35 in arrears that had built up, requiring her to pay weekly instalments of €82. After obtaining the weekly €82 instalment order to discharge the arrears, the credit union found out that McCann was living at a new address on the same estate with her mother, but efforts to serve the order by registered post were returned marked 'notified, no attendance', meaning that the post had arrived but no one was available to accept the registered letters containing the orders.

McCann did not pay any of the instalments and in November 2005 Monaghan Credit Union applied for a court summons for her to be arrested and sent to prison. The order was sought under Section 6 of the Enforcement of Court Orders Act, a law dating back to 1940 that gave judges power to direct that a debtor be imprisoned if they fail to pay an instalment order.

Once again the summons was served on McCann and, as

with previous correspondence, she ignored it. She was absent from Monaghan District Court when a judge directed that she be arrested on foot of the instalment order to discharge her arrears after deeming that her failure to pay the weekly instalment was due to her wilful failure or culpable neglect.

This type and volume of correspondence, and the threat of prison, might normally be expected to bring about some sort of engagement by a debtor; but like thousands of other people up to their eyes in debt, McCann buried her head in the sand.

In all, it had been more than six years and eight months from the first time she fell into arrears when Caroline McCann engaged with the process after a family friend directed her towards the state-run Money Advice and Budgeting Service, which assessed her ability to repay the loan at €10 a week.

At that rate, it would take almost thirty-six years to discharge the debt.

Caroline McCann was, at some level in her dysfunctional and tragic life, aware of her debt and the strenuous attempts to recover it, but she admitted in her witness testimony in the High Court that when the envelopes came through the door from the credit union and their solicitors, she simply burned them. She could not afford a lawyer and did not know that she could obtain legal aid to fight the orders.

The plight of McCann and other residents of Mullaghmatt was mirrored in housing estates and private residences throughout Ireland where people had succumbed to the temptations of easy personal credit, which had been marketed intensely by lenders during the boom years. In 1995, household debt in Ireland stood at 48 per cent of disposable income. By 2009 it had risen to 176 per cent. Even amidst a global loosening of credit, the Irish performance in this area was out of the ordinary: in an international league table of personal indebtedness, Ireland's consumers had moved from 17th in 1995 to 4th in 2008, and in 2008–9 the total level of private sector credit in the economy was about €395 billion.

The downturn in the economy immediately made personal indebtedness a pressing issue for the great number of Irish people who entered negative equity with their homes or who saw their income reduced or eliminated. The effect of the recession on the rate of imprisonment for debt offences was not particularly striking at first, in part because the sort of people who typically end up in jail for failure to repay debts belong to an economic underclass that was largely passed over by the effects of the boom. Such people were always struggling, in good times as well as in bad, and the tangled relationship between poverty and punishment – as borne out by the fact that Irish prisons are, for the most part, occupied by residents from the most deprived postal codes in the country – was a given. But when the state started bailing out Ireland's banks and developers, the contrast with the plight of the poorest members of society became evident to the public.

Between 2003 and 2008 the state jailed 1,138 people for debt-related offences. In 2008 alone, 276 people were jailed for failing to repay their debts, a 37 per cent increase on 2007 and a 60 per cent increase on the 2003–7 average.

This was a significant jump, even though the curve was far less dramatic than those for other indices of debt distress. What was significant about the jump was the emerging gulf between the treatment of consistently poor individuals such as McCann, who were imprisoned for their inability to pay small debts, and the accommodation, through debt write-downs and leniency from creditors, of high-net-worth individuals with multimillion-euro indebtedness. Until the

McCann case in 2009, imprisoned debtors spent an average of twenty days in prison at a cost to the state of €2,000 per week.

A separate but related phenomenon was the imprisonment of people who failed to pay state-imposed fines, and this, too, was a problem that pre-dated the bust: more than 8,000 fine defaulters were jailed between 2004 and 2007.

There was uproar in April 2007 when a heavily pregnant woman from Limerick was jailed six weeks before she gave birth to her ninth baby because she could not pay a €125 litter fine. Jean Kelly, who served a week-long sentence, was also struggling to pay instalment orders after judgment was granted to her credit union over unpaid debts.

The rate of imprisonment for failure to pay state fines increased far more dramatically than the rate of imprisonment for default on private debt: in 2009, 4,806 people were jailed because they couldn't or wouldn't pay court-ordered fines, a massive increase from 2008, when 2,250 people were jailed for this offence, and 2007, when the figure was 1,335.

There was no evidence that imprisonment was an effective deterrent to default: a study by UCD criminologist Ian O'Donnell in 2008 showed that 85 per cent of those imprisoned for defaulting on fines found themselves back in jail within a four-year period.

A TV licence costs €160 per year, but it cost €285 a day to lock up someone who failed to pay the licence fee; and while the sanction of prison struck, correctly, at those who refused to pay, it was problematic because it also struck at those – the poor – who simply could not afford to pay.

The government came under pressure to introduce alternatives to prison after it was revealed that 3,336 people had been jailed for non-payment of fines in the first ten months of 2009. In late 2009 a Dundalk man called Dominic McKevitt was jailed because he forgot to get a €12.70 licence for Nemo, his pet shih-tzu. McKevitt, who lived alone in a council house and volunteered for the St Vincent de Paul, had been given the dog by the Louth Society for the Prevention of Cruelty to Animals. The jailing of McKevitt was a huge embarrassment for the local TD, Justice Minister Dermot Ahern, who had, like many of his predecessors at the Department of Justice, promised to introduce reform of Ireland's archaic debt laws.

Fine defaulters had one major advantage over their civil debtor counterparts: once they had served their time, their debt was expunged. But loan defaulters jailed for non-payment of civil debts still faced their debt when they were released as well as paying their creditors' legal costs and court interest at 8 per cent, resulting in many being sent to prison on multiple occasions for a single debt.

The practice of sending people to jail because they couldn't pay their debts was something that the government had no apparent intention of changing until the McCann case coincided with the country's burgeoning consumer credit crisis. At home and abroad, the state continually justified its debt enforcement regime – despite its obligations under international legal instruments including the European Convention of Human Rights and the International Covenant on Civil and Political Rights (ICCPR), both of which enshrined the principle that nobody should be imprisoned over their inability to pay a debt or to meet a contractual obligation. Every five years the government paraded itself before the Human Rights Committee of the United Nations High Commission for Human Rights, which monitors compliance by governments with the ICCPR and insisted – despite repeated concerns raised by the UN body – that Ireland did not send people to jail simply for inability to pay. Rather, the state argued, debtors were committed because they had failed, either through wilful default or culpable neglect, to obey a court order. In other words, the government tried to assert that the Irish legal system drew a distinction between those who 'can't pay' and those who 'won't pay', insisting that it was only the latter group who were jailed.

On a pure reading of the statute books, the law did draw such a distinction. In practice, however, in most cases it was the underlying debt and the inability to repay it that caused the failure to obey the court order.

The transformation of a civil debt into a de facto criminal offence played out over a number of legal steps. The first step was for a creditor to take legal proceedings against a debtor. If that did not bring about a settlement of the debt, a judgment would be obtained in court. To enforce the judgment, the creditor applied for an instalment order, a process that, in theory, involves the debtor sending in details of their financial position and turning up in court for an assessment of their means. In the vast majority of cases, instalment orders were made in the absence of the debtor. The debtor generally could not meet the terms of the order. If the debtor did not turn up at the arrest and imprisonment hearing, he or she was deemed to have engaged in wilful refusal or culpable neglect of the instalment order.

For decades, the state was loath to amend the legal framework that allowed some civil debtors to be sent to jail. In 1993 and again in 1998, in its appearances before the UN Human Rights Committee in Geneva, its representatives repeated the mantra that imprisonment merely because a person was unable to pay a debt or fulfil a contractual obligation had not been a feature of the Irish legal system since 1872. And every time, a number of leading Irish non-governmental organizations produced shadow reports to contradict the government's stance and offer an alternative view of its compliance with international legal norms.

In 1999 the state finally acknowledged the need for some reform to end imprisonment for civil debts and inability to pay fines. But in the absence of the long-promised reform, the Free Legal Advice Centres, the Irish Council for Civil Liberties and the Irish Penal Reform Trust were among nineteen organizations that briefed against the state before the UN Human Rights Commission in July 2008, almost a year before the McCann case was tried. But the Attorney General, Paul Gallagher, maintained the state's insistence that there was no imprisonment in Ireland for debt and that debtors were only jailed on an exceptional basis for wilful non-compliance. He urged the Committee that any procedural inadequacies in terms of how judges decided what constituted wilful refusal could always be appealed.

In a written parliamentary answer to Sinn Féin TD Aengus Ó Snodaigh on 29 October 2008, weeks after the collapse of Lehman Brothers and the introduction of the Irish banking guarantee, Justice Minister Dermot Ahern said there were no immediate proposals to amend the law in relation to recovery of a civil debt.

Colin Daly had a pretty good idea of what he was up against when Orla Nugent, the MABS debt adviser in Monaghan, called him during the summer of 2006 about the possibility of advising a credit union loan defaulter from Mullaghmatt who was facing jail on foot of an enforcement order.

Daly, a solicitor, is in charge of the Northside Community Law Centre, one of Ireland's most active and influential public interest law groups, offering free advice and representation to people – mainly social welfare clients – in disputes about their entitlements, housing rights and debts.

Daly had no qualms about taking on such a seemingly hopeless case as that of Caroline McCann. In fact, he and his colleagues had been biding their time, waiting for the right case or set of cases to transform Ireland's debt laws through a strategic attack on a body of debtor laws, some of which dated back to 1872.

The first move was to get an injunction preventing McCann's arrest subject to the 2005 committal warrant, on the grounds that Monaghan Credit Union had steadfastly refused to accept the local MABS office's assessment of McCann's ability to repay at €10 a week.

Daly contacted Jeanne McDonagh, the administrator of the Bar Council's Voluntary Assistance scheme under which barristers provide legal services directly to NGOs who advise people who cannot afford legal services. McDonagh in turn cornered barrister Fergal Foley, a high-profile criminal lawyer not known in the Law Library as a bleeding-heart liberal, and asked him to help Daly secure a High Court injunction to prevent McCann's arrest.

Foley agreed, and the injunction was granted by High Court Judge John MacMenamin on 15 September 2006, allowing Daly and Foley to set about preparing the substantive judicial review proceedings challenging the constitutionality of two key provisions of Ireland's Enforcement of Court Orders Acts, which dated back to 1926 and 1940, and their validity under the European Convention on Human Rights.

The nub of the case hatched in the NCLC's offices in Coolock, north Dublin, was that the 2005 order and the laws underpinning it amounted to a conviction of a criminal offence despite the fact that McCann had not been charged with a crime or afforded any of the procedural safeguards that would normally attach to someone about to be deprived of her liberty.

The district judges who had made the orders against McCann, one of whom died before the case was heard, were listed as defendants, as were the Commissioner of An Garda Siochána, the CEO of the Irish Prison Service, the Minister for Justice and the Attorney General.

Monaghan Credit Union was not a defendant in the case but was a notice party to the proceedings, as was the Irish Human Rights Commission, which was granted permission to make observations on the international human rights aspects of the case as an *amicus curiae*, or friend of the court.

In response to Daly's action, the state stood over the committal order, insisted that its Enforcement of Court Orders laws were fair, and demanded to know how McCann had built up almost €20,000 in debt.

As the standard pretrial tit-for-tats took their course, McCann drifted in and out of St Davnet's mental hospital in Monaghan, terrified that the Gardaí would come back and take her away from her children. Her registrar, acting under a consultant psychiatrist at the hospital, advised in August 2006 that McCann's depressive illness was recurrent and she had to attend hospital daily. He also warned that stress would worsen McCann's mental health and strongly urged against imprisonment.

The threat of imprisonment had subsided because of the injunction that had been obtained in September 2006, but McCann's fear of it had not, a fear that was constantly in her mind as the state insisted that it was obliged to defend the constitutional validity of the law. If the state won the case, McCann could still be jailed.

For its part, the state complained in numerous exchanges that McCann had not turned up in court and did not make any attempt to pay a single instalment or try to have the instalments varied to suit her ability to pay. All this was true, of course, and when I first published details of the lawsuit in the *Irish Independent* in the autumn of 2006, sympathy was thin on the ground for the unnamed alcoholic who had drunk the proceeds of her credit union loan. But as the case progressed and the publicity surrounding it increased, Monaghan Credit Union quietly offered to forgive the amount due under the instalment order, while leaving the full amount of debt outstanding.

That behind-the-scenes offer was quietly refused. Had it been accepted, the case between McCann and the state may have been struck out or withdrawn by consent and the issue of jailed debtors let stand for another day. Instead, the case continued through the High Court.

In November 2007, the state's position altered somewhat. It signalled that it would stand over the legislation that was used to ground McCann's committal but would not try to stand over the committal order itself, as this was a matter for Monaghan Credit Union. The Chief State Solicitor's Office, which was representing all of the government parties including the Gardaí and prison service, wrote to Monaghan Credit Union that month to see if it would agree to the committal order being quashed, with the added sweetener that the state parties would bear their own costs in the event that it was successfully quashed.

In the letter, the CSSO revealed that the state's only concern was to ensure that its laws were not declared inconsistent with the Irish Constitution or the European Convention on Human Rights.

Although the European Convention was incorporated into Irish law in 2003, it was done so at a sub-constitutional level, meaning that where any conflict arose between the two systems the Irish Constitution prevailed. But if the law were declared incompatible with the European Convention or the case ultimately ended up before the European Court of Human Rights, unwelcome international attention would have been attracted to the issue and pressure would have been applied on the state to bring its debt-enforcement laws in line with international standards. The government was also uneasy about pursuing a person as plainly vulnerable as Caroline McCann.

'This would appear to be a most unfortunate case where the plaintiff seems to be in the most straitened circumstances,' wrote John Davis on behalf of David J. O'Hagan, the Chief State Solicitor, to Monaghan Credit Union. 'We believe that nothing will be served by having her sent to jail.' The letter also told Monaghan Credit Union that the government was confident that McCann's case would not create a precedent due to the 'wholly unique circumstances of the case', but its move to get the committal order quashed suggested that it knew only too well that McCann's action was a landmark test case that could affect hundreds of others.

Even at this late stage, the state would still not countenance a change in the law – a fact that alarmed the UN Human Rights Committee which, in its concluding remarks in July 2008 following its consultations with the government delegation in Geneva, said that it was 'concerned that the state party does not intend to amend the laws which may in effect permit imprisonment for failure to fulfil a contractual obligation'. Once again, the Committee recommended that Ireland ensure that its laws could not be used to imprison people for their inability to repay debt and fulfil a contract, but once again the plea was ignored.

Almost four years after the original threat to imprison McCann, which was first issued in November 2005, the case opened at the High Court in Dublin before Judge Mary Laffoy.

Mary Laffoy is a highly respected judge who had come to national prominence in 2003 when she unexpectedly resigned as chair of a commission investigating the systemic physical and sexual abuse of children in state-run religious institutions. Her claims that the Department of Education was impeding her work and threatening the independence of the inquiry by refusing to hand over documents to her triggered a sea change in the government's attitude towards the inquiry.

The state was represented by Senior Counsel Michael Cush and Junior Counsel Paul Anthony McDermott. The most noteworthy presence in the courtroom that day was that of Senior Counsel Donal O'Donnell, representing the McCann team. The Belfast-born son of Turlough O'Donnell, a former judge of the Court of Appeal in Northern Ireland, O'Donnell was a constitutional law guru steeped in American jurisprudence from his time as a student at the University of Virginia, where he completed an LLM before returning to Ireland to practise at the bar. O'Donnell had appeared for the state in almost all its recent constitutional cases, including the 'Miss D' case in which a teenager in care sought to leave the country for an abortion because her unborn foetus was unviable. He had also acted for the state in the controversial challenge to the Oireachtas inquiry into Judge Brian Curtin, a Circuit Court judge who had been arrested as part of Operation Amethyst, a Garda sweep on child pornography.

O'Donnell had also been recruited to represent the government in the contentious case in which an estranged couple fought an emotional battle over control of surplus frozen embryos stored in a Dublin fertility clinic; and it was Donal O'Donnell who appeared before seventeen judges at the Grand Chamber of the European Court of Human Rights to defend Ireland's abortion ban. Occasionally O'Donnell would appear 'on the side of the angels', as he jokingly

remarked after he successfully steered the *Irish Times* newspaper through its controversial appeal to the Supreme Court
on its right to protect its sources. The newspaper instructed
O'Donnell to represent it following its revelations that former
Taoiseach Bertie Ahern was being investigated by the Mahon
Tribunal over payments to him when he was Minister of
Finance. The paper was excoriated by the High Court over
its decision to destroy documents despite being asked to
furnish them to the Mahon Tribunal, and was later ordered
by the Supreme Court to pay legal costs of €600,000 despite
the rule that the losing party in an action is liable for the final
bill.

But O'Donnell's victory where it mattered most – in the
Supreme Court – was priceless for the newspaper and vindi-
cated the media's pursuit of Ahern. That O'Donnell and
Fergal Foley were now opposing the state in such an important action was a massive coup for Colin Daly and the
Northside Community Law Centre; and the two barristers'
decision to accept the brief on a pro bono basis through the
Bar Council's Voluntary Assistance scheme did not augur
well for the government's prospects of success.

The striking thing about the Voluntary Assistance scheme
is that few people outside of the Law Library and the NGO
sector know it exists. Many of the barristers who take part
in the scheme carry out their work far from media scrutiny.
Few Voluntary Assistance scheme cases, however, move
beyond the district and circuit courts, and few have the
significance of McCann's case.

Opening the case, Donal O'Donnell compared the
situation in twenty-first-century Ireland to that of the
Victorian era in Britain, before the writings of Charles
Dickens prompted a change in the laws, when people could
be jailed over debts.

The central plank of McCann's case was that the imprisonment order was illegal as it sought to deprive her of her liberty merely on the ground that she could not fulfil a contractual obligation. The government insisted that it was entitled to have a statutory mechanism in place for enforcement of lawfully made court orders and denied the provisions of the Enforcement of Court Orders Acts were unconstitutional or contravened the European Convention. It repeated its refrain that an order for imprisonment could only be made when a District Court judge was satisfied that the debtor had not paid due to either wilful refusal or culpable neglect and said that it had to be presumed that such discretionary powers were applied fairly.

Monaghan Credit Union urged 'a common-sense approach' and proposed the compromise whereby Judge Laffoy would quash the 2005 order and send the matter back to Monaghan District Court.

The credit union said it was prepared to give an undertaking to vary the weekly instalments but insisted that the debt owed would have to be resolved 'sooner or later'.

In light of the credit union's willingness to have the order quashed, the government parties argued that McCann's challenge to the validity of the legislation was moot and urged Judge Laffoy to exercise judicial restraint and not consider the challenges to the Irish Constitution and European Convention at all, a prospect McCann's legal team – keen to establish a useful precedent – would not countenance.

Caroline McCann was the main witness in the case. When called to give evidence, she freely admitted that she had used much of her credit union loan to support her alcohol dependency.

Were the borrowings used for anything else? O'Donnell gently asked her.

A prolonged silence hung in the air before McCann whispered: 'Yes, my baby's headstone and funeral.'

As Judge Laffoy retired to consider her verdict and publicity surrounding the case increased, other jailed debtors gained confidence to challenge their detention. Several days after the McCann case ended the High Court freed a psychiatrically ill mother of four who had been jailed for a month over a €1,500 credit card debt. The 33-year-old woman had seen an advertisement for credit cards from MBNA Bank while she was an inpatient in a psychiatric hospital and had applied for a card, claiming to be working in a local factory. When she received the card she used it to the limit and then failed to engage with the lender or to attend any court hearings seeking to enforce the debt, which ultimately resulted in a committal warrant. In addition to her MBNA debt, she was also being pursued by Bank of Ireland over a €2,000 personal loan, some of which she had repaid.

Her psychiatric health was not her only concern as she had been diagnosed with cervical cancer two years previously and had had to have a hysterectomy performed. When she was imprisoned, she was under psychiatric care and was receiving medication. Her lawyers sought her immediate release under a habeas corpus application and told High Court Judge Iarfhlaith O'Neill that her detention was inappropriate because she had applied for a credit card while an inpatient in a psychiatric hospital and was not in court when the imprisonment order was made. They also argued that they, her legal team, were unaware of any efforts to tell her about her right to legal representation at that hearing.

The MBNA action illustrated the ease with which people on low incomes could access credit during the boom without any real examination of their ability to repay. Just days later, Judge O'Neill was confronted by another jailed debtor, a father of two who asked to be released from prison over his failure to continue paying instalments on a €7,000 credit union car loan on which he had defaulted after he was made redundant. The man had been jailed for a month, and although his partner had raised more than €2,000 from friends to secure his release, she could not raise the entire sum.

Echoing Donal O'Donnell, the man's lawyer argued the whole point of the law should be to prevent people being sent to jail 'just for being poor'.

Judge O'Neill released the debtor, not because he had made out a case for breach of fair procedures or natural justice, but because the judge was concerned at the manner in which the District Court judge who sanctioned the committal warrant had exercised his discretion. Like McCann and an estimated 80 per cent of people facing imprisonment for debt, the father of two had not been present in court when an order was made to commit him. The District Court had to be satisfied failure to pay instalments was due to 'wilful refusal' or 'culpable neglect', but the burden of proof had in fact been passed on to the absent debtors. To shift the burden of proof in what had become criminal proceedings was 'impermissible', said Judge O'Neill, who ordered that the state pay the cost of the action as the problem lay in the operation of the legislation.

Judge O'Neill's remarks about defects in the legislation spelled trouble for the state, but the myth that Ireland did not jail people because they could not fulfil a contract was demolished in its entirety by Judge Laffoy when she issued a 46-page ruling in the McCann case on 18 June 2009.

Laffoy forensically analysed the legal process leading up to a debtor's imprisonment, including the examination (or lack of examination) of a person's means by District Court judges. She noted how neither the summons requiring a debtor to attend court to have their means examined, nor the form of statement of means, gave any warning as to what would happen if they did not turn up or lodge a statement of their means. There was nothing to tell a distressed debtor that they could get legal advice, and they were not told of any other solutions available.

Less than one in ten of the debtors said they understood the consequences of the legal proceedings and the majority experienced health problems trying to keep their debts secret from spouses, children and their families.

Judge Laffoy refused to bow to the request that she simply quash McCann's committal order and send it back to the District Court. She said McCann had already been living under a 'sword of Damocles' for over three years and the issue was not just about how she had been treated in the past, but also about what would happen to her in the future. She could see no reason for denying a debtor facing prison for three months the same constitutional rights as someone facing prison on a criminal charge.

While the judge accepted that the sanction of prison was aimed at debtors who refused to pay, it also struck at those who could not pay; and, like Judge O'Neill before her, Judge Laffoy pointed the finger of blame at the law itself, which McCann's case had demonstrated was 'infected with arbitrariness and unfairness'.

The futility of jailing debtors – at a huge cost to creditors and taxpayers – was not lost on Judge Laffoy, who said she found it inexplicable how the state could countenance the continuance of such a defective scheme of debt enforcement when it could easily introduce a new one incorporating the necessary safeguards.

By the time the McCann case was decided, in June 2009, 186 people had been jailed during that year for debt offences.

The immediate effect of the ruling was the early release of any debtors imprisoned under the struck-down law and the suspension of all committal warrants secured on foot of instalment orders.

The Courts Service was also forced to write to all the chief district courts stating that no further committal warrants were to be issued, and in one sitting in the District Court in Mullingar alone, a judge was forced to adjourn twenty-four enforcement order cases to take stock of the implications of the ruling.

The ruling was a comprehensive victory for the Northside Community Law Centre and those who had long campaigned for reform of Ireland's debt laws as they related to enforcement of court orders.

So comprehensive was Judge Mary Laffoy's judgment and the defeat of the government's stance that Justice Minister Dermot Ahern signalled hours after the ruling that it would not be appealed to the Supreme Court. Far from being taken by surprise by the verdict, the government moved swiftly to respond to the judgment. Within four weeks it had produced a new Enforcement of Court Orders Bill, which incorporated most of the safeguards that Judge Laffoy ruled the old regime lacked.

Although the new bill was crafted to pass constitutional muster, it represented tinkering at best and ignored wider, more pressing calls for reform including an appeal by the Law Reform Commission for a new system of personal insolvency law which would include a statutory, non-court-based settlement scheme for debtors.

The new legislation actually worked to the detriment of single and separated mothers who relied on the enforcement of court orders to ensure their former partners or spouses paid child maintenance as the threat of or, in many cases, actual imprisonment was a vital cog in the wheel of ensuring such payments.

In the first three months of 2010, as a direct result of McCann's groundbreaking legal action, just three people were jailed for non-payment of debts.

In June 2009, President Mary McAleese signed into law a new bill designed to reduce the numbers imprisoned for failing to pay fines. It was badly needed, as almost 5,000 people had been jailed in 2009 for non-payment of a fine, twice the figure for 2008 and almost four times the figure for 2007.

Postscript: *Where are they now?*

Donal O'Donnell SC is now a judge of the Supreme Court, only the second barrister in Irish history to be appointed to the court directly from the bar. *McCann v Judges of Monaghan District Court and Ors* was one of his last cases before he was appointed to the bench.

Colin Daly remains the solicitor in charge of the Northside Community Law Centre.

Caroline McCann settled her damages case against the state, but did not succeed in eliminating her credit union loan. She is still living in Mullaghmatt with her mother and sons.

5. The First Domino

Simon Kelly was livid. It was the summer of 2007, and for days the young developer had been trying to track down Hugh McGivern, a Dublin insurance broker with whom he and his father, Paddy Kelly, had been involved in a number of deals. Now, McGivern was suing the elder Kelly.

The suit related to a deal that dated back a number of years. At the suggestion of McGivern, the founder and director of the IFG-owned credit insurance firm Trade Credit Brokers, Kelly Snr had bought a stake in the Irish franchise of the Spanish fashion chain Mango in 1999. In November 2006, Kelly Snr took over the franchise in its entirety through a share purchase agreement. Under this agreement, separate from the original 1999 deal, McGivern agreed to sell to Paddy Kelly his shares in four companies in Dublin, Cork, Limerick and Belfast that operated the Mango franchise. The share purchase agreement also stated that Paddy Kelly would discharge a €1 million debt owed by McGivern to ACCBank on foot of the Mango operations in five €200,000 tranches, the first to be paid by 30 November 2006.

Crucially, the 2006 deal relieved McGivern from all personal guarantees and indemnities arising out of any of the franchise's debts, as well as from any guarantees and indemnities that McGivern's companies had provided to the landlords of the premises where Mango was a tenant.

Simon Kelly, who negotiated the share purchase agreement on behalf of his father, did not pay much attention to the details. He and McGivern were involved in at least ten other projects together at the time and their administrative affairs were, according to Kelly Jr, 'messy'.

They were not unusual in this. With billions of euros in cheap credit coursing through the veins of Ireland Inc., there was scant regard among many of the country's development and banking elite for small print and due diligence. And such was the trust between Simon Kelly and Hugh McGivern that there were no lawyers present when the men signed the share purchase agreement. According to Claire Callanan, a partner in Beauchamp's solicitors who would represent Kelly Snr in the Commercial Court when the share purchase agreement went sour, it was 'common' that neither of the men's solicitors were aware that the document was being executed.

For his part, Simon was reassured by the fact that Hugh McGivern was not just one of his dad's many business partners.

He was his friend.

But within months of the signing of the share purchase agreement, the storm clouds beginning to form over the Irish economy were testing the limits of many previously happy alliances. In June 2007 McGivern fired off a High Court writ against Paddy Kelly claiming he had reneged on key aspects of the share purchase deal and demanding to be indemnified from all of the Mango franchise's mounting debts.

McGivern complained that Paddy Kelly had failed to release him from the guarantees and the indemnities in respect of the four companies that operated the Mango franchise and that Kelly had failed to pay the first €200,000 instalment to discharge McGivern's €1 million bank loan by the agreed date.

A judgment totalling £108,228 had also been lodged against McGivern by the landlord of one of the companies pursuant to a guarantee he had provided under the relevant lease. McGivern wanted to be indemnified against the judgment and other proceedings that had been commenced against him from similar guarantees. The case was duly entered into the Commercial Court in June 2007.

It was, Simon Kelly told me, the first time Paddy Kelly had ever been personally sued by a partner. This infuriated Simon, who bombarded McGivern with calls, texts and emails with a view to resolving their differences out of court and staving off any public indication that the Kellys, who were among Ireland's top property developers, were experiencing financial difficulties. In the early hours of 5 July 2007, Simon drafted an email to his collaborator which would, he hoped, jolt him into engagement and, with any luck, a settlement. He did not hit the send key on the first version of the email, as he thought it was too strongly worded.

Which it was. One line of the unsent email read: 'We all have skeletons in our cupboards.'

Kelly went back to the drawing board and wrote what he thought was a more measured missive excoriating McGivern's 'bullshit' legal action.

'In the very near term, this dispute is going to move beyond the bounds of a commercial claim and become personal,' said Kelly in his early-morning rant. 'If this happens, I do not care what cost I will bear to make you regret taking this action. You may win in court but it will be to your eternal regret.'

He signed off: 'There are plenty of places that I can hurt you and you can hurt me.' He felt that the revised email, which contained the phrase 'maybe you are smart or maybe you are a crook', was more tempered than the first draft.

The litigation was eventually resolved after two days in the Commercial Court in February 2008, with a €1.35 million settlement in McGivern's favour. Kelly's late-night email blew up spectacularly in his face when Mr Justice Peter Kelly later ruled that it had represented a 'shameful' contempt of court. The young developer had not only penned an email that could be considered threatening or intimidating to McGivern, he had also sent it after McGivern had commenced the legal action some weeks earlier in June 2007.

To Simon Kelly, the email was an expression of exasperation; to Peter Kelly, it was an interference with the administration of justice. Judge Kelly said every citizen has a constitutional right of access to the courts and it was 'of the highest importance' that a citizen who exercises the right to litigate should be able to do so free of threats or obstructions.

'Regardless of how wealthy or involved in business and land transactions one may be, no person is above the law,' said the judge, who required Simon Kelly to make a €20,000 donation to the St Vincent de Paul.

It could have been worse: the judge had been on the verge of referring the email to the Director of Public Prosecutions.

Simon Kelly was not the first high-flyer to be at the receiving end of Peter Kelly's ire. The judge's reputation for trenchant commentary from the bench was established well before he took over as head of the Commercial Court.

In the late 1990s, while in charge of the High Court's minors list, Kelly earned acclaim when he took the government to task over its failure to face up to its responsibilities towards some of the neediest children in the state. For years judges presiding over the High Court minors list could do little more than rail at the inertia of health boards and government departments over their failure to help troubled children in desperate need of care and secure accommodation. When he took over the childcare list Kelly, who was appointed to the High Court at the age of 46, became the government's chief scourge on child law.

In February 2000, frustrated at what he described as the 'scandalous' conduct of the government following a succession of tragic cases that had come before him, he issued a court order, in the form of a mandatory injunction, ordering several ministers to provide additional places for children in special care and support units, to a specific timetable established by the state itself. During one hearing he said the then Minister for Health and Children, Micheál Martin, should be 'not only embarrassed but ashamed' to seek to keep another troubled child in 'completely substandard' conditions. The move provoked outrage in political circles, but to children's rights advocates Peter Kelly was a godsend.

'He has got things done when nobody in the government has,' Fr Peter McVerry, the veteran campaigner on behalf of the homeless, told the *Sunday Business Post* shortly before the government appealed Judge Kelly's rulings to the Supreme Court.

Peter Kelly's stance on behalf of homeless children proved a hit with the Irish public, who were happy to see someone in authority challenge the government's neglect of needy children and act as a moral and legal bulwark for the powerless against those in power. But the Supreme Court clipped Judge Kelly's campaigning wings in December 2001 in a landmark ruling regarding the separation of powers. 'If a judge considers that there has been a failure of the legislature and executive in some particular area of constitutionally significant policy, can he or she on that account "attempt to fill the vacuum" by ordering either of those bodies to implement a particular policy?' asked Supreme Court Judge Adrian Hardiman. Four of five judges ruled against Kelly, concluding that despite acting from the best of motives, he had crossed a constitutional line by telling the executive how to use its resources.

The ruling sounded the death knell for what remained of liberal judicial activism in Ireland. And Judge Kelly's efforts to force the state to make provisions for troubled children had, his colleagues believed, ruined any chances of him being appointed to the Supreme Court.

Perhaps it had, but no one would have imagined that the children's champion would rise to far greater prominence when the Commercial Court, a pilot programme of the High Court to deal with big business disputes, opened its doors for business in 2004. The creation of the Commercial Court was a consequence of the enormous escalation of the scale of business conducted in Ireland during the boom years, an escalation that naturally caused a major surge in the number of business-related disputes coming before the courts. It was designed to deal quickly with cases involving sums in excess of €1 million. Kelly, who once plied a lucrative trade as a libel and commercial lawyer and who helped to design the rules for the new court, was assigned to run it.

Under the old regime, it was not unheard of for commercial cases to languish in the system for anywhere between three and five years after they began. But the new Commercial Court quickly established a reputation for focusing minds and disposing of cases quickly.

The secret of the court's success lay in the brisk, business-like approach it adopted to disputes. Parties were obliged to identify the key issues and prepare focused pleadings at an early stage, and to exchange all documents within strict deadlines. The sheer speed with which Kelly dealt with cases, holding individual solicitors to account for carriage of the litigation under threat of contempt, caught many in the legal profession – and their wealthy clients – by surprise. Kelly was an exacting taskmaster who spent his weekends reading briefs at his home to execute the delivery of cases and expected those coming before him to do precisely the same. He came down heavily on parties where there was even a hint of misconduct, bad faith or trying it on.

In previous recessions, the courts were, ironically, a haven for some ailing businesses: broke companies and sole traders could refuse to pay up safe in the knowledge that it would probably take years for a case to come to trial, by which time they might be in a better position to resolve litigation. But the new Commercial Court's hands-on judicial case management meant that fools – and debtors with no arguable defence – would not be suffered gladly. Within a short period of time, the court had demonstrated that there was a different way of handling litigation in Ireland. International corporations eyed up the new forum, and domestic law firms quietly touted to their global clients that Peter Kelly's Dublin dominion was the quickest place to resolve a business row.

Such was the swift and hugely public nature of the court's operations, the court also led to a surge in out-of-court deals as bankers, builders and investors battled to keep details of their losses and balance sheets out of the public arena of the Four Courts.

From the outset the Commercial Court was inextricably linked to Peter Kelly's personality. A weekly communicant at the Latin Tridentine Mass, the judge brought a quality to the Commercial Court that was notably absent in many deals transacted by the money men during Ireland's boom years: a sense of morality.

According to a statement of wealth produced in March 2006, Paddy Kelly's matrix of partnerships – he was involved in more than seventy of them through his investment vehicle Redquartz at the time – made him worth €2,777,924,435. He was, on paper at least, a €2.7 billion man.

In the overall scheme of things his foray into Mango was child's play, a mere drop in the ocean; but at the time he settled McGivern's case there were five outstanding Mango leases on which McGivern had given personal guarantees. These were now Kelly's responsibility and with the retail market just about to enter into freefall he decided that Mango had to be wound down.

This caused agitation among the landlords of the various leasehold premises, who were torturing McGivern to pay them their rent.

Since the February 2008 settlement with Paddy Kelly on foot of the share purchase agreement, court claims for unpaid rent had been issued against McGivern by landlords in Belfast, Dublin, Limerick and Cork. The 2008 settlement contained a clause allowing McGivern to reactivate his claim against Kelly if he could not enforce his settlement, and the broker brought Kelly back to court seeking to be indemnified from the landlords' actions. In the same month that McGivern reactivated his claim, Paddy Kelly quietly arranged a personal loan with Anglo Irish Bank, with €5 million of it earmarked for the Mango wind-down.

The Anglo credit facility was a lifeline for a developer who was feeling the heat. He was not the only one.

The beginning of the end for Liam Carroll – arguably Ireland's biggest property developer at the height of the boom – might be traced to the dying days of 2007, when rival developer Sean Dunne fired the opening salvo in a €200 million turf war in Dublin's docklands dubbed the Battle of North Lotts.

The dispute could be traced back to 31 May 2007, when one of Carroll's companies, North Quay Investments Ltd (NQIL), entered into a confidential arrangement with executives in the Dublin Docklands Development Authority (DDDA) to develop three corporate office blocks on the former Brooks Thomas site on Dublin's North Wall Quay. Two of the buildings were to house Anglo Irish Bank's new corporate headquarters and Carroll's solicitors, Eversheds O'Donnell Sweeney.

But there was a problem: Carroll's site surrounded on three sides another North Wall Quay site owned by rival developer Sean Dunne, whose opposition to Carroll's ambitious plan would lead to huge problems for both Carroll and the DDDA.

The DDDA had been established by the government in 1997 to attract private investment to the neglected brownfield sites near the mouth of the river Liffey. It had the power to grant exemptions from planning permission, and under its auspices – and amidst a property boom – the docklands were transformed.

The law setting up the DDDA allowed the agency to grant fast-track development permits, known as Section 25 certificates, which allowed developments to go ahead without fear of planning objections from third parties or the public. The authority, which issued around fifty Section 25 certificates a year, was not obliged to disclose which developers it had entered into Section 25 application 'discussions' with; and its planning files, which were meant to be available for inspection, were often unavailable or incomplete. This often meant in practice that by the time the public knew anything about the latest coup by the quays, the certificate had already been awarded.

Liam Carroll originally sought a Section 25 certificate for his development on the Brooks Thomas site in late 2006. The DDDA made it clear that a strip of land on the site would have to be ceded to the agency to be used as a public space in order to ensure compliance with the 2002 North Lotts planning scheme. Carroll did not want to cede the strip, so he abandoned talks with the agency and made an application in December 2006 to Dublin City Council, which, as a matter of course in all planning bids in the area, invited the DDDA to make observations on Carroll's application to it.

The DDDA objected to Dublin City Council that Carroll's plan was not consistent with the authority's planning scheme, and the council rejected NQIL's application.

It was at this point that David Torpey, one of Carroll's key lieutenants, approached the DDDA about applying for a Section 25 certificate. The DDDA's North Lotts master plan allowed for buildings of up to eight storeys in height. Carroll wanted to raise the buildings to twice that size. Carroll now offered to cede to the DDDA the strip of land it had sought in exchange for an agreement by the authority that it would initiate procedures to amend the master plan in order to allow Carroll to apply at a later date for sixteen-storey structures.

Carroll took part in discussions between the NQIL team and DDDA executives, including CEO Paul Maloney and John McLaughlin, director of architecture and planning. Eventually, on 11 May 2007, Carroll lodged an application for a Section 25 certificate towards his development on the Brooks Thomas site. Twenty days later the DDDA executive entered into a confidential agreement with NQIL which provided that the DDDA executive would recommend to its board that the certificate should be granted and anticipated the construction of sixteen-storey buildings on the site.

When the board of the DDDA met on 11 June to consider the Section 25 application, it knew that its executive had been in talks with Carroll and it was asked to note that the executive had entered into a contract with NQIL under which it would be granted the strip of land as an amenity space. But the board apparently was not told of the full contents of the agreement.

While the planning application that was ultimately granted by the DDDA board on 13 July 2007 provided for three eight-storey blocks, Carroll was confident that he would eventually get his own way and built a car park under Anglo's new HQ with enough spaces to provide for the requirements of a sixteen-storey building.

When he first fired off his High Court writ just weeks later, Sean Dunne's main problem with Carroll's development related to access, not height. Dunne had believed that his own piece of land at North Lotts would be accessible from both North Wall Quay and from what he had understood would be a new road running between Castleforbes Road and New Wapping Street, which bounded the two developers' sites to the west and east respectively. He would start building the road from his site and he believed Carroll, as the adjacent developer, had an obligation to continue it.

In his High Court case against the DDDA, Dunne complained of what he saw as a failure in the plan for Carroll's development to provide a route between New Wapping Street and Castleforbes Road. He was also concerned about the potentially adverse effect of 'an industrial-scale basement access ramp'. Dunne claimed that both of these aspects of the Carroll plan would affect a residential development that he was building on his site.

The case, with NQIL as a notice party, opened before High Court Judge Mary Finlay Geoghegan in April 2008 and Dunne was represented by Rory Brady SC, the former Attorney General.

By the time Judge Finlay Geoghegan delivered her verdict in the Battle of North Lotts, on 9 October 2008, the Commercial Court had been transformed from an efficient and busy accident and emergency suite with a sophisticated triage unit into a field hospital overrun with casualties of the failing Irish economy. The US investment bank Lehman Brothers had gone bust in the middle of September, transforming a rumbling crisis in the global financial system into a full-blown meltdown. And at the end of the month, with at least one major Irish financial institution facing insolvency, the Irish government had guaranteed the liabilities of six banks: AIB, Bank of Ireland, Anglo Irish Bank, Irish Life and Permanent, the Irish Nationwide Building Society and EBS. Property prices were plummeting and the banks had stopped lending.

In a 35-page ruling, Judge Finlay Geoghegan found that the confidential agreement made between the DDDA executive and Carroll on 31 May 2007 — before the Section 25 certificate was issued by the DDDA board in July 2007 — gave rise to a reasonable apprehension of bias on the part of the state agency.

The judge ruled that whilst the DDDA had wide powers to secure development, what it did not possess was the power to allow any member of the executive or the board to give any commitment prior to the board's decision on the application. Nor could it grant certificates for fast-track development if the exemption flew in the face of the planning scheme for the area, as she found that Carroll's plans did.

The ruling was a disaster for Carroll, who had already spent €83 million on the North Lotts development, and for the DDDA, which, in a climate of mounting public mistrust of the nexus of relations between banks, developers and the state, was increasingly subject to claims that it had too cosy a relationship with developers. The case also drew unwelcome attention to complaints about potential conflicts of interest between the agency and Carroll's lender and putative tenant for the North Lotts development, Anglo Irish Bank. Anglo's chairman and former chief executive, Sean FitzPatrick, was a member of the DDDA board, and Lar Bradshaw also sat on both boards.

A jubilant Dunne wasted no time after Judge Finlay Geoghegan's ruling in calling on the High Court to tear down Carroll's half-built tower. But Carroll applied to Dublin City Council for retention permission, which was granted; the building intended for Anglo remains a concrete shell.

As a result of the ruling, the DDDA introduced new rules to remedy a series of defects identified by Judge Finlay Geoghegan in its Section 25 procedures; among these was a provision that no member of the authority could enter into any contract with a developer before a Section 25 application was decided by the board.

The North Lotts ruling was a victory for Sean Dunne, but the Baron of Ballsbridge was struggling too.

Dunne became the poster boy for the Celtic Tiger's excess in 2004 when he splashed out €1.5 million on a fourteen-day party aboard the yacht *Christina O* to mark his wedding to former *Sunday Independent* gossip queen turned barrister Gayle Killilea. A year later he paid €380 million for the Jurys and Berkeley Court hotels in Ballsbridge as part of a €1 billion plan to redevelop the Dublin 4 neighbourhood.

The Ballsbridge purchases, probably the most talked-about property acquisitions of the entire boom period, represented a high-water mark in the relationship between Sean Dunne and estate agents CB Richard Ellis. The relationship was prolific: at one stage Dunne's Mountbrook Homes Group conducted eight out of ten deals through CBRE. Willie Dowling, a director at CBRE, had been one of Dunne's closest friends since the mid-1990s, and such was the volume of work thrown CBRE's way by Dunne that he spent half his time or more, at the height of Dunne's buying frenzy in 2005, looking after the developer's deals.

The lines between business and pleasure were constantly blurred for Dunne and Dowling, who often swung by Dunne's mansion on Dublin's Shrewsbury Road to ferry his pal to GAA matches at Croke Park. In a High Court witness statement, Dunne would wistfully recall how he arranged for a private jet to ferry Dowling, his fiancée and their families to Florence. But Dunne's love affair with CBRE ended when the agents demanded that the developer pay €1.5 million to settle their fees for handling the 2006 transactions whereby Dunne became the owner of Hume House.

Hume House is about as ugly as an office block can be. But it is in Ballsbridge, and in late 2005, intoxicated by his audacious hotel raid, Dunne instructed CBRE to acquire the building for him from its owner, life assurance giant Irish Life.

CBRE arranged a series of transactions whereby Dunne purchased the 80,000-square-foot building in Ballsbridge and Irish Life purchased from Dunne the much larger 133,000-square-foot office block Riverside IV, at Dublin's Grand Canal Docks. CBRE sued Dunne over his refusal to pay its fee in relation to the Riverside IV part of the deal. Dunne hit back with a counterclaim alleging that the firm had overvalued Hume House by €35 million. It was the latter claim that created the real legal drama.

CBRE claimed that it told Dunne that Hume House was not worth more than €65 million – the figure that Dunne, through CBRE, bid for the building in January 2006. Irish Life said the bid was unacceptable in light of an offer they had from another, unnamed bidder. Undeterred, Dunne told CBRE on 8 February to submit a revised offer of €90 million, but again Irish Life rebuffed him, asking the estate agents to get Dunne to submit his 'best and final position' by 20 February.

Dunne claimed in a court affidavit that his immediate reaction to the rebuffed €90 million offer was 'we cannot win them all and we already had enough property in Ballsbridge'. However, according to Dunne's statement, 'against his better judgment' he increased the offer to €95 million, though CBRE claimed in court papers that the sum was €92 million. Four days later Irish Life told CBRE that it had received a higher offer which would be considered by the Irish Life board. But the Dunner would not be outdone, and after more talks with Irish Life he instructed CBRE to submit a revised bid of €130 million. Irish Life finally said yes and laughed all the way to the bank.

Dunne and Dowling had a 'slightly heated debate', in Dunne's words, in November 2006 when Dowling raised the thorny issue of fees owed by the builder in relation to the Riverside IV element of the transaction. Over the next couple of months there were a number of meetings between the pair to discuss the matter. Dowling was under pressure to collect fees from his clients to fund the annual staff bonus extravaganza and conscious that without Dunne's fees, he wouldn't get his full allocated bonus either.

When Dowling didn't get his pound of flesh, CBRE hit his buddy Dunne with a High Court summons in November 2008.

On 18 December 2008 the chairman of Anglo Irish Bank, Sean FitzPatrick, was forced to resign after admitting that the bank had for a number of years been transferring personal loans it had made to him – worth more than €80 million at their peak – to the balance sheet of Irish Nationwide Building Society at Anglo's year end, so that the existence of the

loans would not be discovered. Anglo non-executive director
Lar Bradshaw also resigned that day, and a day later Anglo
CEO David Drumm fell on his sword. To complete the
drama, the state launched an emergency €1.5 billion recapi-
talization of the bank on 21 December. In the New Year the
Dáil was recalled to pass legislation to take the bank into state
ownership. Weeks later, Anglo withdrew its emergency credit
line from Paddy Kelly.

Hugh McGivern resurfaced in March, seeking to enforce
his February 2008 Mango settlement and looking for a sum
of about €131,000. At a meeting in the offices of solicitor Ivor
Fitzpatrick on Wednesday 24 February, Simon Kelly revealed
to McGivern and his lawyers that the liabilities of the family
business exceeded the assets. The Kellys were broke.

Questions about the Kelly clan's solvency had been raised
towards the end of 2008 when the Thomas Read Group,
which operated twenty-one bars and restaurants in Dublin
and employed 400 people, entered into examinership with
debts of more than €26 million. The Kellys were directors of
the group's holding company, Guerneville Ltd, but it was felt
that the sheer scale and diversity of their developments could
survive the threat posed by the troubles of the Thomas Read
Group.

In November 2008, Paddy Kelly took to the national
airwaves and, in a lengthy interview with Eamon Dunphy,
regaled listeners with tales of how he owned several Rolls-
Royces and not one but two homes on Dublin's Shrewsbury
Road. He admitted that he owed Anglo hundreds of millions
but insisted this was 'no great burden' to him.

Kelly's €131,000 debt to McGivern should, in the grand
scheme of things, have posed no great threat. But it was
McGivern's insistence that Kelly honour the February 2008
deal that brought Kelly to the brink. The 65-year-old

developer considered deploying litigation strategies to keep McGivern and a shark pool of creditors circling him at bay, but as St Patrick's Day approached he instructed his barrister James Doherty to inform the Commercial Court that he was considering bankruptcy.

Kelly had been bust twice before. He had been bust when he met his wife Maureen, and they were both busted in 1990 when Lloyds of London called in its 'names' to underwrite massive losses. Now, with most of his borrowings backed by personal guarantees, he was more deeply in the hole than ever before.

In the affidavit drafted for him by barrister James Doherty, Paddy Kelly told how the decision by Anglo to stop the flow of credit to him had had a dramatic impact on his ability to access funds. It was, he stated simply in the five-page sworn statement, a matter of great personal regret that he had not been able to honour his financial commitments to others, McGivern included; he added that he was determined to deal with his affairs in an open and transparent manner. Kelly said that he had taken active steps to explore the possibility of instigating a personal bankruptcy process and to implement a personal Scheme of Arrangement under the rarely used 1988 Bankruptcy Act.

A Scheme of Arrangement is a type of examinership process for individuals, where a debtor can apply to the High Court for protection from his creditors with a view to negotiating an agreement that can then be enforced by the courts. But a formal Scheme of Arrangement can only protect a debtor from being sued by his creditors if 60 per cent – in both number and value – approve the arrangement. The advantage of a Scheme of Arrangement is court protection, but the pitfall is the potential for any agreement to be blocked by disgruntled creditors, thereby pushing a debtor into bankruptcy.

Paddy and Maureen Kelly were stoic, but on seeing the headlines in the newspapers hailing his father's financial woes, Simon fired off a text message to McGivern the next morning – St Patrick's Day – stating:

See all the papers. Thanks. Somebody had to be the first to attack Paddy so maybe it is apt that it is you. Simon

McGivern replied by text that he had nothing to do with the articles in the papers, prompting Simon to reply:

It was your motion. Sleep well knowing who you truly are. Good luck with the future.

The admission by Paddy Kelly that he was broke was the first of its kind by a developer since the onset of the credit crunch and the collapse in the property market.

Well, almost.

In January 2009, as the state was about to take over Anglo, the *New York Times* published an interview with Sean Dunne, who the paper described as a man whose 'brazen deal-making and Donald Trump-like lifestyle epitomized the country's euphoric boom'. The paper's business reporter Landon Thomas Jr had spent twelve hours interviewing Dunne over the course of two days and a very late night at Doheny and Nesbitt's, the Dublin watering hole much loved by politicians and businessmen. The piece was full of colourful moments, none better than an account of Dunne bending over to pick a penny up off the floor of the pub.

'I grew up with nothing and I know the value of money,' Landon quoted Dunne as saying. 'The Celtic Tiger may be dead and if the banking crisis continues I could be considered insolvent. But the one thing I have is my wife and children – that they can't take away from me.'

The Irish press had a field day with Dunne's apparent admission that he was almost broke, just weeks before An Bord Pleanála was due to give its decision on Dunne's plans for a development including a 37-storey tower on the Jurys site in Ballsbridge, plans that had received a record number of objections. Dunne immediately moved to clarify his remarks, issuing a press release from Mountbrook which reported what he claimed he actually told Thomas.

'With countries, banks in almost every country and legends of the banking world for over a hundred years going bust in the credit crunch, I would not bet against myself or anybody else being taken out,' Dunne said he told Thomas. 'However, if it does happen, I would like to think that my conservative gearing prior to the credit crunch and the location and quality of my assets present as good a buffer as is possible.'

Landon Thomas Jr then backtracked, telling the *Sunday Independent* that Dunne 'never gave me any impression that he was insolvent and I certainly didn't mean to convey that he was'. But many felt that the developer was protesting too much.

Meanwhile, Dunne's dispute with CBRE was heating up. Shortly after CBRE's writ was lodged in the High Court Central Office in November 2008, Dunne claimed in a replying affidavit that any debt owed on foot of the Hume House deal was owed by Mountbrook Homes Ltd and not him personally – a reference to the fact that CBRE was suing Dunne in a personal capacity.

Dunne counterclaimed for €35 million, alleging that CBRE had told him verbally that Hume House was worth €130 million and that this was an overvaluation.

Sean O'Brien, the head of investment at CBRE, gave a very different version of what had happened. He claimed that Dunne was determined to get his hands on Hume House for 'strategic reasons', namely to increase his stake in Ballsbridge, and said CBRE had never valued the building at more than €65 million. O'Brien said that despite the fact he told Dunne in an email on 3 February 2006 that he could not 'justify significantly more for Hume House' than €65 million, Dunne instructed him to submit a revised offer of €90 million.

Drawing a distinction between a formal valuation and an agent's advice on a bidding strategy, O'Brien insisted that CBRE's advice to Dunne, pursuant to the developer's request, concerned the level that he would need to bid in circumstances where at least one other party was bidding for the site. He also described Dunne's claim that he had acted against his better judgment as 'impossible to credit'.

Arguably the lowest point of the pretrial exchange of claims and counterclaims came in February 2009. Dunne, in a new court affidavit, alleged that CBRE had received a payment from Irish Life in connection with the sale of Hume House. Dunne based this charge on a conversation he said he had had with Gerry Keenan, the chief executive of Irish Life Investment Managers. The developer claimed he picked up the phone to Keenan on 6 February 2009 and, after shooting the breeze with the CEO, asked him how much Irish Life had paid CBRE in fees related to the Hume House deal. According to Dunne, Keenan replied, 'Guess,' and Dunne guessed €500,000. Dunne claimed that Keenan told him he was 'in the right field' before dismissing the developer with a laugh and the words: 'I'd better not say any more.'

Five minutes later, according to Dunne's version of the call, Keenan called back and said that he 'had his head mixed up' and that Irish Life hadn't paid anything to CBRE.

In a signed court statement, Gerry Keenan denied that Irish Life had effectively induced CBRE to get Dunne to increase his offer through the alleged payment of a fee to CBRE, and complained that Dunne had 'an agenda' that he was totally unaware of when Dunne telephoned him.

'I made a simple mistake being led by him [Dunne] in a direction which clearly suited his purpose,' Keenan stated. 'I checked the facts immediately after the telephone call and rang him straight away to apologize for misleading him . . . it became clear to me in the second phone conversation that the clarification that I gave him was not the answer he wanted.'

Dunne demanded all correspondence between CBRE and Irish Life but was rebuffed by the courts.

In early May 2009, weeks before the trial began, CBRE indicated that it was seeking damages for malicious prosecution of Dunne's claims. Irish Life, which denied that it had ever discussed any fee with CBRE, sought its legal costs for being dragged into a case in which it claimed the developer had acted 'despicably' towards it.

The circus finally rolled into town in July, and Dunne, still maintaining his €35 million counterclaim, was to be the central witness. But on the opening day of the case before High Court Judge Mary Finlay Geoghegan, Mrs Dunne (née Killilea) turned up without her husband, who was at home sick in bed.

There were plenty of reasons in 2009 why an Irish developer might suffer from a lack of energy, low levels of concentration and sweats requiring three-hourly changes of bed linen. A suspected case of the dreaded swine flu, which had the Dunner housebound and unable to attend for his big fight, was just one of them.

Judge Finlay Geoghegan refused to postpone the dispute

until the developer felt better. Sean O'Brien, CBRE's head of investment, took to the witness stand and offered a telling insight into how properties were bought and sold for unprecedented prices during the boom years. O'Brien, a former employee of Irish Life, insisted that he had told Dunne that Hume House was worth €65 million; and he told the court that there was 'a world of difference between the *price* of a property and the *value* of a property … The value would be a relevant factor in deciding what price you are prepared to pay, but they could be two wildly different numbers depending on the appetite to acquire the apple.'

Sean Dunne did not just want an apple, he wanted the entire orchard of Ballsbridge. But he never got to tell his side of the story in court. Laid low at home, he agreed to settle the case on the third day – a settlement that included €1 million he had lodged in court earlier in the proceedings and the withdrawal of all claims against CBRE.

It had been a bitter dispute and arguably there were no winners, yet both sides claimed victory. CBRE's Managing Director Guy Hollis said in a press release the firm was delighted with the outcome of this settlement. 'All unfounded allegations have been withdrawn, which fully vindicates our position,' he said.

Mountbrook Homes also issued a press release in which it said that the disputed fees of €1.5 million sought by CBRE had not been paid.

'Sean Dunne and the Mountbrook Group have terminated all dealings and will not be engaging CBRE Ireland or world-wide in relation to any further dealings,' the Mountbrook press release noted.

Not that it mattered. Ireland's property party was well and truly over.

*

Within months of admitting that he was broke, Paddy Kelly had had almost €100 million worth of court judgments made against him. Later in the year Redquartz Boundary Ltd, the property investment company set up by Paddy and Simon Kelly along with financiers Niall McFadden and Paul Pardy, fell into the hands of liquidators.

Most of the first wave of judgments against the Kellys and other developers related to relatively small debts owed to business partners, or to loans issued by foreign banks. Irish lenders had good reason not to pursue developers until their loans were transferred into the National Asset Management Agency (NAMA), a sort of 'bad bank' devoted to buying bad loans from the Irish banks covered by the guarantee, at a discount from their book value but a big mark-up on their current market value, thereby recapitalizing the banks and providing them with fresh liquidity. Foreign-owned banks whose distressed assets would not be absorbed by NAMA had no incentive to be so patient, and began to adopt a much harder line with developers.

Leading the charge was ACCBank, whose Dutch parent Rabobank had been forced to write off €294.9 million in bad loans and to pump €175 million into ACC to make sure it was adequately capitalized. Having made these provisions, Rabobank was keen to wash its hands of the ACC adventure in Ireland, and to get whatever it could from its Irish debtors.

Judge Kelly granted judgment to the bank in May but did not allow the lender to register or execute the orders until the courts ruled on claims by the Kelly family that the way in which the bank had dealt with them had exacerbated their financial difficulties. ACC had loaned €1.5 million to Simon, Christopher and Emma Kelly to invest in the bank's own 'SolidWorld' bonds, whose value had plummeted.

'No wonder the banks are in trouble,' said Judge Kelly.

'The bank was lending its own money to invest in its own product but, if that product went down, where does that leave the bank?'

Most of ACC's €16 million claim related to guarantees the bank maintained were given by the Kellys over loans in late 2007 to Pressaro Ltd to buy the Cablelink/NTL building at Pembroke Place in Ballsbridge. The building was valued in 2007 at €27 million, but less than two years later its value had plummeted to €8.5 million. ACC and the Kellys ultimately settled the action on terms which included a condition that the judgment against Emma would be withdrawn and the bank would not move against Christopher's home in pursuit of its judgment.

The rush by ACC and other foreign banks to secure judgments caused frayed nerves at Government Buildings, where the possibility of fire sales of the assets of major developers was seen as threatening to undermine NAMA. The temperature rose even higher when the Irish Nationwide Building Society, still reeling from the resignation of its charismatic chief Michael Fingleton over its 'warehousing' of Sean Fitz-Patrick's loans, brought a €60 million claim against Liam Carroll relating to guarantees over loans made to his company Aifca Ltd.

The case was the largest personal guarantee action ever to come before the Irish courts, and the Nationwide claim threatened to bring Liam Carroll down.

But somebody else got there first.

6. Not Too Big to Fail

It was the last day of the legal term. Barristers were fleeing the Four Courts and pouring into restaurants and bars around the capital to celebrate their last day of school and an enviable two-month break from the Law Library. A few unfortunates get caught out every year when the High and Supreme Courts try to clear their desks by handing down a flurry of rulings ahead of the new legal year in October, but mostly the Four Courts are deserted by noon at the end of Trinity term.

But on Friday, 31 July 2009 no one was celebrating in Court 6, the hub of the Commercial Court. A sign outside warns against chewing gum in court, but it was mostly lips being chewed in anguish as Mr Justice Peter Kelly approached the bench at 2 p.m. to rule on the fate of Liam Carroll and his Zoe building empire. BlackBerrys in hand, thumbs twitching nervously over the 'send' key, men in dark suits formed a barrier around Carroll's legal team, waiting like awestruck pilgrims in front of Kelly's altar for a sign as to whether the fabled 'shycoon' would be saved or condemned by his judgment.

Two weeks earlier Kelly had sent barrister Bernard Dunleavy, the Junior Counsel representing Zoe, away to find another High Court judge to deal with Zoe's eleventh-hour examinership application. Kelly had just spent a long day presiding over a €78 million debt claim by Irish Nationwide against Carroll and his company Aifca – an action spawned by a row with developer Noel Smyth over The

Square shopping centre in Tallaght. Carroll himself was facing a €60 million debt claim by Irish Nationwide over personal guarantees he allegedly gave to cover Aifca's borrowings, a lawsuit that made front-page news as the largest personal guarantee action ever to come before the Irish courts.

That same day, Senior Counsel Hugh Mohan was defending Carroll in a separate €140 million damages case in Court 7 taken by Smyth's company Redfern against Carroll and two other developers, former IRA hunger striker Tom McFeely and Larry O'Mahony, also arising out of the Tallaght dispute.

Two days after the case opened, and just after Judge Kelly heard the Nationwide claim, Dunleavy approached the bench and asked him if he would consider an examinership application.

Judge Kelly, who appeared unenthusiastic at the prospect of beginning a new case late on a Friday afternoon when he had ninety-one sets of papers to read before the following Monday morning's list, inquired of Dunleavy, one of the rising stars from the junior Bar, the identity of the latest beleaguered entity seeking protection from its creditors.

'Vantive, Judge,' said Dunleavy in a stage whisper.

'Who?' asked Kelly, oblivious to the fact that Vantive – with Morston, a Jersey-registered company also seeking court protection – was the corporate parent of Zoe Developments. Zoe was Liam Carroll. Liam Carroll was broke.

For weeks, rumours had circulated in legal and political circles that one of Ireland's biggest developers would go bust and seek court protection to avoid liquidation and a fire sale of his assets. It was feared such a move by a developer could have huge consequences for the National Asset Management Agency (NAMA), the bad bank for which the government was struggling to secure support.

A fire sale of the assets of any of the large developers before

NAMA was up and running, in an otherwise dead market, would establish a market price for development assets and determine the basis for the write-downs the banks would have to take. This would make it politically difficult for the government to justify paying prices for toxic development loans which reflected, not their actual value now, but rather the hope that there would be asset-price increases as the economy improved.

For the most part, Irish punters knew Liam Carroll as the reclusive former electrical engineer from Dundalk who became one of the richest men in Ireland by building shoebox apartments in Dublin. Carroll focused on run-down areas of the capital where land could be got cheaply from the City Council and where tax breaks were available. Zoe was brought temporarily down to earth by the same Judge Peter Kelly following the death in 1997 on one of Zoe's sites of a young construction worker, James Masterson. The case came to court as a result of thirteen breaches of health and safety laws on the Charlotte Quay site in Ringsend on the same day the 24-year-old carpenter fell to his death. It was not the first time Zoe had been dragged to court over its health and safety record: Kelly had evidence before him of twelve previous convictions for the same sort of activities on three separate sites at Grove Road, Bride Street and Dorset Street. A year earlier, a 71-year-old bricklayer had died after another safety lapse at a Zoe site on the corner of Parnell and Gardiner Street in Dublin. Kelly branded the company that Carroll controlled as a recidivist criminal and threatened to shut down its sites. The directors of Zoe, including Carroll, his wife Róisín and David Torpey, were summonsed to court, and Carroll was forced to appear in the witness box. The judge berated Carroll, saying he had behaved 'as if he couldn't care less' about his workers and the laws of the state.

Memorably, he told Carroll: 'You are entitled to make profits on the sweat of your workers but you are not entitled to make profit on the blood and lives of your workers. You are a disgrace to the construction industry and ought to be ashamed of yourself.' Carroll was asked for assurances, which he gave, to implement a safety plan and cooperate with the authorities who would police it. The judge then asked Carroll whether he had anything to say to the court, but the developer remained mute. His silence prompted a furious reaction from Kelly, who was staggered that Carroll did not apologize for the failures that contributed to Masterson's death.

Faced with the prospect of his sites being shut down, Carroll instantly apologized. Within forty-eight hours and at judicial prompting, Carroll also paid out £100,000 to charity, which Kelly directed towards the St Vincent de Paul and Temple Street Children's Hospital.

Carroll cleaned up his on-site act, and the building continued apace.

Meanwhile, he was extending his business interests in different directions. In 2002 he achieved a hostile takeover of property company Dunloe Ewart, prising it from the hands of Noel Smyth after a protracted and dramatic battle. Dunloe's main assets were almost 400 acres of development land at Cherrywood, adjacent to the newly completed M50 in south Dublin and valued at well over €1 billion, and a top-drawer site at Sir John Rogerson's Quay.

In 2006 and 2007, Carroll built up holdings of almost 30 per cent in the food group Greencore and shipping company Irish Continental Group. The only thing the listed companies had in common was their land banks – and land, not food or ferries, was the commodity that Liam Carroll was really interested in.

By January 2008 Carroll was refinancing much of his

borrowings to support his experimental foray into the stock markets and to meet ongoing liabilities and commitments associated with his developments. By July, work on development sites in Ireland had ground to a screeching halt. Undeterred, Carroll went on an equity buying spree, ratcheting up positions in three listed companies: Aer Lingus, insurer FBD and house builder McInerney. He built up those positions partly through contracts for difference, a financial derivative that makes it possible to make large bets on stock prices with only a modest cash payment.

Six months later, Carroll, nursing heavy losses on his stock market positions, was forced to offload his FBD stake and sell his 5.5 per cent position in Aer Lingus, incurring losses of up to €30 million on the disposal. And then, in October 2008, Carroll suffered arguably his greatest setback to date when the High Court ruled against him in the Battle of North Lotts.

In the nine months between August 2008 and April 2009, the High Court received nine petitions to wind up Danninger, Carroll's main construction vehicle. More serious, however, was the matter of €136 million he owed to Dutch lender ACCBank.

On 29 June 2009 two of Carroll's holding companies, Vantive and Morston, received letters from ACCBank, demanding that he repay €136 million in loans that had been made in August 2007 to Vantive and in January 2008 to Morston. These letters of demand, which gave the companies twenty-one days to repay the loans in full, set in train a series of events that would ultimately lead to the collapse of Ireland's largest developer. The demand prompted Carroll to seek court protection from the companies' creditors, and on 17 July Bernard Dunleavy was sent by Judge Kelly to his colleague Judge Frank Clarke, who granted an order appointing an interim examiner to the

Zoe Group of companies, pending a full hearing of the examinership application.

The purpose of examinership is to offer troubled companies a temporary refuge from their creditors in order to devise a survival scheme. By the time Carroll sought shelter in the courts, fewer than one in three companies survived the process, compared to nine out of ten during the boom years.

Examinership was itself the product of a previous crisis, when another Irish titan was in need of a state bailout.

The Irish government introduced the concept of examinership into Irish company law in 1990 when beef baron Larry Goodman's Goodman International Group was staring down the barrel of liquidation.

Given the potentially catastrophic impact that the collapse of Goodman International Group could have had on the Irish agricultural economy, the government introduced the concept of examinership to facilitate the rescue of companies that faced solvency problems but that could trade profitably again if given a bit of breathing space to raise new investment, sell assets, or otherwise re-establish the business on a stable footing.

The law allowed court protection for between seventy and 100 days, during which time an examiner would investigate the affairs of the company and report on its prospect of survival.

Examinership worked spectacularly well for Goodman, who went on to regain control of the company when he bought out the shareholders who helped him restructure the group; but its relevance was questionable in a situation where property developers – who produced nothing themselves and whose assets, the notional value of which underlay their borrowings, were now worth a fraction of their bubble prices – were hoping to keep going in a dead, capital-starved market.

Until 2006, an average of ten companies sought examinership each year. The number rose to thirty by the end of 2007, and exceeded sixty in 2008.

Attracting new finance was vital to a company's prospect of success in an examinership application, but credit was in short supply when Senior Counsel Bill Shipsey, who had acted for Carroll for two decades, made his case in the hearing before Judge Clarke.

Not since the collapse of Goodman had there been an examinership case in which the wider public interest had been so clearly at issue, with the country's most prolific developer facing liquidation. The hearing lasted less than half an hour during which Shipsey revealed that the Zoe Group, comprising fifty-one companies, owed €1.1 billion to its various creditors and had been forced to seek court protection under the umbrella of its parents and four related companies because of ACC's action. The monies owed to ACC were just over a tenth of Zoe's overall debt, and Zoe's debts were themselves dwarfed by the estimated €3 billion Carroll owed overall through his various business interests. Zoe's largest lender, representing about 40 per cent of the overall debt, was AIB. Bank of Scotland (Ireland) was owed some 23 per cent of the total, Bank of Ireland 9.3 per cent, Ulster Bank 6.7 per cent and Anglo Irish Bank 2.1 per cent.

Vantive and Morston were parent companies of the Zoe Group. They borrowed money from banks, and the funds cascaded down to companies within Zoe in the form of inter-company debt. Curiously, Vantive and Morston, ultimately owned by Carroll and his wife Róisín through their unlimited vehicle Showlay – which did not have to publish its accounts – always had 'negative asset values'. In layman's terms, they didn't trade at all. They had no employees and no income of their own and made losses every year, which were offset against profits in other related companies. The Zoe group relied in its entirety on Vantive and Morston for funding and the acquisition of key assets which were critical to the future of all of Carroll's undertakings. But until July 2009, when Carroll sought the protection of the court, few knew the intricacies of his labyrinthine corporate structure.

After Zoe secured interim protection, the case came back before Judge Kelly on 28 July for a full hearing of the petition. It was ironic that Carroll was relying for the survival of his business on a judge who had, twelve years earlier, threatened to exterminate it.

While Carroll was nowhere near the Four Courts on 28 July, he had crafted the affidavits supporting the petition, warning of the dire consequences of an immediate disposal of properties on to the market. This doomsday scenario was widely perceived to be overstated, as a liquidator with a duty to protect assets was unlikely to dump Carroll's portfolio in this manner. Carroll's real concern related to two key sites in the Dublin docklands, Castleforbes and East Road, over which ACC had first legal charges and which he did not want 'attacked'. He wanted to hold on to them as they were 'absolutely key' to the ongoing prospects of Zoe. The affidavit asserted that the value of the sites would soar once the economy recovered.

Behind the scenes, the struggle to save Zoe was taking a personal toll on the notoriously secretive Carroll. Unbeknownst to the courts or the media, Carroll had attended his GP on 14 July 2009 for a stress-related illness. It had been on that same day that the board of Vantive, namely Carroll and his trusted lieutenants David Torpey and John Pope, had passed the resolution to seek an interim examiner if the threat from ACC did not recede.

The petition had been cobbled together in less than four days and that haste was manifest. The Independent

Accountant's Report, the backbone of any examinership petition, contained a litany of errors – including a statement that Morston had an excess of assets over liabilities of some €293,958 when it should have read an excess of liabilities over assets.

Carroll's Senior Counsel, Michael Cush – who shared duties with Bill Shipsey – argued the case for his survival. Cush, who had represented a series of high-profile clients in the Commercial Court, including a number of developers, opened the petition by stating that the Zoe Group had historically been a very successful property business. Cush attributed Carroll's mercy dash to the courts to credit problems, the downturn in the property market, problems with investments and ACC's rogue streak.

ACC had extended a €62 million loan to Vantive in August 2007 to refinance loans from Barclays Bank and to finance another loan by Vantive to Danninger. In January 2008, ACC sanctioned a second €69.2 million loan to Morston to refinance an existing loan facility Morston held with NIB and to cascade a loan down to allow Peytor, a Zoe company, to acquire what Carroll expected would be his next goldmine, the 6-acre Castleforbes Business Park site at Sheriff Street in Dublin. Both loans were to be repaid within two years or on demand, and ACC ensured it had good security to cover its facility, holding the first legal charges over the Sheriff Street site and the site at 1–3 East Road, another prime 6-acre site in the docklands.

ACC, as a foreign-owned bank, was outside of the state's bank guarantee and thus not subject to government pressure to support the NAMA agenda. While the guaranteed Irish lenders (and other banks in the Irish market) 'held hands' with their big debtors by rolling up interest on their loans and taking a softly, softly approach towards realizing their security, ACC, which held less than 2 per cent of the Irish market, was firing writs. Between January 2007 and May 2009, weeks before it issued letters of demand on Vantive and Morston, it had initiated almost 300 debt recovery actions in the High Court, mostly arising from property-related lending.

As Cush set out his case, the fragile and wholly interdependent nature of Zoe's complex structure was exposed. The business relationship between Vantive and Morston and its offspring was entirely symbiotic. Like a set of dominoes, the Zoe companies could all be felled by a minor gust of wind from one creditor shouting, 'Stop!'

Cush outlined what would become a mantra over the next three months. If the group was liquidated, hundreds of jobs would be lost, Zoe would collapse owing more than €1 billion, and it was unlikely the market could absorb such a large portfolio of properties.

During the hearing, it emerged that Carroll and his advisers, KPMG accountants, had placed a business plan before his lenders in December 2008 to address their difficulties and how these might be overcome in the next few years. The essence of the plan was a new strategy whereby Zoe would concentrate on responding to individual market demand for certain types of development rather than engaging in speculative development. The plan also relied on active management of Carroll's land portfolio to exploit 'planning gain', disposal of most of his residential stock through aggressive marketing and heavy discounts, and disposal of his increasingly compromised equity positions. Non-key assets would also be disposed of.

The crucial feature of the plan was a two-year moratorium on interest payments. All of Carroll's lenders, with the exception of ACC, agreed to the plan. AIB and Bank of Scotland (Ireland), which stood to lose most if Carroll's assets were liquidated, also agreed to provide more loan facilities to buy off his unsecured creditors and thus ward off any other collateral attacks.

The plan confirmed what most people suspected: the banks were willing to roll over for large developers at a time when homeowners and businesses were being pursued without mercy in the courts. Carroll's case exposed not just the scale of that forbearance but also showed that the banks, whose primary function in lending is to assess and manage risk, were willing to make funds available to selected insolvent companies through interest roll-ups and to continue funding certain projects. Evidently they had concluded it was in their interest to keep Carroll alive until NAMA was up and running. The only bank that wouldn't play ball was ACC. It had refused Carroll's request for forbearance and instead served him with threats to begin désastre (liquidation) proceedings against Morston in Jersey and winding-up proceedings against Vantive in Ireland.

Bill Shipsey had laid the foundation for Zoe's strategy in the initial application for an interim examiner before Judge Clarke.

But the initial hearing was little more than an advertisement to the world at large that Zoe was seeking the appointment of an examiner, and it still had to convince another Judge, Peter Kelly, that it was entitled to one.

One of the requirements for the appointment of an examiner is that a company is, or is likely to be, unable to pay its debts as they fall due. In other words, it must be very, very sick. But it cannot be at death's door, and an examiner cannot be appointed where there is an order for the liquidation of the company. In this way, a company seeking the appointment of an examiner is like a patient in an intensive care unit: very ill but at least harbouring a prospect of survival.

It was Cush's contention that Zoe, though seriously ill, could survive. He argued that what was most unusual about this patient – compared to others who sought refuge in the courts – was that its survival plan did not involve writing off debts and had the support of all of its creditors bar ACC.

An examinership application must include a report by an independent accountant that corroborates the view being put forward by the company, outlines how much money is needed to keep the entity afloat during the examinership period, and specifies where that money will come from.

Kelly was unconvinced. This scheme to help Zoe out of its crisis involved 'pouring money' into developments over the next three years when the office market was already 'grossly oversupplied' and the residential market as flat as a pancake, he said. He noted that the report of the independent accountant recommending the survival scheme (and also proposing that the existing senior management at Zoe remain in situ) had been prepared by Zoe's own auditors. 'The captains who navigated the ship on to the rocks are to remain in charge,' he sighed.

He also expressed amazement at the number of directorships held by Carroll and his henchmen David Torpey and John Pope within the Zoe group. The corporate structure was akin to a spider's web, he remarked.

ACC was represented in court that day by Junior Counsel Rossa Fanning. A law lecturer at UCD, Fanning had fast earned a reputation as the first port of call for institutions seeking to recover debts in the Commercial Court. Fanning told the court that ACC was adopting a 'guardedly neutral' position, neither opposing nor supporting the petition, but warned that stance could change if the NAMA legislation, due to be published within hours, was deemed unfavourable towards the bank's interests. Although the spectre of NAMA had loomed large over many actions that had come before the Commercial Court, it was ACC who made the issue explicit.

ACC's stance gave rise to suspicions it was trying to use Carroll as a Trojan Horse to get the six state-guaranteed (and about-to-be-bailed-out) banks to take over the Dutch-owned bank's exposure in Ireland. This possibility was not lost on Judge Kelly, who suggested to Cush that Zoe's problems could be easily resolved if ACC's debts were bought out by his other lenders, thereby avoiding receivership or liquidation. But the government was adamant the Irish banks, owned in all but name by the taxpayer, would not set a precedent for other foreign lenders by removing ACC from the Irish picture.

On Wednesday morning, Carroll got a minor reprieve when Judge Kelly ruled that Irish Nationwide's complaint over the €60 million personal guarantee involving Aifca should go to a full hearing. But Kelly had barely drawn breath when Dun Laoghaire-Rathdown County Council, one of Carroll's joint partners in the development of a science and technology park at Cherrywood, brought an emergency application to restrain Carroll from dealing with or selling any of the lands.

The next day, the eve of Judge Kelly's ruling, four senior ACC and Rabobank executives held crunch talks with NAMA managing director Brendan McDonagh and senior Department of Finance officials. The talks took place at exactly the same time as business journalists were being briefed on the draft legislation underpinning the NAMA bill, which was due to be announced by Finance Minister Brian Lenihan in time for the six o'clock news.

The Dutch delegation was led by Frank Steenhuisen, a risk

director with the bank, who indicated ACC would try to work with NAMA to salvage the best outcome for both sides from the carcass of the collapsed property market. Hours later, Minister Lenihan unveiled the draft bill, but it came with a significant caveat: it was for public consultation purposes only and the Dáil would not be recalled until mid-September to debate it. Lenihan talked tough, warning there was nothing in the planned bill to bail out borrowers. Anyone who owed money would continue to owe it, he said.

As the country pored over the draft NAMA bill, the drama resumed in Court 6 at 2 p.m. on Friday, when Judge Kelly gave his ruling.

'It is sometimes said that when small or modest borrowers from banks encounter difficulties in repaying their loans, then such borrowers have a problem,' began Kelly ominously. 'For those with large borrowings, it is the banks who have a problem. If ever a case demonstrated the accuracy of that proposition, it is this one.' Kelly observed that the sort of forbearance shown to Carroll was 'remarkably absent' with regard to smaller borrowers who, like Carroll, defaulted on their obligations when they fell on tough times. He also poured scorn on Carroll's 2008 business plan, saying that while much of it was written in 'management speak' it all hinged on a promise by the banks not to call in the loans.

Kelly dedicated an entire section of his ruling to the Independent Accountant's Report compiled by Fergal McGrath of LHM Casey McGrath, whose opinion that Zoe had a reasonable prospect of survival was grounded in projections partly based on valuations provided by estate agents CBRE and Hooke & MacDonald, both major clients of the Zoe group. The report predicted a remarkable turnaround for the company: from a €1 billion deficit to a €300,000 profit in less than three years. Kelly described the degree of optimism on the part of the independent accountants as 'bordering if not trespassing on the fanciful' and asked: 'What market is there likely to be over the next three years for the sale of sites even with planning permissions and the sale of residential, commercial and retail units?' Carroll had placed the scale of his portfolio at the heart of the petition, but he had sold only thirty-nine residential units since December 2008.

Kelly cast doubt on the reliability of the valuations provided by the Zoe clients CBRE and Hooke & MacDonald, which he said were out of date, and observed that there was something 'artificial' about Carroll's bid for court protection. In his view, the whole exercise seemed designed to help shareholders whose investment had proved to be unsuccessful, something examinership was not designed to do.

Panic surged through Court 6 as the implications of Kelly's ruling struck home and the banks that had stood by Carroll faced the prospect of sending in receivers. At the back of the court, a handful of Zoe construction workers sat ashen-faced, their fingers trembling as they sent texts to their colleagues at the Cherrywood site and beyond to say it was all over.

But it wasn't over. With great reluctance, Judge Kelly, after adjourning for over twenty minutes, granted Carroll's application for a stay against the refusal of court protection pending the outcome of a Supreme Court appeal against his ruling. ACC cried foul, arguing that it wasn't possible to place a stay against a refusal. Kelly agreed that it was unusual, but allowed the application nonetheless.

In the brief period that Kelly had adjourned to his chambers, Carroll's legal team had dashed to the office of the Supreme Court and had secured a commitment for an early hearing for its planned appeal. The Supreme Court agreed to break its legal vacation and sit on the following Tuesday morning. The court's decision to sit almost immediately after the appeal could be explained in part by the fact that the 100-day examinership clock was ticking, but the willingness to accommodate Carroll also smacked of judicial politics at a moment when details of the NAMA bill had just been published and public levels of anxiety were high.

On Tuesday morning the Supreme Court, led by Chief Justice John Murray, extended the stay and made clear the appeal would be heard quickly. Murray had already read the books of appeal and was unimpressed. In a parting shot, he warned the company to come up with answers to the questions begged by the Independent Accountant's Report.

'Get a new one,' he growled to a bowed but not broken Cush.

The Supreme Court is a forbidding arena. Eminent barristers well versed in the cut and thrust of Ireland's adversarial legal tradition routinely find their finely tuned theses torn apart by the judges. The oral representations by barristers are based on written submissions tendered to the court in advance of a hearing that are sliced and diced by judges before the barristers even rise to their feet to open their cases.

Michael Cush presented Zoe's appeal before a three-judge court led by Chief Justice John Murray, who twice served Fianna Fáil as Attorney General. A former judge of the European Court of Human Rights, Murray is renowned as a shrewd operator with a firm finger on the pulse of political life. To his left was Nial Fennelly, the corporate law expert on the court, who had delivered a significant ruling clarifying the law on examinership in January 2009 which became the template when the surge of new cases hit the courts. Mrs Justice Susan Denham, the last liberal on the court following the retirement of Mrs Justice Catherine McGuinness, was seated at Murray's right-hand side.

When the Supreme Court sat down to hear the appeal against Judge Kelly's refusal, it was clear Zoe faced a difficult challenge to dismantle the factual and legal analysis that had led to Kelly's dismissal of the first examinership bid. The court, which only considers points of law and does not retry the facts of a case, was also now part of the wider political maelstrom arising from the banking bailout that had not died down despite the publication of the draft NAMA bill.

The parliamentary process proper had not even begun as politicians availed themselves, to the incredulity of the public, of their usual long summer vacation. Demands to recall the Dáil in August to debate and enact the NAMA bill at the earliest opportunity were ignored. In the politicians' absence, the Supreme Court was being asked to make a decision that could have major knock-on effects with regard to public policy and on the wider economy.

In theory, the Supreme Court was only being asked to consider an appeal against a refusal of examinership to a very large group of companies. In practice, it was stepping into the shoes of the putative NAMA, arguably the most contentious political and legal issue in decades.

It was expressly being invited by Liam Carroll's Zoe Group to make a decision about the impact of its collapse on the wider economy, and there was a possibility – in the absence of a body of law designed to deal with such a major economic event – that the Supreme Court would legislate from the bench, even if it did not intend to do so.

If the court granted protection to Zoe on the strength of a seemingly hopeless survival plan, it might stand accused of crossing the constitutional line, bending the law to accommodate a political crisis and using the coercive power of the state to enforce policies desired by government mandarins.

Just prior to Cush's opening statement that Tuesday morning, lawyers representing the Revenue Commissioners quietly informed the Supreme Court that four days earlier Vantive had discharged a €764,900 payment owed to the taxman, prompting the Revenue to take a neutral stance on the appeal. There had also been subtle but critical changes in attitudes among the creditors, with five banks – including Zoe's largest creditors AIB and Bank of Scotland (Ireland) – changing their position to what Cush described as 'active support' for the examinership application. Cush complained that Judge Kelly had failed to give sufficient weight to the level and type of support being offered by the companies' lenders: seven out of Zoe's eight lenders were supporting the companies by providing finance to pay off third-party unsecured creditors. The banks weren't just protecting Zoe from third-party attacks; they were agreeing 'in principle' to provide finance for ongoing development and had agreed to a moratorium on repayment of debts by rolling up interest repayments for two to three years.

The Chief Justice queried the 'very vague' claim by Cush that the banks would finance all of Zoe's outgoings. The assertion that the banks had agreed 'in principle' to provide finance for ongoing development did not detail what the actual commitments given to Zoe by the banks were.

Cush persevered, complaining that Judge Kelly had relied on his own views on the property market instead of heeding two December 2008 valuations provided by agents CBRE and Hooke & MacDonald. But these valuations, which had formed the basis of the independent accountant's opinion in the original examinership application, had never actually been placed before the High Court. Nor had they been produced to the Supreme Court, and this fact was seized upon by Judge Fennelly, who cut Cush short to point out that the Supreme Court had been given no information whatsoever on the property valuations that underpinned the appeal.

What hope have the companies if the valuations are made public? asked Cush. Murray responded that the valuations could have been tendered in confidence to the court and not made public if there were concerns about commercial sensitivity.

In a rapid series of exchanges, Judge Murray honed in on each of Zoe's grounds of appeal and observed that not one creditor – banking or otherwise – had actually said it believed the companies had a reasonable prospect of survival. They supported the appeal, but it seemed their support was based not on any genuine belief that Zoe could survive, but rather on the calculation that they needed it to survive until Zoe could cross the NAMA line.

There would be no need for an appeal at all if it weren't for ACC, said Cush in frustration, prompting Judge Murray to reply that the bank was only exercising a right that Carroll had given it.

Having made little headway with the claim that Carroll had the support of all but one of his banks, Cush claimed Judge Kelly had misunderstood the companies' current financial situation and projections, had made no reference at all to evidence that the property market could not absorb the Zoe properties if court protection was refused, and had failed to give due weight to the impact of the collapse of Carroll's companies for 'many others'.

The debate returned to the topic of the mysterious valuations, whose absence was becoming a major problem for Carroll's legal team. Carroll was asking the Supreme Court to make a judgment based on valuations he had withheld from the court. The entire report of the independent accountant, including the valuations that underlay it, had been based on assumptions about the property market that could not be tested by the court. Judge Denham, in her first interjection, pointed out that the whole basis for the appeal seemed to be the banks' forbearance; she also defended Kelly's entitlement to make observations on the property market based on the caseload he handled every day of the week.

It comes to this, said Cush: the banks had seen the business plan and they supported the examinership bid. With increasing impatience, Judge Murray reminded Cush that the Supreme Court was not a court of first instance. Could new evidence about the bank's support actually be heard? Should the chief executives of the banks be sworn in to give evidence? The prospect of AIB's Eugene Sheehy or Bank of Ireland's Brian Goggin being summonsed to the Supreme Court to clarify their support for Carroll caused momentary excitement, but Murray resiled from such a possibility as an appellate court could not hear new evidence.

Cush stuck to the broadcasting maxim. You tell them. Then tell them. Then finish by telling them what you've already told them.

You know the valuations are in place, you know they are from reputable valuers, you know the banks have seen them, he told the all-powerful triumvirate that would seal Carroll's fate.

Liam Carroll believes it will work, said Cush, sounding less confident now.

In contrast to Cush's rather laboured appeal, ACC conformed to type: short, sharp and ruthless. Rossa Fanning was again present, assisting Senior Counsel Lyndon McCann.

McCann outlined the bank's position. It had not seen the business plan and had downgraded its attitude towards the examinership bid from guarded neutrality to opposition pending the publication of the draft NAMA legislation.

ACC's war was not with Carroll alone. Having considered

the draft NAMA legislation, ACC concluded that what was contained in it, even if ultimately amended by the Dáil, could be prejudicial to its position. In layman's speak, ACC was informing the court that NAMA – through its write-downs on toxic debts – could adversely affect the bank's chance of fully recovering its loans. McCann rubbished the idea that the apparently high level of bank support for Carroll indicated a reasonable prospect of survival. In an aside, he mused that the banks probably had their own motives for wanting a controlled explosion of Zoe's assets via NAMA rather than a liquidation.

Far from warding off a third-party attack, McCann suggested that the supine banks' actions could give rise to charges of fraudulent preference, where an insolvent company intentionally prefers one creditor over another. He highlighted the folly of a nationalized bank, Anglo, agreeing to give Carroll an extra €8 million loan facility to pay interest on AIB's loan towards the construction of its planned new headquarters.

The big lacuna for ACC, as well as the Supreme Court, was the failure of Carroll to put the property valuations, or evidence supporting its belief in a coming upturn in the property market, before the court. ACC said it was baffled by the lack of views from economists. Interest rates would soon be ratcheted up and any 'scheme of arrangement' with creditors would as a consequence require more borrowings, which would in turn further dilute the value of the security held by ACC over Carroll's prime assets.

Cush mounted a brief reply to ACC, but his task was difficult: he had been instructed by Carroll to defend the indefensible, and with both hands tied behind his back. What the Supreme Court and ACC did not know was that Carroll, against the advice of his lawyers and other representatives, would not permit the valuations to go before the court at all, not even on a confidential basis.

The Supreme Court retired, promising to return with a judgment at 5 p.m. It was expected the court would give its judgment orally and provide its written reasons at a later date, a common practice in urgent cases; but just before 7 p.m., Murray returned with his colleagues and a 32-page written ruling. It fell to Murray to break the bad news: Zoe had lost its appeal and was staring down the barrel of liquidation. No doomsday scenario, no catastrophic warnings about hundreds of job losses and a flood of properties into a dead market, could save it.

The Supreme Court found that it was not possible for it to reach any conclusion about the prospects of survival of the companies as a going concern in the absence of any evidence about the likely future development of the property market.

The opinion of the independent accountant was, it found, explicitly based on a number of assumptions, none of which had been verified by evidence.

The independent accountant had not expressed any opinion about the valuations; the valuers upon whose reports Zoe had made the assumptions had not given any evidence and their reports had not been given to the courts.

The basis of the banks' support had not been articulated and Carroll had not established that his strategy for the future orderly disposal of the key assets of the company were 'credible or reasonably viable'.

The appeal had failed; Zoe would be liquidated.

The Supreme Court is an appellate court and its decisions are final, but that did not stop Carroll's lieutenants David Torpey and John Pope, under the direct instructions of Róisín Carroll

– their de facto boss in her husband's absence – from mounting an audacious legal challenge to circumvent the Supreme Court's ruling.

Solicitor Neil O'Mahony, from the firm Eversheds O'Donnell Sweeney, was one of the authors of Zoe's comeback. The possibility of bringing a second petition for court protection was first canvassed during a conversation between O'Mahony and Eamon Richardson of KPMG, who had devised Carroll's business plan. That evening, Cush and other advisers to the Zoe group were summoned to a meeting and the possibility was teased out. The discussions continued through the night and the following morning.

The *Irish Independent*'s former deputy business editor, Ailish O'Hora, published a splash on Friday morning revealing that Zoe was going to mount a second bid to set aside the Supreme Court ruling. The *Star* newspaper's Robert Cox exclusively reported that Carroll had been hospitalized the previous evening. The reports prompted a handful of reporters to descend on a nearly deserted Four Courts, which had only one duty judge, Eamon de Valera, hanging around in his chambers in case any emergency applications needed to be heard.

The Central Office of the High Court was informed of a new petition for court protection. If the papers were not properly lodged in the office, no petition could proceed, a fact highlighted by a seething Judge de Valera when at 9.20 p.m. a dozen lawyers led by Cush burst into Court 12.

Cush, who had been planning to catch a late flight to Kerry, looked exhausted, as did his legal colleagues and Carroll's co-directors Pope and Torpey, who had worked night and day to file the petition before the statutory deadline expired at midnight.

ACCBank, led by solicitor Jane Marshall of McCann

FitzGerald solicitors, looked none too happy to be back in court over its intractable debtor, given the seemingly unappealable Supreme Court ruling and the fact that a provisional liquidator had already been appointed.

Carroll's legal team applied to seek the emergency appointment of an examiner to the six companies including Vantive and Morston that had featured in the original application, and a seventh Zoe company called Royceton. De Valera opened his night-time court with a terse 'Goodnight, everybody'. He listened attentively as an apologetic Cush began an impassioned ninety-minute plea for Zoe to be re-granted court protection. Cush explained that Carroll had been hospitalized and was unable to give instructions but that Pope and Torpey had residual powers to oppose the winding-up of the company – notwithstanding the appointment of Declan Taite as provisional liquidator of Vantive and Morston. Taite sought sweeping powers to appoint new directors, secure assets and gain control of Zoe's massive rental income.

The basis of the latest bid was new evidence of bank support, up-to-date valuations of Carroll's residential and property portfolios, and a new Independent Accountant's Report prepared by David Wilkinson of KPMG. These, Cush said, proved the group had a reasonable prospect of survival. Goodbody Stockbrokers' chief economist Dermot O'Leary had also produced a report predicting the world economy would pick up in 2010, with Ireland to follow in 2011. AIB, Bank of Scotland (Ireland) and Anglo Irish Bank were now explicitly stating that they were prepared to inject more cash into the insolvent group. AIB revealed it had advanced further funds to Zoe, while Bank of Scotland (Ireland) confirmed it had given an additional €50 million since last December.

Cush also produced letters of support for the bid from one

of Carroll's employees and a subcontractor, and added that he would submit the revised valuations to the court provided they were shielded from the public. De Valera was unconvinced and grappled with the problem of being asked to reopen a case already decided by the Supreme Court. Carroll had already had his day in court and, in record time, had his case decided by the Supreme Court. Now he was back, albeit under his wife's instructions, trying to mount a second bid with new evidence as well as material that had been available during his first failed bid but withheld by him.

De Valera knew he was in legally difficult terrain. 'I have to maintain the integrity of the system here,' he chided Cush, adding that his mind was sharper at midday than at midnight.

The judge's frustration was matched by that of ACC's Jane Marshall, who accused the Zoe petitioners of an abuse of court process and of having treated the Supreme Court as an 'advice on proofs' – legal speak for a test run – for the bringing of a new application which would address the deficiencies identified in the earlier cases.

As the clock inched closer to midnight, Pope and Torpey looked nauseated with tension and fatigue. Miraculously, de Valera allowed the seven companies another day in the High Court, but only on the strict understanding that they would not do anything to prejudice ACC's position before the hearing. It thus fell to another High Court judge, John Cooke, to pick up the Zoe baton and decide, first and foremost, whether it was legitimate for Zoe to petition the High Court for a second time in circumstances where the group had already been refused protection by both the High and Supreme Courts on foot of its first application.

On Thursday, 20 August 2009 Judge Cooke, who had served on the European Court of Human Rights, was told Carroll had been impaired due to stress when he opted to omit important information from his original petition, including detailed valuations from CBRE and Hooke & MacDonald and material on the future prospects for properties owned by the group.

This was a tricky issue for Cooke because stress – in the absence of a diagnosed psychiatric condition – has never been viewed as a reason to reopen or relitigate a case. Many an alcoholic or drug addict has had to make crucial decisions about their defence in criminal trials while mentally impaired, and criminal convictions cannot be overturned because a defendant ignored the advice of his legal team. This was not a criminal case, but the same basic legal principles applied.

For the latest hearing, Carroll's son Conor, who at 23 had served as a director of six of his father's companies, attended court, sitting unobtrusively in the first-floor gallery of Court 1.

Pope revealed to the court that in the weeks prior to the original bid, he and Torpey had been worried about Carroll's 'ill health', which they now claimed resulted in his decision-making capacity being affected. The description of Carroll's condition was vague but the inferences from the language used by Pope indicated he was somehow of unsound mind when he refused to accept advice.

Róisín Carroll, who weeks earlier had appeared in an instantly iconic *Sunday Independent* photo shielding her visibly ailing husband from the camera outside their Mount Merrion home, submitted a brief statement saying she too had been concerned about Carroll's health in recent weeks.

Cush submitted in confidence two doctors' letters, one of which revealed Carroll attended his GP three days before the first petition on 17 July but neither of which offered a clinical diagnosis.

Zoe, having apparently learned its lessons from its previous court rejections, now presented a raft of new evidence before Judge Cooke that seemed to tick all the Supreme Court's boxes. The new petition contained affidavits from valuers claiming that if the firms were liquidated and their assets sold in a short space of time, it would have adverse consequences for the market generally. The new survival plan generated by KPMG's David Wilkinson, like its predecessor, was contingent on continued finance from Carroll's banks and a moratorium on capital loan repayments. Cush also suggested that the as-yet-unborn NAMA could have an impact on the future level of credit available to the companies.

One of the country's most influential estate agents, David Cantwell, a director of Hooke & MacDonald, had evaluated Carroll's residential portfolio. He estimated that property prices had fallen by 40 per cent since the market peaked in 2007 but suggested 150 residential units could be sold every year with only a 10 per cent fall-off in the original sales price by the time Zoe would resurface and enter solvency in 2011.

Lyndon McCann, for ACC, accused Zoe and its directors of making a deliberate tactical and strategic decision to withhold the crucial business plan and property valuations in their original case, which amounted to abuse of court process. He also accused Pope and Torpey of trying to distance themselves from a bad decision: they were directors of the company and had 'acquiesced' in the strategy by allowing Carroll to dictate an approach that they had now abandoned.

In his ruling, Judge Cooke said that company law permitted the Zoe companies to make a second attempt to appoint an examiner. He said that 'past mistakes and misjudgments, and perhaps misconduct' on the part of their directors did not affect the statutory interests of the companies' creditors, employees and other companies that had business with them. He took into account ACC's serious reservations, but noted how the overwhelming majority of Zoe's creditors, employees and business partners supported the new bid.

'There is a clear imperative in allowing the petition to proceed to be heard,' he said, but added that the full hearing would decide whether the defects discovered by Judge Kelly and the Supreme Court in the first application could be answered by the new material tendered into court by Zoe.

Carroll appeared to have beaten the system again.

As they prepared Zoe's latest bid for court protection, Bill Shipsey and Michael Cush knew they were entering uncharted waters. Liam Carroll was by now completely indisposed and out of reach of his legal team and lieutenants as Róisín Carroll had decided that her husband was not well enough to communicate with anyone.

The two lawyers had thrown everything possible into the new petition, which was to be heard by High Court Judge Frank Clarke. So too had ACC, which recruited Professor Morgan Kelly, the outspoken UCD economist whose dire analyses about the perilous state of the Irish economy years earlier had proved eerily accurate and had become a thorn in the side of the government.

Asked by ACC to provide his opinion as to the likely path of Irish property prices in the coming years, Kelly predicted that property price falls would be 'large and prolonged', with values possibly falling to between one-third and one-half of peak values – levels not seen since the mid-1990s. ACC also engaged as independent witnesses Sean McCormack, the director of professional services at DTZ Sherry FitzGerald, who specialized in valuations for secured lending. Simon Coyle, a partner in Mazars, was also asked by ACC to give an opinion on the Independent Accountant's Report compiled for Zoe by David Wilkinson. Coyle concluded the new report did not provide sufficient or reliable evidence that the companies or any part of them had a realistic prospect of survival as a going concern.

The latest action pitted some of Ireland's best-known property experts against each other, and the huge divergence of opinion between them went to the heart of the difficulties NAMA would later encounter. Enda Luddy, a director of CBRE who had evaluated Carroll's commercial property portfolio for Wilkinson, hit out at McCormack's bleak assessment and denied the property sector was 'on its last legs'.

The December business plan had outlined the need for the Zoe Group to access development funding of €345 million, but ACC complained that new letters of support handed into court as part of the new petition were 'tepid' at best and in the case of AIB – Zoe's largest creditor – amounted to nothing more than what ACC described as 'an indication of willingness' to consider any fresh loan application at any given time in the future. ACC urged Judge Clarke not to confuse the other banks' supportive stance with any genuine belief in the long-term commercial future of the companies. ACC also urged the judge to conclude that all the evidence indicated not a revival of Zoe's fortunes but a relentless decline in asset values, an increase in liabilities and a determination to trade whilst insolvent.

Outside the Four Courts, opposition politicians were growing weary of Carroll's court outings. Eamon Gilmore, the Labour Party leader, lamented the absence of any legal representation of the taxpayers' interests at the hearings. Zoe's runs into and out of the courts were predicated on a doomsday scenario where his fall would have alarming consequences for the property market and the wider economy, but despite this apparently appalling vista, the public interest was not represented, Gilmore argued. He had a valid point. It is common practice in civil litigation for the Attorney General to be joined as a defendant or notice party in cases where the public interest may be threatened.

The task facing Judge Clarke – and ultimately NAMA – was best summed up by Dermot O'Leary, Goodbody Stockbrokers' chief economist, who said it was neither feasible nor appropriate for the court to make any final determination on which of the various competing viewpoints was correct. But this was precisely the task that NAMA would have to undertake. Zoe's endless efforts to avoid liquidation exposed the quandaries facing NAMA, including what to do with regard to lenders outside of NAMA who chose not to cooperate with it. Irish developers were invariably multi-banked, and not all of their lenders were or would choose to be NAMA candidates. The state's solution to the banking crisis was based on the hope that no lender would break ranks.

It was, perhaps, Liam Carroll's misfortune that, for Zoe's third attempt at salvation, it drew Frank Clarke to appraise the new and improved petition. The one-time Fine Gael supporter and former chairman of the Bar Council, the representative body for the country's barristers, Clarke was playing a blinder as the chairman of the commission setting out the arguments for and against passage of the Lisbon Treaty in the second Irish referendum, to be held that October, when Zoe sought refuge. Clarke was labouring under an enormous workload before Lisbon II but was well used to presiding over high-profile business cases. He had already won international acclaim for his handling of some of the fallout from the Bernard Madoff affair, as European victims of the fraudster flocked to the Commercial Court in Dublin to try to recover their investments.

Before he was appointed to the bench, Clarke had himself dabbled in the property game along with many barristers and judges, many of whom had lost their shirts in the process. As a horse-racing steward, he was also well versed in the risk involved in taking a punt. And beneath his gregarious exterior were the skills of a forensic accountant.

Clarke devoured and demolished the figures produced by Zoe's bean counters. He excoriated the KPMG report, complaining there were so many inaccuracies in it he had great difficulty assessing it. KPMG had insisted Zoe would have sufficient rent roll to pay its overhead and interest costs, but Clarke did the sums himself and concluded the group would need more rental income. The report also calculated that Zoe would record a surplus of some €2.84 million for the first seven months of 2011 once the rolling of interest was considered, but Clarke calculated that Zoe would instead generate a loss of €3 million.

Shipsey requested a brief adjournment and corralled Pope and Torpey for a conference outside. After an hour and a half, he returned to court and conceded that Clarke's calculations were correct.

Although the examinership clock was still ticking, Frank Clarke took his time to consider Zoe's fate. On 10 September 2009 he refused Zoe's second application, severely criticizing the way in which certain figures had been presented to the court by the companies.

The judge carved up the Independent Accountant's Report which formed the backbone of Zoe's second case for examinership and said the figures were 'either presented in a very poor way or just plain wrong'.

The following day the judge gave detailed reasons for refusing court protection when he delivered a 74-page written ruling. He described as a 'significant flaw' in the business plan the fact that interest rates had been calculated to remain at just 1 per cent over the next two years or so, despite the predictions of economic experts that rates would rise. Even a rise of half of one per cent would add €4 million to the companies' interest bill.

Judge Clarke also noted that even though the business plan envisaged an interest moratorium for two years, the group would still have to pay the interest when it emerged at the other end, which he said could have 'a devastating impact'.

Clarke, who had also warned of a 'recipe for procedural disaster' involving a rush by creditors if Zoe was not wound up in an orderly process, placed a stay on his order winding up Vantive and Morston when Zoe said they would appeal against his order. ACC was livid and Rossa Fanning insisted Zoe's litigation stop immediately. The bank, in the face of Zoe's unprecedented bid to have a fourth bite of the cherry, revived an earlier threat that it would cross-appeal Judge John Cooke's earlier decision to allow Zoe a second run in the High Court.

The proceedings had descended into farce, but such were the stakes involved that Zoe would not accept defeat, and the Supreme Court reluctantly agreed to extend the stay until 2 October, when it would hear both appeals. Despite two refusals of court protection, Zoe had by now entered day sixty of the examinership process and was on the verge of limping into NAMA, whose passage from bill to law was coming closer.

The Zoe saga had been 2009's summer blockbuster, a three-month odyssey which not only captivated the public but illustrated the problems that would be faced by NAMA in trying to determine how to manage troubled property portfolios. In the end, though, the thrilling ride ended with little more than a whimper. The Supreme Court ruled that Judge Cooke should never have allowed Carroll a second chance to bring a petition, thus nullifying Zoe's appeal against Judge

Clarke's ruling. The Supreme Court said it was unimpressed by the medical evidence tendered and gave little weight to Pope's opinion that Carroll's mental health was impaired. There was little more the court needed to do, given the forensic dismissal by Judges Kelly and Clarke of Zoe's bids. Chief Justice Murray, while stopping short of accusing Carroll and his directors of bad faith, ruled that the Zoe companies had nonetheless consciously and deliberately withheld information from the court that was within their possession or could easily have been obtained.

It was a measure of Liam Carroll's zeal and self-belief that he thought he could take on the legal system and succeed. One of the biggest measures of his self-confidence and faith in a comeback was his return to his cherished building sites, directing orders, just weeks after the Supreme Court sealed his fate.

7. Nemesis

By the first half of 2009, the profile of Ireland's judiciary had undoubtedly been raised as a result of the bust. Peter Kelly and his High Court colleagues who presided over commercial cases had gained a reputation for an ability to cut through the obfuscations of business people who sought to evade the consequences of contracts they'd signed and loans they'd drawn down.

But in June of that year, the judges found themselves in the spotlight for a different and less pleasant reason: it was revealed that only nineteen out of the country's 148 judges had opted for a voluntary pay cut in lieu of a mandatory pension levy that had been imposed on all public sector workers as part of the government's attempt to address a dramatically widening budget deficit.

There was one class of public servants that was exempt from the measure. Article 35.5 of the Irish Constitution states that the pay of a judge shall not be reduced during his continuance in office. The objective of the constitutional ban is to safeguard the independence of judges by ensuring that they are not subject to political pressures, favours or retribution. The Attorney General, Paul Gallagher, advised the government that the pension levy could not be made applicable to judges because it was tantamount to a pay cut.

As a mark of solidarity with her compatriots President McAleese – who was also constitutionally exempted – volunteered a 10 per cent pay cut, forgoing €32,500 of her €325,000 annual salary because of the economic crisis.

Following the announcement of the levy the Chief Justice, John Murray – who earns €295,000 a year, almost twice as much as the Chief Justice in the United States – arranged a voluntary scheme with the chair of the Revenue Commissioners, Josephine Feehily, whereby judges could make voluntary payments on a monthly, quarterly or annual basis in lieu of the levy. The sum could be equivalent to what they would have paid in any given year if the levy applied to them, or it could be significantly less. Either way, the public would never know who paid what or how much they paid as all details would be confidential.

The judges, some of whom had lost not insignificant sums dabbling in bank shares and property, came under significant public pressure to take what amounted to a voluntary pay cut. Some senior judges felt that the bench should respond en masse and, like McAleese and others, show a unified front and defend the reputation of the judiciary by taking a unilateral 10 per cent cut. Others feared that failure to contribute might affect their future career prospects, despite the fact that the decision to make a contribution – or not – was meant to be confidential. And yet others resisted the idea. The salaries enjoyed by judges – €243,000 a year for a High Court judge and €147,000 for District Court judges – fed a public view that those who did not contribute, at a time when their (generally lower-paid) colleagues in the public service had no choice in the matter – were elite untouchables. Many judges – particularly those who had been making more money as barristers than they'd earn on the bench – took a different view.

Inevitably, the media demanded details from the Revenue Commissioners on the uptake of the voluntary scheme for judges and, following repeated requests including applications under the Freedom of Information Act, the press office complied in June, revealing that nineteen judges had contributed a total of €60,000 to the scheme.

The timing of the release was disastrous for the Chief Justice, who was unveiling a €50,000 designer range of judicial robes to his colleagues at the five-star Adare Manor Hotel and Golf Resort in Limerick when the press release hit the news desks. The Chief Justice had commissioned fashion designer Louise Kennedy to create a new range of designer robes for the country's judges, following in the footsteps of the Former Lord Chief Justice Nicholas Phillips in Britain, who had hauled his judges over the fashion coals a year earlier by kitting them out in continental-style gowns created by fashion designer Betty Jackson. The new Irish robes, colour-coded by Kennedy to designate judicial rank, marked the first-ever break from the judicial garb inherited from the British.

Rumours of ermine fur draping judicial shoulders were greatly exaggerated, but the robes – and the inconvenient timing of their launch – received a lukewarm reception.

The revelation of the judges' modest contributions prompted a national outcry, and within forty-eight hours several government ministers had taken to the airwaves to condemn the low uptake. Health Minister Mary Harney expressed her disappointment and Minister for Defence Willie O'Dea said the judges were showing a 'poor example'.

Kieran Mulvey, the chief executive of the Labour Relations Commission, also rowed in on the debate, stating that he would expect 'from a moral leadership perspective' that all judges would have made the voluntary contribution by the end of the summer.

Opposition politicians and legal scholars cast doubt on the Attorney General's interpretation of the constitutional question, noting that the pension levy was clearly not aimed at the judiciary per se or at any individual judge, and one Fianna Fáil backbencher called for a referendum to amend the Constitution on this point.

The severity of the backlash prompted the Chief Justice to take the unusual step of issuing a press release to counter allegations that the judiciary were elitist and lacked moral authority. 'Unfair and misleading statements have been made concerning the position of the judiciary such as to the effect that all those who have not yet made a voluntary contribution have refused to do so,' said Murray. 'Although the making of contributions is necessarily voluntary and the decision of each judge with regard to them must be a matter for him or her, I expect that as the arrangements put in place by the Revenue Commissioners are allowed to operate according to the terms laid down by them, there will be a strong and continuous participation in it.'

In time, and under sustained pressure, most but not all judges took part in the voluntary scheme; but the affair had undermined confidence in the judiciary at a time when solidarity was needed most.

As he donned his clerical vestments in preparation for John O'Dolan's requiem Mass, Fr Peter Finnerty tried to hold back a tide of grief.

O'Dolan, one of Ireland's leading developers, had always told Finnerty – his best friend since nursery school – that if his business went bang he would simply start all over again. Instead, in February 2009, he hanged himself – only hours after visiting a psychiatrist to help him deal with the pressures arising from his financial problems. His body was found in a disused horse shed on the Barna Road in Galway after a frantic search by family and friends.

In the months leading up to his death O'Dolan had confided

in family and friends that he was struggling to cope with the economic downturn and disclosed that he was under 'enormous pressure' from one of his lenders, Bank of Scotland (Ireland).

Only two years earlier O'Dolan and three other investors had paid €28 million for the man-made Island of Ireland, part of The World, a property development on a man-made archipelago off the coast of Dubai. The next year, aping the success of Irish developers who had engaged in a reverse colonization when they snapped up landmark sites in London, O'Dolan bought the Island of Britain in the same development for €23.5 million. The archipelago, a sorry monument to the hubris that inflated the Dubai property bubble, is now sinking under the weight of the financial crisis.

Although O'Dolan was under pressure in relation to the Dubai investments, the 'last straw', according to a friend of his, was the decision by Bank of Scotland (Ireland) to appoint a receiver over Kinlay House, the hostel he owned in Eyre Square, Galway.

'Losing Kinlay was like losing a child,' the friend said.

The son of a distinguished surgeon, O'Dolan had attended St Paul's School in Raheny, north Dublin, where he and Finnerty were in the year below Marty Whelan and Gerry Ryan, who would go on to become RTÉ broadcasters.

He had his first business success in Galway, as founder of Mullery O'Dolan & Doyle, which became one of the biggest auctioneering firms in the 1980s and 1990s.

By 2000 O'Dolan's wealth had soared and he was often seen driving around Galway in his beloved Aston Martin, the one he had taught his son Robert to drive when he was just 13.

At the height of his success he was being wooed by banks as target-driven managers salivated at the profits to be made on the back of successful deals.

But when the market turned, the goodwill dried up.

John O'Dolan felt under siege.

Initially, O'Dolan – who in 2006 donated an apartment in the Canary Islands to the charity Turning the Tide of Suicide – thought he could ride out the storm. Although the going was tough, he was engaging with all of his lenders. But he told friends that he felt the debt management process was demeaning.

So concerned were O'Dolan's family and friends that they sought medical intervention for him.

'They were watching him,' Fr Finnerty said. 'They wouldn't let him out of their sight, wouldn't let him out on his own, but he slipped out quietly that Friday morning.'

On the day of O'Dolan's funeral, the Church of Christ the King was packed with family, friends, neighbours and an array of figures from the property, legal and business worlds through which O'Dolan had moved with ease.

John O'Dolan's was not the first high-profile suicide amongst property developers: that grim distinction fell to Patrick Rocca, the 42-year-old developer and socialite who shot himself at his home in Castleknock in January 2009 as his wife Annette ferried their two sons to school.

In Ireland Rocca, the scion of the eponymous Italian tile company, was best known for being the brother of Michelle Rocca, a former Miss Ireland winner and Eurovision presenter who herself was best known as the wife of singer Van Morrison. Patrick and Annette Rocca were a golden couple in their own right, lending their helicopter to former American President Bill Clinton.

Although Rocca had not been one of Ireland's top developers, his death was reported in an array of foreign media including the *New York Times*, the *International Herald Tribune* and CNBC. At home and abroad, the media could not resist the Van Morrison and high-society connections. The *Times* of London reported that Rocca's suicide has 'sent shockwaves through the beau monde of Dublin's wealthy cocktail society'.

The media also could not resist making the assumption that Rocca's suicide had been the result of pressures arising from his heavy indebtedness. However, his family denied that money worries were related to his demise, and publicly condemned what his widow described as 'callous speculation on why and how he took his own life and misinformed commentary on his financial affairs'.

In the absence of direct evidence it was impossible to link any particular suicide to the pressures of debt and a crashing market, but in March 2010 the Irish Property Council claimed that it could directly link twenty-nine suicides to the turmoil engulfing the property and construction sector; and data released by the Central Statistics Office in June 2010 revealed that deaths by suicide had soared from 424 in 2008 to 527 in 2009: the largest ever annual hike in recorded suicides. Recession-related debts, depression and relationship breakdown were identified by mental health advocates as the leading causes for the 24 per cent spike in suicides.

On Thursday, 30 April 2009 *Sunday Independent* journalist Ronald Quinlan doorstepped Paddy Kelly outside his home in Shrewsbury Road. The two then got into Quinlan's car, and the journalist quizzed the affable developer while his Dictaphone ran.

'The banks are being bailed out and they are putting the boot in right, left and centre, destroying businesses,' said Kelly. 'They're not lending and they're getting away with telling lies.'

Kelly claimed that the banks had kept pushing him to

borrow more and that the only security they were really interested in was his home, plus personal guarantees.

Kelly's remark was telling. Personal guarantees (PGs) were an integral part of Ireland's 'name lending' bank culture during the boom. Pioneered by Anglo and aped by the rest, PGs played a similar role to solicitors' undertakings, greasing the wheels of the boom by facilitating near-instant approvals of credit.

In pre-Celtic Tiger Ireland it could take weeks and months to evaluate the potential of a venture, stress-test the project and the borrower, run decisions by credit committees and, once approval was granted, put in place the necessary security and then verify it. But PGs became the hallmark of fast and lazy banking: borrowers were literally betting their houses that their schemes would work, and bankers were happy to accept their word for it.

'Personal guarantees were crazy,' said one developer who crashed and burned with debts well exceeding €100 million. 'You would want to be Rockefeller to be able to cover them. The banks knew that. They were lazy bastards.'

The reason why banks insisted on PGs was because they allowed banks to chase all of a borrower's personal assets, including their family home, if individual borrowers and company directors who signed them personally guaranteed the debts of their firms.

In theory they acted as a comfort blanket, ensuring that a borrower's word was their bond, but far from being an optional extra requested in addition to core security, developers complained that PGs were forced upon them: no guarantee meant no loan.

More than that, developers claimed that banks made soothing noises that PGs were just paperwork for their files, and no one had ever been chased on foot of one.

Even though PGs were meant to be stress-tested against a borrower's full statement of wealth including an in-depth picture of their entire assets and liabilities – both personal and corporate – in practice the system provided very little security at all.

As with solicitors' undertakings, there is no central register of personal guarantees. Borrowers giving PGs were under no obligation to disclose if they had given another bank a PG, which meant that multiple claims could be made on the same assets if the overlapping guarantees were ever called in – as would likely happen if a borrower got into serious difficulty. The wealth statements were often cobbled together by accountants based on what their developer clients told them they were worth, and independent valuations of properties underlying the wealth claims were often insufficient or non-existent.

For the most part, PGs were not worth the paper they were written on, as there was a symbiotic relationship between borrowers and their corporate vehicles.

Many developers' personal wealth depended on how well their corporate ventures and individual projects fared. If their business collapsed so too did their personal wealth, rendering them unable to meet the guarantees.

In other countries, such as Britain and America, they were rarely deployed, but Irish bankers could not get enough of them, and everyone from experienced developers to amateur speculators who signed up to them was convinced they would never be called in. But they were, and when ACC forced the Irish banks' hands, they got very, very personal.

What underlay many of the decisions to enforce PGs was a complete breakdown of trust and confidence between bank and borrower. If a debtor played ball, the banks tried to come to informal arrangements to keep the parties out of court; but if there was any suggestion of bad faith or other deterioration in the banking relationship, the guarantor felt the full force of the law.

'They [borrowers] singled themselves out,' said one lawyer involved in debt recovery proceedings for banks. 'They singled themselves out by sticking their heads in the sand. Sometimes the banks had no option.'

It was Irish Nationwide Building Society who kick-started the PG spree in earnest in the Four Courts in June 2009 when it tried to secure a €60 million summary judgment against Liam Carroll's company Aifca over loans provided by the bank for the development of The Square shopping centre in Tallaght. INBS claimed Carroll had executed an 'irrevocable' guarantee on 29 September 2006 for payment of all liabilities of Aifca up to €60 million, and that it had only granted Aifca a term loan facility on the strength of Carroll's PG.

Although INBS succeeded in July in securing a €78.6 million claim against the company, its €60 million personal action against Carroll was thrown out of the fast-track commercial list in December 2009 after Judge Peter Kelly described INBS's attitude towards handing over documents in its claim as 'cavalier'.

The action is now languishing in the normal court list.

Although personal guarantees were meant to be the last stand, they soon became the only port of call when borrowers stopped servicing loans and asset values collapsed.

Hotelier Hugh O'Regan became the first tycoon to be hit with a successful PG claim. O'Regan was a leading figure in the pub trade who, ironically, had been credited with getting out when the going was good when he sold his Thomas Read Group chain of bars in 2005 for €30 million to a consortium which included Paddy and Simon Kelly.

The Dubliner had been blessed with an extraordinary run of luck throughout his business career, always appearing to be in the right place at the right time. He used a €19,000 inheritance from the sale of his dead mother's home to get a foothold on the property ladder, buying a house in Rathmines and later moving to Sandymount, the Dubin 4 enclave where homeowners made a killing when property prices surged.

It was against his Sandymount home that O'Regan raised a loan in 1988 to buy a tiny Temple Bar pub along with his brother Declan, just as the city-centre district was about to be transformed into a Mecca for noisy hen and stag parties.

During the 1990s O'Regan rode the wave of the economic boom and a population spike of twenty- and thirty-somethings, opening up iconic pubs such as Thomas Read's, Hogan's, Searson's, the Bailey, Pravda and Life. He also built the Morrison, an upmarket boutique hotel styled by designer John Rocha, out of the ashes of the old Ormond Print Works on Dublin's north quays, and won a lucrative contract to run a string of pubs at Dublin airport.

As he climbed the ladder of success, the entrepreneur was part of a series of high-profile legal spats and even dared to take on the might of the Irish brewing industry in 2000 when he set up bartrader.com, an online business aimed at selling wholesale drink to publicans at lower prices than the breweries. Publicans loved the idea and hundreds signed up as O'Regan ploughed €2 million into the venture, but was forced to back down when the breweries threatened to drown bartrader.com in a sea of litigation.

O'Regan sold out his pub interests at the top of the market in 2005, but he could not resist the temptation to invest his fortune elsewhere. The jewel in his crown was a 330-acre site in the foothills of the Dublin mountains that he renamed

New Spring Field; through his company Dashaven, he planned to develop the site into a mountainside resort with a 129-bed hotel, restaurants, golf and leisure facilities, yoga studios, a theatre, office and conference facilities. History showed that Kilternan had been unkind to previous investors, including the late supermarket tycoon Pat Quinn, but that did not deter O'Regan, who borrowed almost €170 million from Irish Nationwide to develop the site.

By spring 2009, the newly nationalized Anglo Irish Bank began to take a closer look at his €80 million worth of personal and company borrowings and his prospects of repaying the loans.

The picture was not pretty. Work on Kilternan, though 90 per cent complete, was stalling and No. 8 St Stephen's Green – the former Hibernian United Services Club, which O'Regan aimed to convert into a private members' club – was well behind schedule. And, of course, the value of all his property holdings – like everyone else's – had plummeted.

Desperately trying to keep all his balls in the air, O'Regan sought solace in the arms of Irish Nationwide, the main backer of the Kilternan project. In April INBS issued Dashaven with an offer letter of €180.5 million which would allow O'Regan to refinance several loan facilities in relation to the project and inject another €10 million to finish work on the site. As part of the INBS deal, O'Regan promised to release monies to the lender from Clubko, the vehicle behind the St Stephen's Green club, and provided additional guarantees and indemnities from Thomas Read Holdings (TRH), the holding company for a cohort of O'Regan interests including the Morrison Hotel.

The terms of the deal, designed to reduce Dashaven's debts, pacified Irish Nationwide but set alarm bells ringing for Anglo, which had funded TRH and Clubko. Anglo's loans to Clubko and TRH were backed up with security over the company's assets, a security which would not just be diluted by the INBS deal: in theory, Anglo, because it had funded TRH and Clubko, would find itself in a situation where cash flow from companies that owed money to it would be used to pay off loans owed to a rival bank. In this way, its loans could operate as a guarantee for O'Regan's loans to INBS.

The proposed deal was a bridge too far for Anglo, which called in its debts on 23 July 2009 after a round of intensive negotiations with O'Regan, giving him twenty-four hours to repay all of his debts. The next day Anglo appointed Martin Ferris, a veteran insolvency practitioner, as receiver over Clubko and TRH.

Anglo had backed him all the way for more than fifteen years, but the cosy relationship had turned uncomfortable after the government guaranteed the liabilities of Anglo and six other banks in September 2008.

That same month, just as O'Regan was due to close the St Stephen's Green deal, Anglo demanded a revised valuation on the property, a demand which O'Regan claimed was a delaying tactic designed to give the bank an excuse to back out of funding the deal.

Immediately after Anglo appointed Martin Ferris as receiver, O'Regan began a battle to save his empire, sending his lawyers to the home of High Court Judge Vivian Lavan on 26 July, a Sunday, to secure the appointment of an interim examiner to protect Clubko, Dashaven and TRH from his creditors, including Anglo.

O'Regan had no Independent Accountant's Report, the backbone of any petition for an examiner, but somehow managed to get the 100-day clock of court protection ticking when Judge Lavan approved the appointment of

Kieran Wallace, the head of insolvency at KPMG, as interim examiner.

It was one of Wallace's briefest gigs.

O'Regan's survival plans included a write-down of trade and inter-company debts and the refinancing of Anglo's loan to Clubko, but its backbone was the drawing down of Irish Nationwide's €180.5 million loan offer which the society, now under new management with a mandate to sanitize its loan book, reneged on. The withdrawal of the offer after the interim examiner had been appointed torpedoed O'Regan's fight for survival and on 6 August he threw in the towel and placed his three companies into liquidation. This move drew protests from Anglo and Irish Nationwide, which maintained that receivers could liquidate him just as well and for a lesser sum.

Anglo's pursuit of O'Regan did not end with the collapse of his empire: in September 2009 the bank moved a €37.5 million judgment against him for personal guarantees he had given in relation to loans received by TRH and Clubko.

The case came before Judge Kelly on 12 October 2009, days after the new law term commenced. The judge had just signed two massive contracts for a new hospice in west Dublin in his capacity as chairman of the St Francis Hospice. A €15 million bank loan to be funded entirely from future public donations and a €19.4 million building agreement may have given him a more vivid sense of the challenges and pressures faced by bankers and business people than he would have had before; but nothing could have prepared him for the onslaught that greeted him and his colleagues when the Commercial Court opened its doors for the Michaelmas term.

In just under two hours, Judge Kelly accepted into the commercial list more than €300 million worth of fresh claims.

Such was the scale of new cases, almost 100 in all, that Kelly
had been forced to post a notice on the website www.courts.ie
warning lawyers that it was unlikely even a portion of the
pending motions could be facilitated in one day.

Most of the cases, including the €37.5 million summary
judgment application against Hugh O'Regan, related to the
collapse in the property market, and what worried commercial lawyers most was the continued absence of ordinary
decent business rows seeking entry to the commercial list.
The re-emergence of purely commercial rows instead of
multimillion-euro debt actions would, in its own way, suggest
some sort of underlying economic activity; but they were
few and far between.

The morning kicked off with another lawsuit lodged
against Thema, the Irish-registered fund that was suing the
Irish arm of banking giant HSBC for €1 billion over its role
as custodian of funds affected by New York fraudster Bernard
Madoff.

Such was the speed and control with which High Court
Judge Frank Clarke was mastering the fifty-plus Madoff-
related cases before him that Ireland had unwittingly become
the European hub for Madoff lawsuits.

'Madoff strikes again,' said Kelly as three international
finance firms sought to recover from HSBC an account worth
€54 million.

O'Regan wasn't in Court 6 for round one of his legal difficulties with Anglo – more was to come when the bank
pursued him over the Morrison Hotel – nor, indeed, were
the vast majority of debtors being pursued by their banks.

For the most part, there was nothing to defend.

Some businessmen under fire did fight back. One such was
Michael Daly.

A former partner at Grant Thornton, Daly quit the accountancy firm in 2004 in a hail of publicity, bringing some key staff with him. Having advised several Limerick developers, including Pat Whelan and Brian Cusack, who built the Clarion Hotel in the city, Daly decided to get in on the act and founded the Fordmount Property Group, which became one of the biggest development firms in the midwest and was backed to the hilt by Anglo.

Fordmount constructed more than €300 million worth of property in Limerick including the landmark Riverpoint Development, the Savoy Hotel and The Park nursing home in Castletroy.

At one stage Fordmount was worth more than €100 million, earning Daly a coveted slot in the *Sunday Times* Rich List.

Along with Daly, who was a 50 per cent shareholder in Fordmount, four solicitors in the Limerick law firm Dermot G. O'Donovan and Partners each had a 12.5 per cent stake. The first big sign that Fordmount was in trouble was in June 2009, when Daly resigned from the Fordmount Property Group and four of its subsidiaries. Adrian Frawley, one of the four solicitor-shareholders, took over management of the group after Daly's departure, but in December Anglo installed a receiver over the group, whose net liabilities now stood at more than €200 million.

Despite the fact that all five men were shareholders of Fordmount, initially Anglo only moved against Daly, who succeeded in convincing the Commercial Court that he had an arguable defence to the case, one that would cause a huge headache for Anglo.

When the bank moved an €84.4 million PG case against him arising from some €170 million in unpaid property loans owed to it by Fordmount, Daly insisted that his other partners should also be sued.

The solicitors had succeeded in keeping their heads down and the law firm had even managed to get selected to act on the NAMA legal panel, carrying out the due diligence the agency needed before it transferred loans and acquired assets. The fact that Fordmount's assets were in all likelihood destined for NAMA was not lost on some of the group's unsecured creditors, who protested to RTÉ's *Liveline* that the firm had a conflict of interests. Builder Seoirse Clancy, owed €1 million by Fordmount, complained to Joe Duffy that he had been 'left holding the baby' since Daly's resignation and said the solicitors' appointment to NAMA was inappropriate due to their own involvement in Fordmount.

The firm denied any conflict and stated that their interests in the company had been disclosed in their NAMA tender, which itself raised questions about the manner in which NAMA had handled professional appointments. Within days the firm had resigned from NAMA, stating that its work could not 'be in any way distracted by matters of public debate'.

It was a good call, as one of the central planks in Daly's defence when Anglo came chasing after him was that Dermot G. O'Donovan and Partners were at all times the legal advisers to the Fordmount group and his own personal legal advisers.

In a five-page handwritten letter intended to avert a summary judgment against him, Daly implored Judge Kelly for a full hearing in which he could contest Anglo's application.

'There are no circumstances in which I would have entered into a loan or a guarantee without the five of us being party to it, yet now I find that I am the only one being summonsed in respect of the guarantees,' complained Daly, who scrawled in the left-hand corner of page 2 that where his name was mentioned in mortgages it was on behalf of the group because 'DGOD's wanted to be hidden'.

The missive, which at times read like a tortured stream of consciousness, was an embarrassment for Anglo, already under pressure over the quality of its lending and its cosy relationship with developers.

'In twenty-five years of dealing with the banks I was never asked for a statement of affairs,' said Daly who, €84.4 million in the red, had nothing to lose. 'The bank [Anglo] knew my personal guarantees were meaningless in the context of the level of business we were doing with them and now that there is a problem the first port of call is the guarantee,' said Daly, who claimed that his case illustrated a blatant disregard for security on the bank's part.

Daly's complaint that he had never been advised by either Anglo or DGOD about the nature of the personal guarantees he signed rang hollow, as he was an experienced accountant and developer who had signed the loans and drawn down the loot. But it was enough to get him across the line, and the case proceeded to a plenary hearing in April 2010, a case which was robustly defended by Anglo.

When the case opened before High Court Judge Peter Charleton, Daly, who had applied to the Legal Aid Board to fund his action, pointed the finger of blame at Anglo and claimed that he had easy access to senior figures in the bank including former chairman Sean FitzPatrick and former CEO David Drumm. Daly painted a detailed picture of the bank's lending culture that was entirely consistent with the stories one heard about Anglo at the height of its powers.

According to Daly, Anglo wasn't just a bank, it was your partner. He told the Commercial Court how he had been a 'favoured developer' who could just pick up the phone at any time and get finance from Anglo to activate whatever deals he was looking into.

Daly claimed that Anglo was extremely anxious to lend to him in 2006 and 2007 when Fordmount was spending more than €300 million on Irish commercial projects and more than €100 million on German adventures.

He claimed that he did not apply to borrow, but that Anglo would routinely meet with him to plan the group's future projects. Drumm, he said, made it absolutely clear to him that funds of up to €500 million were available to the group.

Daly sought to impress on Judge Charleton Anglo's allegedly cavalier attitude towards PGs, claiming that he relied on oral assurances that they were a secondary or lesser form of security that were regarded as a formality and would never be relied upon.

Maurice Collins, Anglo's Senior Counsel, dismissed Daly's claims about his access to senior executives as 'irrelevant' and his account of the bank's attitude towards PGs as 'incredible'.

Within weeks Collins was back on his feet in the Commercial Court after Anglo finally moved against the four solicitors, suing each of them personally for €21 million under PGs they had allegedly executed. The four men contended that they were not liable, as Daly was the group's 'agent' in relation to the guarantees and they had had no direct dealings with the bank – a claim Collins described as 'wholly implausible'.

As Judge Charleton reserved his judgment in the Daly case, the Anglo case against the four solicitors over the €165 million in unpaid loans made to companies and partnerships linked to Fordmount opened in July 2010 before Judge Kelly.

On day one of the hearing, Thomas Dalton capitulated and consented to a €21.4 million summary judgment order against him. But his colleagues Dermot O'Donovan, Michael Sherry and Adrian Frawley, who were also being sued for €21.4

million each, opposed the case. They claimed that senior Anglo executives had given assurances that their personal guarantees were 'empty' and mere 'form-filling exercises', exercises they said were carried out by Anglo to keep its files right and to keep the compliance people happy.

The men's barrister, Bernard Dunleavy, told Judge Kelly that it would not help the court at all to rely on what he described as the general probabilities as to how 'normal' bank managers might behave when seeking PGs for multimillion-euro loans. Anglo was not a normal bank, said Dunleavy, adding that its decision to extend loans of €21 million to each of the solicitors without anyone in the bank even lifting the phone to talk to them about their PGs appeared to have been standard practice at the bank.

Like many debtors who found themselves in the courts, the three solicitors said that they never expected the bank to rely on the PGs, and pointed out in their defence that Anglo had failed to produce any evidence from its senior executives to contradict their claims that the PGs would never be relied upon. But Anglo insisted that the men were experienced professional solicitors and that it 'beggared belief' that they did not understand what was involved in signing guarantees. The men were, said Anglo's Senior Counsel, Maurice Collins, informed participants.

Judge Kelly ruled that O'Donovan, Sherry and Frawley had an arguable defence and sent the case forward for trial in early 2011.

One man who almost beat the banks – or one of them at least – was Niall McFadden, the corporate financier and founder of investment firm Boundary Capital who had choreographed some of the biggest deals during the Celtic Tiger years.

In 2005 McFadden had teamed up with Paddy and Simon

Kelly to form Redquartz Boundary (RQB), the property investment company whose big deals included snapping up the Marriott Hotel Resort on the world-famous PGA Sawgrass golf course in Florida for $220 million in 2006.

Between 2005 and 2007, at the height of the boom, McFadden brought three companies to the stock exchange. In 2005 McFadden's Boundary Capital floated Veris, a property services firm, and a year later he floated Siteserv, a building services company on the Alternative Investment Market in London.

In May 2007, just months before the subprime crisis took hold in America, McFadden and his wife Leisa Benner, a joint shareholder in the venture, floated Boundary Capital.

The flotation was a huge success, and within a week shares in the private equity firm had soared by 15 per cent; but just a week after the listing McFadden sat in the office of an oncologist in Dublin who told him he had melanoma, the most serious form of skin cancer. McFadden was given a 50/50 chance of recovery.

The wizard spent the rest of the summer in a haze, working out big transactions negotiated in the early part of the year and trying to come to terms with his diagnosis and treatment. The deals he brokered were among the biggest he had ever put together, including the €21.3 million acquisition of classified ad bible *Buy and Sell*, which had been bought by Naldin, a Boundary-related company, with the help of an €18 million loan from NIB.

In October 2007 Boundary Capital took a 28 per cent stake in the Dublin department store group Arnotts for €40 million. The Anglo-backed move came after a bitter boardroom dispute between Arnotts' owners, the Nesbitt family, led by Senior Counsel Richard Nesbitt, and long-term investors the O'Connor family. The prize for all – the Nesbitts, Boundary and Anglo – was the €750 million Northern Quarter, a development in central Dublin that was set to become home to 47 new shops, 17 cafés, restaurants and bars, 189 apartments and a 152-bed four-star hotel.

McFadden rounded off the year, along with Paddy Kelly and RQB, by teaming up with developer Sean Mulryan's Ballymore Properties to buy the Thames Royal Docklands development for a cool £155 million.

In their first annual report, Boundary Capital's directors had warned investors that the valuation of property assets was 'inherently subjective' and real estate investments 'relatively illiquid', meaning that a general economic downturn could have an adverse material effect on the group. The fact that those observations were not merely annual-report boilerplate was abundantly clear by the end of July 2009, when National Irish Bank moved against RQB, demanding €8.5 million from Kelly, McFadden and former Anglo executive Paul Pardy over personal guarantees they gave for an RQB overdraft facility to buy properties. (A handwritten note on the guarantees stated that the banks would not move after any of the men's family homes.)

In October McFadden succeeded in having the personal judgment action against him deferred when his lawyers told Judge Mary Finlay Geoghegan that he had an arguable defence. NIB opened a second front against McFadden, lodging a €6.3 million summary judgment action against him over the funding of the *Buy and Sell* takeover deal which the bank claimed had been sealed on the strength of the financier's personal guarantee.

At the heart of the dispute was a three-month bridging facility extended to Naldin and personally guaranteed by McFadden, who also promised not to reduce his assets below €20 million. A handwritten note was incorporated into the guarantee stipulating that the guarantee only related to the *Buy and Sell* deal. The three-month bridging facility, which was to be replaced with equity investment, rolled over nine times, and Naldin was placed into examinership in June 2009.

NIB insisted on sending a summons server to his home to serve notice of the legal proceedings. McFadden was in London when the servers descended on his home, frightening Leisa and their children. In a rage, McFadden called NIB and told them that he had instructed them to liaise with his legal team. It was then he decided to move his family to London.

The case was hard fought, with NIB accusing McFadden of relocating to London 'to avail of what was perceived to be a more debtor-friendly bankruptcy procedure in England'. The bankruptcy tourism charge – the first time a high-profile figure had been accused in court of moving abroad to avoid their debts – was probably unfair: McFadden had moved to London in part for the sake of his young children, and he had defended every action against him and turned up in court whenever he was required to do so.

For its part, NIB had good reason to try to avoid a full plenary hearing before High Court Judge Frank Clarke. The only witness in the action was Kenneth Dobson, the head of NIB's corporate banking unit, who had been forced to admit that he had never met McFadden before accepting the personal guarantee in 2007 and had never even spoken to him about the PG before it was accepted by the bank as collateral. Dobson had no role in the drafting of the guarantee, which was left to the bank's solicitors.

McFadden lost the *Buy and Sell* case (and later the RQB one as well), but in raising a number of uncomfortable issues for NIB he set a trend for challenging PGs.

With four companies a day going out of business in Ireland in 2009, there was little cheer in the air; but the country's spirits were lifted that autumn when two cheeky twins from Dublin, John and Edward Grimes – aka Jedward – took the TV talent contest *The X Factor* by storm. The teenagers' talent, or lack of it, divided public opinion in Britain, sparking pro and anti campaigns on Facebook; but when they were booted out of the competition, almost everyone agreed that their only crime was enthusiasm.

As 2010 began another set of identical twins from Dublin was making headlines. The last thing Simon and Christian Stokes expected when they sought court protection for their private members club Residence was accusations that they just might be corporate criminals.

The twins – the only sons of Jeff Stokes, the owner of the Unicorn restaurant in Dublin, and Pia Bang, the former owner of the upmarket boutique on Grafton Street that bore her name – had enjoyed huge success during the boom with their city-centre restaurant Bang Café, which they opened in 1999, when they were just 24. Always dressed in sharp suits and perfectly coiffed, the twins were Trojan workers, front-of-house men who poured their hearts and souls into their business.

The next big deal for the Stokes twins was the purchase of the Clarendon Bar from developer Bernard McNamara for €2.7 million, but this venture did not go well. After a costly refit the brothers sold it back to McNamara, only to lease it back from him for €420,000 a year.

Their next venture was Residence, a private members club which they opened in May 2008. The idea of opening a new private members club at the start of what looked like being a deep recession seemed insane, but Residence soon became a popular haunt of celebrities and Celtic cubs who still had some disposable income to hand. Membership was not cheap – an annual subscription of €1,600 and a €250 joining fee – but more than 1,450 corporate types and aspiring socialites flocked to its doors. Members were badly needed as Residence's start-up costs were astronomical, including an annual rent to developer landlord Johnny Ronan of €225,000 a year and a €3.4 million fit-out.

The twins' trouble began, unbeknownst to them, when their financial controller made a claim for the refund of VAT to the Revenue Commissioners without providing any underlying documentation. Revenue chased Residence for the papers, and a new financial controller, who had been installed in July 2009, discovered that the club was not due a refund but was in fact indebted to the taxman because it had underdeclared VAT to the tune of €200,000 and PAYE/PRSI payments of €170,000 up to June 2009. This led to a bill of €472,000, including penalties – a bill that Missford Ltd, the holding company for Residence, could not pay – and triggered a full Revenue audit in September 2009 that reassessed the total debts owed to it by Residence over the previous twelve months at some €1.2 million. In December 2009 the Revenue seized Residence's bank account.

This move prompted the twins, on 5 January 2010, to seek court protection from their creditors via examinership.

Zurich Bank, which had loaned the twins €2.3 million backed by personal guarantees, supported the Stokes' petition and the Revenue – the twins' biggest creditor – adopted what it described as a 'very guardedly neutral' stance.

Hundreds of Residence members bombarded the twins with offers of support and pleaded with interim examiner Jim Stafford to keep the club alive, but any chance of entering the safe harbour of examinership was blown apart when Peter Kelly learned that Residence had not been passing on its fifty-eight employees' tax and PRSI payments to the Revenue.

Some €800,000 destined for the taxman had been spent on capital expenditure for the club. Independent accountant

Paul Wyse quietly informed the judge that, regrettably, many companies were doing the same thing, in essence using taxpayers' money as working capital.

The twins, who attended the court hearings, were anticipating some sort of a hammering, but it was widely expected that the examinership petition would cross the line. They hadn't been aware of the diverted tax until the Revenue audit, but as directors they bore ultimate responsibility for the club's affairs.

Judge Kelly took a dim view of the fact that Missford, in breach of its covenants to Zurich, had loaned €616,000 to Mayfair Properties, the company that operated Bang Café, and Auldcarn Ltd, the company that had owned the Clarendon Bar. Now Bang had gone wallop and Auldcarn was also placed into liquidation with debts of €2.7 million.

Peter Kelly's ruling on Residence was one of his harshest. He withdrew court protection and directed that papers in the case be sent for investigation to the Director of Corporate Enforcement. The judge, who in an earlier hearing said Residence had 'operated under a form of thieving', said examinership should not be allowed when it was likely to have a beneficial effect for 'delinquent directors' nor was its purpose to provide directors with 'a ready form of absolution' in relation to corporate wrongdoing.

'There must come a time when companies that have flouted the obligations of company law, revenue law and their obligations to employees, should not be allowed to call in aid the very legislation they have ignored so as to save the enterprise,' said Judge Kelly as the twins stared at their shoes.

Kelly also spoke harshly of the accountancy profession, saying it was high time it abandoned what Wyse had told him was a 'normal' convention of treating tax money as working capital.

Outside Court 1, Simon and Christian Stokes engaged in a heated debate with their legal team over whether or not to appeal Kelly's ruling to the Supreme Court. Eventually, after lunch, they returned to Kelly and told him they would not appeal.

The demise of the Stokes twins' mini-empire received a massive level of media attention, but in some ways it was a very common story. The Revenue had lost €202 million in 2009 as a result of liquidated companies being unable to pay their income tax, PRSI and VAT bills. Of that sum, an estimated €150 million was lost through fraud or what the First Interim Report on the Loss of Fiduciary Taxes Arising from Abuse of Limited Liability described as 'the phoenix system' whereby directors fail to pass on taxes they collect and hold in trust for the state. The report, which was being finalized as the twins sought court protection, revealed that the Revenue had written off €1 billion in PAYE, PRSI and VAT between 2000 and 2009, as much as 15 per cent of that revenue lost through the activities of rogue or crooked directors who used the tax money to support their enterprises before they went bust.

More than 500 suspected 'phoenix' companies were being monitored by the Revenue when Residence sought court protection. By then the examinership bar had been raised extremely high, due to the dearth of possibilities for companies seeking fresh investment. Judges were also increasingly sceptical of the projections of independent accountants, which were often dismissed as overly optimistic.

Some legal observers felt that Judge Kelly's decision reflected a new harshness in the interpretation of examinership law, and that past judges had shown a greater willingness to grant court protection as a means of saving jobs even where company directors had disregarded their obligations to the

Revenue, had been dishonest or had broken company laws.

In 1991, a year after Ireland's examinership law had been introduced, a case came before the High Court in which the Revenue complained that the directors of a company had lied about a host of issues. Judge Declan Costello excoriated the directors of Selukwe Limited for their lack of candour and good faith when they petitioned the court for protection, but ruled that the protection of jobs – thirty jobs in this instance – far outweighed the directors' bad faith and misconduct.

Judge Costello directed that the two company directors resign as part of the survival plan and said he had serious reservations about the proposals and the company's future. Still, he ruled that the overriding factor was jobs and, despite all his doubts, placed the company under court protection.

'I do not think the court should turn down the proposals if there is any prospect of saving those jobs,' said Judge Costello.

Judge Kelly, however, evidently took the view that the job prospects of the employees of Residence were not in any more jeopardy under the control of a receiver than they were under the twins.

Given that Residence had debts of €4 million, had failed to pay its taxes and had not made a profit since it began trading, he might have had a point.

As the noose tightened around the necks of Ireland's business titans, the Four Courts heard all manner of explanations for failures to pay tax or read small print. Some were more plausible than others.

Jimmy Mansfield Jr, the playboy son of Falklands scrap merchant turned property tycoon Jim Mansfield Snr, raised more than a few eyebrows when he tried to avoid repayment of a €6.28 million development loan to AIB. Jimmy Jr, the former lover of Katy French, the model and socialite who died from a cocaine overdose in 2007, told the Commercial Court that he had literacy difficulties due to leaving school at an early age and possibly having dyslexia. A psychologist's report confirmed that he had average intelligence and the reading age of a 7-year-old.

Mansfield Jr claimed that he had never read a book or newspaper and needed his parents or brother to explain things to him and could not understand the term 'jointly and severally liable'.

Judge Kelly, who later dismissed Mansfield's novel defence, marvelled at how someone who was illiterate could serve as a director of twenty-three companies. And fly a helicopter.

The hardest yard for many borrowers who came before the Commercial Court was disclosing their full statement of affairs when compelled to do so by court order. One property developer who fell into this category was Greg Coughlan.

Coughlan was the chief executive of Howard Holdings, a Cork-based property firm whose other principals were Brian Madden, the finance director, and Brendan Murtagh, the veteran businessman who co-founded the building company Kingspan.

In May 2009, a week after Howard Holdings made an €11 million settlement with investors in an unsuccessful development in Poland, EBS brought a €31.5 million action against the three men over loans – backed by personal guarantees – to buy and develop 32 acres of land at Little Island in Cork.

As Christmas drew near the men entered into intense negotiations with EBS and reached a settlement – only to be hit with a separate €27.7 million claim by Loparco, a consortium of investors who had pumped huge sums into a number of Polish companies managed by Howard Holdings.

The EBS settlement was severe, requiring a US$60 million

fund-raising drive and the handing over to the lender of *Looking Towards the Lake*, a painting by the artist Jack B. Yeats.

The Yeats was handed over, but the fund-raiser, which required the men to pay €250,000 a month to the lender, rising to €300,000 a month from March 2010, never materialized and EBS went back into court to reactivate its claim, now demanding €33 million.

Summary judgment was granted to the building society on 25 January 2010. Two days later Loparco went into the Commercial Court and accused Murtagh, Madden and Coughlan of ruthlessly exploiting court procedures, stalling their case to allow EBS to get in first and register its claim.

Loparco found itself at the wrong end of a judgment scramble for the men's assets. The trio, now facing debts of €61 million, denied manufacturing a phantom stay to deny Loparco their judgment, but it mattered little if there was an abuse of court process or not.

It didn't matter because all three, who had gone on a personal guarantee spree – advancing more than twenty-five PGs to back investments – were broke.

The reversal of Murtagh's fortune was stunning: a man whose net worth was once calculated at €271 million was now – after an unsuccessful investment in Smart Telecom and major property-related losses – €353 million in the red. The titan was at least forthcoming about his insolvency and came out with his hands up, avoiding a cross-examination in court over his assets.

Madden, acting without any legal team, worked through the night to determine just how broke he was. But Coughlan, who complained to his doctor that he had 'a feeling of impending doom' about it all, turned a blind eye to court orders demanding that he provide a statement of his assets needed by Loparco to execute its judgment.

Gardaí were dispatched to Coughlan's luxury home, 'Fast-net', overlooking Kinsale Harbour, to serve him with his court orders. It was, according to Detective Garda Jason Wallace – who took Judge Kelly on a virtual, *MTV Cribs*-style tour of the house with its indoor swimming pool – 'located on a beautiful spot'.

Ten times Gardaí came looking for Coughlan at 'Fastnet', all to no avail. Intelligence they received indicated that Coughlan's wife had been in the area in recent weeks, but she wouldn't answer their calls on her mobile phone.

They persisted in their visits to the couple's home. On one occasion they saw two shih-tzu dogs in the pantry, on another they heard the crashing of plates, and during another they 'found evidence' that a room was being painted. Kelly ordered the investigators to break into the house to see if Coughlan was actually there.

Kelly also made a groundbreaking decision to allow the Loparco investors to appoint a receiver over Murtagh's pension fund. Whatever about securing judgments, banks were generally queasy about enforcing them and didn't like to move against a citizen's home or his pension.

Murtagh's pension was a self-administered Approved Retirement Fund, under which the holders may make personal investment decisions and draw down funds as needed, rather than wait for an annuity as they would with an ordinary pension. Creditors cannot gain access to the funds in a regular pension – which is usually set up as a trust – but they can gain access to funds in ARFs, which are classified as personal property.

In all, Murtagh had about €831,000 in his ARF and Loparco wanted it.

It was hardly worth the pursuit: owed €28 million, the most the Loparco investors would receive was €30,000 a year, barely a drop in the ocean. But they convinced Judge Kelly, who placed charging orders over Murtagh's fund and other shares, and delivered a scathing attack on the Cavan man's bid to protect the last vestiges of his wealth.

Aged 64, Murtagh sought to retain shares and the ARF, valued at between €700,000 and €1.2 million, so that he could cover 'reasonable' living expenses: not to maintain the lifestyle he once enjoyed but to put food on the table. Kelly, who observed that two houses had been transferred into Murtagh's wife's name, was having none of it, and said he found it hard to see how Murtagh would need the assets he wanted to hold on to for reasonable living expenses as the term that was understood by ordinary people.

He claimed the entrepreneur was 'an example of those wealthy persons who never seemed to be satisfied with what they had but seemed to require more and more'.

He added: 'Such persons had apparently forgotten hubris is followed by nemesis.'

8. All Roads Lead to Anglo

Poring over disintegrating photographs of Dublin's Sandymount Strand, Lorna Kelly remembers how she learned to swim in its clear waters and played on the seemingly endless beach which was used by thousands of Dubliners in the 1920s, 1930s and 1940s as their holiday resort close to home.

The quality of the seaside snaps has greatly deteriorated over time, but Kelly, a local historian now 85 years of age, has a crystal-clear recollection of Sandymount Strand from the years before its Ringsend corner was reclaimed to create the 'Poolbeg peninsula'. This became home to the capital's main refuse dump, which would provide the contaminated foundations for the 24.9-acre Irish Glass Bottle site – which would in turn eventually be sold to property developers for €412 million in the most ruinous single deal from the years of Ireland's property bubble.

Lorna Kelly has an advantage over those who sought to perform modern-day alchemy by turning the toxic site into property gold: she has seen it all before.

'It [the IGB deal] was a land-grab, but for more than fifty years the loss of beach and sea in our area has been nothing more than a consistent land-grab,' says the still active and long-serving committee member of the Sandymount and Merrion Residents Association (SAMRA).

For almost fifty years Kelly campaigned against development on the site of the former municipal waste dump, and tells those trying to understand the story of the disastrous purchase of the now virtually worthless site that it is necessary to dig very deep.

In its heyday the Irish Glass Bottle Company, along with its former subsidiary Waterford Glass, employed up to 5,000 people in Ireland, and almost 400 were employed at the Ringsend plant. But the business deteriorated over the years and in 2000 IGB asked its landlord, the state-owned Dublin Port Company, to change the use of the site from the manufacturing and storage of glass to providing warehouse facilities for third parties in the port area.

At the heart of that dispute, and of everything that eventually happened on the site, were the terms of IGB's 99-year lease with Dublin Port.

The lease, which was not due to expire until 2065, included restrictive covenants, meaning that the landlord retained a say over how the land was used; and Dublin Port insisted that the terms of the lease excluded warehousing and distribution.

Dublin Port was uneasy about the Irish Glass Bottle Company's motives in seeking a change of use. The company pleaded in letters to its landlord that it was constantly reviewing the development of its business, but Dublin Port had not been provided with any detailed plan by IGB and it was not clear what the company actually proposed to do. The landlord came to the conclusion that increased warehousing would not lead to any increased revenue, and noted that IGB was already the owner of one of the largest warehouses in the area, which was not fully occupied. As a result, IGB launched a legal action on 6 April 2001 against the Dublin Port Company.

The following year, with the litigation in train and the question of the future use of the site still unresolved, the IGB plant was taken over by Ardagh Glass, a publicly listed recycling company headed up by Paul Coulson, a former tax consultant. Coulson immediately set about changing what he perceived as outdated work practices at the site, prompting a hugely controversial seventeen-week strike at the site. His long-term plan was to take Ardagh private and divest the glass business to foreign shores. This ultimately led to the Ringsend factory being closed in 2003, with the loss not only of almost 400 jobs but also the Republic's sole glass recycling plant. Ardagh Glass was renamed South Wharf plc.

The now idle plot of land looked like a developer's Utopia: 24 acres of brownfield in Dublin 4, Dublin's most exclusive postal address, and just 3 kilometres from the city centre. The legal row over the use of the site finally reached the Four Courts in 2003. Coulson had inherited IGB's legal action against Dublin Port, although the litigation continued to be moved in the name of the Irish Glass Bottle Company Ltd.

On 2 February 2005, High Court Judge Mella Carroll delivered her ruling. In a short judgment she dismissed the South Wharf claim, noting that whereas in 2001, when the initial application was made, the then leaseholder, the Irish Glass Bottle Company, was actually manufacturing glass, a year later it was not. IGB, now South Wharf, had failed to demonstrate that Dublin Port had unreasonably withheld consent to change of use. Judge Carroll also observed that the site was 'very valuable' and, without explicitly naming it, unmasked the agenda underlying the case: namely the property play at stake for both the Port Company, the site's freeholder, and South Wharf, which wanted to exploit the site's value through its leasehold.

The ruling was a major setback for South Wharf which had, with the assistance of real estate specialists Jones Lang LaSalle, put together a team of lawyers, town planners, architects and tax advisers to maximize the potential development value of the site.

All was not lost, however.

Three months after Judge Carroll's ruling, Minister for Enterprise Micheál Martin introduced emergency legislation in the Dáil to add the Industrial Development Authority, Shannon Free Airport Development Company and Údarás na Gaeltachta to a list of agencies that would not be bound by the constraints of Ireland's Landlord and Tenant Acts. The move arose from a desire to close off a loophole – identified by the Law Reform Commission as far back as 1989 – whereby a company holding a long-term lease from a state body could sublet the property to a third party, which could in turn become entitled to acquire the fee simple interest. By this means the third party would no longer be subject to any restrictive covenants – relating, for example, to the nature of the enterprise to be pursued on the property – that the state body had put into the original lease.

Coulson seems to have been alerted to the existence of the loophole by Minister Martin's amendment, which did not cover the Dublin Port Company. South Wharf, evidently believing itself to be in a strong position because of the loophole, applied to buy the fee simple of the IGB site for just 5 per cent of its commercial value. In July 2005 it confirmed that one of its subsidiaries had applied to Dublin Port to acquire full ownership of the site, stating that it had been advised to seek full ownership under the relevant provisions of the Landlord and Tenant Acts.

The Dublin Port Company resisted this, and in the summer of 2005 a fresh legal battle loomed. Recognizing that a sale of the site for development would be enormously lucrative – and would be impossible as long as Dublin Port and South Wharf were fighting in court – the two parties settled the litigation and agreed that they'd jointly sell the site, with South Wharf getting just under two-thirds of the proceeds and the Dublin Port Company getting the rest.

The sale of the site for €412 million the following year netted the state, through the Port Company, a tidy sum of €138 million; South Wharf walked away with €274 million, and Coulson netted an estimated €30 million personally from the deal.

In any other era, a €138 million boost to the state's coffers – from a site on which the Irish Glass Bottle Company had been paying less than £10,000 a year in rent just a few years earlier – would have been a good news story. Instead, the sale of the site to Becbay, a consortium led by Bernard McNamara and Derek Quinlan and bankrolled by Anglo Irish Bank and the Dublin Docklands Development Authority, became a fiasco of unprecedented proportions in which everyone – apart from Coulson and Jones Lang LaSalle, which boasted on its website of the 'remarkable prescience' of their advice to their client – was a loser.

The Dublin Port Company and South Wharf first put the Irish Glass Bottle site out to tender in September 2006. The first Bernard McNamara heard about it was in late September or early October 2006 when Brian McKiernan, the head of Davy Private Clients, called the Clare-born developer and asked him if he would be interested in fronting an investment for the acquisition and development of the Ringsend plot. McKiernan told McNamara that unnamed private clients of Davy's would be prepared to provide the necessary equity funding. The corporate finance wing of Davy was, meanwhile, advising Coulson on the sale.

Within weeks of the decision by Dublin Port and South Wharf to put the site out to tender, Davy had produced a

confidential information memorandum for would-be investors. 'This transaction offers the opportunity of
participating with one of the most prolific and successful
developers in the country in the development of the largest
and most high-profile property to become available in
Dublin 4 in decades,' enthused Davy, which said the site's
potential included up to 3.25 million square feet for the
construction of retail and commercial premises and more
than 2,000 apartments.

Apartment prices in Ireland's 'mini Manhattan' would
begin at €500,000 for a one-bedroom unit, rising to €850,000
for a three-bedroom apartment. Davy investors were offered
a staggering 17 per cent compound return after the investment matured in 2014.

Davy trumpeted McNamara's virtues and tantalized its
clients with the allure of a third-party investor, 'a prominent
Dublin-based property investor who is a co-investor with
Bernard McNamara on a number of other projects'. The
mysterious third party turned out to be Derek Quinlan.
Investors would receive a compound return equivalent to 17
per cent a year for seven years via a loan stock arrangement,
with the principal guaranteed by McNamara.

Davy also found time to pay homage to the DDDA, noting
that it had attracted investors from home and abroad to avail
of 'never-to-be-repeated development opportunities' due to
its fast-track planning powers, which 'guarantee the authority's ability to make things happen for its development
partners'.

The most comical aspect of the memo, in light of what we
now know, was Davy's assertion that the commercial and
retail property markets were set for further growth and its
claim that not enough homes were being built in Ireland at
the time. 'Although the supply of new homes has increased

significantly in recent years, it is still not satisfying demand and prices continue to rise,' Davy reassured the would-be investors, noting that the age profile of the Irish population was continuing to drive demand for new housing.

The memorandum stated that McNamara had used current market prices in his projections even though the properties would not be sold for a number of years, and noted that property values could be affected by factors such as interest rates, economic growth, fluctuations in property yields and any changes in the laws. Investors were warned that there was no guarantee that they would receive back their original investment 'or anything at all' and advised that there was no guarantee that any of the exit strategies outlined in the memo would be 'available or practicable at exit'.

Investors were also warned of risks relating to the high level of bank borrowings that would be required to fund the investment, the necessity of decontaminating the Irish Glass Bottle site, and the fact that no planning permission was in existence in relation to the proposed development. But the memo did state that the DDDA had 'confirmed that they will seek to have Section 25 of the Planning Acts applied to the site. If successful, this means that the development of the site will be an exempt development for the purposes of the Planning Acts.'

Altogether there were ten risk factors identified. The property market was number one. Number two, under the heading 'Guarantor Risk', was Bernard McNamara, who was to guarantee the investors' principal.

'Although we understand Bernard McNamara is currently of significant net worth, there is no guarantee that will be the case should the guarantee ever be called upon,' the potential investors were warned.

*

Becbay, the consortium that purchased the Irish Glass Bottle site for €412 million, comprised Bernard McNamara, with a 41 per cent share, Derek Quinlan, with a 33 per cent share, and the DDDA with a 26 per cent stake. Becbay sealed the deal by buying the entire share capital in South Wharf, providing a bonanza for Coulson and his shareholders. In all, the acquisition cost €424.4 million. McNamara and Davy pumped €57.5 million into the deal, the DDDA €32.19 million and Quinlan's Mempal some €46.31 million. Loan facilities were to be provided by Anglo to the tune of €288.4 million, although this debt was ultimately financed jointly by Anglo and AIB, and almost €36 million extra would be borrowed towards the cost of cleaning up the former dump.

McNamara had acquired a 41 per cent stake in the biggest property deal ever conducted in the capital despite having put up hardly any of his own cash.

The loan stock issued by Donatex, one of McNamara's companies, was held by Davy Property Holdings as trustee and agent for the unnamed Davy investors. In September 2008 the loan stock was transferred from that company to another, Davy Estates Limited; and in March 2009 it was suddenly transferred on once again, to Ringsend Property Ltd, a company registered in St Helier, Jersey.

The last of these transfers was made ten days after developer Paddy Kelly was revealed in the High Court as having gone bust, and at a time when McNamara himself was fending off rumours that he had hired bodyguards to protect him from eastern European gangs seeking to recover debts on behalf of angry subcontractors. The market had turned; everyone connected with the Irish Glass Bottle site purchase was in trouble.

★

The Davy investors' loan stock instrument had an important caveat: McNamara would have to immediately redeem the stock and make accelerated payments to the investors if, amongst other conditions, Becbay did not apply for the necessary Section 25 certificate from the DDDA or if it had not been granted planning permission from Dublin City Council for the commencement of the development within thirty months of the January 2007 agreement. When that condition was not met, Ringsend Property Ltd, the Jersey-registered company representing the Davy clients, demanded more than €95 million from McNamara's Donatex. Unsurprisingly, given the lack of movement on the IGB site development and the general collapse of the property market, Donatex did not pay.

In a letter McNamara wrote on 15 October 2009 to Tony Garry, Davy's CEO and a long-standing personal friend, he conceded that the failure to secure planning permission was a 'technical breach' of the financing transaction; but he castigated Davy's move as premature. McNamara tried to explain to Garry why Becbay was not in a position to obtain either a Section 25 certificate or planning permission and implored Davy to wait until the outcome of separate proceedings he had lodged in the High Court against the DDDA.

In his case against the DDDA, McNamara claimed that he would not have become involved in the Irish Glass Bottle site deal in the first place if the DDDA's chief executive at the time, Paul Maloney, had not made representations to him that the agency had the ability to fast-track any application for planning permission. He contended that the DDDA had failed to implement a planning scheme for the site, rendering it impossible to even consider a planning application to Dublin City Council and therefore making it impossible to secure planning permission via this route within the thirty-month deadline.

He contended that Becbay was unable to apply to the DDDA for a Section 25 planning exemption because of the High Court's October 2008 ruling in the North Lotts case involving Sean Dunne and Liam Carroll. McNamara interpreted Judge Mary Finlay Geoghegan's ruling to mean that the DDDA had no power to issue Section 25 certificates in circumstances where it was also involved as a developer in that project.

McNamara had sued the DDDA for €108 million – the value of the claims which he said the DDDA's actions had exposed him to – and implored Davy to wait until his action against the DDDA concluded; but the investors would not entertain such a proposition. In an affidavit that formed part of his defence against the Davy action, McNamara's legal team named ten investors he believed had been procured by Davy, in a move described by Davy director David Goddard as 'scandalous' and 'inaccurate'. The names named by McNamara included the crème de la crème of Irish business: Martin Naughton, the founder of Glen Dimplex; Lochlann Quinn, the former AIB chairman; Tipperary biotech guru Louis Ronan; Barry O'Callaghan, the Cork-born chairman of Education Media and Publishing Group (EMPG), the international company which grew out of educational software firm Riverdeep; and the Coolmore Stud, led by business magnate John Magnier.

Like McNamara, Naughton, Quinn, Ronan, O'Callaghan and Coolmore all pumped €5 million into the deal. The developer also identified a second category of investors who parted with €4 million each to join the Ringsend party. They included Bernie Carroll, Larry Keating, the Gowan Group and the four children of the late Noel Keating's Kepak meat processing dynasty. They also included Kyran McLaughlin, the deputy chairman of Davy Stockbrokers.

One of the most high-profile figures in the Irish business world, McLaughlin is chairman of Elan and a director of a number of companies including Ryanair and O'Callaghan's EMPG. The naming of McLaughlin as a Davy investor was uncomfortable for the company as the firm had both advised Coulson on the sale and put together the group of investors to participate in purchasing it.

Goddard was furious over McNamara's claims about the identities of the Davy investors – which journalists were free to publish as they were made a part of legal proceedings – but to this day Davy will not confirm who is on its list.

Sensational as it was, McNamara's list could not stave off Judgment Day. On Friday 18 December 2009, Judge Peter Kelly ruled that neither Donatex nor McNamara had made out an arguable defence to the Davy investors' claims, and the developer was hit with a personal judgment of €62.5 million. Judge Kelly cited Judge Finlay Geoghegan's judgment, which acknowledged the DDDA's entitlement to enter into discussions with developers prior to Section 25 applications but did not allow it to make any commitment to a particular course of action, and found that it could not be given the wide interpretation that McNamara gave it.

Thus began Bernard McNamara's odyssey to insolvency.

The developer, who had spent forty years building up his father's eponymous Michael McNamara and Co. construction company and then establishing himself as one of Ireland's top property developers, was, according to close friends and advisers, devastated by Davy's pursuit of its €62.5 million personal guarantee action against him, the largest such action ever to come before the Irish courts. Once one of Ireland's richest men, he was now facing the possibility of bankruptcy on foot of a debt he could not pay.

Davy moved immediately to protect the judgment by telling Judge Kelly that it intended to call evidence to show McNamara's financial situation had deteriorated. This was true, but McNamara was loath to reveal the details, and in a desperate bid to stave off execution of the judgment he offered the Davy clients €100,000 a month – an offer dismissed as paltry by the investors.

On Christmas Eve the investors received a letter from McNamara's solicitors stating that he was broke, that he had no unencumbered assets and that he had used all of his personal assets to shore up his businesses and support more than 1,100 employees. Again he implored them to hold fire until his DDDA action was heard.

Again they refused.

The full scale of his indebtedness was not revealed until early January, when the courts reconvened and McNamara made his way out to RTÉ's Donnybrook studios where he gave an impassioned interview to *Drivetime* presenter Mary Wilson.

'My head is on a plate and that is where it has to be,' he told Wilson, noting that he was broke to the tune of €1.5 billion.

'There are people who say "you live in a fancy house". I'm willing to get out of my house, or whatever it takes,' he said. McNamara told Wilson it was 'possible, probable' that he would have to sell the lavish family home on Dublin's Ailesbury Road. When asked whether his personal worth once topped €300 million, he replied that he was told he was worth that by 'all these valuation experts and chartered accountants'.

During the boom, he said, he had been aggressively targeted by bankers saying: 'We'll give you the money. Would you like to do this, or that, or whatever the case might be?'

After considering a Supreme Court appeal against Judge Kelly's ruling, McNamara abandoned the prospect on 13

January 2010. Normally when a judgment is entered against a defendant, it takes immediate effect; but after McNamara's €1.5 billion confession, the war with Davy entered a new and more subtle phase.

McNamara may have been broke, but Davy did not believe that he had lost everything and suspected that, contrary to his assertions, the developer had debt-free assets that they could pursue through the courts. Davy demanded that McNamara provide a full statement of means which, in time, could be laid before the courts.

The firm gave him a week to set out a detailed schedule of all of his assets including any property in which he had a legal or beneficial interest, whether held in his name or through any companies or trusts, and over which he had any degree of control or to which he had any form of contractual entitlement, 'wherever they may be in the world'.

The investors wanted the estimated current value of any of his assets, the liabilities, whether he held them solely or jointly, and details of all property transfers between 2005 and 2010 to family members or 'connected parties', as well as transfers of assets to any companies he owned, controlled or was associated with.

'We assume that this information is already readily to hand as no doubt Mr McNamara has prepared a similar document for NAMA and his funders,' Davy noted in a tart letter to McNamara's legal team.

Davy's real target was the family construction firm, Michael McNamara and Co., where it suspected much of Bernard McNamara's wealth was retained. During his RTÉ interview, McNamara had insisted that the company he inherited from his father was unaffected by the Davy action and was engaged in a number of projects that were generating an income stream. Davy demanded, under threat of seeking a court order to force him to provide a statement of affairs, details of McNamara's shareholding in Michael McNamara and Co. and a number of related companies; but the developer insisted that his construction company was outside Davy's ambit, its financial health 'irrelevant' to the panel. McNamara implored Davy to sign a non-disclosure agreement if he furnished certain details, but it refused.

Davy insisted that McNamara had extensive assets, held personally as well as through Irish and offshore companies and through a range of partnerships and joint ventures including one in Qatar. He was a director of 138 Irish companies, many with significant land holdings; but as many of the companies had unlimited liability, they struggled to ascertain McNamara's true worth or lack of it.

Finally, in May 2010, after intensive negotiations and a series of adjournments, the dispute between the investors and McNamara was settled on confidential terms. Under the deal, McNamara was obliged to swear an affidavit of means and provide Davy with details about all his assets and interests.

One of the strongest weapons in Davy's arsenal was publicity: if McNamara did not cooperate, they could make public certain information that he did not want disclosed. Davy promised not to leak any of the details of McNamara's wealth to the media, but they refused to sign a non-disclosure agreement.

Theatre director Jimmy Fay was planning to bring *Macbeth* to the Abbey in Dublin in February 2010 when Anglo Irish Bank, the national theatre's biggest corporate sponsor, started a dramatic production of its own.

The 'Scottish play' explores the corrupting force of unchecked ambition and the betrayal of loyalty, themes that were oddly suited to the demise of the Celtic Tiger and its runaway bank. As rehearsals got under way at the Abbey, Anglo moved against its former chief executive David Drumm.

David Drumm was a surprise candidate to replace Sean FitzPatrick as Anglo's CEO in 2005, at the tender age of 39. FitzPatrick, in a move contrary to normal principles of good corporate governance, became chairman of the bank. Within two years of taking over as chief executive, Drumm had doubled Anglo's already healthy profits. But by the end of 2008, Anglo's shares were worthless and Drumm and Fitz-Patrick had resigned on foot of the revelation that FitzPatrick had for a number of years been hiding millions of euros' worth of personal loans from Anglo on the balance sheet of Irish Nationwide at the year end, so that the existence of the loans would not be revealed. Now, Anglo was suing Drumm over loans it had made to him that had gone into arrears.

In court pleadings Drumm claimed that following his appointment as CEO he was told by FitzPatrick that he had to increase his Anglo shareholding 'in order to show confidence in the bank'. At that stage Drumm already had 37,000 shares. With a €1.2 million loan from the bank he bought an extra 50,000 shares at €20.08 per share.

Two years later, at the end of May 2007, Anglo's share price was tanking and Drumm exercised 200,000 share options at a price of €4.27. Between June and November 2007 he was paying €30,000 a month to service the Anglo loan account, €12,000 in interest alone. His overall debts amounted to €1.8 million.

By January 2008, the credit crunch was tightening its grip. Northern Rock had been nationalized, Bear Stearns had collapsed and Anglo found itself at the centre of a massive storm of negative media coverage and market pressure as short sellers – speculators betting on Anglo's share price going down – targeted its shares.

According to Drumm, Sean FitzPatrick felt the bank's directors should make a show of confidence by buying the bank's stock or exercising share options. Several executive and non-executive directors did so, according to Drumm, using loans from the bank to fund the purchases. Drumm himself agreed to exercise 500,000 share options, and got a €7.65 million loan from the bank to fund a new share purchase.

It was a non-recourse loan, which only allows a lender to pursue the borrower's collateral, worth a fraction of the value of the loan. (In contrast, recourse loans allow a lender to go after you for the full amount that you owe.) Drumm's non-recourse loan was secured against the value of his shares. You couldn't make it up: a bank giving its chief executive loans to buy shares in its own stock, and 'securing' those loans against the shares.

In late December 2008 and early January 2009, amidst the furore arising from FitzPatrick's loans, a review of all Anglo directors' loans was undertaken. Following the review, Anglo and Drumm – who had resigned and was unable to service the loans – now agreed that the loans were recourse; Drumm would later tell Judge Peter Kelly that the non-recourse terms of the original 2008 loan facility were 'an error'.

It was crucial for the bank and Drumm to clarify the error: uncorrected, it might have left both parties facing difficult questions. This is because the Garda fraud squad had begun an investigation into €300 million in non-recourse loans given by Anglo to ten high-profile clients to buy its own shares, a scheme that on the face of it gave rise to suspicions that the bank had perpetrated a fraud on the market in a desperate bid to prevent its share price from collapsing. No detailed explanation was given by either party for the 'error', but both were at great pains to stress to Judge Kelly that that was all it was.

On 7 January 2009, Anglo issued a new facility letter to Drumm stipulating that it was a recourse loan, which would allow the bank to move personally against Drumm and his assets for the entire value of the loan. When the negotiations over the repayment of the loan broke down, Anglo brought two legal actions: one against Drumm over non-repayment of the loans and a separate action against him and his wife, Lorraine, in which the bank sought to set aside the transfer of their Malahide home into Lorraine's name, a move the bank claimed was a fraud on Drumm's creditors.

Drumm, now living in Cape Cod, Massachusetts, and preparing for a lengthy court battle with his former employers, was not the only former Anglo executive feeling the heat. Other leading actors such as Willie McAteer, Anglo's former finance director, and Pat Whelan, its former head of lending, were also negotiating the payback of their loans from the bank. But, for now, Drumm was the only executive being pursued in the courts.

As the case was transferred into the Commercial Court, Drumm – who counter-sued – complained that the bank had taken an overly aggressive stance towards him and alleged that private information which he had given to Anglo had been leaked to the media to 'harass and humiliate' him.

He felt wronged that Anglo believed he had moved to America with his wife to evade his responsibilities, wronged that the bank suspected he had transferred their family home into Lorraine's name in order to evade his creditors, and wronged that Anglo had withheld a deferred bonus he said was owed to him from 2006.

He felt betrayed that details of a private meeting between him and the bank's new chief executive, Mike Aynsley, in October 2009 were published in the *Irish Times* and he accused the bank of betraying his confidence and breaching his privacy, an accusation Aynsley denied.

The Drumm litigation – which is still before the courts at the time of writing – was the first major legal battle between Anglo and a former executive, but it was not the last. On 11 March 2010, as Jimmy Fay put his actors through the final weeks of rehearsal for *Macbeth*, Anglo launched a €70.4 million lawsuit against Sean FitzPatrick, Ireland's most famous hero turned villain. Seven days later FitzPatrick was in Garda custody, being quizzed by members of the fraud squad.

Like the murderous tragedy about to unfold at the Abbey – and like a so-called 'raid' of Anglo's headquarters by officers from the Director of Corporate Enforcement, assisted by Gardaí – the confluence of the litigation by the nationalized bank against FitzPatrick and his arrest a week later had a staged feel about it. The arrest coincided with revelations that Anglo was set to transfer at least €28 billion worth of toxic property loans to NAMA.

In custody at Bray Garda station, FitzPatrick, who had engaged leading criminal law solicitor Michel Staines to advise him in relation to the criminal investigations, gave detailed answers to Gardaí and was released without charge after thirty-one hours.

The arrest of FitzPatrick, which was followed several days later by the arrest and questioning of Anglo's former finance director and chief risk officer Willie McAteer, was the first high-profile detention of a senior banking figure. It came fully eighteen months after the government guaranteed the six Irish banks, fifteen months after FitzPatrick and Drumm resigned from Anglo over the revelations about the hiding of FitzPatrick's Anglo loans on the balance sheet of Irish

Nationwide, and fourteen months after it emerged that Anglo had conspired with Irish Life and Permanent in a deposit swap intended to make Anglo's balance sheet look healthier at its year end in September 2008.

It was no small coincidence that the lawsuit/arrest combo came just weeks before Anglo posted the biggest loss in Irish corporate history. The ballpark figure, €12 billion, was leaked well in advance to various newspapers in the hope of softening its impact on public opinion.

It didn't really work.

On 31 March 2010, Anglo reported results for the fifteen months to December 2009. Losses for the period were actually €12.7 billion. That morning, readers of the *Irish Daily Star* were treated to a screaming headline: 'They deserve to be shot'. The controversial headline accompanied a picture of FitzPatrick and former Irish Nationwide chief Michael Fingleton. The paper later appealed to its readers not to take its suggestion literally, but others joined the fray, pursuing FitzPatrick when he flew to Marbella, where he was dubbed the 'pariah on the playa' by the *Irish Daily Mirror*. The paper also superimposed a mock 'For Sale' sign on his Greystones home with the words 'angel of debt'; and a story went around that diners in restaurants where FitzPatrick ate with his wife and family insisted that he leave, or else they would.

Whatever way you looked at it, FitzPatrick's fall from grace was spectacular. He was not, contrary to some media portrayals, solely responsible for the collapse of the Irish economy, but he had cemented his position as the face of Irish banking and of the bust through various misjudgments, most dramatically his October 2008 interview with RTÉ's Marian Finucane, when he refused to apologize to the taxpayer for having to bail out the banks.

'It would be very easy for me to say sorry,' he told the

presenter just days after the government's unprecedented decision to guarantee the banks. 'The cause of our problems was global so I can't say sorry with any degree of sincerity and decency, but I do say thank you.'

Anglo's lawsuit ensured that it would be seen as taking a tough stance against debtors, in keeping with its newly nationalized status. But FitzPatrick – under investigation by a host of agencies including the Garda fraud squad, the Director of Corporate Enforcement and the Financial Regulator – moved to take his personal financial woes out of the media spotlight by seeking court protection from his creditors, and tried to make a deal with them in private.

Under the little-used 1988 Bankruptcy Act, a debtor can petition the courts for what is known as arranging debtor status, a sort of personal examinership. One advantage of such an approach is that the process can be conducted in secret. If FitzPatrick successfully pitched a deal to Anglo, now owned by the state and under the control of Finance Minister Brian Lenihan, the taxpayer might never know the details of it. On the other hand, this approach had a big disadvantage: if the creditors refused his deal, he would be instantly declared bankrupt.

In April 2010, High Court Judge Brian McGovern refused to allow FitzPatrick's case to be heard in private. On 12 July, following a brief hearing that he did not attend, FitzPatrick was declared bankrupt.

During a routine morning of misery in the Commercial Court in early 2010, a barrister confirmed to Judge Peter Kelly that the plaintiff in yet another debt recovery action was Anglo.

'Of course,' said the judge, pursing his lips. 'All roads lead to Anglo.'

It has often felt that way in Ireland in recent years; and some of the roads have been rockier than others.

For years, the 103-kilometre stretch from the headquarters of billionaire Sean Quinn's empire in Cavan to Anglo's headquarters on St Stephen's Green in Dublin was paved with gold. Sean Quinn loved Anglo and Anglo loved Sean Quinn. The country's richest man loved the country's sexiest bank so much that he gambled most of his fortune building up a massive 25 per cent stake in the bank using financial derivatives known as contracts for difference (CFDs).

CFDs allow investors to speculate on the price of a share without having to own the share (the conventional means of taking a 'long' position, or betting that its price will go up) or to borrow it in order to sell 'short' (the conventional means of betting that it will go down). To take a long position in a stock via a CFD, the investor need put up only a fraction of the value of the underlying shares (the 'margin'), typically around 10 per cent. So, with a 10 per cent margin requirement, an investor could take a position in €100 million worth of shares by depositing with his broker a margin of only €10 million up front.

This gives the investor enormous leverage – the ability to take a big stake in a company with a relatively small deposit. But leverage works in both directions. If you take a long position in a stock via a CFD and the price rises, extraordinary profit margins can be achieved. But if the price falls, the losses can be particularly painful. If you own shares that lose their value, the one consolation is that the money is already spent. If you take a long position in a share via a CFD and the share price falls, you face a 'margin call' – a requirement to put up additional collateral or else close out the contract. Closing out the contract in such a situation forces the investor to crystallize his loss.

That was the situation in which Sean Quinn found himself in the early part of 2008. Quinn had quietly built up a 25 per cent stake in Anglo using CFDs, and now Anglo's share price was tanking, due largely to aggressive short selling. On St Patrick's Day alone, Anglo shares dropped by 15 per cent. In July, Quinn crystallized his losses on three-fifths of his stake – representing 15 per cent of the bank's shares – by converting the CFDs into an ordinary 15 per cent shareholding.

The move cost him €2.5 billion.

Around the same time, terrified that a disorderly unwinding of Quinn's position would cause its share price to fall even further, Anglo loaned €451 million to ten long-standing clients of the bank to allow them to buy the remaining 10 per cent of the bank from the brokers who had issued Quinn's CFDs. As with the original non-recourse loan to David Drumm, these were non-recourse loans, 'secured' against the shares whose purchase they were to fund.

Quinn was a local hero turned national business icon. The former Fermanagh football captain became a demigod in Cavan, the heartland of his empire which employed 8,000 people worldwide in a matrix of businesses that stretched from cement and glass to hotels, pubs and insurance.

But there was also a side to the mighty Quinn Group's culture and approach to doing business which one High Court judge described as cynical, calculated and ruthless. In 1999, Meath County Council granted planning permission to Lagan Cement, a rival to Quinn's own cement company, to build a factory at Killaskillen in Kinnegad. Quinn surreptitiously gifted £30,000 to the Ballinabrackey Residents Action Group to fund legal action opposing the grant of permission by Meath County Council. The covert payments and the group's relentless legal pursuit of Lagan were deemed an abuse of process by Judge John Quirke.

Judge Quirke crossed swords with another branch of Quinn's conglomerate, Quinn Insurance Ltd, in January 2009 when the insurer abandoned a seven-year fraud claim against a paraplegic.

Quinn claimed that John Deegan sustained his injuries, which caused him to be confined to a wheelchair for life, in a fall from a third-storey balcony in Ballymun flats in 2001. In fact, he was injured in a crash involving a car owned by a holder of a Quinn Insurance policy.

The married father of five spent a month in an intensive care unit and almost died, but spent the next seven years battling Quinn Insurance, which finally abandoned its fraud claim and settled for close to €2 million after Judge Quirke said it was a 'very serious' matter that such grave allegations were made in open court by a 'well-resourced company' when there was no evidence to support them and the company possessed a Garda report stating that there was no such evidence.

In the same week that Quinn Insurance withdrew its fraud claim, Sean Quinn, under sustained media pressure as a result of his disastrous bet on Anglo and fending off rumours about the solvency of his insurance group, was portraying himself as a victim in an interview with RTÉ's Tommie Gorman.

'We feel the media frenzy around the Quinn Group is totally outlandish, outrageous,' he complained to Gorman. 'We have no idea why this agenda is to get Quinn.'

The media inquiries into Quinn's finances were valid, as later events would demonstrate. The mythology surrounding Sean Quinn, perpetuated by the man himself, was that he lived a simple life and would not bet more than €5 at his weekly card games with friends. The truth was that he had been gambling billions he did not have to build up his disastrous stake in Anglo.

The first time the public knew that Sean Quinn was

officially in trouble over his exposure to Anglo was in October 2008, when Quinn Insurance was fined €3.25 million by the Financial Regulator – the biggest penalty of its kind ever – after the insurer failed to notify the watchdog of loans it had made to related companies.

Sean Quinn was hit with a €200,000 fine personally and was forced to step down as chairman of the insurer after a loan of €288 million was made by the insurance arm to help fund his costly conversion of CFDs into a 15 per cent direct shareholding in Anglo. The Anglo punt was a personal bet, but he had used his company's reserves – designed to protect his customers – to pay for it.

New insights into the reasons for the unprecedented fine emerged in 2010 when the watchdog, headed up by a new boss, Englishman Matthew Elderfield, took High Court action to place Quinn Insurance into administration.

The courts were out of term and deserted on 31 March when a small team of sober men in suits descended on the duty judge, John Cooke, and asked him to place Quinn Insurance into provisional administration.

The judge agreed to appoint Michael McAteer and Paul McCann of the global accounting and consultancy firm Grant Thornton as provisional administrators after lawyers for Elderfield told him that the solvency cushion at Quinn Insurance had been 'wiped out'.

When news of the appointments broke there were fears for the wider Quinn Group's 5,500 employees, and more than one million Quinn Insurance customers. McCann and McAteer were dispatched to Cavan with a team of officials to begin the task of taking over the firm, but not before the board of the Quinn Group issued a letter to all government ministers castigating the move as 'highly aggressive and unnecessary'.

For two weeks the Quinn Group and its employees railed against Elderfield's decision to place the insurer into administration. Hundreds marched on the Dáil and Quinn told RTÉ that Elderfield's decision was one of the biggest errors in the history of corporate Ireland. He even rang *Prime Time* to say the Quinn Group had plenty of money and was not looking for money from anyone.

He was in a blind panic.

In Cavan support was wavering too, along with Quinn's nerve. The initial anger at Elderfield gave way to a suspicion that maybe it was their boss and his inexplicable multibillion-euro share gamble that had placed their livelihoods on the line.

Elderfield moved against Quinn shortly after taking up his post as Financial Regulator, but the staff of the watchdog had been monitoring the insurer intensively prior to his arrival. After the record €3.25 million fine in October 2008, the Financial Regulator applied pressure on Quinn Insurance to deliver a financial plan to restore its solvency margins. Quinn Insurance had been struggling to meet its solvency ratios for some time and was already in default of a prior agreement reached in May 2008.

In early December 2008 Quinn Insurance asked the regulator to consider a number of proposals designed to enhance its financial position, and €70 million was pumped into the company as a result of a reinsurance agreement with a related company. The firm battled its way throughout 2009 and reassured the regulator that it was making huge progress on its UK business. It sought time to 'exit unprofitable lines while increasing premium in profitable lines'.

The regulator gave Quinn Insurance a chance to restore its solvency and trade out of its difficulties, but by December 2009 the insurer was telling regulatory officials that it was likely to fall below its solvency margin requirement by the end of the year.

A meeting was held during which Quinn Insurance admitted that its anticipated profits had not materialized in the UK private car insurance business and conceded that its solicitors' professional indemnity book in Britain was also struggling. In all, Quinn Insurance lost €44 million on insurance writing in the UK in 2009.

On Christmas Eve Quinn Insurance sent an email to the Financial Regulator in which it stated that the Quinn Group needed a waiver from its banks in relation to the group's year-end debt covenants. The request represented a crisis for the Quinn Group: any breaches of debt covenants would entitle the Quinn Group's banks and bondholders to demand immediate repayment or force the group into a renegotiation of its debt terms, which could trigger its collapse.

The regulator knew of the potentially calamitous effect reneging on covenants could have, and immediately demanded that Quinn Insurance draw up contingency plans in the event of the collapse of the entire Quinn Group.

The insurer submitted its doomsday plans by 29 January 2010, prompting a response to those plans by the regulator on 17 February. Two days later, a meeting was held with key Quinn Insurance executives to discuss the plans. The regulator demanded more information regarding the contingency plan for the Quinn Group.

On 22 February, Quinn Insurance received another letter from the regulator informing it that it had to provide the regulator with a financial recovery plan to restore the insurance wing of the beleaguered group to a sound financial position. This plan was then rejected by the regulator, which said Quinn's projected investment returns were very optimistic and its profit forecasts unrealistic.

On 12 March Jim Quigley, chairman of Quinn Insurance, received a call from the regulator to say its latest plan had been rejected. A letter issued the same day said that the regulator was unconvinced that the plan was realistic, sustainable or prudent.

A series of emergency meetings followed and Quinn Insurance, desperate to stave off intervention, offered to sell properties to reduce its exposure. A new plan was submitted on 22 March and rejected by Elderfield the next day. An even greater bombshell was dropped on the regulator when Quigley picked up the phone to Patrick Brady, the head of insurance provision at the Financial Regulator, on 24 March. Quigley told Brady that over €1.2 billion had been put up as collateral to guarantee the liabilities of other companies in the Quinn Group. The guarantees had the effect of reducing the value of the insurance firm's assets by almost half a billion euro, effectively wiping out the insurer's solvency cushion. This news proved the final straw for Elderfield, who moved to bring Quinn Insurance under state control.

In April Anglo Irish Bank, which stood to lose the most from Quinn's collapse, offered to put up €700 million as part of a financial restructuring package. The plan would see €150 million injected into Quinn Insurance and €550 million used to pay off bondholders.

But the plan faced huge hurdles, not least because it would involve a bankrupt bank, which was itself dependent on multibillion-euro taxpayer bailouts, stepping forward to bail out a man who had dipped into his insurance company's statutory solvency cushion in order to fund his stock-market plays. The government, which had asked Anglo to formulate proposals to save the insurer, eventually concluded that this was too grotesque a scenario to stand over politically, and the Quinn bailout did not come to pass.

The political pressure brought to bear on Elderfield and his Assistant Director General for Financial Institutions Supervision, Jonathan McMahon, during this period was staggering. The two Englishmen had been imported into the Central Bank to turn around a discredited regulatory apparatus, and their introduction to Ireland's gombeen-style politics was a baptism of fire. But the men persevered even as Anglo and the Quinn Group bombarded them with numerous half-baked plans to solve the group's problems. On Monday 12 April, minutes before High Court President Justice Nicholas Kearns was due to preside over a full administration hearing, lawyers for Quinn Insurance submitted a series of lengthy statements robustly defending the management of the company and taking the Financial Regulator to task for what was perceived to be unnecessary action. Sean Quinn was said to be relishing the opportunity to defend his realm.

On 13 April, the Quinn Group was still preparing to fight administration and was awaiting a response from the regulator to its court submissions. That afternoon, Elderfield told an Oireachtas committee that he would not back down on his plans and denied that he had been 'heavy-handed' with the insurer.

Hours after the Dáil committee meeting, Elderfield met with Murdoch McKillop, the London-based corporate restructuring guru who was appointed by the Quinn Group as interim executive director to steer the conglomerate through the difficulties posed by the administration threat to Quinn Insurance.

The meeting took place at the regulator's office late on Wednesday night, and less than twelve hours later the Quinn Group abandoned its court battle.

Appointing full-time administrators, Judge Kearns said

that he was neither accepting all the assertions made by the regulator nor rejecting any claims by the insurance company, a finely tuned judicial remark that could not conceal the fact that the regulator had won and the mighty Quinn had lost.

Epilogue

Saturday, 3 July 2010

The main attraction at the Irish Women Lawyers' Association inaugural seminar on white-collar crime, UCC law lecturer Shane Kilcommins was rushing off to Dublin airport to catch a plane to join his wife and children on their summer holidays, but not before he fielded a few questions from the floor.

For more than half an hour, speaking under the heading 'Crime in the Suites vs Crime in the Streets', Kilcommins had argued that the threat to Ireland's national security posed by wrongdoings in the corporate and banking sectors, along with political corruption and misconduct in the environmental or health sectors, was as serious, if not more serious, than that posed by street crime and organized crime.

Serious regulatory failures in the Irish banking sector had led to the near collapse of the economy. It had brought with it hundreds of home repossessions, the scourge of negative equity – by the end of 2010 an estimated 350,000 mortgage holders will owe their banks more than their houses are worth – and widespread job losses, with unemployment at 13 per cent (and rising) as the Dáil broke for its summer recess. It had heralded the possibility, once again, of mass emigration, bringing with it fevered whispers of a lost generation and warnings about the detrimental knock-on effects on social cohesion and the provision of health, education and housing services.

Kilcommins warned that the dramatic initial costs arising from the bailout of Ireland's banking system could, in time, pale in comparison to the almost unquantifiable social costs of a deep recession wrought, at heart, by the state's failure to regulate the banks.

'To date, we have adopted a very narrow understanding of what constitutes a threat to our security, fastened to a very traditional outlook that views white-collar wrongdoing as having rather benign effects,' said Kilcommins. 'We quickly need to develop a more nuanced understanding that jettisons such traditional thinking.'

Kevin Prendergast, the Corporate Compliance Manager of the Office of the Director of Corporate Enforcement, Ireland's company law watchdog, conceded in his presentation to the seminar that in the organization's ten-year history, it had never secured a single successful prosecution for insider trading or market abuse. Fraudulent trading had been on the statute books since 1963, but had resulted in only four or five attempted prosecutions since then.

It was 'undeniable', said Prendergast – whose office had told the High Court just days earlier that it would take at least two years for prosecutions, if any, to emerge from its investigations into Anglo Irish Bank – that there would be huge difficulties in bringing white-collar crime cases before a jury.

As the Q&A drew to a close, as Kilcommins pressed delegates on the contrast between the lack of state resources deployed to tackle regulatory offences and the extensive apparatus for tackling organized crime during the Celtic Tiger years, he was interrupted by a tongue-in-cheek quip from Senior Counsel Mary Ellen Ring.

'Wasn't Anglo Irish and its carry-on organized crime?' suggested Ring. When the laughter subsided, Ring continued: 'Is there a way of taking what are clearly [regulatory] breaches, defining them as offences and bringing those offences before a court within a time frame and in a way that would allow twelve members of the community [a jury] – or at least one member of the community possibly [a judge] – to make a decision before society's faith is totally undermined in the prosecution of criminal offences of this nature?' she asked.

This time, no one laughed.

It is three years since Judge Peter Kelly directed that files on rogue solicitors Michael Lynn and Thomas Byrne be sent to the Garda fraud squad. The High Court files were sent to the Gardaí because the judge believed they contained prima facie evidence of white-collar crime. Yet at the time of writing, not one rogue solicitor has been formally arrested and questioned by Gardaí, let alone prosecuted or convicted in the criminal courts, and Judge Richard Johnson's requests for information on the bonuses enjoyed by the bankers who lent to Lynn and Byrne have gone unanswered.

In monetary terms the wrongs of Lynn, Byrne and their ilk were soon eclipsed and overtaken by the events of September 2008, when the Irish government introduced its €400 billion bank guarantee. The initial shock at the fact and scale of the guarantee gave way to anger about the conduct of Ireland's banking elite. Now Gardaí are investigating the back-to-back deposit wheeze between Anglo and Irish Life and Permanent, as well as the controversial winding down of Sean Quinn's stake in Anglo, which bears all the hallmarks of an illegal share support scheme. It remains to be seen what, if anything, will come of these investigations.

For almost two years after the collapse of Lehman Brothers, the Irish government sought to perpetuate a myth that the collapse of the investment banking giant, and the financial mayhem it caused, was the immediate source of Ireland's ills. The Lehman myth was refuted in May 2010 when Patrick

Honohan, the new Governor of the Central Bank, delivered a report on the Irish banking crisis which concluded that the essential characteristic of our problem was 'domestic and classic'. At least two banks, Anglo and Irish Nationwide, were marching headlong towards insolvency, with or without Lehman.

But well before the Honohan report, the Lehman myth (and others) had been gradually picked apart in the courts, where the public was presented with ample evidence that the Celtic Tiger was little more than a mirage: a massive pyramid scheme.

Acknowledgements

This book was not my idea, and I cannot claim credit for it. That credit goes in part to my *Irish Independent* colleagues Frank Coughlan and Peter Carvosso, who commissioned me to write a series of features about the Commercial Court for the newspaper's Weekend Review.

It was a copy of one cover story, 'Snapshots From The Court That's Writing The First Draft Of Celtic Tiger History', that Brendan Barrington, my editor at Penguin Ireland, was clutching in his hand when I first met with him and Michael McLoughlin, Penguin's MD, last year to discuss this project.

I am grateful to Michael and Brendan for spotting its potential; to Michael for all his support and for driving me to completion when I was, no doubt, driving Penguin to distraction; and to Brendan for guiding me through the difficult terrain that is the editing process and reminding me that there are no short cuts to any place worth going to.

Thanks also to my literary agents Faith O'Grady and Lauren Hadden from the Lisa Richards Agency for their help and support, especially when my energy levels were at a low ebb.

I would receive no thanks but possibly plenty of legal writs if I were to attempt to thank those that deserve it most: the countless barristers, solicitors and others who work in the administration of justice who have helped me on this journey.

They cannot be identified as most would face disciplinary proceedings, or worse, for being identified in any way with me. In any event, all interviews and meetings with such sources were conducted in the strictest confidence. I am indebted to those members of the legal related professions and other contacts who have given generously of their time, insights and expertise. You know who you are.

Special thanks to the Bar Council of Ireland, especially Jeanne McDonagh and Michael Collins SC, its former chairman. Thanks also to Ken Murphy, the Director General of the Law Society, for his never-ending engagement with me – even though I have, at times, been an unwelcome thorn in the side of solicitors.

Thanks to Gerry Curran and his colleagues at the Courts Service for providing me with up-to-date data about the courts; to Colin Daly and his staff at the Northside Community Law Centre and to Noeline Blackwell, Paul Joyce, Michael Farrell and Yvonne Woods at the Free Legal Advice Centres, who are all working at the cutting edge of legal protection for the disadvantaged and shared their experiences with me.

James Treacy and Greg Connell from BusinessPro, publishers of *Stubbs Gazette*, deserve special mention for sharing their data and insights with me.

One lawyer whom I can publicly acknowledge without fear of retribution or excommunication is Colleen Coughlan, Barrister-at-Law, who assisted with research on this book. I am grateful to her for her time, diligence, professionalism and support, generously given whilst maintaining her own busy practice.

Thanks too to Deirdre Kilroy, Caroline O'Connell and Hugh Garvey at LK Shields Solicitors for legal advice received in the early stage of this project.

Writing a book can be an isolating experience, but I have been helped through it by an amazing network of friends and colleagues who have provided invaluable support. I cannot thank you all. I am especially grateful to: Maddie Grant BL, Rob McMahon, Elaine Byrne, Emma Callanan, Jimmy Costelloe, Michael O'Higgins SC, John Kettle, Mary Heaney, Jer O'Mahony, Catherine Ghent, Eimear Noone, Craig Garfinkle, Kirsten Sheridan, Orla Clayton, Cian O'Neill, Jayne Maguire, Fiona Donohue, Sarah Williams, Emily Brand, Trevor Donovan, Gary Daly, the Harcourt Literary Foundation, the Glen Belles, Paddy Carberry, Cormac McConnell, Pat Larkin, Pat McParland, John Connolly, the Supergirls, Stephen Kennedy, Ciara McGuigan, Catriona Duggan, Claire Duggan and Stephen Cahill.

Special thanks to the Grant, Noone, McArdle-Shine, Hogan, Dunne and Hammond families and to my great friend Br. Alberic Turner at Bolton Abbey.

Anne 'Chica' Devlin, Ciara Burns and Ann Forde, thank you for keeping my feet on the ground; and thanks to all my colleagues in the Dublin Symphony Orchestra and the Serafina String Quartet.

Thanks to the staffs at the National Library and to my fellow authors who have provided crucial support and advice: Scott Millar, Shane Ross, Pat Leahy, Matt Cooper, Remy Farrell BL, James Downey, Mike Soden and to my writing mentor Aine McCarthy (Orna Ross) who has supported me unwaveringly throughout my writing career.

My journalism colleagues have been superb, especially those who cast a critical eye over early drafts of chapters. For this editorial and emotional support I thank, in addition to the entire *Irish Independent* newsroom: Maeve Dineen, Emmet Oliver, Shane Phelan, Thomas Molloy, Gemma O'Doherty, Neil Callanan (*Sunday Tribune*) and Simon Carswell (*Irish*

Times). Thanks also to Dara Flynn, Tom Lyons, Alish O'Hora Kathleen Barrington and Tom McEneaney.

Special thanks to Carol Coulter of the *Irish Times* and the entire pool of court reporters, in the Four Courts and beyond, for their support and advice.

It would be unfair to single anyone out, but I will make an exception: Mary Carolan from the *Irish Times* has been an absolute rock throughout this process, both as a friend and a colleague. Her generosity with her time and her knowledge has exceeded all expectations and I cannot thank her enough.

I could not, of course, have completed this work without the support of my employers, the *Irish Independent*, in particular editor-in-chief Gerry O'Regan and news editor Shane Doran, who gave me their patience and support and tolerated my absence from work while I was writing the book.

I am also eternally grateful to my former colleagues and mentors at the *Sunday Times* and other papers who have helped me in my journalism career. They are too numerous to mention, but special thanks for sticking with me in the early days go to Fiona McHugh, John Burns and Frank Fitzgibbon, as well as Paul Drury at Associated Newspapers.

My family know, I hope, how much I appreciate their support in this and all endeavours I have undertaken.

My parents, Frank and Marion, gave us the best start in life anyone could hope for. To my sisters, Karena, Caoilfhionn and Saorlaith, thank you so much for tolerating my prolonged absence from family life at home in Newry. Aoife, my twin, to whom this book is dedicated, has practically been a co-author and proves every single day that she is the better half.

I look forward to spending more time with my nieces and nephews, Tiarnan, Caitlin, Shea and Jack, and hopefully my goddaughter, Ruby K. McMahon, will soon learn that Auntie Dibs is not a book.

Finally, this book could not have been completed without the support of its protagonists: the individuals whose very private crises have played out in the public arena of the courts. Many have spoken to me, in confidence and otherwise, about difficult events in their personal and professional lives and for that I am truly grateful.

Index